KERRY HEAVENS

Karen,

Find yourself a
#GoodBoy!

love
Kerry Heavens
♡.

Published by Kerry Heavens.

Will

First Edition

ISBN-13:978-1539366423
ISBN-10:1539366421

Published by: Kerry Heavens
Editing: Mandi Gibala
Cover Design: Rebel Graphics
Model: Andrew Biernat
Photographer: Wander Aguiar

For Gigi

SATURDAY 30TH MAY
PROLOGUE

"William, before you go," Mum reaches into her pocket and pulls out a business card. "George wants you to give him call."

"George?" My heart almost stops.

"George Goldsmith," she says softly as if to break it to me gently.

Of course I know which George, if you say George around here, everyone knows which George. That was not the point of my question.

"Why?" That was my question…why, why, *why*?

I feel the weight of the card as she places it in my hand. It's heavy, it oozes class, but it's not the weight of the paper I feel. It's the weight I've learned not to carry all in one load anymore. The weight of missing her.

As I take the small, embossed card, the weight lands squarely on my shoulders again.

All of it.

Every bad choice, every cowardly decision, all the longing, all the guilt and on top of it, the sour cherry. The fact that I still think I did the right thing for her.

I scrub my hand over my face.

Mum shrugs in her typical fashion. She has run 'Mary's'

the bakery/cafe that is the hub of the village, for over thirty years. The shrug is the symbol of her favourite phrase, 'it's none of my business dear', I hear it echoing in my head and I know it's going to be useless pleading. "Give him a call and find out for yourself," she says instead.

Fuck.

I put the heavy card in my pocket without looking at it and I nod, my shoulders slump.

Fuck, fuck, fucking fuck.

"George Goldsmith," he answers officiously.

"George, it's Will— William." Ugh! Tell him which Will you fucking idiot. "Middleton." I confirm. "Will Middleton." For pity's sake, I've just paced my kitchen for an hour trying to figure out why in the hell he would want to talk to me and planning what I'll say to each scenario in my imagination, and I fluff the opening bloody sentence.

"Will, thanks for calling back. How are you?"

"I'm good thanks, and yourself?"

Damn it. I don't want to know how he is.

He might be over the moon. He might be planning a wedding for his beautiful daughter. Hell, he might have done that two years ago and now he's welcoming a first grandchild. All of which, I. Do. Not. Want. To. Know.

Which is precisely why I wasn't going to ask him how he is. It's too dangerous. 'How is business?' was the safe question. I had planned for this! Not that I know the first thing about what he does, but it was safer than 'how are you'? And I blew it.

"I'm well thank you. Listen, your mother tells me you're

going into business for yourself?"

Inside, I do the biggest sigh of relief.

Business. He wants to talk business.

Thank fuck.

My heart receives a kick of adrenaline and starts racing having been stuttering for the past hour. "Yes, that's right, my cousin Spencer and I have been thinking about it."

"Well, you know the only way to really make money is to work for yourself. You're wasting yourself working for someone else."

"That's what we figured."

"You're doing the right thing."

"Thanks." I think. Was that the purpose of this? To give me business advice?

"Listen, I'm looking for contractors to undertake a fairly sizeable extension. I'm about to get on a flight, but I'll be home Tuesday, would you and your business partner be able to come to the house and discuss it?"

"I, um…we haven't really got started yet George, we both still work for other people right now."

"Casual labour from what I understand and your cousin is freelancing, so he can walk away from that pretty easily. I'd say you were perfectly lined up to take on your first project, wouldn't you?"

"Actually, I've been project managing for a firm." I don't know why I need him to know I'm more than just a labourer. It just seems important. You know, because I want him to know that although I was never good enough for his daughter, I'm better than he assumes.

"Yes, but it's still contract by contract isn't it? It's not difficult for you to walk away."

"I suppose." Yeah, he doesn't give a shit about my eligibility for his daughter…who is probably married and happy by now anyway. This is business.

"Good," he says like the deal is done.

Jesus, wait. "But George, how do you know we'll do a good job? We have no references. You don't know what we can do."

"The two of you rebuilt your parent's garage last year, correct? You did a lovely job. I have faith in you."

"It was a single garage, George, not a Georgian mansion."

"Your cousin is an architect, am I right?" I roll my eyes. Clearly some skewed information he got from mum while she was waxing lyrical about her highly accomplished nephew.

"He's a structural engineer."

"So between you, you have a lot of building knowledge."

"Well, yes."

"And you have contacts, you can pull a team together?"

"Yes, absolutely."

"Will, I like to support local business as much as I can. You won't get a much better opportunity to start out than this. It's a huge job. Do it well, it will get you a lot of recommendations. I'm a solid customer, I'm fully aware of the pitfalls of small business, I'll pay for materials up front and you won't have to chase me for invoices. It's as good as a business loan. I trust you. I'd like you to come and see the house, give me a quote and have your cousin draw up plans. Once the plans are approved with the local council, you can both quit your day jobs and get started on your future."

"I'll…um…need to talk to Spencer."

"I'll see you on Tuesday, say, seven?"

I can hardly argue can I? "Ok, see you then."

"Excellent." He hangs up, leaving me feeling bewildered.

Talk about out of the blue. Fuck knows what I'm going to do. This is an amazing opportunity, Spencer will shit. But I don't know if I can do it. I mean, I see George around often enough, we say hi, but working on his house? Won't that be awkward? What if Mags comes over? I don't even know where she lives now, I don't ask. All I know is that wherever she is, she stays there. We never see her and it's probably because of me. I know it's selfish, because this is such a big opportunity for both Spencer and I, but I don't know if I can put myself in that situation.

What am I going to do?

I hear Spencer's key in the door and decide I need to think on it before I tell him, because once I do, it will be a done deal. He walks in silently, stops in front of the coffee table, lets go of everything in his hands and drops into the chair opposite me. His files and plans slide sideways and spill off the table into a heap on the floor and he doesn't even look at them. He stares at the ceiling.

"I've got to get another job," he says after a long moment.

"Bad day?"

"Worse journey home."

"Want a beer?"

"Yeah, if you could put a beer in this hand," he wearily lifts his left hand an inch off the arm of the chair. "And some pizza in this hand," he lifts the other hand. "I'll do the rest."

"Go shower, I'll order a pizza."

"But it's so far!" he wails childishly.

"Dude, I'm not carrying you."

"Just get that cushion and smother me then, I don't think I can carry on."

I look at him for a second and I know what this would mean to him. Fuck it, I can't be selfish. I know what I need to do.

"I can do better than a cushion."

He lifts his head in interest. "You have a gun?"

I roll my eyes and hurl a cushion at his head. "I've got us a job."

SATURDAY 22ND AUGUST

Finally.

I nudge Mags with my elbow, as she puts a plate back in the cupboard. She turns in time to watch Spencer and Jazz's feet disappear up the stairs.

The four of us have been together all day and Spencer has pretty much been too frightened of Mags to put a foot wrong, so he and Jazz have had no time alone. After a month apart and having only just reconciled, I was surprised when Spencer suggested we all have dinner together this evening when the shop closed, instead of whisking Jazz away and having his wicked way with her. I guess he was nervous and dinner bought him more time. It's kind of sweet in a way, and I wasn't complaining, I was keen to buy a little more time myself. Mags and I have spent so much time together preparing for the shop opening lately, I'm going to be sad now it's over.

Surprising Jazz was all Mags' idea. Jazz had been too afraid to take the leap and open her own business, but Mags had so much faith in her best friend. And Spencer really stepped up. He may have messed things up with Jazz on a grand scale, but I'm very proud of the way he pulled himself together.

He has worked day and night for the last month renovating

Mum's old bakery in secret. We managed to convince Jazz that it had sold and the new owners were doing it up. All the while we were furiously working behind the scenes to get her Chocolate empire started.

Spencer took on all the work, knowing she may never take him back, he just wanted to make things right somehow. That really shows that he cares about her and I know she feels the same despite their differences. I hope this is the start of something good for them

At least I have a few more weeks work on the house. After that, who knows what will happen.

She hasn't said what she plans to do now. I think it's safe to assume that now Jazz has her business in the village, she will be around more. But she hasn't said she's going to move here and I'm too much of a coward to ask.

"Do you think they'll sort it out?" Mags asks with a grin as she watches them run upstairs.

"I think that looks promising," I reply. "But I bet there's no talking."

Mags gives me a withering look. "Is there ever any talking with them?"

"They'll get there."

She smiles. She is so beautiful. Smiling back at her, I feel envious of Spencer. Yeah, I said it, lucky bastard. He may be completely devoid of social grace, but at least he can express himself. Times like these, I want to tell her how beautiful she is, but that wouldn't be fair. I guess I'm lucky, I mean she doesn't hate me, we're close. That's more than most exes have and I like it, but it's so damn hard when I want more.

"They're going to be loud aren't they?" She groans.

"Yeah." I laugh, pausing as I almost offer her a way out. I can't, it will be hell. But then I look at her and that's all it takes for me to throw caution to the wind. "Hey, come stay at mine."

"I think I might take you up on that," she replies without hesitation or innuendo.

I turn to put the plates in a cupboard and press my eyes closed. It's good that she feels comfortable saying yes to staying the night with me. It's tragic that there isn't even a hint of suggestion in the way she says it. I guess I only have myself to blame. Finishing the clearing up we were left with when the horny lovebirds vanished, I switch off the kitchen lights and follow her into the hall.

"I'm just going to go and grab a few…" She pauses on the bottom stair at the unmistakable sound of Jazz moaning. "…yeah, you know what? You can lend me a t-shirt," she concludes, grabbing her bag and jacket and heading for the door. "You coming?"

I glance up the stairs once more.

Lucky, lucky bastard.

"Will?" Mags urges.

Jazz cries out Spencer's name and I back away from the stairs. "Right behind you," I tell her grabbing my keys.

Clicking her seatbelt in to place, Mags looks up at me. Her eyes glinting in the darkness. "Are you sure this is alright?"

"Yeah, totally fine," I babble, hoping she can't sense my reticence. "I'm not mean enough leave you there listening to that all night." My voice threatens to give my nerves away and I laugh to cover it. That just makes it worse. If she wasn't watching me I would probably slam my head into the steering wheel. Hold it to-fucking-gether.

Quietly, she places her hand on my knee and squeezes. "Thanks."

It's impossible to hide my surprised flinch and I could kick myself as she slides her hand away.

We drive home in silence. On top of my awkward behaviour, knowing that we have sleeping arrangements to discuss and that I have to find her a t-shirt to sleep in is grating at me. She stayed over once before. That was ok. But it was ok because we fell asleep accidentally, woke up at 3am to the sounds of Spencer and Jazz going at it and were both too tired to do anything other than fall into my bed. I lent her a t-shirt that night too, but I can't give her that one again. If I did, she would know that it hadn't been washed since. It smells like her and I want to keep it that way.

As for having her in my bed again…I can't do it. I'll have to take the sofa. Last time, I just watched her sleep and tried my best not to hold her. And when I say tried my best, I mean I totally caved, pulling her in close. I had my excuse ready just in case she busted me out. I would've pretended to have been asleep and unaware that I had her in my arms.

"You alright?" she asks softly as I turn the car into my road and pull on to my driveway.

I was lost in thought. "Yeah, I'm good," I reply brightly. "I was just thinking about what film we could watch."

Mags yawns. "If we don't fall asleep again."

"It has been a long day hasn't it?"

"Worth it though," she grins.

She's right it was. Jazz loved the shop, Spencer managed not to be a dick all day, which was a minor miracle. He has tried to sort his life out before, but I guess losing Jazz was a wakeup call for him. Maybe she's the one.

"Yeah it was worth it." Climbing out of the car, I find myself again on the cusp of a conversation I've been dreading, it's starting to become awkward that we haven't talked about it. I put the key in the door, trying to sound as nonchalant as possible. "I guess you're sticking around?"

She screws up her nose, but with a suppressed smile. "Looks that way."

"Poor you." I try to sound light. "Wrenched from the city and forced into small village life again. It's a huge sacrifice to make for a friend are you sure you're ready for how dull life really is here?"

"It's always been home here and I was bored of city life. I can write anywhere and if this is where Jazz needs to be, then I'm here. Plus, it has certain other appeals." Barely visible in the low light, a flirtatious smile pulls at the corners of her lips as she casually shrugs off the remark.

I feel my face get hot. Jesus Will, pull yourself together! Thankfully I hadn't hit the light switch yet, hopefully it's not as glowing as it feels. That's assuming she meant me when she said certain other appeals. I have no fucking idea anymore. Change the subject Will, for the love of God!

"Ah yes, your writing. So when do I get to read some of it?"

"I don't know if you're ready for that."

"Ok, now I'm more intrigued."

"Yeah, well, you can stay that way. I can't have the inner workings of my mind being examined by people I know."

"Jazz has read it though I assume."

"Jazz is different."

"Fine." I laugh. "I'll just look you up on Amazon."

"You can try, I use a pen name."

"Hmmm, interesting. What could you possibly be writing that you have to hide behind a pen name? Is it filthy?"

"Well obviously."

"Yeah, but come on, it's the age of 'mummy porn,' isn't that what they call it? None of that stuff is taboo now."

"This isn't exactly mummy porn."

I narrow my eyes. "Hmmmm, the plot thickens."

"Keep dreaming, Middleton. It's not happening."

"I will get to the bottom of your dirty little secret, Miss Goldsmith."

She shakes her head walking into the living room and making herself at home on the sofa.

"Here, find a film, I'll make us a tea." I toss the remote control onto the sofa beside her.

"Ooooh, we are so rock and roll," she says as I leave the room.

"Village life Mags, I warned you." I call out from the kitchen, picking up the kettle and filling it with water. Village life that looks like she is going to be a part of…Yesss! I pump my fist. Not exactly sure why, because that brings me more problems than if she was leaving, but let's face it, I like her.

"Don't know if I can be arsed with a film. I just want to curl up," Mags says suddenly from behind me.

"Fuck!" I jump. Dropping a scalding hot teabag onto my sock. "Shit!"

"You ok there jumpy?"

"You are a ninja woman, you scared the crap out of me."

"Sorry." She laughs. "I'll have to get a little bell or

something."

Yawning again she sets me off. "Why don't you take your tea up to bed?" I ask, handing her the mug, handle first, so that she doesn't burn her hands.

She frowns. "What are you going to do?"

I shrug. "I'll make myself comfortable down here."

"For the night?"

"Yeah, it's fine, you have the bed."

"Did you not like being big spoon last time then?"

Fuck, does she know I spooned her? "I just thought it would be better if…" I mumble, panicking.

"Better if what?" She frowns.

"I don't know Mags. I'm just trying to do the right thing." I sigh.

"Good," she says firmly, turning to walk out of the kitchen. "Then you'll come up with me and stop being silly. We're way past sleeping on the sofa don't you think?"

"Yeah I guess." I grab my tea and go after her, feeling like I've being told off by the teacher. Flicking the light switches off as I go and following her up the stairs, I'm cursing myself for this stupid, stupid idea.

Mags laughs, looking at her watch. "It's not even nine-thirty."

"We worked our arses off last night Mags. By the time I dropped you home and got into bed it was two am and we've been running around all day. I say we deserve a stupidly early night."

"I know, but it's pretty sad isn't it. We had a lot to celebrate tonight and we all end up in bed by nine-thirty."

I clear my throat. "In vastly different circumstances I

might add."

"Yeah," she agrees, with what I could easily convince myself was a hint of regret. But I know I'm only seeing what I want to see.

I hook her up with a t-shirt and pack her off to the bathroom while I find something to wear to bed. Something with a padlock maybe, I think to myself as I rifle through my drawer.

"All yours," she says as she comes back in the room. I tense, trying hard not to show that she startled me again. I'm wound up so tight I must look like a freak. I quickly head to the bathroom to get away from the tension I'm creating.

I return to the bedroom to find her sitting back against the pillows in bed, with the duvet pulled up around her, hugging her tea and surfing through the channels on my TV. I carefully climb in beside her so as not to jog her mug, propping my pillows the same way she has hers.

I lift my tea off the bedside table and wrap my hands around it. "Aaaahhhh." I sigh as the wave of relaxation filters through my tired body.

"Good isn't it?"

"Heaven." I grin, sipping my tea. "Oh! Go back!"

"What?" she asks, re-tracing her steps through the channels until she comes to Point Break about twenty minutes in. "Sweet!" She smiles.

"Young, dumb, and full of cum," I laugh. She looks at me deadpan for a second and I kick myself for once again letting my guard down and relaxing too much in her presence. Then she laughs and I sigh with relief.

We settle down and enjoy the film and each other's

company. The bed adds a weird dimension, but it has been quite easy like this between us since she came back. We have managed pretty well to put our history behind us and I've realised how much I've missed her. Not just as my girlfriend, but as a big part of my life. She was my best friend.

When the film finishes, I realise she has fallen asleep, so I switch off my bedside lamp, leaving the room lit only by the TV. I study her face and my hand reaches out without permission to stoke her hair. I realise just in time and reach for the remote that is resting on the bed the other side of her instead, trying not to wake her. But I end up brushing her breast with my wrist as I lift it over. She stirs and I panic, pulling my arm back quickly, muttering "oh shit." Of course it was totally an accident, but in my fluster, I drop the remote on her.

"Mmmmph," she murmurs, waking up.

"I'm so sorry Mags, I'm such a klutz." Moving to pick up the remote from her chest, I realise far too late that I can hardly see. I'm groping around for the remote, only it's not the remote I'm feeling… "Bollocks!" I whip my hand away.

She lets out a sleepy laugh while I put my hands in the air to show they are where she can see them. "I'm so sorry."

"What are you sorry for?"

"Because this was awkward enough and now I've groped you."

"You call that groping?" She laughs again, this time a throaty provocative sound which has me watching her in the flickering half-light of the TV. Damn, that laugh. I feel it in a rush every time I hear it and it causes...stirrings.

Shit, this is going to be a long night. Once again I'm

actually jealous of Spencer. He would say something tremendously crude, like, 'fuck me, that laugh makes my cock hard. You'll have to suck it better.' And he would either get a slap or a blowjob, but he's happy to take his chances because the odds are reasonable. I wish I could do that. I've got a gorgeous girl in my bed, someone who means a lot to me, but here I am rooted to the spot by fear and self-loathing and left to spend the night in the torturous company of my raging hard-on.

"I prefer my groping a bit firmer, Middleton. You'll have to try a bit harder than that."

Is she flirting, or am I just kidding myself? Jesus. "I…erm…" I close my mouth. You sound fucking pathetic Will. Something about her lately reduces me to a snivelling idiot. I swear it never used to be this way. A real man would have her pinned to the bed by now. That's not really my style. I think if I were to have any chance with her, a little manning up is probably called for but I just don't know if I have it in me.

"...on my face."

"Huh?" I blink, searching for a clue as I realise she had been speaking and I wasn't listening.

"I said, you're staring, have I got something on my face?"

"Oh, no...I was just..."

"Just what?"

She reaches over and takes my hand, pulling it closer to her body. I watch it, wondering what she is going to do with it.

"Will?"

"Huh?"

"You're impossible to read, do you know that?"

"I don't mean to be," I mutter. I can't even look at her now, this is a fucking disaster. She wouldn't find me so impossible to read if she could feel what I'm hiding under the covers. Like I said, I'm not Spencer and I'll probably be nursing this for hours.

"Don't you..." she pauses, then huffs, shaking her head she lets go of my hand.

Oh bollocks, now she's annoyed. Why is she annoyed? "Don't I what?"

"I don't know," she sighs. "Don't you ever think about..."

My heart almost stops. I hardly dare hope. All that is done between us. Isn't it?

"You know what, never mind. It's in the past, I guess it's better off there," she says shaking her head.

Shit.

She's thinking about us too?

And now she's turning away from me and I'm losing my chance…

Deep breath, here goes... "Being with you?" I finish for her.

She turns back to face me and I try to gauge her expression in the dim light.

"Yeah I do, all the time in fact." It's out there now, no point in playing it down. "It's pretty much all I think about."

There is nothing but silence from her.

Balls.

I close my eyes and clench my fists. I'm so stupid ruining things when they were getting manageable. Sighing, I look up at her just as the TV flickers to something bright, which casts its light across her face. Her eyes are fixed on mine and she looks terrified. I can tell in that instant that she doesn't feel the same. Shit, shit, shit.

"I'm sorry, I shouldn't put that on you. It's not your problem."

"Put what on me?" She frowns.

Oh god, this isn't happening right now. Why couldn't we have this conversation in broad daylight, across a table? Why now when I've said she can stay here? And we are in bed of all places. I need to be away from her before I make this any worse. "Nothing," I reply. Flicking the covers off me, I make to stand but I feel her hand around my wrist pulling me back down.

"Where are you going?" she asks, sounding frustrated.

"To give you some space."

"I don't bloody want space!" she snaps.

"Then what do you want Mags? Because I'm fucking confused." I don't mean to sound so irate, but I can't tell what's going on in her head at all.

She stares at me. I feel like I've bared all and she's still giving me no clue. I'm just about to pull my arm out of her grasp and walk away, when she leans in and presses her lips to mine.

All my resolve, all my hesitation goes out the window and I have her under me in a split second, pushing my tongue between her parted lips. It's so unlike me, but I'm only human, I can only take so much longing before I break. Taking what I have needed for so long, I try to put my doubts out of my head. I know I'm not who she needs me to be and I can't ever be, but right now I don't care.

I've been alone without her. I can't do it anymore. I need her.

"Thank God," she gasps when I let her breathe. "I thought you didn't want me."

"Feel how much I want you now?" I grin, pushing the hard fact of my arousal against her.

"Uh huh." She giggles, pulling my face back to hers.

I let myself relax into her, loving the feel of her body pressing against mine and kiss her, taking my time. I've wanted to do this for so long. Her hands find their way under my t-shirt and her nails lightly draw across my back sending a shiver down my spine.

I pull back from her lips, smiling as she opens her eyes. The light from the TV doesn't do justice to the searing flecks of gold in her green eyes, but I have that indelibly marked in my memory, I don't need to see it right now. There are however, things I do want to see. This might be a one shot deal and I'm not walking away from this wishing. Lifting off her enough to find the bottom of the t-shirt she's wearing, I help her off with it, burying my face in her neck. She smells just like I remember and I want to eat her.

Holy shit! I didn't mean eat her, eat her…but fuck, I could, if she'll let me.

Hers was the first clit I ever licked and I think even back then I was pretty good at it. It's worship in it's purest form and I doubt any man has ever worshiped her like I did…do…and now I could remind her. I try to take my time making my way down, I want to bury my face between her legs like, yesterday. I'm aware that I'm rushing, a couple of kisses here and there as I ease down her body, but I can't slow down.

Reaching her underwear, I'm already intoxicated by her heady scent. I grasp her knickers in both hands and peel them down, stopping dead in my tracks when I see that she is completely bare and as if this isn't almost more than I can take right now, she has the word 'Focus' tattooed, just…there above her…you know. Like she knows she will have an intoxicating effect on whoever is lucky enough to read the word. I'll be honest, it's the one thing I can't do right now. I think I might have swallowed my tongue.

I can't describe what this does to me. I'm sure it has some deep meaning, but fuck…what was I doing? Oh yeah, I was about to worship her like she has never been worshiped before. Show her that anyone else who has tried was simply pretending, because this is from the heart. Except now, I have performance anxiety. I mean, look at her. Stunning, and so boldly confident in her sensuality, that she has an instruction tattooed right by her perfectly waxed and ready…Je-sus! I can't even think the word.

It's her pussy. P-U-S-S-Y.

Right now, I think the only pussy around here is me.

This is what she's doing to me. I can't even think of her in the same way as I would think about anyone else. It's like she is sacred ground and I must tread respectfully. But look at her. Brazen when you think about it.

I don't want to think about it.

How many people do you suppose have almost choked on seeing that sight for the first time? That's not a brand new tattoo, people have seen it. Ok, I'm going to hyperventilate in a minute. Stop thinking about how many people she has had sex with!

“Are you just going to stare? Or do you have a plan?”

I look up at her. Propped on her elbows, looking down at me with a mischievous smile.

There is nothing I can say to that. I have no idea who she is anymore. The last thirty seconds have rewritten everything I thought I knew about her and I’m so turned on it hurts.

She raises her eyebrows, a gesture which says ‘well?’, oh shit I need to do something before she speaks again and adds fuel to this already out of control fire. Keeping my eyes locked on hers, I close the couple of inches between us and take her clit straight into my mouth.

She gasps and then groans as I sweep my tongue across it. Burying my face in her delicious…come on, you can think it…pussy.

This is crazy, she’s not so precious I’ll defile her with my thoughts. She has a tattoo practically on it for fuck’s sake, she’s no angel. She drops her head back, moaning. It’s a dirty, unashamed sound that resonates deep inside me. I close my eyes, come on Will, you can do this. This is your thing, your zone. She is moaning already, listen.

She’s incredible and the fact that she just took on an air of terrifying mystery just adds to her appeal. Now all I need is for her to pull my hair and I think I’ll be done.

God, I hope she doesn’t pull my hair, I don’t want to embarrass myself.

Fuck. Focus.

Oh the irony!

That’s it, I can’t do this anymore.

I pull away from her and crawl back over her. I feel calmer above her, more in control of myself. But then she takes my face in her hands and kisses me. Licking my lips with a moan and cleaning her…yeah…no…can't think it.

Jesus. Who is she? She used to be so sweet. She was *never* this person. I like this person.

Speaking of physical attention, I'm now aware of where she is rubbing up against my straining boxers and I need to get inside her. Pulling myself away from her hands, I raise up onto my knees and rip off my t-shirt. She's pulling at my boxers before I've got the t-shirt over my head and I let out a croaky sound as her hand wraps around my length. I pause for a moment, looking down at her and appreciate the sight of my beautiful Mags spread out before me, my hard cock in her hand. I enjoy it for only for a second, then I shift so that I can ditch my boxers and reach across and open my bedside drawer, feeling around for a condom.

"Wait, I'm…"

Got it. I pull one out and shove the drawer shut. "Allergic to latex," I finish for her. "I know." I hand the packet to her and she takes it slowly. 'Latex free' it says on the plastic, but she doesn't read it, she just looks at me.

"You remembered," she says softly.

"Of course I remembered." Like I could forget. She had a bad reaction and I wasn't going to risk that again. Ever. Better to just buy non-latex than have to worry.

A slow smile spreads on her lips and she pushes me back onto my side of the bed, quickly turning the tables so that I'm laying back and she's over me. She doesn't bother with the pretence of kissing her way down my body, she goes straight for what she wants, which apparently is my dick in her mouth.

Fuck me.

She only teases, just a taste, but damn, her mouth. Even someone like me has a hard time not grabbing her hair and forcing her further down. She knows I want it too because she smiles up at me as she releases me with a pop and runs the tip of her tongue around the head. She pulls away, when I try and push forward into her mouth again, shaking her head and smiling. The denial is really hot.

It's just what I need. She needs a man though, a real one. Someone rich and powerful who is her equal in life and doesn't want permission to come. But right here and now, I'm the one she wants and I can play along for tonight because in this moment none of that matters. She rips open the wrapper on the condom and rolls it on quickly. Crawling up me until her lips brush over mine, her tongue licks into my mouth at the same time that she sinks down on to me with a muffled moan. I thrust slowly into her, kissing her and wrapping my arms around her to hold her close. She begins to meet my slow thrusts with a grind that is just another level.

I gasp.

She places her hands on my chest and pushes up out of my grasp, where she is fully seated and in control. My hands slide down her sides and come to rest on her thighs and I watch, mesmerised as she begins to rock. For a while I just can't take my eyes off her, but then losing myself in the feeling, I close my eyes. I'm buried deep inside her and her motion has me almost in a trance, so when she leans forward, gripping the bed frame and her nipple brushes my lip, I'm startled.

I lift my head slightly and take it into my mouth, sucking on it, which makes her moan and grind harder. I get lost in it again, sucking on whichever nipple she presents and pinching and rolling the other, until she switches again. While she never ceases that grind.

I'm so close, I grab her hips, helping her to grind harder, faster. Her throaty groans build and she stretches forward again, resting one hand on the bed frame, feeding her nipple into my mouth with the other. I suck greedily as she steadies herself on my chest.

"Bite it," she whispers.

I don't hesitate to carry out her order, sinking my teeth into the sensitive flesh. It seems to be just what she needs. She tenses and her nails dig into my chest as she explodes, biting into my skin and affording me that slight edge I need.

I erupt inside her.

She rides me breathlessly through the waves of pleasure, until it subsides and she lowers herself onto my chest, panting.

And in that moment, all there is, is us, and even though I know it's futile…I think I love her.

I put my bag down on the stool in the kitchen and look up guiltily as Jazz appears in the doorway giggling. A horny looking Spencer clamped to her back with his face buried in her neck and his hands everywhere. It’s seriously early, I wasn’t expecting them to be up. I thought I’d be able to sneak back in.

Jazz stops and Spencer looks up, raising his eyebrows.

"You were out early," Jazz remarks.

"Or home late," Spencer mutters, returning his lips to her neck and forgetting I'm even here.

Now Jazz's eyebrows shoot up. "Where were you?"

"I crashed at Will's. It beat listening to you two all night.” I use the word ‘crashed’ as casually as I possibly can. Trying to make it sound as innocent as it was supposed to be.

Spencer's eyes lift to meet mine and I can see his smile even though he refuses to stop nibbling on Jazz. The smile says he thinks it was more, but then, this is Spencer. He’s always going to think it’s more. I look away, feeling tired and like I need a hug.

“You ok?” Jazz asks, shaking Spencer off and coming over to put a hand on my shoulder.

“Yeah, just tired,” I reply.

"Didn't get much sleep?" Spencer smirks.

"I slept just fine thank you. In case you've forgotten, we've put in a lot of late hours this week," I snap. Spencer holds his hands up in surrender. Awesome, now I doth protest too much. I turn to Jazz. "I'm going to go and jump in the shower, we have a busy day."

"Ok, I'll make you a tea when you come out."

I make my way upstairs and into my bathroom to turn on the shower. Catching sight of myself in the mirror I pause. Why do I look so fazed? Last night was incredible. We fell asleep wrapped in each other and woke this morning at the break of dawn all smiles and gentle kisses. But it feels off. The kiss goodbye was awkward. Am I just reading into that? He seemed ok, he said he'll see us at the shop this morning, so he's not avoiding me at least. It's just, you know, we haven't talked and every minute that puts itself between now and when I left him makes the feeling of dread I have grow. I still don't know what last night means. And if it means nothing— no, I don't want to go down that road. I need to keep it casual, not get too invested.

I'm all about casual. I never get invested. Remember? There is a really good reason for that…and I fucked him last night.

Get it together for fucks sake. Don't lose your head.

"Are you ready for another day, Miss Chocolatier?" I grin as I enter the kitchen, sounding much refreshed after a nice hot shower.

"Yes!" she beams. "I'm so excited. I was a bit overwhelmed yesterday, I'm looking forward to taking more of it in today. Shall we head down there soon so I can get started? I'll make you breakfast there." Then she frowns. "Oh no, I don't know where anything is!"

I put my hand over hers, "Jazz, relax. The girls are coming in early too. I'm sure they can rustle up some bacon sandwiches or something. You just focus on getting your head around things. Someone needs to make the chocolates remember? That is your main priority today."

"Ok," she sighs. "Maybe I'm still a bit overwhelmed. Thank you again for doing this for me." She squeezes my hand from beneath, with her thumb.

"I just did the bit you weren't brave enough to do. You'll be doing all the work. You can do this Jazz. I believe in you."

She pulls her hand away and says brightly, "Ok, shall we go before I start crying again?"

I laugh, "Sure, I'll just get my bag." Then I realise for the first time that we are alone. "Where's Spencer?"

"Oh he went home to have another shower."

"Another shower?"

She smirks. "Yeah, we had one earlier, but then we got all dirty again."

I glance at the clock on the wall, "Jazz its ten to eight on a Sunday morning, how can you possibly have needed two showers already?"

She bites her lip to suppress the smile.

"Oh god," I groan, picking up my bag and slipping it over my shoulder. "Spare me the details."

"Speaking of details, anything to report from your sneaky night out?"

"Nope." I turn for the door, hoping that is the end to it.

"Bullshit!" She catches up. "You look shifty."

"I'm naturally shifty looking Jazz, it's a curse from my father's side." I keep walking until we reach the front door.

"Uh huh," she says barely controlling the mirth. "I'll find out," she warns. "I always find out."

"There's nothing to find out Jazz. We had a cuppa and watched Point Break."

"And?"

"No and!" I snap, wrenching open the door.

"Ooookaaaay! Easy there, you'll rupture something essential."

"I'll rupture you in a minute!" I grumble, erupting into a very reluctant giggle as I do.

Jazz is laughing as we walk to the car. "So you aren't ready to talk about it yet, obviously." I shoot her a look and climb in to the passenger side as she goes around. As she sits in her seat, she adds, "I'll ask you again later."

I huff. "Perfect."

Having shown Jazz where to park at the rear of the shop and how to unlock the doors and deactivate the alarm, we get to work. It's still quiet in the village and we had put 9am on the sign because we were still finding our feet, but by 8.30 we decide there's no reason not to open the doors. The sun is shining and a few people will be milling around soon enough. I'm just carrying a table out the front when I hear his voice.

"Hey," he says in his gentle way that sends a warm feeling all through me. "We were coming to help, you should have left this for us." He takes the table from me and places it down, then he moves closer and reaches forward, tucking a strand of my hair behind my ear and looking at me with a soft smile. “Hi.”

“Hi,” I reply quietly, keeping my eyes locked on his.

“Scuse me, coming through,” Spencer calls as he bumps my behind with the other table, knocking me into Will’s arms.

“Careful dude,” Will scolds, catching me against his chest, where he simply holds me to him.

“Sorry, I tried, but you two are in the way, making misty eyes at each other.”

“We are not,” argues Will, still holding on to me. “Just be more careful will you.” He eases me away from his body and looks down at me. A small smile playing at the corner of his lips. "You okay?”

I nod.

"Are you two done?" Spencer cuts in to our moment and I look up to find him well and truly wedged in our personal space.

Will huffs. "You're a dick, do you know that?"

"I've heard mention of it once or twice before.” He smirks. "Now," he says cheerfully, "I didn't get up at dawn to watch your sickly PDAs all day. Chop chop! We have shit to do.”

“Oh look at you!” I tease. “So motivated. I’ve never seen you like this Spencer. Wanting to do things for other people. It’s sweet.”

“Pft! I’ve got you breathing down my neck about moving appliances and finishing the kitchen. I’ve got Will nagging on about getting back on site and I just came here to watch Jazz play with chocolate. The sooner we get organised, the sooner I can do that. Okay?”

I look back at Will and smile. “It just warms your heart

doesn't it?"

"His benevolence knows no bounds," Will agrees.

"Oh kiss my arse, the pair of you. Honestly, the sooner you get it over with and fuck, the better for all of us," Spencer retorts.

Both Will and I try hard, but the reflex is to exchange a guilty glance. As we tear our eyes apart a fraction of a second later and try to pretend they didn't meet at all, we both know deep down, it's too late to hide it. Spencer averts his eyes, trying to mask a smile and leans in really close.

"I saw that," he whispers triumphantly and saunters back inside the shop.

Will rolls his eyes. "I'll deal with him," he says heading after him.

I stare after them for a second. Deal with him? Why does he need to deal with him? Are we keeping this a secret? I only averted my gaze because I didn't want Spencer stomping all over it before we even had chance to talk about it. Maybe Will just wants to bury it. Very quickly, the dread settles in.

Oh god, what did we do?

I take a deep breath and go back inside. Spencer and Will are in the kitchen, Jazz wanders out carrying clean trays with an amused look. She opens her mouth to speak and a voice from behind me cuts in.

"I've heard this is the place to be right now," says the deep well-spoken voice. It's one I know so well. "Are you open?" I turn around with the biggest smile.

"JJ!" I shriek and run at him, launching myself into his strong arms in the doorway so that he has to take two steps back into the street to save from falling. He wraps me up in a huge hug and lifts me off the ground.

"How are you doing, Shrimp?" he asks, his face still buried in my hair. "Think you can just come back and not tell me?"

I look up at him guiltily as he sets me down. "No not at all, I just didn't know I was staying at first. I was going to call you now that we are, you know, once we were settled."

He his dark eyebrows form a frown and he folds his arms across his broad chest. "Almost two months, I heard."

I cringe. "Sorry, I've just been busy."

He grins that glittering smile that occasionally overwhelms his otherwise serious face. "It's ok Shrimp, it's just good to have you back."

"Have a coffee with me? We can catch up," I ask.

"Sure," he smiles.

SUNDAY 23RD AUGUST

I recognise his obnoxious, cut-glass accent the second he speaks and my back straightens. I turn to see Mags literally throw herself at him and my shoulders slump. "Perfect," I mutter.

"Uh dude…" Spencer warns.

"Yeah I know." I sigh.

"Aren't you going to do something?" he says, coming to stand beside me to observe the spectacle.

"There's no point," I reply, not talking my eyes off the scene.

Spencer pulls his eyes away for a second, looking me up and down. Then he goes back to watching Mags and JJ. "For you maybe," he concedes. "But I could take him."

"Dick," I murmur.

Neither of us can stop watching.

I'm watching in resigned disappointment as the love of my life reacquaints herself with Prince Charming.

Spencer is fascinated. "What is he wearing?"

"Jodphurs."

"Why?" His tone is incredulous.

"He rides horses."

"But why are they so tight?" Spencer adjusts as if he is

experiencing sympathy dick pain.

“I have no idea. Maybe baggy trousers freak horses out.”

“He looks like a character from a BBC period drama.”

“I know. Talks like one too.”

“Twat.”

“Yep.”

“So what are you going to do?” he asks, turning to me when Mags stops pawing the pain in my arse.

I watch them for a minute, sharing a joke and I see from the way he looks at her, his feelings haven't changed. He wants her. He always has. There’s no way I can compete with him. He is right for her in a way I never will be. “Nothing,” I sigh. “There’s nothing I can do.” Then I turn away. “Come on, we have a shit load to do today,” I tell him.

He stares at me for a moment. Then he mutters, “if you say so,” following me to the back of the kitchen.

I keep busy and try not to keep looking up through the kitchen doorway. And when I do, I try to ignore the fact that his hand has squeezed hers across the table a few times. His eye contact never falters. I may as well give up, I can’t compete, I should never have tried. He was out of sight, out of mind. That was too good to be true. I need to pull myself away before it’s too far gone.

When he finally goes, Mags comes looking for me. I tense when her hand lays on the small of my back, straightening and banging my head on the counter top I’m working beneath.

“Ouch!”

“Oh shit, sorry,” she says, pulling her hand away.

Immediately I miss it. It felt possessive and I liked it. Just like me to see things that aren't there. “It’s not your fault.” I have to be strong. I have to tell her. But not here, not today. I’m too tired. Suddenly, the exhaustion of the past few weeks catches up with me. I’ve been carrying the job at her dad’s place, helping out here, wanting her so much it hurts, not sleeping…I’m done. I need to sleep and not dream because if I do, it will be of her and that’s no rest.

She pauses for a moment behind me, not speaking and I pretend to be engaged in some screw tightening that requires every shred of my concentration.

“Are you ok?” she asks.

“Me?” I act surprised by the question. “I’m fine,”

She waits a moment longer, then says, “okay.” And then she walks away.

“Smooth dude.” Spencer slides in beside me.

“Shut up, Spencer.”

“And we’re done!” Jazz calls from the front door as she turns the sign over. She comes over to the kitchen door and slips her arms around Spencer’s waist, giving him a squeeze.

“You heard her people,” he barks. “We’re done here, so off you go. I’ve got business to attend to.” He hoists Jazz, who’s squealing, over his shoulder and stands looking at us expectantly. “I mean it, I’ve had all I can take, this is MY time. Now get out…unless you like to watch.” He flashes his wolfish grin at the girls behind the counter, who are doing their best to clear up quickly.

The two girls, who worked for mum and have stayed on to work for Jazz, both blush. I know they both have big crushes on Spencer. It’s painfully obvious, since they both used to get all flushed and quiet as soon as Spencer would stroll in doing his 'God's gift' act. Now that he is being all caveman, I don't think they know what to expect. I mean, it's not like he's going to throw Jazz down on the counter and fuck her right now…Jesus, who am I kidding? That's exactly what he's going to do.

I have to step in to stop him now, before he crosses the line. "Okay, how about you go home and we'll lock up?"

"Excellent choice." He winks as he heads for the door. I grimace.

"Wait, my bag!" Jazz shouts, wriggling in his grasp.

"We'll bring it," Mags calls back.

"Sorry about him ladies," I mutter apologetically to the girls. "He has no self-control."

"Aww, leave him alone," Mags scolds.

I give her a flat look. "You've changed your tune."

"He's in love, it's sweet."

I scoff, "Yeah and to hell with public decency, right?" I pass her in the doorway as I go to, switch off some lights.

I feel her hand slide around me as I'm flicking the last switch. "Nothing wrong with a little public indecency," she purrs.

Holy shit.

I feel that thought shiver through my body and I can't control what it does to me. Just the thought of dangerous sex with her and I'm already caving.

"I was thinking," she says quietly, so only I can hear. "Why don't we…" she trails off as a huge yawn grips her.

I seize the opportunity while it's available. "Both go home, take baths and have early nights?" I say with more excitement than I feel. "I couldn't agree more." I grin, hoping to smooth it over. This is brutal. I'm going to have to actually sit her down and look her in the eye while I tell her that I think we made a mistake. I don't want to, but I have to. I've been through it before and I knew better than putting myself through it again. This is for the best.

"But I…"

I press my finger against her lips. "Shhhh. We both need sleep, we haven't had enough for days. Go home, sink into bed and I'll see you in the morning."

She nods, the disappointment clear on her face. "Okay."

She watches me for a moment, her shoulders sinking. My eyes roam her face. What I wouldn't give for things to be different. I ache for her. I thought it had gone away, but I guess I'll just have to learn to live with it. Better this than letting her rip out my still beating heart.

"Good, now go home, I'll lock up."

She sighs, but she doesn't argue. Picking up their bags, she turns to leave and I just can't let her go. I grab her arm and pull her back to me, crushing my lips to hers. She melts into my arms and I pour everything I feel into the connection between us. When I pull away, her chest is heaving. She looks up into my eyes with confusion, because although I tried, there was no hiding the goodbye in that kiss.

MONDAY 24TH AUGUST

Arriving early to the site, I take the cowards way out and start mixing mortar. This means that even if she comes out and tries to talk to me, I can't stop or it will set and be unusable. When Spencer arrives I'm already attacking work like a man possessed.

"Bang goes me living out my princess and the stable boy fantasies," Spencer says, looking up at the house wistfully.

It's his first day back on site after his month away and while I'm sure he is very happy with how things are going between him and Jazz, I guess it's only just dawned on him that she's no longer the rich bitch he'd been fantasising over at work.

He looks at me and the light comes on. Pointing from me, to the house, he grins.

"Don't," I warn him.

"What? Lady of the manor fucks the construction worker. It's the perfect little freaky role play scenario for you."

"That's it, rub salt in the wound why don't you." He doesn't get it. I don't want to live out any fantasies. For me, it's a harsh reality that I wish wasn't true.

"Oh come on, it's funny."

"For you." I grumble.

"You were out early," he says, wisely changing the subject.

"I couldn't lay there listening to you two for a minute longer." I grumble, throwing down a trowel full of mortar and scraping it into shape before thumping a brick on top with too much force.

Spencer's eyebrows raise, but he doesn't respond, so I continue to work, a little aggressively.

"What did those poor bricks ever do to you?" Mags' voice startles me.

"Just trying to catch up now we are back to full output." I give Spencer a pointed look, then I sigh and turn to face her, because she hasn't done anything wrong.

"Hi," she offers, the uncertainty clear in her tone.

"Hey," I reply with a tight smile.

"Do you have time for a cuppa?"

"I'm um…" I hold up the board of wet mortar in my hand and shrug. "It'll dry out if I stop."

She nods in understanding.

"No it's ok, you go," Spencer butts in, walking over and taking my trowel from my hand. "I'll take over." He grins. "I'm better at this than you anyway."

I could cheerfully murder him at times. I turn to hand him the board and cut him a look which expresses my desire to maim. He returns with one of his sarcastic 'you're welcome' grins.

I turn to Mags. "Looks like I'm free."

"I'll go and put the kettle on," Mags replies.

"Milk and one sugar!" Spencer calls out. Arsehole.

I follow her into the kitchen, reluctantly. The uneasiness

between us is not cool. I caused it, I know, but I don't know what else to do. She sets about making tea without a word and I realise it's going to be down to me to do the talking. I hate that, but since I'm the one with the issue I guess fairs fair.

"Why did you change your mind?" she says abruptly, pulling me from my thoughts. She doesn't turn to face me though, she just stares out of the kitchen window and down the long drive.

I don't know what to say. I wasn't expecting her to call me out, just like that. I thought I'd have to do some creative explaining, but she just knows. The guilt I already feel is worsened by the fact that she can see though me so easily. I search my empty head for something that sounds like a good reason, but all I find are my own insecurities, all of which are guaranteed to make her feel worse. While I'm dithering, she turns and fixes me with her hurt eyes.

I open my mouth to speak, but close it again.

She nods. "It's ok. Really. I get it. You don't want this."

"No, I…" She watches me expectantly, but I have nothing.

She sighs. "Will, you're going to have to tell me what your real problem is, I can't guess."

I look at my feet. Then mumble something I can barely even make out myself. It'll sound pitiful, so I can't even let the words fully form.

"What?" she snaps.

I lift my head and look her square in the eyes. She is understandably annoyed, but I feel the same way. I have to let go of something I really want. *Again.* Where is the fairness in that? But it is what it is. "I said, I'm not good enough for you."

She stares at me, speechless.

"I'm not Mags. Don't try and deny it."

Her brows furrow. “Are you serious?"

I just shrug. "I don't want it to be true, but you know it is."

"Have I *ever* made you feel that way? Because if I have then please forgive me."

"It's not you," I tell her, walking over to her and taking her hand. She tries to pull it away, but I don’t let her. I need to say this. She needs to understand. "When I'm with you," I continue, "I can believe it isn't true."

"Because it's not!" she protests.

"Mags, I'm not part of your world."

That's the final straw for her temper, she wrenches her hand from mine. "The money again? Is that all you care about?”

I watch her, fuming over this old wound which I’ve reopened. It’s not just the money, but it’s better that she doesn’t know that. Jealousy isn’t something I’m proud of and nothing she ever did made me feel this way. It was him. JJ and the fact that I’m not on a level to compete with him. I’ll stick with my story, the money is still a valid argument. I wish she would see it how I see it, but she thinks it doesn’t matter. And it might not right now, but I’m a realist and later down the line, when it counts…whatever, we have been through this. I’m not what she needs.

“Get out.”

She looks up and straight into my eyes. I try to speak, but she cuts me off.

“GET OUT!”

I sigh, but quietly leave.

Spencer looks up as I stalk past, but he carries on the

brickwork and lets me fume silently to myself. I need a distraction.

At lunch time, Spencer forcibly shoves a sandwich in my hand to stop me working and even then, I only stop to chew and swallow. I need to work. I need to forget and I need to move on.

The unmistakable thunder of hooves on the earth, pulls me out of my brooding and I turn to see my worst nightmare galloping across the open land that backs on to the rolling lawn behind the house. My blood boils, he is riding one horse and leading another, which I recognise as Mags' horse, so they must be going to go for a ride together.

How nice, that didn't take long.

That creature hates me I swear. She used to try and get me to ride with her, but horses and I are not compatible. Obviously she has JJ for that. Just another glaring example of how different our worlds are.

Mags steps out onto the terrace, dressed for riding. I hear Spencer choke at the sight of her in her jodhpurs. They aren't so funny on her.

"Damn," he says under his breath. I ignore him and watch her. She doesn't look this way, she heads straight for him.

"Hey, Shrimp!" I hear him call in his ridiculous booming voice, as he reaches the gate and dismounts.

I don't hear her reply, since she speaks like a normal person. I see him wrap her in a warm hug and hold her for far too long. Then I watch in horror as he pulls back and looks down at her, frowning, then pulls her in tight to his chest and looks up at me. He looks me in the eye while he kisses the top of her head.

Fucking perfect. He's enjoying it. I've handed her to him on a plate and he is being a smug bastard about it.

"Are you going to stand for that?" Spencer asks incredulously.

"Not a lot I can do."

He puts his arm around her and leads her back towards the horses, glancing once more in my direction with contempt, before he turns his attention fully back to her, I force myself to look away.

Spencer shakes his head, but remains tight lipped. So unlike him. I go back to attacking bricks with vigour.

The silence stretches out and I can almost feel him rehearsing the argument in his head. I know in a minute he is going to let rip and I can't deal with him spouting off when he doesn't know shit about this whole situation.

As he opens his mouth, I hold up my hand. "Can we not please?"

"I'm just saying, get your head out of your arse and tell her the horse dude has to go!"

I scoff, shaking my head and turn to go and get a new bag of cement.

"Don't be a baby. What's the big deal?"

I drop the bag and stare at the house. "Dude, she lives in there." I throw my arm towards the house. "Right now, she's off galloping around the country side with His Royal Perfectness. I'm the hired help, don't you see? This is how it's always going to be. Why would she want me? I mean, look at me."

He looks me up and down and folds his arms across his chest.

"If you're fishing for compliments mate, you've come to the wrong person. You're a fucking state, not gonna lie. But she obviously digs it."

I sigh. "Yeah, but for how long?"

Spencer frowns.

"Look, she'd come to her senses eventually and go off and marry the 4th Earl of Twatsville. That prick never goes away."

"Is he her ex or something?"

"No." I sigh, giving in to the self-pity. "He is her future. Can we just drop it now?"

"You have a very vivid imagination do you know that? Where do you get this crap from?"

"It's a fact. She's not mine anymore."

"Yeah well, you can't get all bent out of shape, you dumped her to come and let your hair down in Australia with me."

I stare at him for a second. He really is clueless. I shake my head, feeling suddenly bitter for what I gave up, but I choose not to go there. He lives in Spencerworld, the effort it would take to deliver cold hard fact into that grey matter of his really isn't worth it.

"What?"

"Nothing," I mutter.

"No come on, what?"

"Please, drop it."

"You obviously have something to say. Let's hear it."

I look up and the self-centred prick is standing there with his arms crossed, waiting to shoot down whatever I say. Well let's see if he's got something to say about the truth. "I didn't dump her to come and let my hair down you selfish bastard. I abandoned her and couldn't ask her to wait for me, when I knew she deserved better than me."

Spencer looks at me like I'm missing the upside. "Yeah, abandoned her to come on a beautiful one year shagfest with your dear old cousin." Then he grins and bangs me on the back.

I see red. All the things I've sacrificed come bubbling up in a rush and my fist connects with his face before I realise I took a swing. I immediately put my fists up to try and deflect the blow I know is coming, but instead he tackles me into the wall. The other guys rush at us, pulling us apart and in the scuffle, I hear Spencer saying, "It's ok, I deserved it."

What in the hell?

The guys back away cautiously and then disperse, when it's apparent that Spencer isn't going to retaliate.

He touches his cheek and winces.

There is silence while we both catch our breath.

I can't believe that just happened, I bite back the urge to apologise. I'm too nice. I'm not a violent person, but he did indeed deserve that.

"You ready to get it off your chest?"

I sigh. "I didn't abandon her to go and have fun in Australia." I say, sounding defeated.

Spencer waits, but when I don't offer more, he toes the sand covered cement floor and stares intently at his boots. "I think it will be good for both of us if you say why you really left her."

I stare at him. Seriously, who is this guy and where is the idiot I only tolerate because we are blood? When he finally looks up at me I know he's right. It needs to be said.

"I left her to save you from going under."

He nods, looking back at his boots. "Have you told her that?"

"Yeah, I have actually. While you and Jazz were taking pot shots at each other then getting busy, we've had some really good talks."

"And that didn't make a difference?"

I shrug. "I broke her heart. Do you think it really matters why?"

"Well yeah, when it was an entirely selfless act, I think it does."

Entirely selfless? I think to myself. Hmmm. That's when my conscience kicks in. Damn it. "Yeah, well, it wasn't entirely selfless."

"Oh?"

Thinking back to that time, part of me thinks it was entirely self*ish*. "No." I scrub my forehead with the heel of my hand. "I had my reasons."

"Care to share?"

"Ugh, where do I start? I wasn't good enough for her."

"So you keep saying. Do you think you'll end up believing it one day?"

"I believe it now. I didn't always think it. I used to believe it didn't matter, but there were always tiny issues that cropped up from us being from such different backgrounds. The parties, the occasions, the dinners. Things I wasn't invited to. But guess who was always there?"

"Horse Boy?"

"Yep. Any time she had a 'family thing,' he was there, suited and booted. The times I was included I felt so out of place, but not him, he was in his element, with all his ‘may I have this dance?’ bullshit. I started making excuses in the end, until eventually we had it all out. Big fight.”

“And then what happened?”

“Well then it all went wrong really quick.”

“How?”

“It was some debutante ball. It was a huge deal with all her rich friends, she had grown up wanting to go and after my strop of the century, she suddenly didn’t seem at all bothered about going. Her dad was bugging her, JJ was bugging her and I could tell she was avoiding going so she didn’t hurt me. I told her she should go. What I should have said was, I would take her. I didn’t mean I wouldn’t go, I just meant she shouldn’t not go on my account…I don’t know. I was stupid. Anyway, the next thing I know, she’s going. With Prince Charming.”

“And you didn’t try to stop her? Tell her you meant you’d take her?”

“Nope, instead, I had the freak out of all freak outs, quietly to myself. Realised I was never going to be good enough and that all the time JJ was willing to put the effort in, I couldn’t compete. You had a well timed break down and I did a seemingly selfless disappearing act.” I sink down on a pile of sacks and let my face fall into my hands.

Spencer, surprisingly, laughs. “What an idiot.”

I nod. “I expected to come back from Australia and find them on the cover of OK magazine with cheesy smiles, showing off the spot where the Titanic clipped the diamond.”

“And what did you find?”

I rake my hands through my hair. “She was gone.”

“Exactly. You were out of the picture and nothing

happened."

"You don't know nothing happened."

"And you don't know anything did."

"Oh come on. Her family and his have been cozied up for years. George thinks the sun shines out of his arse. It's practically an arranged marriage."

"I don't hear any wedding bells."

"Give it time."

"Yeah, but George is a smart guy. Do you think he would have thrown you two together this summer if he thought Horse Douche was better for her and was in the wings waiting for his shot?"

"Yeah I know," I sigh. "I have thought that and its messed with my head." It's the only thing that bent my resolve when I first saw her again and now look at me, my resolve got crumpled and thrown in the bin, while I ruined it all by sleeping with her. "Anyway, it's too late now. I've well and truly blown it with Mags."

"You don't know that."

"Yeah I do. She just threw me out and promptly rode off into the sunset with the hero."

Spencer looks up at the sky and smirks. "The sun is still up drama queen. When she gets back, talk to her. You don't know if this guy is even interested in her."

"I've been back all this time and not seen hide nor hair of him even though he's only down the road. Now she's moved back and he's immediately sniffing around again…what does that tell you? He wants her and he has what it takes to get her."

"Does he though? And so what if he does? Be the one she wants and he will have to get used to it."

I sigh and stand back up. “He is from her world, it’s what she’s supposed to do. I’m just making things a bit easier on myself.”

“How?”

“By being the one that gets used to it.”

“You’re a dick, you know that right?”

“Takes one to know one.”

“Yeah, it does, so I can say with great authority, you’re being a dick. She clearly doesn’t care that you’re covered in plaster, drive a shit car and are a little on the weedy side.”

I raise my eyebrows.

He holds up his hands. “Just my opinion.”

“Is that so?”

“You could do to bulk up a bit dude, it’s a fact.”

I shake my head. “Just because I’m not a meathead like you.”

“Whatever, you’re being an idiot. Sort it out.”

“Uh huh. Ok.”

“Don’t let him get to you, he’s not worth it. I mean what does he have to offer her?”

I laugh. “You mean besides wealth, status, a shared passion for horses and let’s not forget, the family blessing.”

“That’s all overrated, what does he even do besides wear tight trousers and have floppy hair?”

“He runs George’s stables.”

“So he’s basically a farmer.”

“There’s a bit of a difference between mucking out old nags and thoroughbred management, Spencer. His Royal Highness doesn’t get his hands too dirty, trust me.”

“And Mags is into all that?”

"Yeah, she loves to ride." I turn to go back to work and end up staring out towards the fields, wondering if she is having a good time. If she hasn't seen JJ since she has been back then she hasn't ridden in a long time. She must be loving it.

I suddenly feel the need to leave. I can't be here when she gets back. I can't see how happy she is doing something she loves, with him. And I can't watch if he makes a move. "I think I'm going to go home. I'll make it up, I just can't…"

"Yeah ok." Spencer says behind me.

"Thanks."

"Is he seriously royal?" Spencer blurts as I pack up my stuff.

"56th in line to the throne, or something."

"Jesus. You're fucked."

"Cheers mate."

"You're welcome."

Stretched out on my bed, staring at the ceiling, I glance at the clock again. He's late. Just then, I hear the front door slam. I listen for a while as he crashes around the kitchen. I want to go down there and question him about what I missed. Did she look ok? Did he kiss her? Or worse, did he go into the house with her? Hell I know that knowing the details will only hurt. I shouldn't torture myself.

Minutes later he climbs the stairs and appears in my doorway, eating an apple and holding an open book, deeply engrossed in what he's reading.

I raise myself up on an elbow and watch him. Seemingly unaware of my presence, even though he is standing in the doorway of my room, he bites into his apple and keeps his eyes fixed on the page. His eyebrows shoot up and then he continues chewing, turning his attention to the next page.

"What are you reading?" I ask, breaking the silence.

He looks up in surprise almost as if he didn't realise where he was. He turns the book over and glances at the cover. "Your girlfriend's latest book." Then he turns on his heel and heads for his room.

I frown, my…I don't…WAIT! I leap up and scramble after him, tearing the book out of his hand before he reaches his door. It's too easy, he let me have it, he was just dangling the carrot, but I don't care.

"How did you get this?"

Spencer shrugs. "Jazz had it in her room."

"So you stole it?"

"I'll put it back," he says unconcerned.

I turn it over in my hand and stare at the cover. 'Gigi King' is the author's name. King was her mother's maiden name, it figures. I feel a swell of pride in holding her book in my hand and fan the pages, scanning the sheer volume of words produced by someone I— by an old friend. I stop on a page and my eyes land on words that immediately set my pulse racing. Then I feel Spencer looming over me. I give him a sideways glance and hurry to my room.

He is right behind me. "She's a filthy one your girlfriend."

"She's not my—" I sigh. "Just go away Spencer."

I walk into my room and he tries to follow. "Leave you alone to 'read' you mean?" He laughs, doing air quotes with his fingers when he says the word, read.

I press my hand into his face and push him out of my

doorway, closing the door on him once he is out.

"There better not be any pages stuck together when I get that back!" he shouts through the door and I stick my middle finger up even though he can't see.

Taking a deep breath, I look down at the book in my hand. It looks filthy as fuck. A black and white image of the backs of a woman's legs. She's wearing stockings, those ones with the fucking line up the back. Shit. And the fuck-me-heels. But it's her stance that gets me. In charge, confident and from a single finger hangs a pair of handcuffs. The thought crosses my mind that the legs could actually be Mags' and I toss it on the bed as if it burnt me.

I run my fingers through my hair. What am I going to do? I can't read it, this is all bad enough as it is. I can hardly think when I'm around her, I want her so badly. But I've messed it all up now. Can I really have her dirty thoughts in my head torturing me?

I look down at the book.

Can I not?

"Have you tried to see it from his point of view?"

I fix Jazz with a glare. "Really? You think I'm the one being unreasonable?"

"No not at all," she backtracks. "I'm just wondering if a bit of empathy might calm you down a little so you can see the bigger picture."

"Which is?"

"That he clearly likes you, but he's letting some deep insecurities get in the way."

"I don't need to empathise to see that. It's bullshit. He slept with me knowing damn well that he would pull away afterwards. That's just wrong. He's messing with my feelings."

"Mags, until about two months ago, I didn't know you had any."

"Thanks!"

She rolls her eyes. "You know what I mean. Until we came here, you were only too pleased to have one night of pleasure and then pull away. You did it all the time. In fact, you got downright annoyed if they even wanted your number."

"This is different though."

"Yeah, obviously. It's different because you care. I've

never seen you do that."

"For good reason. The last person I cared for was Will and look where that got me. I'm careful now."

"Careful? You make it sound like you use protection against unwanted pregnancy, STDs and the dreaded feels."

"That's exactly what I do."

Jazz tries not to laugh but it beats her.

"Shut up, it's not funny."

"I'm sorry." She tries to look serious. "All I'm saying is, he clearly likes you, can't you talk to him? You might be able to overcome his insecurities together and have banging hot sex."

"I tried that today, the talking to him part. There is just no reasoning with him. He's set on not being good enough for me, whatever that crap means. It's all a smoke screen."

"I agree, there is more to it than he is saying. But don't you want to find out what that is?"

"I just don't see why I should be the one to drag it out of him. I gave him the perfect chance to tell me and he blew it. I'm done with him."

"Oh Mags."

"Don't 'oh Mags' me. I can't go through this again."

Jazz studies me. It's clear she has more to say, but thinks better of it right now. "I tell you what, I'll run you a nice bath, and you try and relax. Maybe you'll feel more like talking it through tomorrow." She leaves the room and misses me shake my head at her. She doesn't know what it took to put Will behind me and I'll be damned if I let him do that to me again.

Uggggggh! I'm so mad I could scream. If the money is such a big deal to him, then I shouldn't give a shit what he thinks.

But where does he get off telling me that he's not good enough for me? I make those decisions, no one else. My blood boils and suddenly I can't fight the urge to have it out with him.

'Where are you?'

'I'm sitting in my car outside Will's.'

'Oh, LOL. Your bath is ready.'

'I'm sorry, I just really need to sort this out.'

'Don't worry, I agree, you do. But why are you sitting outside?'

'I don't want to go in.'

'Then come home.'

'No. I have to do this.'

'Ok.'

I fling open my car door and climb out, slamming it as I stomp up the path. I ring the bell and it takes forever before I hear someone coming. The outside light comes on and door opens. I squint in the glare because my eyes had adjusted to the darkness in the fifteen minutes I sat in my car fuming and deciding whether or not to get out.

"Hey Mags." Spencer grins.

"He in?" I scowl.

"Uh, yeah, he's in his room. I know you know where that is." He performs an over exaggerated wink, standing aside to let me past.

Yeah, yeah, very funny wise guy. I push past him and start up the stairs.

"Mags," he calls after me, his tone more solemn.

I halt on the third step, but I don't turn around. "What?"

"Look," he pauses. Is Spencer Ryan about to get serious? "I know he's a total dipshit, but he really cares for you."

Damn it. I'm trying to be angry here, don't give me a reason to back down. "He has a funny way of showing it," I reply and then carry on up the stairs before he can say anything else.

I don't bother to knock, I just open the door.

Will is sitting in the armchair in the corner by the window, reading. He looks up in shock.

"Mags!" He says jumping to his feet.

I put a finger up to silence him. I only have so much patience and I need to get this out before he makes it worse with a stupid comment.

Then I notice what he's holding.

Shit, no!

"Where did you get that?"

He closes it and looks at it guiltily. "Um, I..."

I walk towards him. "I'm serious. How do you have it?"

"Spencer found it in Jazz's room."

"Give it to me," I bark, trying to take it from him.

He holds it behind his back and I lunge for it, crashing into him so our bodies are pressed together. He doesn't relinquish it and I pull my face back to look at him. When his eyes flit to my lips, I know it's too late to move out of his space. His lips are on mine as I try to voice my objection and I hear the book drop to the floor. His arms sweep around me, caging me in and my lips part involuntarily to allow his tongue to find mine.

I press my hands against his shoulders, bracing myself to push away and catch myself lingering in the kiss.

No. I push him off me, annoyed at myself for giving in. "Wait!"

We both step back gasping.

"I'm sorry, I—"

"No, stop with the 'I'm sorries.' I can't stomach another one." I glance at the book on the floor. I don't know how much he's read, but this is bad. So bad. I need to say what I wanted to say, get that bloody book and get out. I take a deep breath and look him in the eye. "You don't get to say who is good enough for me and who isn't. I decide. Me. If you don't feel good enough then that's something you need to figure out, because it's not my problem. You can't sleep with me then say it won't work, then kiss me when I come to have it out with you." I shake my head. "Fuck, Will. What is going on with you?"

He drops his gaze, but doesn't respond.

"You're being really unfair, do you know that?"

He nods but doesn't look up.

"You think if you say you're not good enough for me, I'll agree with you and make walking away easy on you? Is that what you want? You think if you hurt me enough I'll do the hard part for you so that you can be a coward and you don't have to have the balls to say you don't want me?"

He raises his head abruptly. "What? No!"

"Well what then, Will? Because that's how it feels."

"You wrote a book about us," he says softly.

I close my eyes and wince. "Don't change the subject."

"I'm not."

"You shouldn't have read that." I shake my head, wanting to back away as he takes a step towards me.

"It's us." He dips his head to try and make eye contact.

I sigh and meet his eyes. "It's just a story."

"It's *our* story."

"It's nothing like our story, she's a—" I blush, it hits me hard and fast and I can't hide it as I feel the warmth radiate from my cheeks. I look away, not able to bring myself to say that she is a domme and he lives to please her. What will he think of me? I can deny it all I like but it's obvious that the submissive in the book was based on him, down to the fact that he left her to go to Australia. From that point on though, it's purely fiction. When I wrote it, I hadn't seen him for years. There was no way it could fall into his hands. I would have kept it in my head if I thought for a second…

Fuck me.

My ex just read the fantasies that I still harbour for him. Ok, it's an exaggeration of the fantasies I harbour, but still. It seemed like such a good idea. It was the perfect set up for the second chance love story that my publisher was looking for. Will was the ideal basis for a submissive male. Not that that's how I saw him, it's just…oh god!

I've taken an innocent story and made it just…dirty.

And he read it!

Kill. Me. Now.

“I know what she is,” he says. “What I want to know is, where did all this come from?” His tone is so soft, I feel compelled to look at him again.

I shrug. “It’s fiction.”

“Really?” He steps in close, stealing the air from around me and I gasp shallow breaths trying to survive while he lingers.

It's unbearable to be this close again knowing it will all end. So closing my eyes, I lie. “Yes.” The word is a whisper.

I can feel how close his face is and I imagine his lips pressing against mine and how impossible I will find it to push him away. Then suddenly the air is clear and cold and all his warmth has left my space. I open my eyes expecting to see him walking away, but he isn't there and then I glance down.

I gasp, stepping back when I see him on his knees.

"Whoa! What the hell are you doing?"

He doesn't reply. There is no reaction, his eyes stay fixed to the floor.

"Will?"

Still nothing.

"Get up, Jesus Will." What does he think? That I'm her? That I'm going to dominate him? I'm no domme. Sure I write a good game and yeah, I've fantasised about it. Maybe I do naturally take the lead in bed, but I've never put it into practice…I mean men just don't fall to their knees...not in the real world.

Then it hits me that I'm missing the point.

He's kneeling.

For me.

My heart pounds and my palms start sweating. Maybe it's his fantasy too? I flex my fingers, imagining slipping them gently into his hair, closing my fist and pulling sharply to make him look at me.

But I couldn't. This is the real world, I remind myself.

And still he waits.

Eons seem to pass and he is unfaltering.

I lift my hand, wondering if I really could, but pull it back.

"Come on Will, this is silly."

Nothing.

"Will," I plead.

Finally, instinct more than anything moves my hand forward, he flinches ever so slightly as I make contact and it thrills me. Something inside me takes over and I fist his hair. "Damn it, Will, look at me."

Suddenly he looks up. His eyes are glazed with desire and I definitely didn't have to yank his hair, that was all him. It was my command. I said look at me and he looked at me in a heartbeat. It was hot as hell, but he is living in a fantasy that doesn't exist and it makes me more cross with him.

"It's. Just. A. Story." My fist tightens in my frustration and he lets out a sigh of pure pleasure.

"I want to know how it ends," he whispers.

I pause, staring into his eyes. Which version? The fictional story, or the one that's real? I feel all the power I ever fantasised about having, right at my fingertips. But what about all of his ridiculous issues with my money and lifestyle? What about the fact that he rejected me? I can't go through it all again, it hurt too much. I glance down at the book laying on the floor beside him and decide.

Let him have his stupid fantasy.

"You'll have to keep reading then," I reply, releasing his hair. I can hear him scrambling to his feet as I reach for the door. He puts his hand firmly on it to stop me from opening it. I can't bring myself to look at him because I know it will weaken my resolve.

"Let me go," I demand calmly.

"I can't," he gasps, as if this revelation is a surprise to him. "Please, Mags."

"Please what?" I turn abruptly. His hand falls away from the door and I open it to leave. "Please give you another chance to sleep with me so you can make me feel like shit again tomorrow when you remember I'm not what you want?" I snap. "Or please take you back so you can make me feel like shit on a daily basis until you decide it's over again and fuck off round the world?"

This is a pointless conversation. Nothing changes the fact that he can't handle my lifestyle. Why? Who the hell knows. I am not going to put myself in that situation again. I don't understand any of this. I never did. And trying to figure it out is both hurtful and exhausting.

"No," Will frowns. "None of that. You are what I want Mags. You always have been."

"Really? Then you need to work on how you express yourself, because leaving the country indefinitely sends a powerful message."

He drops his eyes.

"And this bullshit today about not being good enough for me. When are you going to stop making excuses? I can't change who I am or where I come from. I don't think I have ever shoved it in your face. It's not that you aren't good enough for me, is it? It's that I'm not good enough for you."

"No!" He roars, putting himself between me and the open door. "You, you're…you're everything. I just can't give you the life you come from. Not like—" he cuts himself off abruptly.

"Not like…?" I push impatiently, folding my arms.

From across the hallway Spencer coughs loudly through his open door, "Horseboy."

"What?" I frown, staring over Will's shoulder. This is just perfect, I didn't realise we had an audience.

"Fuck off Spencer." Will snaps, without turning around.

"What does he mean?"

Will sighs, but doesn't say a thing.

"Fine, if telling me the truth is too much then I'll just leave."

"No wait, please don't go."

"Well then tell me what he means."

Will glances behind him to Spencer's open door. "Will you come back inside so we can talk about this privately?"

I shake my head. "No. If you have something to say, spit it out so that I can go."

"Ugh god, this soap opera is getting so BO-RING," Spencer exclaims stalking towards us. "He means your horsey friend with the floppy hair. This idiot thinks he isn't good enough for you because you will eventually settle down in a castle with Ponyboy. There, I said it, are we done now?"

"Seriously Spencer, what did I ever do to you to deserve this shit? All I've ever done is help you out." Will looks genuinely hurt as I watch the exchange in shocked silence.

"Exactly," Spencer replies looking pleased with himself. "You told me to pull my head out of my arse, so I'm returning the favour. You're welcome. So now that I've saved us all at least a month's worth of excruciating back and forth and guessing games, I'm going to see my girlfriend."

Will opens his mouth, then closes it again.

"Fuck me," Spencer mutters under his breath as he trots down the stairs and grabs his car keys. "All this drama and it's not even anything to do with me. I'm the one who has it all sorted? Who'd have thought they'd fucking live to see the day?" He pulls the front door closed behind him, leaving us both in stunned silence.

"Was he being serious?"

Will blows out a long breath that just confirms that Spencer was telling the truth.

"JJ? Wh—" I can't even… "I haven't seen the guy in I don't know how long, then one coffee and a ride and that adds up to me wanting to marry him?"

"It runs deeper than that Mags. I can see how much he wants you Mags and realistically, I can't compete with that."

"Deeper? What do you mean?"

He stares at me for a long moment. "Honestly?" he asks quietly.

"That would be a refreshing change," I challenge.

"Who was that on the phone love?" Mum asks, startling me. I hadn't heard her come in the back door.

"Auntie Liz."

"Oh does she want me to call her back?"

"No she called to speak to me."

"Oh?" She looks intrigued.

"Yeah, she's worried about Spencer. She really wants me to go down there at the weekend."

"You should, you haven't seen him in a long time."

"I doubt he will be at all interested in seeing me. The reason we've hardly spoken is that bitch of a girlfriend he thought the sun shone out of. What makes you think he wants me down there gloating that she turned out to be the bitch I thought she was?"

"Well you don't have to gloat dear."

I groan. "I'm not saying I will, but still, he won't want me down there."

"If Auntie Liz thinks he will, maybe you should go."

"Auntie Liz doesn't have a clue. She wants me to go to Australia with him."

"I thought he'd cancelled it?"

"He did. She thinks he needs to do it regardless. And she wants me to go with him."

"For how long?"

"I guess for the year, I don't know."

"Oh."

I can see the worry on her face. "Don't worry mum. I'm not going. I have stuff going on here that I can't just leave." I see her frown deepen and sigh reluctantly. "I'll go down there at the weekend and drag him out of his room. He just needs cheering up that's all, I don't need to go to the other side of the world for that."

She squeezes my shoulder and offers a concerned smile. "Maybe the trip would be good for you too," she says heavily.

"Why do you say that?"

"Because…" she hesitates.

"What?" I demand.

"Well don't you think some time away might do you good?"

"Are you trying to get rid of me?" I joke, trying to deflect her true meaning I know she is tiptoeing around. Things have been pretty intense lately, I've been wrapped up in my insecurities. My fear that Mags might perhaps eventually want someone more suited to her lifestyle. Someone like the jumped up, mini aristocrat that hangs around like a bad smell, just waiting to snatch her away.

"Of course not. I don't relish the thought of you being away for so long. But you're a young man and I would hate it even more if you missed out on a big opportunity over a girl. Don't get stuck in your first relationship, when you have your whole life ahead of you." She smiles, trying to soften the blow, but there's no hiding her point. She thinks Mags and I won't last, so maybe I should take this opportunity.

I want her to be wrong. Mags and I are strong.

I can almost believe it.

Deep down, I know she will ultimately marry money, and I'm not money. I don't mean she's obsessed with material stuff, it's just a lifestyle thing. This guy, he's her people. Their dads golf together, the families holiday together on private islands in far flung archipelagos. They share common interests and passions that their upbringing has given them access to. I'm just not part of that world and some things are hard to fight.

And it built up. It came spilling out. I didn't say I was jealous of the aristocrat, but I let my growing insecurities get the better of me and made her feel like she was in the wrong for wanting to be part of her circle. And now she's acting like she has no interest in this debutante ball thing that's coming up. She has worked hard for the last year, doing charity work and etiquette stuff for it. It was something her mum was into, so she really wanted to do it in her memory. It would have been something they prepared for together. But now, she says it's a stupid, snooty tradition that she's not interested in. All because she wants to prove to me that she and I are not from entirely different worlds.

I realise what an arsehole I was about it and I've told her she should go. I've tried to convince her that she should do it for her Mum, but I don't think she's really hearing me. So I'm going over there to try and convince her to go with me. I owe her that.

"Don't worry Mum, I'm fine, and I'm not going anywhere." I hug and kiss her and turn to leave.

"Just give it some thought," she calls out after me.

"I will," I reply, already out the door. I have to get to Mags and ask her to a ball.

"I've got something to tell you." Mags says as she greets me at her front door.

"Me first," I counter, eager to see her face light up.

"No, this is important," she insists. "You were right, the debutante ball is something that would have made mum so proud, she wanted me to do it and I will. But don't worry—" she says as I open my mouth to interrupt. "JJ has kindly agreed to escort me, so you don't have to go through the whole nightmare."

I catch myself before my face falls.

Don't be a dick Will. Just don't be a dick.

Of course he's fucking kindly agreed, I bet he couldn't wait until I screwed up so he could jump in.

But I won't be a dick. She looks so happy.

"That's great," I manage.

No, It's not great.

I didn't mean you should go with just anyone.

Him.

I meant you should go with me.

A roar of laughter comes from the doorway to Mags' dad's office. I look up to see him throwing his arm around JJ with a huge smile. With his free hand, he shakes JJ's and gives his shoulders a pleased-as-punch rattle.

"You won't regret this George," JJ tells him.

"I know I won't son. Welcome to the family."

And there it is.

My heart hits the floor so hard, I can't even see straight.

JJ is standing beside Mags the next thing I know.

"What was all that about?" She asks, mirroring his goofy grin.

"Your dad just offered me a job! I'm going to be training to manage his stables while I study."

Of course, 'welcome to the family' meant his staff. So stupid. But then as Mags squeals and hugs him in congratulations, the feeling overwhelms me again. He is never going away. He is always going to fit in more than I do. It's a suffocating feeling, I want to tear out my hair and scream.

I realise I'm being spoken to, too late to register what was actually said.

"Huh?"

"Isn't it great?" Mags repeats.

"Oh yeah, great."

"And don't worry buddy," he smiles. "I'll take great care of her at the ball." And then he slaps my arm like we are in this thing together.

Fuck my life, I feel like I'm choking and no one notices.

"I've got to go," I murmur.

"Okay," Mags replies, looking confused. "Will I see you later?"

Thinking fast, I look her straight in the eye. "That's what I came to tell you. My cousin, he's er...going through a really bad time. My Auntie is worried he might do something stupid. I'm going down there. He needs me."

"Oh, Okay, when will you be back."

"I don't know. I'll text you." And then I turn and leave, trying not to look like I'm making a break for the getaway car.

When he finishes his walk down memory lane, I stare at him in disbelief. Putting aside the ridiculous the notion of JJ wanting me, I feel the rage bubbling up. Fuck who else wants me, if he wants me then he should fight. "So what you're saying is, I'm not worth fighting for? Even in a fight you *think* you can't win, it's not worth at least trying?"

"I didn't say that."

"Well actions speak louder than words Will."

"I was just protecting myself."

"From what?"

"Heartbreak."

I shake my head, defeated. "I've never thought of JJ in that way and he has no interest in me either. It's pretty obvious you just don't want to be with me, you need to stop making excuses. I'm going to go." I try to leave and find him moving in close, blocking my way.

"I wasn't making excuses. I—" He pauses, swallowing. "I was a fool," he whispers.

"You're telling me." I huff, remaining rigid while he tries to wrap me up in his arms.

"Please Mags, don't go."

"Give me one reason to stay."

"I could give you a thousand."

"And yet you take one look at JJ and you freak out?"

He sighs. "I can't help it. Seeing him around you just makes me think that if he really tried, he could have you and honestly Mags, I'd never recover."

"So instead of having some faith in me, you take the cowards way out and make me think it's something I've done to make you feel unworthy."

"Something along those lines, I guess."

"That's really shitty, Will. All this time, I've felt responsible."

"I'm so sorry, Mags. I never meant to hurt you. Please give me another chance?"

"And what will you do with it?"

He takes my hand and looks me square in the eyes. The fire I see in his makes me come alive. "Never let you go," he rasps.

I catch my breath because despite myself, it's what I want to hear. And even though he is the reason I have a wall up, he is the only reason that I would tear it down. So while I know

I'm probably going to get battered, I allow a crack to form. It was going to form anyway.

"Why should I believe you? Earlier today, I was too good for you, now this," I say bitterly. "What's changed?"

He flushes red and looks away. Shame maybe? Because I brought up his awful display earlier. I don't know. I wonder if I will always have to examine his every nuance for evidence that he is covering some vague insecurity that will come out and bite me when I least expect it?

"I see," I say when he doesn't respond. I try to push past him but he stands firm.

"I was being stupid," he says firmly. "Pushing away the most precious thing I've ever had because I was a coward. I'm going to fight for us Mags. I'm going to fight for you." He looks sincere. I wish I had Jazz here so we could analyse it together.

"I don't know Will. I don't know if I can trust you to follow through. I can't keep getting hurt by you not believing in us."

"I know I don't deserve it, but I'm asking you to try me. Put me to the test."

"And if you fail?"

"Punish me," He says quietly, lowering his eyes.

I gasp. My body and mind simultaneously react, only in opposite directions. "Will, for heavens sake, you can't make this about sex! This is serious," I snap, while fighting the need to squeeze my thighs together. Is he for real?

"I know it is and I'm deadly serious. Try me," he glances down at the book on the floor. "If I fail to have faith in us, punish me however you see fit. Correct me. Remind me I'm yours." He looks up, straight into my eyes.

I cannot believe he is quoting my book at me. From the look of him though, he means it.

MONDAY 24TH AUGUST

"I know this should be about my commitment to making this work between us," I sigh. "And it is, honestly, but I can't help myself. How could I not see it? It's obvious." I reach for her hand and she doesn't pull it away. "I always knew you were perfect for me but I never believed I was perfect for you. Until now. Now I see that all those years ago, without us knowing, something in me recognised something in you and needed it. No wonder I never got over you. *That* is what has changed. *That* is why I know I have to fight for us. Not because of the mind blowing sex I think we could have, but because I know now that I can be something you need, despite the rest."

She looks like she hasn't heard a word I just said. "This is a lot to take in Will, I need to go," she mutters.

"Mags, please."

"I'll…" she trails off.

What?

Call me?

See me tomorrow?

See me around?

She obviously can't find the appropriate words. I don't want her to make a promise she can't keep, nor do I want to hear a goodbye. She doesn't have to push past me this time, I stand aside, defeated. If she doesn't want to be here, I can't make her stay.

I hear the front door close and let out a long groan, scrubbing my face.

Fuck.

It can't end like this. I need her and even though I've had a hard time seeing it, I think she needs me. And yeah, ok, JJ might want her. He might even think he can get her. But—Then it hits me like a thunderbolt…No one is better for her than I am.

I grab my phone off the bedside table and open my conversation with her and to my surprise, I find that she's already typing. My heart leaps. What's she going to say? I sit on the edge of my bed, waiting.

Knowing that she is just outside, but had to get away from me is an awful feeling, she could be about to tell me she never wants to see me again. I try to hold on to the hope that there is still a chance for us.

'Punish you?'

I stare at my phone. I thought it was going to say 'It's over'. This is not what I expected. Evidently I take too long to answer because she starts typing again.

'So you're into the submission thing?'

I take a deep breath. This is something I have never admitted to anyone. Spencer teased me for weeks after he used my laptop and saw something I'd been watching, but no one really knows. Not even the girls I've been with.

'Yeah.'

'For how long?'

'Mags this is crazy, come inside, we need to talk things through.'

'I can't think in there. How long?'

I sigh. It hurts, but I deserve it.

'I don't know, always I guess.'

'You didn't used to be.'

'Didn't I?'

'You tell me.'

'I think I always have been, I didn't know all that really existed, I hadn't had my eyes opened. But I was into you, and now it all makes perfect sense.'

'Who opened your eyes?'

'No one.'

'So how do you know?'

'I just know, it appeals to me.'

'But you've never submitted?'

'Never.'

'Good.'

I smile. Hope fills every crack in my confidence. I love how possessive that was. It totally wasn't jealousy. It was a warm hug of possessiveness that gives me the first real taste of that thing I have always fantasised about. Being owned.

'Have you ever dominated? Like really, properly?'

'Nothing beyond being bossy.'

I swallow. It's agony to think of her being bossy in bed with someone else. But I can't expect she's been celibate the last five years. I'll take it. If she'd had a sub before, it would have killed me.

'But it's there though isn't it? I mean I've read your words. Don't tell me this doesn't tempt you. You asked me what has changed. It's this. I have always known you are perfect for me, but I've never believed I was good enough for you, until now. Now I see we are perfect for each other. That I'm what you need just as much as you are for me. That's how you can trust me to follow through. I'm going to fight for you. I swear.'

There's a really long pause.

'Mags?'

'I'm going to go, I need to think.'

Fuck.

I throw myself back on the bed and cover my eyes with my arm. This is such a mess.

"You alright Mags?"

I jump and look up to find Jazz standing in the doorway. "You're home early."

"The joys of a catering business. Early start, early finish. I'm getting to grips with things now, I don't have to stay as late. You look sad, did something happen?"

"I'm ok."

She frowns, moving towards me. "No you're not, I can tell. Is Will still acting like a knob?"

I just sigh. To be honest, I don't know if it's Will acting like a knob or me.

"I'm sorry, I suck." She sits beside me and takes my hand. "You need me and I'm not here."

"No, no you don't suck, I'm fine, honestly. I went for a ride earlier and I hit my word target, I've had a nice day."

"I do. Between work and seeing Spencer, I haven't been around at all." She looks upset with herself. "I didn't even stay up last night to see how you were after you went over there to yell at Will. All I know is, you were in your bed asleep when I left this morning. I'm the worst friend ever. Are you two still not talking?"

"Jazz, you're busy, I made you busy. I'm ok. And it's not

that we aren't talking exactly. It's just that I told him I needed to think."

"About what?"

"Honestly, it's fine. There's nothing to talk about."

Jazz stands up. "Right, this is clearly an emergency. Tea or Margaritas?"

I giggle. "Don't tempt me. I've been staring at that tequila all day, but I have more work to do."

"Ok, I'll get the kettle on, you? Spill." She turns sharply and heads for the kitchen, pausing halfway and turning back to me. "Come on," she says expectantly and waits until I groan and get up to follow her and sit on a bar stool.

"So?" she demands.

Jesus, maybe I should have opted for the tequila.

"So, I was annoyed—"

"Annoyed? Is that what we're calling it?"

"Yeah, ok." I blush. "I was pretty angry, but I think I had every right to be. He was blowing hot and cold."

"So you went steaming in and ripped him a new arse?"

"That was the plan. Only...I was quite thrown off by the way I found him."

Jazz grimaces. "Eww, was he wanking?"

"No. He was curled up in a chair, deeply engrossed in a book. By the way, did you know your boyfriend stole your copy of Blind Faith and gave it to Will?"

"What?" she gasps, slapping her hands over her mouth. "I'm going to kill him," she says decisively.

I nod. "Uh huh."

"Oh my god Mags, I'm so sorry, he is going to die, I promise." She shakes her head.

"It gets worse."

"How?"

"It was that book, of all books..." I swallow. I've never told her this, much like I never told her about Will. She was my new life away from that hurt, so I didn't taint it, I just moved on.

"Why does it matter which book it was?"

"Because Blind Faith is about Will."

Her eyes go wide. "Nooooo!"

"Yep."

"No!"

"It doesn't become less true if you keep saying no."

"Oh my fucking god."

I nod, letting her absorb the revelation.

"So did you—? I mean, was it with Will that you got into—you know, all that?"

I chuckle. "God no, Will was Mr. Sweet-and-Innocent." Was, I think to myself. Can he really be so different now?

"So how was Blind Faith about him?"

"It was based loosely on us up to the break up, not much. I made the rest up, the second chance aspect and all that is fiction."

She raises her eyebrows and whistles. "That's some serious shit you made up about a real person."

"I know. I never thought he would see it. We lost touch, I moved away. I use a pen name for a bloody reason!"

She visibly cringes as the guilt touches her again. "Again, I'm sorry. Had he read much?"

"It looked like well over half."

"Oh fuck."

I bury my face in my hands, because although I'm dealing with it now, if I think too carefully about the words I know he has read, mortification will creep in and take hold and I don't know if I could face him again, even if he does seem to get a kick out of it.

"Maybe he didn't really read it, maybe he was just skimming to the juicy bits."

"Nope, he read it."

"Oh no. How did he take it?"

"Ugh," is all I can manage as I recall how he took it. I cover my face. I still can't believe what he did.

She wrenches open the fridge and gets the milk out, slamming it on the counter angrily. "Honestly Mags, I'm so sorry. He will be punished severely."

"That's not necessary. It might have worked in my favour, but you don't need to tell Spencer that, his ego is barely manageable as it is."

"Really?" she looks surprised.

"I don't know, maybe," I cringe.

"What does that mean?"

"Well, it only might have, it's too soon to tell."

"You're being cryptic," she says pouring milk into the two steaming cups.

"Will knew right away it was about us, I denied it, but he had read enough. And now he thinks that I have fantasised about dominating him all these years."

"Haven't you?"

"No!"

"Really?" She looks utterly unconvinced.

"I may have let fact inspire fiction a little, but it is just a story. I have not been dreaming of what could have been all this time. I moved on. Clearly, he doesn't see it that way, but it's the truth."

"Mags, you've not had anything with more substance than a one night stand since him. I wouldn't call that moving on, I'd call that utter avoidance."

"Are you really in a position to judge?"

Ignoring my deflection, she hands me my tea and takes a seat beside me. "So what did he say?"

"Nothing," I pause to take a sip. "He fell to his knees."

Jazz chokes on her tea. "He what?" she wheezes.

I bang her back. "He fell to his knees."

"What, like in the book?"

"Yep, assumed the position, eyes to the floor, wouldn't look up at me no matter what I said."

"Damn, what did you do? I'd have died!"

"I— Oh god, this is way too much information."

"You what? Come on Mags you can't stop there. I tell you everything."

I close my eyes. "Ok, but you CAN'T tell Spencer. He'll torment Will."

"I wouldn't, you know that."

I nod.

"So?"

"So I—" I cringe, but I suck it up. "I pulled his hair and ordered him to look at me."

"Oh my god," Jazz squeals. "Did he do it?" She is wide-eyed and brimming with excitement.

I nod, a shy smile curling my lips.

"Oh shit. So then what? Did you make him lick your

shoes?"

"No!"

"Well what happened? I bet it was good."

I shake my head. "It was more complicated than that Jazz. He'd rejected me, I was angry with him, he was all over the place. I ended up walking out of there. I needed time to think."

"Jesus Mags, you just left him on his knees?"

"No we talked a bit first."

"Damn."

"What?"

"If you'd left him on his knees it would have been hot."

"Oh my God! You're enjoying this."

"Just a little." She laughs. "Then what?"

"That's it. I left. There is nothing else."

"So you left him last night and you haven't spoken to him at all today?"

"I said I needed to think. He hasn't tried to talk to me. Either he is respecting it, or he is done with me."

"I highly doubt he's done with you Mags, I mean, from the sounds of it, he was damn keen on the idea. He is probably terrified to put a foot wrong. Poor boy."

"Poor boy? Why are you sympathising with him? I'm suffering here."

"What you gonna do?"

I set my cup down on the counter and stare at it. "I really don't know."

"That's what the face was for?"

"What face?"

"That sad face you had on when I came home."

"It's not sad, it's just," I pause. I almost don't want to give voice to it.

"Come on, you know you can tell me."

I sigh. "It's just that before, he was pulling away, rejecting me. He hurt me Jazz. And now, he's certain."

"That's good right?"

"I hope so."

"But?"

"But what if he's just excited by the fact that I write femdom erotica?"

"Mags, who wouldn't be excited by the fact that you write femdom erotica?"

I give her a flat look. "I'm serious. I can't handle him changing his mind again."

"Give him a chance. He seems like a good guy and from what Spencer has told me, you don't have anything to worry about."

I narrow my eyes. "Hmmm and what has Spencer told you exactly?"

She laughs. "Just that he really likes you and that he's into some, I quote, 'freaky shit'."

"And that's it?"

"Mags, we haven't exactly reached the long cosy nights chatting by the fire stage of our relationship yet. We haven't even been on a date."

I can't help but laugh, it's true, for all they've been through, they've only really been together properly, with no games, for a few days.

Jazz lays her hand over mine and gives me a comforting squeeze.

"Think if you have to, but don't think too hard. This seems

like a no brainer to me. He's just there," She nods to the door, where we can hear the sounds of them working. "He seems to really like you and damn would you two have hot sex."

I pull my hand away. "Is that all anyone around here ever thinks about?"

"You know you would, so don't give me shit for stating a fact."

"Well it's not the most important thing. I'm looking out for myself. I can't put myself through that again."

"Maybe it's you who is putting the emphasis in the wrong place. Who says this has to be so serious? Hmm? Maybe this should be more about sex. You're young, you know how to have a good time, where did all this heaviness come from? So you fell for him hard once, you were practically a kid. You're different people now, you've grown up. Enjoy each other. That's what life is for."

I nod absently. I don't know if I can see it that way.

I need more time to think.

Will

FRIDAY 28TH AUGUST

"Spencer, can you go and tell Mags that we need to turn the power off for half an hour?"

"You sure you wouldn't rather find your balls and do it yourself?"

I take a deep breath. Life is shitty enough right now without clashing with him. "I'm busy with this." I wave my hand towards the electrician who I am not really helping at all; I'm just trying to look busy. I hope he just buys it and shuts up.

"Ok," he nods. "It's been almost a week you know?"

I turn back to the electrician who is waiting for the go ahead to cut the power. I can't look at Spencer's disappointed face. "I'm perfectly aware of how long it's been. Could you go and tell her?" I hear him walk away and let myself relax a little. Another battle won. It's hardly a win though is it? More like another avoidance achieved.

Like I don't know she hasn't talked to me for a week. I'm bloody dying here. All I've done the past week is check my phone, stare at the house and read. I have read all of her books. The one about us is my favourite. Ok it isn't about us, it's based around our story up to a point, but god if it could have been us it would have been my dream come true. A dream is all it will ever be though. Otherwise she would have talked to me by now.

Part of me is giving her the space she asked for, the rest of me is shit scared to talk to her because I know it will only be so she can say that we made a mistake, the past is in the past and the stuff in her book is just fiction not fantasy.

I've spent the week lost in her fictional world and I would give anything to make it real.

Anything.

"She says it's fine, do it." Spencer calls from the kitchen door. I turn, expecting him to be walking back towards me, but instead, I see him stepping back inside the house and closing the door behind him. What the—?

It's an eternity before he emerges. An eternity I have to at least pretend to be helping the electrician and look like I'm occupied with something other than staring at the kitchen door. When he finally comes out, he looks like he has been up to no good.

"What did you do?"

"Nothing," he frowns. "Why do you automatically assume I've always done something?"

"Because you usually have."

"You're paranoid."

I watch him for a moment. He is unusually quiet for Spencer. If he had done something bad, I would expect him to be more goading. Maybe I am just paranoid.

But it's been a week. A week!

I'm just out here, she's just in there, what the fuck? Maybe I gave her too much space. How was I supposed to know how much she needed? She wasn't very clear. She said she needed to think, how long does it fucking take?

Limbo sucks.

Any other guy would have called her by now, or gone in there days ago. Or more to the point, most guys would have said fuck this and moved on…and there is the problem. I'm not most guys. I'm not what she needs. I thought for a perfect moment I might be. There in my room, on my knees with my hair in her grasp. I let fantasy mask reality for a moment and I believed that maybe everything about me that I have always seen as a letdown to womankind, might just be her thing.

But she is never going to call.

"Mate, I think that's you."

"Huh?" I look up, snapping out of my thoughts.

"Your phone." Spencer rolls his eyes like I'm some sort of moron.

I frown and look around. Sure enough, I can hear it, but I can't see it. I start scanning all the surfaces around me. Fuck, where is it?

Spencer shakes his head. "And they say you are the more evolved of the two of us." He reaches around me and pulls my still ringing phone out of my back pocket. "Well look at that," he smiles looking at the screen. "You can thank me later." He shoves the phone at me and I grapple with it trying to turn it the right way. I catch a glimpse of Mags' name on the screen as I almost drop it.

"Motherfucker," I growl as I fumble with it, finally getting it to my ear.

"Bad time?" Mags replies.

"Oh! No! Not you, sorry…I—" I shut myself up and take a deep breath. "Hi."

"Hi."

"How's it going?" I ask, feeling like it's most inane question ever.

"Pretty well. How are you?"

"I'm good."

Lie.

Pathetic, stupid, lie.

I open my mouth to correct myself—

"Would you like to have dinner with me?" she asks, stopping me.

"Yes." There's no hesitation.

"Are you free tonight?"

"Yes I am."

"Good. Let's meet at the pub at eight."

I open and close my mouth a couple more times. "Yes, okay."

"Okay, see you then," she says quietly.

"Yes see you then."

I disconnect the call and stare at my phone. Did that just really happen?

"Everything ok?" asks Spencer knowingly.

I look at him for a long moment. "What did you say to her?"

"Nothing."

"Bullshit Spencer."

"She asked how we were doing out here, that's all."

"And?" I demand after giving him plenty of time to tell me more.

"I merely told her we were running a little behind and that we could do with everyone focused on the job right now. I never even mentioned your name."

"That's it? You didn't tell her I've been a pathetic mess?"

"Mate, she has windows." He laughs.

I narrow my eyes. "I hate you sometimes."

"Yeah I know. But the rest of the time you realise how awesome I am."

I scoff.

"Is that ungrateful bastard for, 'yes Spencer, you are awesome, thank you'?"

"Whatever." I turn away, going back to what I was doing. "I have work to do. Apparently I'm underperforming."

I fiddle with the menu again, straightening it up, so it's square with the table edge. A drop of condensation rolls down my glass and lets me know I've been sitting here a while. She isn't late. I was just stupidly early.

I ordered her a wine, that too has condensation and I resist the urge to use a napkin to dry it off. I will look like a right weirdo if she arrives to find me polishing her wine glass, with the wine in it. Instead I look at my watch and check the angle of the menu again. I don't even know if she wants to eat here, or just meet here. I got her a drink, I mean, it's safe to assume that if you meet in a pub, a drink is required, isn't it?

I got the menu just in case.

She said dinner.

That's good, I think.

'Fuck off and die' could be taken care of with a text. "Thanks but no thanks' merely requires a call. And if she was just meeting me for 'it's not you, it's me' then she would not have suggested dinner.

Right?

I'm fucking dying here.

I got the table in the corner so we could talk if that's what she wants to do, but what if she doesn't see me? I arrange my seat a little better so that I'm more visible from the door, and straighten the menu again.

"Hey."

I jump at the sound of her voice. "Hey," I smile, standing to greet her, panicking inside about whether to kiss her. What's the protocol when greeting someone you've slept with but now can't even look in the eye? I'm not sure. When you hope beyond hope that she will allow you to kneel at her feet, it kind of throws all other social conventions out the window.

But when I look at her, her smile makes everything ok.

She looks different.

Powerful.

I'm probably just seeing what I want to see, but she is fucking stunning dressed all in black. There is nothing cliché about it, just pure power.

Social convention isn't something I need to worry about in the end. While I'm standing here catching flies, she leans in and places a light kiss on the corner of my mouth. It's not a peck on the cheek, it's not a kiss on the lips, it's right between formality and affection and what it tells me is, she isn't pulling away. There is hope.

And then as she leans further into my space, she whispers. "Sit."

I feel his body tense as I kiss him. All the nerves I came here with seem nothing in comparison to the tension he is carrying and something that feels remarkably like instinct kicks in, I feel like I know how to soothe him. Don't ask me how, this is new territory for both of us, but I feel it inside, like I know what he needs.

"Sit," I whisper firmly. There is no mistaking that it's an order, however softly I delivered it.

My heart is hammering in the pause after. God, I hope I'm handling this right. I thought we were just going to talk, not…you know, get started.

Then the tension seems to bleed out of him and he sits heavily back in his seat. It was the magic word, like I entered the right passcode and a door opened. I place my hand lightly on his shoulder and then remove it, not knowing how to handle myself. Maybe I should praise him, but it's too soon to find the words. One step at a time.

I take the seat opposite him and he watches me slip my jacket off. When I meet his eyes, they seem to say thank you and I return a small nod.

"I got you a wine, is that okay?" he says, nodding to the glass. The nervous energy vibrating from him again.

"It's lovely thank you." I reply. I can't help the smile as I see that my approval relaxes him a little more.

"How have you been?" he asks.

"I've been ok. How about you?"

"I've missed you," he says quietly.

I smile softly. "I had some thinking to do."

"I know you did. I was starting to think that you might not reach a conclusion."

"Who says I have?"

"You called me. You're here. That's enough for now."

"For now?" Heartened by the hope in his voice, I lean forward and dip my head to keep his eye as he tries to look away. "That sounds to me like you plan to get more."

A flush of colour creeps across his cheeks and I raise my eyebrows. I don't know where my challenge came from. This was not my agenda, but being here with him, and with this new found knowledge of each other. My agenda seems to have died on its arse.

"I just—" he cuts himself off. Clearing his throat, he sits straighter. "I would very much like more, Mags. But for now, I'll take whatever you can give."

"That's brave of you." I smile suggestively. "You don't know what I'm capable of." I almost feel bad, he is being so sweet and considerate. I can really see he is trying and now I'm the one making it all about sex. But Jazz was right. When did this get so heavy? I came here still carrying some of that weight, but seeing him for the first time in almost a week, it's like something has clicked.

"I'd like to find out." His voice is laced with desire.

"Just like that? No discussion?" Leaning back in my chair

and lifting my wine to my lips, I watch him. It's hard to know how seriously to take him. I have no clue how far I could take this. Hell, I have no clue how far I'm brave enough to take it.

He shakes his head and picks up his beer. "I've seen enough to know."

"Know what?"

"That I trust you."

I frown. "You have seen a little, that's all."

"No, I've seen it all."

I pause after taking another sip and a few seconds pass before I swallow.

Will smiles. He sits forward, seeming more self-assured. "I've read them all Miss 'Gigi King.' Every last word. I'll admit Blind Faith is my favourite, but you are a very talented writer, with a very vivid imagination."

"You've read them all?"

"Yep."

"Shit."

"Why shit?"

"Because no one was supposed to see any of that."

"Well, according to your rankings, people have seen. Many people."

"Yeah, but not real people!"

"You mean no one who knows the real you knows what you have written?"

"Well no, people know, just—"

"Just not the people you've written *about*."

"Well yeah." Bloody hell, I came in so strong, why am I the one feeling on the back foot now?

Will shrugs. "Oh well, so I know. The secret is still safe

from anyone else you've written about. What's the big deal?"

I swallow. My mouth is suddenly dry. "You are the only real person I've written about, Will."

His shy smile warms my heart, but I don't miss the hint of triumph there too. "Well, I'm honoured."

I laugh. "Yeah, I'm still having trouble getting my head around that. I would have thought you'd be horrified. I mean, some of the things—" I can't even talk about it. It's mortifying.

"Well…surprise! I loved it."

"Surprise indeed. Where did all this come from Will? Who are you now?"

"I could ask you the same question."

Touché.

"But does it matter?" he continues. "I like who you are. I want to know you better."

I smile.

"Some of the things you wrote…"

"Oh God." Bringing my hand up to my face, I cringe.

I feel Will's fingers on mine and my hand is gently lifted away. I still can't open my eyes until he squeezes my hand and I realise he is still holding it, stroking it with his thumb. My eyelids flutter open and I gaze at his thumb moving gently back and forth over my skin.

"Some of the things you wrote," he repeats. "Are my wildest fantasies."

I look up at him and study his expression.

"My dreams come true." He shakes his head as if he is lost in a conversation with himself. Then he looks at me again. "I never thought I could share that with anyone. Admit it even. I've pretended my whole life to be a 'normal' guy, to fit in.

But that's not me. What you wrote feels more like me then I have ever allowed myself to feel." He pauses, swallowing hard, not breaking eye contact. "I want to find out who I am and who I can be with you."

I came here to talk about our break up and find out if he really thought we could try again, but that all seems trivial now. I want to find out who I am too and I want to find out with Will. I take a large sip of my wine. He needs me to lead this and I'm just as nervous as he is. "Shall we order?" It seems a bit wicked to leave the conversation hanging there like that, but it won't do him any harm to dangle there with it for a few minutes.

"Sure," he frowns. I can see the confusion written in his features. It makes me smile, and I'm smiling when he looks up and hands me the menu, which only adds to his confusion.

I glance quickly at the menu, I'm not in the least bit hungry, but I will not be picking round a waify salad because of my lack of appetite. He needs to see confidence and strength. I snap the menu shut. "The steak looks good."

He twitches at the snap of the menu. Perfect.

"The steak is good here, I think I'll have the same. Let me go and order." He stands to go to the bar, and I let him. The dominant deep inside me pinches me to let me know that this kind of thing wouldn't wash in a real D/s relationship, but I shut her up. What does she know? She is the product of unreserved research. She has never had to handle this shit in real life.

He returns with a couple of fresh drinks and takes a seat. I've had a few minutes to prepare, but that doesn't make this any easier. Nevertheless, I take a long drink and centre myself.

"So tell me which of your wildest fantasies I wrote about."

He looks embarrassed. I've put him on the spot. Good. I'm looking for the real him and I won't find him with his guard up.

"All of it," he stammers.

I quirk my brow in an unmistakable gesture that says 'you can do better than that' and he sighs.

"Okay. I like that you took my— his, sight."

I can't help but laugh inside at his correction. I know perfectly well that he sees the character in the book as him, even though past the point where they/we broke up and he went off travelling, he is entirely fictional. There was no way I could know how close I would come to the truth. It's like the character is a self-fulfilling prophecy. "Wait, your fantasy is to be blind?"

"No, of course not. But it was hot that he couldn't see at times. It was clever how you did that."

"I needed to bring— him home for a reason. The accident was a good reason to cut his trip short and bring him back vulnerable. It created a situation where he had to put his faith in her because he had no other choice. And all the things he had been resisting seemed easier to handle once he gave himself to her."

"Yeah, I liked that. The way there were things he wouldn't have done because he was too worried what it said about him, but then suddenly she was the only focus of his world and he had to trust her to make sure it would be ok."

I nod. "It's funny how other people's opinions of us hold us back so much in life."

"Yeah," he agrees sadly.

And there it is. It stirs something inside of me. A determination.

Conversation turns to lighter things and I find my appetite when the food arrives. I'm finding it almost impossible to imagine a time when I didn't see the submissive in Will. The longer we talk, the clearer it becomes in all aspects of him. I can see what he needs. I don't know how. It's not like I'm qualified to say with any certainty. I never saw it before, but now it's obvious. And it's even more impossible to have predicted what it would do to me. I want, no, *need* to nurture that in him. I can feel a strong sense of protection forming. He needs to be dominated and I think I'm up for the challenge.

When we leave the pub, Will slips his hand into mine. "Thank you," he says sweetly.

"What for?"

"For calling me. For having dinner with me." He laces our fingers together. "For not thinking I'm a freak."

Anger sparks suddenly. "You are not a freak." God I want to protect him from that.

"Some people would think so."

"Some people? Do you really care what 'some people' think? Who are they? Why do they matter?"

"I don't know, it's just—"

Without warning, I tug him down the side of the ancient pub building and shove him against the wall. He grunts as the air is knocked out of him, but the shock gives me time to position myself against him, pinning him to the old stone wall.

"Mags what are you doing? Someone will see!"

"And all they will see is a girl kissing a guy she likes." I press my lips to his before he can answer and claim him in a rough kiss, my tongue forcing its way in as he whimpers with need.

My hand drifts downwards to find him hard and getting harder by the second. I lavish a few strokes on him and he tries to shy away.

"What? You don't like being touched?"

"No, I do," he gasps, "but—"

I stroke him harder, lifting my other hand to thread my fingers through his hair.

"What are you afraid of? That they will see a woman in control? Taking what she wants? And you, loving it?"

He doesn't respond. The only sound he makes are the ragged breaths as I stroke over his straining cock through his jeans. His eyes darting left and right, scanning for people who will probably never come. He needs to let go of these worries. To hand them over to me. And he gave me the perfect idea.

"I think you need a lesson in trust, Will." I glance around, before pushing him further along the wall, into a pocket of shadow, behind a bush. We aren't completely invisible, but that's kind of the point.

"What are you—" he begins to protest, until I give his dick firm squeeze and he chokes on the words.

"Shhhh. Trust, Will," I whisper. "Trust."

I slip the black silk scarf with the skull print from my neck and lift it to his face. He flinches, but doesn't object, so silently, I proceed to blindfold him.

It seems to settle him. He is still wound up tight and trembling, but I get the sense that it's more from excitement than fear. "Better?"

He nods.

"Better because you know I'll take care of you?"

"Yes," he whispers. "I trust you."

"Good boy." I balk at the words as they leave my lips. It feels right, but strange and faintly cringe worthy to call him that. The way he moans however, tells me he doesn't see a thing wrong with it. I smile to myself a little triumphantly. Check me out!

I take one more look around. There's no one who will see us and as long as he is quiet, we'll be fine. Turning back, I watch him, lips parted breathing hard from nothing but the sheer excitement of it all. I take his mouth in a deep kiss again. I can't help myself. He looks so perfect in the dim light. "Quiet and still," I tell him and he nods, his breath hitching at the command.

Slowly, I unfasten his jeans, watching his face, not wanting to miss a moment of his first surrender. He gasps as I touch him where he is practically bursting out of his boxer briefs, but I don't linger there long. When I slip my hand past the waistband, he actually holds his breath and I watch with glee as he waits for my touch. Several seconds pass and he doesn't take a breath. I feel the power build, knowing every cell in his body is poised waiting.

Waiting for me.

His sole focus is me.

When I grant him my touch, the air leaves him in a rush.

Knowing I am all that exists to him, even in this short moment, is more incredible than I ever expected it to feel. I control everything: his pleasure, his safety, his wellbeing, even his self worth. It's a heady power trip, but it means everything. I hold it all in the palm of my hand and I promise myself silently that I will never take a moment like this for granted.

I pull his boxers low enough to fully expose him to me. I'm not going to fritter away this first for both of us, with an under-clothes fumble. He needs to feel the fresh air on his shaft and balls. He needs to trust me.

He shudders as he feels it. I watch him silently. I can read it all in his expressions, Panic, then acceptance and finally, trust. I stroke him and he sighs. Such a good boy I think to myself, but I don't voice it. No reason to spoil him.

As my hand moves faster over his hard length, a moan escapes him.

"Quiet," I hiss and he presses his lips together, only for them to drift open again in silent bliss.

It's a privilege to watch him so raw as he builds higher and higher.

His soft sounds bringing my attention to my own need for the first time. I've been so caught up in attending to his. His gentle sighs are making me ache and I think I'm more turned on than I have ever been in my life. I have to decide whether to let him finish here or take him home. I was planning to go home alone tonight. I was planning to be sensible and strong. Tonight has not turned out at all how I planned.

Even as I left the house, I wasn't sure that we would necessarily be able to fix things between us. I was hoping that we could, but it didn't feel at all likely. I'd turned everything he'd said over and over in my head and weighed it up. It looked good, it sounded amazing. We could be together again and he wouldn't hurt me AND I could live out my fantasy with a willing submissive. But the nagging doubt was there still.

And then I saw him.

In all his delightful submissiveness.

I mean I really saw it, for the first time, and all that changed.

But part of me still thinks it would be better not to rush things. Says the woman in a pub carpark with a blindfolded man's cock in her hand.

"Mags," he whispers urgently, his jaw hanging open with the un-moaned sounds of his pleasure. "Please, I need—I—can I come?"

My chest tightens. I love that he asked so much, I nearly ruin the whole thing by thanking him. He is going to make a good little sub. I just hope I can live up to him.

In the moment I decide. I'll make him choose. "I'm not stopping you…But…"

"But?" he gasps. "I—please Mags."

"You have a choice."

He lifts his head from where I lay against the cold stone building, as if in doing so, I would see the look in his eyes.

Frustration. I know it's there behind the silk barrier.

"What's my choice Mags. Please," he begs, hurrying me, before it's too late.

"You can come right now and that's perfectly okay…"

He groans now, desperately and wantonly.

"Or?"

"Or, you stand there and take it until I decide to tuck you back into your jeans, still hard and wait for a bigger reward." I increase my speed. "Your choice."

He draws in a sharp breath, punctuating his rhythmic pants.

"So? Which is it to be?"

"I— Oh God."

"He can't help you, Will. Are you going to choose?"

He nods, pain written on his face.

"Are you ready to come?"

"I'm so ready."

"It's a quiet village, maybe no one will see if you come all over my top. Or maybe we'll bump into the vicar on our way home, who knows?"

Will lets out a whimper. He's right there, I feel him tense in my hand.

"Are you going to let go?"

He releases the breath he's holding. "Fuck!" he growls. "No."

I release him suddenly and he sags, fighting for breath. His hard cock stands straight out from his hips, twitching from the lost orgasm. His desperation can still be heard in every breath he draws and I watch him proudly. It takes a hell of a man to fight that urge and I even gave him the choice. Scenes I have written swamp my thoughts suddenly, and I smile thinking of the possibilities that suddenly feel less of a fantasy.

Will is reality.

I reach up and pull the knot free from the scarf and he blinks in the darkness as it slides off. Still breathless, he straightens and the corner of his mouth tugs up in a half smile.

I stroke his cheek. I want to tell him how proud I am of him, but I don't know how to not sound ridiculous. So instead, I lift his boxers back up and attempt to restrain his rock hard erection. He winces, I imagine it is hell. He groans as his jeans come up and adjusts himself before I pull up the zip.

"Good boy," I whisper, running a finger along the pronounced shape behind the denim.

He snaps then and lunges for me. Capturing my face in his hands and parting my lips with his. He devours me hungrily, showing every ounce of his need. I let him have the control for a moment because he has done so amazingly well tonight.

"Thank you," he whispers as we pull apart. And he means it. He really means thank you for driving him to the brink and not letting him go. He means thank you for holding the power and giving him what he really needs.

He is perfect and I can't believe I get to help him find himself.

"Let me walk you home." He smiles, and offers me his arm.

I smile back and link my arm through his and we set off through the village back to my house. I already know I'm not going to invite him in. I think we need to pace ourselves. Knowing that he will accept that graciously is the greatest feeling going.

I won't tell him he is not to touch himself when he gets home. I'll work up to that for another time. Besides, thinking about him taking care of himself when he gets home, while I do the same, is pretty hot.

SATURDAY 29TH AUGUST

Vibrations from beside me stir me awake. I reach out with my eyes still closed, for my phone in it's usual place on my bedside table and I open my eyes when I find it isn't there. It's in bed with me somewhere, which is unusual for me since I always charge it at night and keep it on the bedside table, but I smile as I remember why it ended up sharing my bed.

Before I fell asleep, she text me asking if she could see me today. Of course, I agreed. It's a long weekend and I wouldn't want to spend it with anyone else. Then after agreeing to talk in the morning a final text came through. It simply said: Goodnight x. And it was accompanied by a grainy photo of her in bed. It was just of her face, smiling up at me, her hair splayed around her on the pillow, but I stared at it for a long time after replying, until finally my eyes drifted closed.

I locate my phone under the covers and squint at it as I bring it up to my face. The first thing I see is Mags' name and my stomach tightens. Unlocking the screen to read the message, I smile when the last thing I had open yesterday greets me. Her sleepy face.

'Good morning.'

'Good morning, how are you?'

'I'm feeling good this morning. I've been up sitting on the terrace writing for the last couple of hours. How are you?'

I glance at the time, thinking it must be mid-morning and I slept in, but it is only eight thirty.

'You were up early, I only just opened my eyes.'

'Sorry, did I wake you? I was feeling inspired, I couldn't sleep.'

'I can't think of a better reason to wake up than to talk to you. Tell me about this inspiration.'

My dick stirs at the thought of the words that might have come from her mind in the last couple of hours. I want to read them.

'It's nothing really, I just wanted to get my words down early today so I had a clear day.'

'You write every day?'

'I try to, it doesn't always happen.'

'I guess you have to be in the mood. I don't know how it all works.'

'Yeah, I was in the mood this morning.'

Now I really want to see what she has written.

'Do I get to read it?'

'Bloody hell no! It's nowhere near ready for other eyes.'

I pout, to myself.

'No pouting.'

I laugh, looking around my room even though I know it was just a good guess.

'How the hell? Are you spying on me?'

'You forget how long I've known you. You pout.'

'Do not.'

'Do too.'

Still chuckling, I sit up.

'So what do you want to do today?'

'Spencer wants to meet at the pub this afternoon when Jazz finishes work.'

'How have you spoken to Spencer already?'

'He's here. He's in the gym.'

'Oh.'

I'm not jealous of Spencer or anything, I just wish I'd got to wake up there too.

'I told him to knock himself out, use the gym, have a swim and a sauna. Then he's going to help Jazz in the shop.'

'You're spoiling him.'

'Or...I'm a genius and I'm keeping him busy.'

'Because?'

'Because then you're home alone.'

I frown at the phone. I wish I was more awake, so I could understand how this benefits me rather than just pampers Spencer.

'I thought maybe I'd come over and bring you breakfast.'

Oh!

'If you want me to that is.'

'I'd love that. But you don't have to bring breakfast, I can make some. Or we could go out.'

'I don't think the general public will be at all appreciative of how I intend to eat it.'

'Oh.'

Is that the best you can do Will? Really? Oh?

'Is that a yes?'

'Yes!'

That's a fucking hell yes.

'Please.'

I add hastily.

'Ok, be there in 30 x'

I look at the time. Shit.

No longer feeling sleepy, I throw off the covers and race to the bathroom. I turn the shower on and brush my teeth as it warms up enough to step in. A quick wash is all I allow myself, totally ignoring the semi hard state that just her texts have left me in. I leave the few days of scruff on my face. I kinda like it.

Making my way back to the bedroom, I slip a pair of boxer briefs on and rub the excess water out of my hair with my towel. I catch sight of myself in the mirror and turn to face my reflection, running my hand over my flat stomach. There are defined abs there, but they aren't flashy, deep cut abs. They're more subtle. As is the V that cuts beneath the line of my underwear. I do a physical job and I eat well, I'm just lean. I make fists with my hands and flex to try and bulk out my shoulders, then release them with a sigh and turn away. I need to get dressed.

I pull out some jeans and slip them on, but as I zip them up, I realise they're a bit final. She made it sound like she wanted to…I don't know…stay in.

I slide them off and fold them, returning them to my drawer. I select a T-shirt from the drawer above and lay it on the bed. I can't answer the door in my boxers with a semi, that's not very classy. Way more Spencer's style. Instead, I opt for a pair of loose sweats. Making my bed and dropping my wet towel into the washing basket, I take one more look around to check it looks nice in here, before I pick up my T-shirt and head for the stairs. I need to check on the kitchen, you never know what kind of state Spencer has left things in.

But the kitchen is spotless.

I stand and look around me. Well this is a first. I flip the kettle on and set out two cups, glancing at the time again. She will be here any minute. And sure enough, just as I'm stirring the tea, she rings on the door. I start to head towards the hallway when I remember my T-shirt and double back to grab it. I'm still pulling it on as I reach the door and even I can't miss the way Mags' eyes fall on my stomach first before I pull it all the way down. Once it's out of view, her eyes make their way up to mine.

A soft smile lights her beautiful face. "Morning."

"Morning," I reply, staring at her with a smile of my own.

"Can I come in?"

I realise I'm blocking the door, drinking her in. "Sure sorry." I stand aside and she bends to pick up one of those picnic baskets with the two flap tops. "Here let me take that for you, it looks heavy."

"Thanks," she says, handing it off to me.

"What is it?"

"Breakfast."

She steps inside and I close the door with my free hand. "You didn't have to do that."

"And you didn't have to do this," she chastises with a raised eyebrow, reaching in to lift the hem of my T-shirt with her finger. "I should have specified, breakfast in bed." She steps towards me looking hungry and I clutch the basket handle and will myself not to gulp audibly. She takes the basket from my grip. "Take it off."

I hesitate for the slightest of seconds and her expression tells me not to question her, so I lift it over my head and drop it to the floor.

Shit, it was clean on, I should have folded it. It taunts me from the floor.

I need to get a grip.

"Better," she says, settling the basket on the hallway table and closing the gap between us until she is only an inch away. She trails her hand over my chest and follows the same path my critical eye took in the mirror only a few minutes ago. I hold my breath when she reaches the line of hair that drops below my boxers and follows it with a fingernail until it disappears. She dallies there for a second, toying with the stretchy band, but then she lifts her head and I breathe again.

Having her in my space like this is surprising. I normally keep people out of my space, but it feels like she belongs there, or rather it belongs to her. Maybe that's why I have so vehemently protected it from everyone else. It's hers.

Remembering last night with fresh clarity, I expect to feel mortified, but I'm not. I didn't ask for any of it, if I had it would have been different. Forced somehow and all for my benefit. But that's not how it was at all and I'm seriously grateful for the sweats right now because even though they are hardly doing anything to hide my predicament, boxers would have been highly inappropriate.

"Let's eat," she says suggestively. Maybe it wasn't all that suggestive, I don't know, it felt like she meant eat me.

"Sure," I reply, clearing my throat. I step towards the kitchen and she puts a hand on my arm.

"Where are you going?"

"To the kitchen."

She shakes her head slowly and nods up the stairs. "I just told you, I meant breakfast in bed."

I wait for a second before I reply. Maybe I shouldn't question, or hesitate. I don't know, we haven't set any rules… "But I made us tea."

Her face breaks out in a grin. "Ok then," she laughs. "You can bring that up."

She doesn't follow me into the kitchen and when I come back to the hall with the two cups, she isn't waiting for me. My T-shirt is still laying pooled on the floor where I dropped it. It makes me cringe, but I force myself to let it slide. What's she going to think of me if I'm down here tidying up instead of up there with her? So I take a deep breath and try not to spill the tea with my trembling hands as I climb the stairs.

When I enter my room, she is standing, looking at my desk. She ghosts her fingers along the edge of my Macbook and I watch her until the side of the cup starts to burn my knuckle. I cross the room and set one mug down on the coaster I have on my bedside table, then I open the drawer beneath and bring out another coaster for the second mug.

When I look up, I discover she is now watching me.

"You like things neat don't you?"

I suddenly feel like I am on trial. "It only takes a minute to straighten things up, it's nicer that way," I reply, trying not to sound too defensive.

Mags nods in understanding and then keeping eye contact, she pushes the corner of my MacBook so that it's at a funny angle. I swallow. Then she walks towards me.

Her expression is a challenge.

I shift uncomfortably.

But she turns her attention to the basket sat on the corner of the bed. She hops up into the middle of the bed and throws a couple of pillows together against the headboard. Then she pats the bed beside them, signalling for me to sit.

I position myself carefully where she indicated, discreetly pulling one strewn pillow more central behind me as I settle. When I look at her I see she noticed from her satisfied smile. She's got my number now. I feel like I've handed everything she needs to know about pushing my buttons and I wasn't even prepared. I didn't even think to guard it.

Bollocks.

I wasn't this bad before, she probably never noticed. But there is something about hiding what you really want from everyone and anyone, that makes you keep things under control.

She wants to mess with that…okay. It's no big deal. I'd walk over hot coals to be with her. These challenges are my coals.

She ignores my discomfort and innocently sets about unpacking breakfast.

Onto my white sheets.

A tupperware box of something I can't make out.

Strawberries.

Raspberries.

My breath catches in my throat.

She meets my eye, then looks away.

That's ok. It's fine.

"I thought I would make you an old favourite." She lifts

the tupperware box and opens the lid, sending a waft of that cinnamony goodness I was reminiscing about up to my nostrils, and a sprinkling of sugary badness onto my duvet.

I tense, I can't help it. It's my worst fucking nightmare. I mean, why stop there? Put sand in my sheets why don't you.

"Oops," she dusts the sugar away. At least, she thinks she does. All she does is spreads it further.

But it's ok. I would walk across hot coals…

"You ok, Will?"

"Huh?"

I look up.

"Your hands are all balled up. Am I making you tense?"

I don't reply. It was almost rhetorical anyway.

"I made you cinnamon french toast bites." She smiles.

She did it because I said I love them. And I do. On a plate. In a kitchen.

She shuffles until she is reclining beside me and shows me inside the box.

It does look good, it just makes me tense. And you'd think that with one of my biggest triggers happening right now, it would have killed my hard-on, but not even close.

I'm hard as rock. It's how she has control you see. It's unconventional, subtle, but so effective. She knows she is messing with me. I don't think she knew going in, but the way she has turned it to her advantage is actually a turn on.

I know, I need my head examined.

She picks up a cube of sugar dusted french toast and begins to offer it to me, then she jerks up, dropping it back in the box, "Oh! I almost forgot." She dumps the box of french toast bites on my chest and I have to grab it to save it from falling. "I brought maple syrup."

I let out a groan and she giggles.

"Now, I had planned to pour this into your belly button and dip the french toast in it. But I can see that that will probably give you a coronary, so I think I'll just dip it in here."

To my relief, she doesn't pull out a bottle of syrup, but instead a small pot with a screw lid she decanted some into. I laugh, some of the tension falling away.

Mags turns serious for a moment. "Is this stressing you out too much?"

I shake my head. "No, I'm fine." I hold the box with one hand and use the other to try and ease the strain in my boxers, not thinking it will draw her attention straight to it.

She quirks an eyebrow. "So you are."

I cringe. "Sorry, I uh—"

"Don't be sorry. I like it."

I shift uncomfortably.

"Is it my mere presence that has made you hard?" She flutters her eyelids and flicks her hair with heavy sarcasm. "Or is it the way I'm fucking with you?"

"Both."

Her nod tells me she is surprised and gratified to be having this effect on me.

She hands me the pot of syrup and quickly peels back both my sweats and boxers, exposing me fully with no prelude. My hands are full and she is so fast, I don't try to object and before I know it, she's pulling them down my legs and throwing them over her shoulder with a smirk.

There is a pause and she watches me. I feel like I should shrink under her gaze, but it's having the opposite effect. She reaches into the basket and draws out her scarf from last night.

"If you like I could blindfold you like last night."

I shake my head before I think through my answer. "I want to see." Maybe not being able to see would take away some of the anxiety, but I know that's what is making me so hard. I want to see her have that control over me. Even if it's not proper control.

"Okay." She shrugs, returning the scarf to the basket. Only, she doesn't. She reaches into the basket and pulls out a second scarf. "You can have your eyes today, but I want your hands in exchange."

I have no words. I want to tell her she can have any part of me, any time she likes, but I can't find a way. I just watch silently as she crawls over me, her loose fitting sweater gaping at the neck, giving me a perfect view of what's underneath. She lifts the food out of my hands and places it on the bed beside me and remarkably, I couldn't give a shit.

She settles astride me, completely ignoring my hard cock between us. I hiss as the coarse seam of her tight black jeans, rubs over my head carelessly. She is focused on lifting my wrist and positioning it against the headboard, stretching it away from my body, but not fully extending it. When she is happy with the position, she takes one of the scarves and wraps it around, tying it off. She moves to the other side doing the same and I watch, feeling every movement.

She sits back and admires her work.

"Now are you going to chill out and enjoy this breakfast I made you?"

"I'll try."

She narrows her eyes. "I think you mean, yes Mags."

"Yes, Mags."

"Good boy."

Fuck. Me.

Those two words are all it takes. I shift beneath her trying to get some relief. If it weren't for her clothes, I could slip inside, but having her fully dressed over me is somehow hotter.

"Down boy." She laughs, pressing a hand on my chest.

She brings the box back up and rests it on my chest, rocking against me in a very deliberate way. Nothing registers on her face at all. She knows what she is doing, she's just acting innocent. Opening the pot of syrup, she sits it inside the box with the french toast. Then she lifts one of the crispy little cubes out and dips it, carefully letting the excess drip off, before lifting it to my mouth. I anticipate the flavour, they are like little pieces of doughnut heaven.

I take it willingly and close my eyes as the taste takes me back.

Oh my god that's good.

She places the next piece in her own mouth and very deliberately licks the sugar off her finger and thumb. I shift. She notices.

Next she dips a new piece and halfheartedly chases a drip of syrup trying to stop it falling, but when it lands on my chest she can't hide her glee.

"Oops," she grins as it drips again. She places the piece in my mouth and then slowly leans forward and licks up first one drip, and then the other. She lingers there, circling my nipple with her sticky tongue and then placing a light bite above it. I watch, wishing she would bite harder. But she moves away too fast and is dipping the next piece while I'm still panting. She leans right in with it this time, teasing me, letting me open my mouth for it and then whipping it away into her own mouth. The syrup drips off my lip where she touched it and rolls slowly down my chin. It's killing me. She watches it thoughtfully while she chews and swallows then reaches forward, catching it on her tongue and retracing its path back to my lip where she captures my mouth in a deep kiss.

I close my eyes and get lost in her.

I'm not aware of when she puts the food down, I'm just aware of both of her hands on me.

I moan when her hand wraps around me and pull against the ties on my wrists, not to escape, but to remind myself that this is real.

"Does that feel good?"

"Yes," I gasp.

"As good as last night?" she works her hand up and down.

"God, yes."

"You liked that, didn't you? Being out in public with no control."

I exhale and try to focus on her words, but all I can do is feel.

"Answer me."

"Yes, I loved it."

"I know you did. I loved it too. You must have been desperate for relief." She changes her grip on me and pumps her hand. I was. I wanted to take her to bed so badly, but she placed her hand on my chest at the door and kissed me lightly again at the corner of my mouth and then she whispered goodnight. Chaste but full of promise. It wasn't a rejection, not after what had happened. If anything it was a compliment. Her way of saying I know you can take it. That probably sounds fucked up.

"Is this how you took care yourself when you got home? Thinking about my hand on you, out where anyone could find us."

"No," I manage, thrusting up into her hand.

"Then tell me how, I want to hear all about it."

"I didn't."

Her hand stops. "Really?"

"Don't stop," I plead.

"You didn't do anything last night after you left me?"

I thrust into her hand, trying to keep this feeling. "No nothing."

"Why?"

I pause too. I was so fucking hard, but I felt on top of the world. Like I was in the midst of the perfect 'to be continued.' It would have been emptier walking away fully sated somehow. And I didn't even think to touch myself. It was hers, that arousal. She did it to me. She owned it. And she didn't need to tell me, I knew.

This is really not the time to have this conversation, but she waits for my answer so maybe it needs to be. "Because you didn't say I could," I reply quietly. Then I feel embarrassed and my defences come up, I try to sit up more, but I'm tied down. "I know that's not normal. It's just—" I stop myself. She won't understand. Why should she?

"You want someone to tell you when you can and can't?"

Slowly, I nod.

She smiles suggestively "I really like that," she says with

a sadistic hint to her tone.

I stare at her in disbelief. I know there are people who live this life, but I never expected for a minute for someone like her to accept me for who I am, never mind feel the same way. This is too much, too dangerous. I feel like I could open every corner of myself to her and it would be ok.

Slowly Will. You don't want to push her away.

"So you have had no relief at all since I touched you last night?"

I shake my head, still willing her to keep going.

"What if I refused you again?"

I groan and shift beneath her, probably giving her all the answer she needs. "I could live with that," I reply regardless, trying to keep my voice as level as I can.

"Wow," she sighs somewhat in awe.

Her hand starts to stroke slowly again and I bite my lip, whimpering at both the sensation and at having pleased her. My mind wanders, if she is surprised I didn't finish myself off, does that mean that she did? Images of her fill my head. Her fingers relieving that pressure of unfulfilled arousal. I want her to tell me about it. Finding my voice to ask, she cuts in in front of me with a question of her own.

"You must be pretty desperate now?"

I pause, not knowing how to answer. Yes, of course I am. I always am around her. Sometimes it's unbearable. Before when there was no hope, it was consuming and painful, with no chance of respite unless I took off again. Now...Now it's desperate in a different way. She might not let me have a release, but that wouldn't mean I'm not getting what I need. By denying me, she's meeting a need. If she grants it, she's meeting a need.

If she refuses me, I'll both live and die.

It's fucking complicated and my dick is in her hand and my hands are tied to the bed and I can't work through this right now, so I just nod.

I am desperate.

For what, I don't know.

But I trust her to give it to me.

The breakfast forgotten, I slide my grip up his length slowly and watch him as he watches it slide back down. He is desperate, but I'm not convinced it's for relief. Every man I have ever been with has had only one goal in each sexual conquest. To get off. That's it. Sex without it is unfinished business. Those are rules I can understand. I have always lived by them. It's basic.

This it's all new. I've studied it in theory, but in reality, I don't know what to do with it. He's saying I could leave him hanging again and he would be ok with it. What am I supposed to do with that? Sex has suddenly become an intellectual game. It doesn't begin and end with one encounter, to then be put on ice until the next time. Now it feels like more of a running score. A points tally I'm in charge of. I'm not sure I was ready, but still, here I am, in charge. Keeping score.

He did so well last night, therefore I suppose I owe him a reward. Simple right?

Wrong.

See I don't know what a reward to him would be right now. Give him pleasure? Or give him another chance to impress me? How am I supposed to know without asking him and totally killing the moment? My head is spinning by the time I come back to him. He is in heaven, my hand has been stroking him languidly while my thoughts have been whirling. He has no clue what's going on in my head. He's just surrendered.

To me.

"God, you're perfect," I whisper.

It just slips out. I didn't mean to share it, but his needful moan tells me what it does to him. That's when I get it. It really is more about pleasing me than a climax. That pleasing me is the reward. Not just in fiction, where it's easy to write something like that and suspend disbelief. But here where it's real, this living, breathing, fucking delicious man wants to please me more than he wants his own relief.

And now I have to stifle a moan. I want him so badly.

Letting him slide from my grip, I enjoy the fact that his dick stands straight up by itself. He's as hard as stone and it's all for me. I get up off the bed and strip off my top and bra. He watches me intently, it feels good to have his attention. I try feigning indifference for the sake of a dominant air, but it doesn't feel right. I really don't think it's me. I love all the different facets of BDSM, but I am finding through my writing and from having this amazing man tied to his bed, desperate to please me, that I am not personally into the more degrading side of the act. I'd rather he saw me keenly drinking in the sight of him, than hoping I would cast my distain in his direction.

I turn my full attention to him and stare at him greedily. I want him to feel how much I want him. He shifts under my gaze. I can see he feels my hunger and he is nervous. Good. I want him to feel wanted, not comfortable.

Slowly, I slide my jeans down my legs and kick them

aside. Making my way to the side of the bed I continue to look at every inch of him, his perfect body tied down for my pleasure. I run my thumbs under the band of the lace knickers I wore especially, so that I have his full attention there and then slip them off. I press one knee into the mattress beside his thigh and throw the other leg over him, my knee landing amongst breakfast things. Nothing comes to any harm, but I can see him tense.

"Do you want to move that stuff?" he asks nervously.

I laugh. I know he isn't really concerned if it's in my way or not, more that I'm going to send it all flying. But I deliberately sidestep his point. "No it's fine, it's not in my way."

"Are you sure?" he all but pleads.

"Maybe you should have taken the blind fold offer, then you wouldn't be trying fighting the need to manage everything."

He looks up at me and sees the amusement on my face. "I'm sorry," he half-laughs.

"Good, now relax."

He nods.

I haven't yet settled myself onto him, I'm still kneeling above him. I take him in my hand and hold him firmly, giving him a few strokes. I'm so wet from just the sight of him and I want him to know it. It can be his reward for last night. He pleased me, I want him to feel it against his skin, not through a barrier.

Begin to direct his head and he tenses.

He clears his throat. "The condoms are in the drawer."

My eyebrows raise.

He swallows.

"Who said you'd be getting inside me?"

He pauses. "Sorry, I—"

"Do I need to gag you?"

Just the extra hardening I feel in my hand is enough to tell me that the idea appeals to him, but he moans too. I can't hide my smile. "I want to learn all of your fantasies, Will" I tell him, not thinking to hold the thought back. "I want to know everything."

"Do you?" he asks sceptically.

"Yes. I want to know so we can explore them together."

He pulls at his wrists. "We're doing ok so far."

I tilt my head in challenge. "Just ok?"

His cheeks flush. "Perfect."

"Clearly not," I shake my head, leaning over the side of the bed and reaching for my underwear.

"No, no, I didn't mean—" he shuts up when I force my balled up knickers into his mouth. He just stares at me, his chest rising and falling rapidly. His cock throbbing in my hand. Black lace hanging carelessly from his stuffed mouth.

I smile. "Better?"

Slowly, he nods, his eyes locked on mine. His breathing the only sound in the house. I can't believe we've got this far. Yesterday I wondered if we could ever be more than friends again and now we are pushing boundaries all over the place.

Now, with his obsessive worries silenced, I lower myself onto him, guiding him to my folds, briefly. Just long enough that his eyes go wide and his body tenses as his sensitive head passes between my lips and becomes slick from my arousal. But I don't let him inside. I let his head pass through my lips and then slide them along his shaft, letting my hand fall away. He sighs and his body starts to relax.

The weight of my body presses his cock against his stomach and I begin to roll my hips, sliding up and down his length, rubbing my clit along his hard lines. He is purely mine to take my pleasure from, lying there willing to be used. I moan as it dawns on me, I can't lose. I take my pleasure and he gets his.

I rest my hands on his chest and start to take it.

I briefly consider talking dirty to him, but the slick sounds of his entire length passing between my lips over and over, are a huge turn on, so I get lost between that and the feel of him hard beneath me.

Raking my nails over his pecs has him writhing and his hips press upwards with a subtle but constant pressure. I can feel the tremble of him suppressing the urge to rut against me. I keep him there, battling with himself while I use his perfect body to get off. It's what he wants and I deliver.

His muffled moans come thick and fast between his laboured breaths, he's close, but I know he will try and hold back. My own moans are free and clear, I'm going to come. I dig my fingers into his chest as I grind myself hard on him, and go crashing over the edge, I feel him harden and then the unmistakable pulse of his release between us. He grunts into my underwear and I continue to rock, riding out my own pleasure and ignoring his.

Through my breathless gasps I can hear his grunts turn to pleading moans, because I don't stop my rocking, I still have waves of pleasure crashing through me and I plan to ride each one. But it's too much for him, too sensitive.

Shame. He didn't have permission. Good thing he's gagged so he can't really object. The tension in his body provides the perfect pressure against me and I shudder as the final wave hits.

"Yes!" I groan.

He whimpers and squirms, pulling at the scarves on his wrists. When I slow to a stop, he sags still moaning through his ragged breaths.

I catch my breath and finally look him in the eyes. I see fear there, then hope as he searches my face and finally something that feels like adoration when I finally smile.

I sit back and trace my finger through the streaks on his abs. His abdomen quivers at my touch and I tut tut, shaking my head. "Did I give you permission to do this?"

He shakes his head.

"Bad boy. Hmm, I'm going to have to think up an appropriate punishment now." I smile.

He closes his eyes and swallows.

So that's one reward given: the chance to impress me again.

One punishment due for coming without permission.

But yet…I want to reward him too. I didn't forbid it and he pleased me. How could he not please me? Bound, gagged and in absolute heaven. And I got mine.

I lean in close to his ear. "I'll let it slide for now, since you were a good little fuck toy, even if you couldn't control yourself."

He groans.

I love how easy it is to make him putty in my hands, I could certainly get used to it. I reach up and untie his hands, stroking the marks on his wrist until he pulls it away and unapologetically wraps his arm around me, pulling me against him. Pinned to him, I reach up and pull at the scarf until his other wrist is free.

With both hands free, in one swift move, he rips my knickers out of his mouth and smashes our lips together, winding his fingers in my hair and pulling me tight to him.

I don't mind at all, it feels good to know that what we just did was what he needed.

His tongue thanking me in a way words can't.

When he lets me free, we are both panting again.

His smile says thank you.

Mine says any time.

Words aren't needed at all.

I peel myself off him, we're both sticky and sweaty, I look around us at the strewn breakfast things. There isn't really any damage, a few crumbs perhaps and some sugar I can see he isn't going to get over. "Come on," I tell him. "Let's shower, then clean this mess up and change the sheets."

He groans with desire. "Are you trying to get me hard again?"

I laugh. "Down boy."

"So what did you two get up to today?" Jazz asks.

Will smiles at me shyly.

"I made Will breakfast in bed." I reply, watching the surprise register on his face.

"Aww. That's so cute."

He wasn't prepared for us to be telling people, I could tell from the way he sat on the opposite side of the table. But he is pleased. I can see it in his eyes. I smile back, flashing a knowing look. He blushes and I want to climb across the table and show him how fucking adorable I think he is.

Spencer laughs into his pint, bursting my bubble. "Yeah and then you probably got the five hour lecture about food in the bedroom from the Princess here, who can detect a grain of sand in a fucking mile of bedding." He shakes his head, amused. "Take it from someone who shared a room with him for a year in close proximity to beaches, Will does not do food, nature, animal, mineral or vegetable, or texture of any kind in the bedroom."

Hurt flashes in Will's eyes and he has that look of defeat I've noticed him have so often around Spencer. He tries not to let it show, but I've been studying him more than he realises and I see it. And this time, when he makes eye contact with me across the table, he can tell I saw. It hurts me to see Spencer do that to him. He always has to have a laugh at Will's expense.

"So did you get frogmarched down to the kitchen and told never to darken his duvet with your toast crumbs again?" Spencer continues, highly amused by his own jokes in true Spencer fashion.

I take Will's hand, openly across the table and give him a supportive smile. I'd like to know why he lets Spencer get at him like that, but I won't question him here.

No.

Instead, to his astonishment, I put Spencer firmly in his place.

"Actually," I turn my deadpan expression on him. "He took it like a good boy. It was delicious. Shame most of it went to waste when it got forgotten."

Spencer, for once, has nothing to say. He just looks incredulous as the amusement slides off his face. I doubt he is the least bit shocked that someone else around here will talk about sex the way he does. He is just used to having the upper hand the whole time and although Will has done alright up to now hiding it, I for one have noticed the effect it has on him

Will does look a little embarrassed at what I just said, but I mean, it seems unlikely I'm serious. Spencer isn't sure if I'm kidding or not, but there is no way he's going to probe deeper. He knows enough about what I write to fear the answer. I wasn't going to share any details at all. They are nobody's business but ours, but seeing Spencer taken down a peg or two, seems more important than modesty.

Dismissing Spencer by looking away, I wink at Will and he smiles appreciatively.

I could seriously get used to this.

"Well aren't you something special? He must be more smitten than I thought. I've seen him lose his shit over an innocent midnight snack before."

Will rolls his eyes and finds his voice. "That was not an innocent midnight snack. That was a bed full of popcorn…and—" he stops himself.

It's good. He shouldn't keep defending himself to Spencer. Maybe now he sees I have his back, he will take less of his shit.

"What did you have to do?" Spencer continues addressing me, oblivious to Will's issues. "Tie him to the bed?"

Will almost chokes, but I chose not to answer him, though I would, happily. But he's not worthy.

"There's my girls," says a deep voice from behind me.

"George!" Jazz grins, jumping up.

"Dad," I turn, getting up. "What are you doing back? I wasn't expecting you until tomorrow night." He comes over and kisses me on the top of my head and I wrap my arms around his waist.

"Hello darling. I took an earlier flight. I thought I would come and see how the renovations are getting on before New York next week," he replies, leaning in to kiss Jazz in exactly the same way. "How is my favourite chocolatier?"

Jazz giggles. "I can't wait for you to see it George."

"I'm very proud of you both."

George turns to Spencer and Will. "And boys, how are things going?" He offers his hand and they each shake it.

"Good, good," they reply in unison.

"The windows are in, we are water tight. So it's just finishing." Spencer tells him. It's good to see him off guard. My dad is a pussycat, but he can be very intimidating. There is just an air about him. I enjoy watching Spencer shrink in his presence.

"The decorator came by yesterday, we gave her a date she and her team could get in." Will tells him, more confident. He knows my dad well and Dad likes him a lot.

"Excellent."

"Sit down George, I'll get you a drink," Will offers.

"No, you relax, I'm not stopping, I just got off a plane, I'm on my way home to get out of this suit. I was just passing through the village and saw you, so I thought I would stop and invite you all to a get together at the house on Monday. We have some celebrating to do." He squeezes Jazz's shoulder.

"And since it's a bank holiday, what better way to spend it than afternoon tea on the lawn?"

"You don't have to do that George, honestly." Jazz blushes.

"Nonsense, it's done." George says firmly. "The caterers are booked, it's all organised. I would like to purchase some of your finest chocolates if I may Jazz. It will be a great chance for you to show off to some potential customers."

"Ok, I'll bring a box."

George laughs. "Bring a few dozen my darling and send me the bill."

"A few dozen? Dad, what did you do?"

"Nothing." He grins. "A small get together that's all. I'm proud of my girls."

"Uh huh." I frown, shuddering at the thought of all the country club cronies I bet he has invited.

"I'll leave you too it and see you later," he says kissing the top of my head again to stop me from objecting. "And I'll see you all at the party…I mean small get together." He smirks.

"Bye Dad," I groan.

"You ready?"

I jump out of my skin and jab the mascara brush into my eye. "Fuck." The sting has me screwing my eyes tight shut.

"Shit, are you okay?"

"Yeah," I wince and carefully open my eyes and look at myself in the mirror on my dressing table, inspecting the damage. One bloodshot, watery eye and black eyelash prints circling both eyes. Brilliant.

Jazz makes her way over to me and shoos my hand away from the makeup remover wipes. She plucks one out of the packet and standing over me, sets about carefully removing the smudges from my eyelids. Next, without saying anything, she picks up one of my brushes and dabs it in the eye shadow on the table. She works in silence and fixes both eyes. "There," she steps back satisfied.

I turn to the mirror and give her a tight smile in the reflection. "Thanks."

"No problem. Why so tense?"

I draw in a long breath, holding it, because when I let it go, I'll have to give voice to my fears. Finally I give in to it. "Because it was all this that pushed him away before and it's going to happen again."

"Oh calm down, you don't know that. He's a big boy, he can handle a small party."

I nod to the window and she looks out across the garden where dozens of white clothed tables are set out in rows, under the shade of ancient oaks and out into the sunshine. People haven't even arrived yet and it already looks terrifying.

"Ok, not a small party, a fucking huge party. But still, it's not like it's going to happen every weekend. I don't think he's going to freak out. Just chill will you?"

"It's just that we're only just starting something. Now is not the time for a reminder of why he ditched me in the first place."

"It's going to be fine. I'm here, Spencer will be here, Will isn't going to feel out of place. Just relax."

I puff. Easy for her to say. "Come on, let's just go and get this over with."

"I had no clue you even owned a polo shirt," I laugh as Spencer comes down the stairs.

"I do classy."

"Of course you do."

"Will there be beer at this thing?" he grimaces.

"I should imagine so. George puts on a good party."

"Yeah, to be honest it sounds like it's going to suck. Why do we have to go again?"

"Um, because George gave us a huge break and he invited us. And because the party is for your girlfriend, jackass."

Spencer flashes me a conspiring look. "Not just my girlfriend."

"No, well…"

"You're welcome by the way."

I roll my eyes.

"Mags and I are…" I don't know what we are.

"Fucking, thanks to me, and you know it."

"Oh my God," I mutter under my breath.

Spencer cups his ear. "Sorry, I didn't quite hear you."

"Thank you Spencer," I voice in an insincere tone.

"If it wasn't for you…" he prompts.

"If it wasn't for you," I sigh. "I don't know where I'd be."

"Upstairs crying and masturbating probably. Definitely not getting the sexual education of a lifetime from a hardcore dominatrix that's for damn sure." His eyes are wide and he genuinely believes that little bit of Mags' book he read was autobiographical.

"Spencer—"

"Lalalala!" He holds up his hand, shutting me off. "I don't want to hear it. Don't burst my bubble, just thank me sincerely and keep your trap shut."

"Thanks."

"That's better, it's about time I got some recognition around here. I'm fucking great at this shit and everyone should know it."

Shaking my head, I pick up my keys. "We should go."

"Ugh, fine whatever, lets get this nightmare over with."

"Don't be shy Princess," Spencer says, shamelessly eye fucking Jazz as she comes around with a plate of her chocolates. "These aren't for you, they're for all these insanely rich people George knows. You can get them whenever you want."

Spencer snakes his hand around her thigh and runs it up indecently high. "They aren't the only thing I can get whenever I want, am I right, Princess?"

"Spencer!" Jazz steps away. "Behave yourself." She takes a seat, happy to be out of the crowd. And when I say crowd. I mean a hundred, two maybe? I'm scared to ask. All I want to know is how George managed to pull this together with two days notice. I guess he is just the kind of guy who draws a crowd. The kind you change your plans for. Clearly.

"Who do I have to sleep with to get some more of these little sandwiches then?" he looks around for a waitress, coming eye to eye with a passing waiter.

"That would be me, sir," he offers a wry smile. "More sandwiches was it? Anything else?"

"Er, no thanks, just the sandwiches," Spencer mumbles.

"Leave it with me." The waiter walks away, amused. He's probably going to spit in them now. Cheers Spencer.

"Are you okay?" Mags asks, taking my hand under the table.

I nod and smile. "Are you?"

There's tension between us. It's not her fault. This situation just falls very heavily into my 'I'm not good enough for her' issue. She's tense because she thinks I'm freaking out. I'm tense because she thinks I'm freaking out. Then there's the fact that on some level, I'm freaking out.

I know I don't have much to worry about. In fact, sitting here today, I've stared to realise how little Mags has in common with most of these people. As old friend after old friend has arrived and been so happy to see her and so keen that she comes along to whatever it is they used to do together, I get that old feeling that this wedge between us might never go away.

So yeah, there's tension.

I'm trying to clear it. So is she. But it may be that we are both just trying too hard. We just need to relax and stop second guessing each other.

"You're not, I can tell," she whispers close to my ear.

I turn and look her in the eye, still holding her hand. "I really am fine, stop worrying about me. Enjoy the party."

She looks me over, sceptically.

"You're looking for it. It's not there." I laugh. "Have some faith will you." I tell her ironically.

She frowns, not buying it. But I'm saved by the bell, or rather the old friend.

"Mags darling! How are you?"

Mags gets up to greet the friend and I lose her to the conversation.

"*Mags dahling,*" Jazz mocks under her breath and Spencer and I both crease up with laughter.

"Aww, is Princess jealous?" Spencer strokes the side of her face and she slaps his hand away with a frown.

"No," she snaps. "These people don't know her. It's all a show and she hates it."

I wish I had Jazz's confidence. It seems to me like, love it or hate it, it's her life and it's whether there's a place for us in it long term that scares me.

I promised her I'd have faith. I promised her I'd have faith. I promised her I'd have faith.

I take a deep breath.

These people may think she is one of them, but I know that Jazz is right. None of them really know her.

'Tally-ho' style laughter breaks out across the garden and the three of us turn in its direction to see JJ and a group of friends looking to be having a jolly good time.

I groan.

Perfect.

Of course I knew he would be here. I was just enjoying the moment while he wasn't.

Now that it has my attention, I'm surprised I managed not

to hear his obnoxious tone dominating everything, this far. He has his little group enthralled with something and they erupt again. As the laughter dies down, he looks this way and his eyes settle on Mags. He smiles to himself and watches her, then he breaks away and catches my eye. The smile drops off his face and he stares for an intense moment, before looking away.

"Jesus christ, that's it." Spencer stands, I assume to go over there and rearrange JJ's face.

Jazz grabs his wrist and stops him half way out of his chair.

"Sit the fuck down." I snap.

"He needs to be told," Spencer frowns.

"No he doesn't. He doesn't have what he wants, I do. Let him look."

"Oooh, listen to you!" Spencer laughs, the anger draining out of him. "Mr. Confident." He places his hand on my shoulder in false sincerity. "Again, you're welcome."

I swipe his hand off my shoulder and scoff. "Whatever."

"That's okay." He laughs. "Seeing you happy is thanks enough."

I ignore him and sip my beer.

I can't help looking over at JJ's table again though and watch him sip his champagne. I look down at the bottle of beer in my hand. Says it all.

But…I promised her I'd have faith.

"Who brings dogs to these things?" Jazz asks no one in particular.

"Huh?" I look up, thankful to be pulled out of my thoughts.

Sure enough, someone over by JJ's table has brought two little dogs and they are playing in the spaces between tables.

The smaller of the two is just a puppy, he's really cute. He bounds around excitedly, all over the older one and she just stands there with a bored expression. Then she drops down and starts …cleaning herself. I mean she really goes to town. Has she no shame? Abruptly she stops and jump up, scampering over to JJ's table, obviously they belong to one of his friends. She winds herself around JJ's feet and when he looks down to pet her, she jumps right up onto his lap and starts to lick his face. Instead of pulling away in disgust, JJ welcomes it, letting her lick all round his mouth.

I can't stifle my laughter and end up choking on my beer.

"What the hell is the matter with you?" Spencer asks as he reluctantly bangs my back so he doesn't have to explain to my mum that he just let his cousin drown in beer.

After I take a good lungful of oxygen, I glance back at JJ and see that he is blissfully unaware and happily accepting 'puppy kisses' as I can hear him calling them. It's too fucking funny.

Shame! Couldn't have happened to a nicer guy.

"What's so funny?" Spencer nudges me. Apparently I was the only one paying attention to the dog spectacle.

I cover my mouth with my hand so I can talk discreetly. "That dog which is currently making out with Horseboy, just spent a considerable amount of time licking her…what is a good word for dog vagina?"

"Pooch cootch," he says casually because obviously he just has a phrase like that on hand for any occasion.

I start to choke again and he takes the bottle from my hand. "Ok, let's put this down, no need to waste perfectly good beer because I'm a comic genius."

"I don't know how you come up with this shit." I cough.

"I know it's a gift."

"You ok?" Mags asks, sitting down beside me, her friend finally gone.

"Yeah, I'm fine. Beer went down the wrong way that's all."

"Do you need another beer?" she asks Spencer. "I'm out of champagne," she says, waving her empty champagne glass and standing to go in search of drinks.

"I can get them," I offer, even though there are a dozen waiters around.

"No it's fine, I need to go to the little girl's room," she insists and Mags follows her. I feel guilty, but I'm relieved when she walks away, the tension is getting to me.

I look over to watch her walkaway, because really, who can get enough of watching her? And I'm just in time to see JJ following the girls across the lawn, into the house.

Brilliant.

Took my eyes off her for two seconds and he goes chasing after her.

"Well if you're not going to go and put him straight, maybe I will," he says seeing the same thing as me, putting down his drink. A mere second later he is getting to his feet.

"No Spencer, you won't. And it has nothing to do with me being too much of a pussy before you say it. It is because I trust Mags and I want to prove that to her, so sit down, shut up and drink your fucking beer."

He raises his eyebrows at me but he sits and picks up his beer and we drink in silence.

"Enjoying the party gentlemen?" George takes a seat in

Mags' chair, cutting into the intense atmosphere.

"Very much, thanks for inviting us," Spencer replies, being unusually pleasant and forthcoming with the grown up conversation.

"I'm glad you could make it," George says, sitting back and sipping his champagne. "You're doing a wonderful job, I'm very pleased with your work. I was right to have faith in you."

"We're about a week behind, but we are making up time, I'm sorry." I offer. We were a hell of a lot more behind after Spencer's sabbatical, but we really pulled it out of the bag. I think we will catch up if we knuckle down the next couple of weeks.

"Nonsense, you're behind for a good cause. You made a superb job of the shop as well and I'm thrilled that Jazz is finally putting her talents to good use."

I'm happy he thought it was as important as we did. Because it was a gamble. As much as he loves Jazz, personal business really shouldn't come before work and Spencer's disappearing act could have cost us. It's all fine now. I just need to finish this job off to the standard I want to set for ourselves. I'd like to earn George's respect, that's all. More is a stake here than our business relationship.

I think.

"And I hope you've been looking after my girls," he adds, as if able to read my thoughts.

Spencer offers him a conspiring grin. The idiot. Can't he see that George thinks of Jazz as a daughter?

"Of course," I cut in.

"Good," he laughs. "Oh here they come now," his volume

is intended for them to hear as they approach. “My angels.”

Spencer laughs unreservedly. “Angels. That’s funny.”

George tactfully ignores the comment and I flash him the ‘shut the fuck up now before I kill you’ look.

Fuck my life. I’m trying to make a good impression here and he’s going to fuck it up before I even get started. At some point I might have to approach George as the would-be-suitor of his daughter. I don’t know what he will think. Honestly, he should probably smack me for even thinking the word suitor and tell me to take a hike and make way for a real man. Today is not the day I fancy finding out. I don’t know what Mags has told him, but since we have had no discussion on how we would categorise this, I assume she hasn’t told him much. I’m tense enough. I could just do without shit for brains acting like…well…himself.

Mags smiles as she reaches the table and slides her hand around my shoulder. My skin prickles. George obviously knows, she wouldn’t be touching me like this if he didn’t. I can’t help my smile. Where the hell is Horseboy? I need him to see this too.

“You sit down darling,” George says vacating Mags’ seat. “I’m going to go and find myself some more champagne.”

“You don’t have to run off Dad. I’ll get you a refill.”

“Please allow me,” Horseboy appears out of nowhere, summons a waiter and then insists on being the one to pour George’s drink, which he does with all the poise and flourish of an outright knobhead.

What a cock.

George smiles with something between amusement and pride. He shakes his head and throws an arm around JJ’s shoulders. “I can always rely on you, son.”

Son.

It’s like a dagger to my heart. And the way he tugs him closer into his side and keeps smiling his approval is the twist that almost kills me.

Son.

George sees it. He sees a future with JJ as part of the family. I don’t think he has anything against me. I’m just not his ‘son’.

“So tell me how we are going to do at Ascot next week,” George asks him.

I tune out the conversation and stare at my beer. I can’t sulk here. She deserves better. I promised. No more of this JJ shit and have some faith. That’s all she wants. I need to show her.

While I’m composing myself, I feel her hand slip away from my shoulders and she takes a seat. She pulls her chair in closer and places her hand on my thigh beneath the crisp white tablecloth.

“You ok?” she whispers.

I look up at her and smile reassuringly. “I’m fine.”

I can read the concern in her expression and I know she knows I didn’t take the son comment well. The weird thing is, I expected her to be cross, but she seems to get it. Her hand squeezes my upper thigh and I see a twinkle in her eye.

“Sure?” she asks seductively, almost prompting me to have an issue she can use to her advantage. Her hand inches up, faintly brushing over my dick, which was just minding its own business and now wants in on the discussion.

“I’m sure.” I stop her hand, with mine. There are too many

people around. Her dad is standing a foot away.

"I have a punishment in the bank and you look like you need reminding," she says ignoring my attempt to halt her fingers and stroking over my hardening cock.

"Not here, please." I stop her with more determination.

She suppresses a smile and frowns. "That's not how this supposed to work you know."

"I know. But you can't with your Dad standing right there. I guess now you have two punishments in the bank."

"I can count," she says, masking her satisfaction with a stern look.

I try not to smile. We stare for a moment, her eyes still challenging me although her hand has stopped. It's a shame. I'd give anything right now, but even though I stopped her, it was just enough of a reminder. Enough to make me focus. So what if he calls Horseboy son? It's me she wants to punish…in the good way.

"Well I should mingle." George's voice cuts back into my thoughts. "I have chocolates to promote and builders to recommend. I'll leave you all to get acquainted," he says with a grin, patting JJ on the shoulder fondly one last time and turning into the crowd. Leaving JJ just standing there, looking at us.

Awkward.

"JJ, you haven't been properly introduced," Mags says reluctantly. "This is Jazz, my best friend." Jazz stands briefly to receive the double air kiss, like it's some kind of blessing he is bestowing on the commoners. Thankfully it's just air kisses, or I'd have jumped in to stop him getting pooch cootch on her.

"This is her boyfriend, Spencer," Mags continues.

Spencer offers him sceptical nod, but notably withholds a handshake. God he's an arse. I love him.

"Nice to meet you both," JJ returns.

"And you remember Will." Mags adds, hesitantly.

"Of course, how are you Will?" he holds out his hand and then it's up to me to not be the arsehole and stand up and take it.

Pussy, I scold myself as I do. Wouldn't life be cool if I gave no fucks and could just do the Spencer nod and not have guilt to deal with?

There is something menacing in JJ's handshake. He doesn't squeeze too hard, but he kind of holds on too long and the eye contact is weird. Is it a challenge? It doesn't feel very intimidating, yet I definitely feel there's a message in his stare. I extract myself, confused. I know he wants Mags, but does he realise I'm in the way of that now? He doesn't seem all that bothered if he does.

"I missed you at the stables this weekend, Shrimp," he tells her, his attention to me going out like a light.

"Yeah, sorry, I was busy."

Tell him you tied me to the bed, tell him you were busy with your fuck toy, tell him! I plead in my head. I would love to see his face. But of course, she doesn't tell him because that would be crass and she is anything but.

"Oh well, tomorrow maybe? We could go for a hack?"

"Maybe, I'll let you know." I sit back down and focus on my beer while he tells Mags she needs to ride with him every day, because she's all rusty. Ride him is what he really wants. He wishes. She isn't available anymore. Maybe thats why she avoided riding this weekend, because she doesn't want to tell him about us. That he lost. Maybe she isn't ready to let the option go? Or maybe I'm doing what I just swore I wouldn't do again and not having any faith in us.

Brilliant. Failing already.

"Anyway, I'll leave you to your friends," he says pointedly, making it clear we are not part of the gang here and in the absence of her claiming me as anything other than friend, he makes the most of the term. I shoot daggers into his back as he walks away. In my head, yelling *I'm not her friend I'm her fuck toy!*

Mags sits back down and there is an awkward silence for a moment until Jazz jumps in and fills it, teasing Mags about her old friends. "Were you seriously friends with these people?" she mocks.

Mags giggles and pats Jazz's hair. "Aww is baby girl feeling threatened?"

"Pft! As if," Jazz retorts. "These bitches wish they knew you like I know you."

Mags laughs. She's beautiful and animated. It's the first time I've seen her relax since I got here.

"What the fuck was that?" Spencer hisses beside me while the girls are distracted.

"What was what?"

"The way that floppy haired idiot shook your hand."

"It was weird, right?" I'm glad I wasn't the only one who noticed.

"Why did he stare you out like that? It is a posh people thing? Pistols at dawn and all that shit?"

"I don't know." I grumble. "I hate him."

"He's a twat. I would have clocked him in his porcelain jaw if he'd looked at me that way."

"Yeah well, I was thinking about Mags. She likes him."

"No accounting for taste."

This day doesn't seem to end. We had to get up from our table, not to mingle, just to prevent deep vein thrombosis. It's impossible to casually wander without mingling, especially with Mags in tow. Everyone here wants to know when 'the scene' can expect her back. I can see her growing tired of it. She takes my hand, squeezing it and I stroke the back of her hand with my thumb. I'm thinking she might be as done with this party as I am, but now she's holding my hand, I kind of want to stay and flaunt it.

You see what JJ reduces me to?

"Oh, Will," George calls as we near the group he is with, beckoning us over.

We oblige and he introduces us to his friend Lina who likes what we have done with the extension. George quickly extracts himself to give us room to talk, but as he walks away, a couple of others join the group and I almost groan when I notice one of them is JJ, settling himself right into the huddle on the other side of Mags.

Talk of business is light of course, this is a party. JJ watches intently. I feel very on display and can't relax like I should if I want to sound confident in our abilities, but she takes our card anyway and seems interested. Actually, she seems very interested. Mostly in Spencer it has to be said and I look on with interest as he fights the urge to use his sex appeal to secure a job. It's funny to see him like this, with a girlfriend who is enough for him. It's a shocking level of maturity I have been noticing more and more since Tunagate. Maybe he has grown up. Jazz, to her credit, seems amused by the whole thing.

Despite Spencer's admirable attempt at professional conduct, she continues to flirt, regardless of Jazz by his side. "Goodness you have a lot of tattoos," she blushes, swooning.

Spencer looks down at his arms, both covered in tattoos. "Yeah, I suppose so."

"I like them," she gushes.

"Me too," he grins.

I suddenly want to get out of here. I mean what does this have to do with anything? I squeeze Mags' hand unconsciously expressing my awkwardness and she squeezes back answering my awkwardness with her own. I can't look at her, because I'm supposed to be part of this bullshit conversation. But I want to beg her with my eyes to take me away from this. It's literally my worst nightmare.

"Will, do you have any?" Lina turns to me.

"No, I'm afraid not." I try to sound friendly, but I'm done with this whole day. I just want to get out of here and go somewhere quiet with Mags.

"How about you Lina, do you have any?" Spencer asks, amused.

Fuck my life. I want to pinch his ear and drag him away. What kind of questions is that?

JJ chokes on a laugh.

"No. I've always wanted one," she replies.

"Really?" JJ splutters. "You?"

"Yes absolutely," she returns, smiling at JJ's shocked

expression. "But I don't think I'd enjoy the pain."

"Oh, it grows on you," Spencer tells her with a sadistic grin.

JJ interjects. "You just have to *focus* on something else, right Mags?" he nudges her knowingly and winks.

I don't hear anything else that's said, I watch it all in muted slow motion.

He's seen her tattoo.

She lied to me.

I let go of her hand, put my beer down on the nearest table and walk away.

I take a route around the outside of the party and around the side of the pool house, in an attempt to get away from people as fast as possible. I'm heading down the maintenance path towards the garages we have been keeping our tools before Mags catches up with me.

"Will, where are you going," she demands. Her voice bursting my bubble of silent chaos.

"Will!"

I pause, hearing her approach, but I don't turn around.

"What on earth was that all about?"

"You lied to me."

"What?"

I turn, facing her. "You told me you'd never been with him. You lied."

He frowns, her anger showing. "No I didn't. I have never been with JJ. That is the absolute truth."

"Then how has he seen your tattoo?"

Realisation dawns and some of her annoyance is replaced with amusement, though I fail to see anything funny here.

"He hasn't seen it. He knows about it. It was him that encouraged me to get it actually, but he has never set eyes on it."

"Oh sure."

"Are you serious?" she challenges. "You realise—" she stops herself.

"What?"

"It doesn't matter. JJ has never seen my tattoo. He encouraged me to get it because he thought it would be good for me."

"Good for you?" I'm confused.

"Yes. I've had some hard times over the last few years. Times I could have done with having mum around for support," she says pointedly. I feel a huge pang of guilt knowing I was responsible for at least one of those hard times. "When I was stressed, or frightened, or sad, she used to tell me to focus. Focus on the positive, focus on me, focus on what is important. JJ thought that having that as a tattoo would help keep her with me."

Oh.

My mind is flooded with all my wrong assumptions, but it still doesn't feel right. "But it's on your—" I glance around, before hissing, *"pussy."*

"It's hardly on my pussy, its inside my bikini line."

"Pft. Must be a tiny bikini you wear."

She lets out a frustrated growl. "I chose a place where it would always be hidden, alright? My Grandma would be disappointed if she knew I had it. She's old. I don't want her to die disappointed with me, so I put it somewhere no bikini, however tiny, would ever show it, so that she would never have to know I'd 'violated my natural beauty.' It's important to her, but this was important to me. I found a compromise." She inclines her head. "Of course you would think that a tattoo there makes me a slut."

"No, I—"

"Save it, Will." She shakes her head, getting ready to walk away. She stares at me, her chest rising and falling rapidly.

I'm an idiot.

I reach for her hand. "I'm sorry, I panicked."

She pulls her hand away from my fingertips as the make contact.

"I jumped to conclusions. I was wrong."

"Do you know how much that hurts?"

I hang my head and close my eyes. "I'm really sorry."

"You said you'd fight for me and look at you. Running away at your first doubt. You're never going to change."

I want to beg for forgiveness, but I don't deserve it. This is over, she is never going to trust me now.

"Go home Will."

I look up at her sorrow filled face. "Mags, I—"

She shakes her head sadly. "Just go home." Then she turns and walks slowly back the way she came, to rejoin the party.

TUESDAY 1ST SEPTEMBER

The phone buzzes beside me where I left it when I fell asleep. I kept it close in case she messaged me, but she didn't.

That's probably Spencer telling me not to bother coming to work today, I'm not welcome. He never came home last night, no text, nothing. I guess they all sat around discussing what a loser I am for throwing it all away.

What am I going to do?

I feel for my phone between the pillows and my hand bumps the book I stayed up into the small hours re-reading. I don't know why I'm torturing myself. We aren't going to get such a happy ending. I've seen to that now.

Reaching for my phone, it's like a kick in the teeth when I see the message.

'I'm going to be out today, if you need me
for anything on site, it will have to wait
until tomorrow. M.'

Talk about cold. I guess I deserve it, but it hurts. I've lost the love of my life, the most precious thing I've ever had and now I'm just expected to go back to business like I'm not dying inside? I sigh. Yeah, apparently that's exactly what's expected and since I have to work on her house for a little while longer I'll have to suck it up I guess.

'No, it's fine, everything is running
smoothly. W.'

I refuse to use the words, 'I don't need you'. I just can't do it. I drop my phone and haul myself out of bed reluctantly. I suppose it's a small mercy that she won't be around today. I don't think my heart could take it.

I hear Spencer come home as I leave the bathroom and I close my door so that I don't have to deal with him. No doubt he knows by now that Mags won't forgive me. When I'm dressed, I make the bed, retrieving my phone and fin another message from Mags sitting on my screen.

'Good. Please use the day to get your head
straight so that we can talk later. x'

What the…?

She'll still talk to me after all of that? Part of me wonders why she would bother. I haven't showed any faith in us. I really don't deserve it. I wish I did.

As I run through the dreadful events of yesterday in my head, I know I have some big issues to work through. Maybe that's what she means when she says use the day to get my head together. Maybe she wants me to resolve my issues before we can talk? My issues are with him, not her. For that to happen, I would need him to disappear. He isn't going to just go away and he isn't going to stop wanting her. How can

I resolve that?

By telling him to back off?

I need to tell him to back off.

Determination that I have never felt before, all of a sudden takes over.

"Spencer, I'm going to be late for work." I yell, dashing out of my room and down the stairs.

"Oi!" He calls down the stairs. "We have a schedule to keep, you can't just go swanning off."

I turn and lean so that I can see him peering over the bannister. "Yeah, a schedule I kept up on my own for the last month so now you can pick up the slack. I'll see you later."

"Hello?" I call out.

A horse shuffles and snorts in a stable beside me and I eye it suspiciously. It baffles me how people put their trust in these animals. They are so foreign to me, I can't connect with them at all. Plus, they stink.

I hear the sound of sweeping coming from the end of the long line of stable doors housing George's prize thoroughbreds. As I approach the last stall, wet straw is brushed out in front of me. I stop short and wait for the stable hand to finish so I can pass.

To my surprise JJ appears in the doorway, broom in hand. Well I never, he does get his hands dirty. To look at him you'd never know though, he is still immaculate.

"Will?"

Caught off guard, my determination seems to have vanished. "Hi, I err…"

"If you're looking for Mags, she isn't here."

"No, I was, um, looking for you."

"Oh?" His eyes burn into me and I want to run.

I clear my throat. "Yeah, I wanted to have a word, but I can see you're busy, maybe I'll…" I begin retreating.

Coward.

"Wait," his command echoes through the cavernous building and despite myself I stop. "I can finish this later, what's up?" He leans the broom against the stable door and places his hands on his hips.

Fuck. For this to work, I had to take command. I had to say, *'Now look here, keep your eyes off my woman.'* Ha! Who the hell am I kidding? I've never been, nor will I ever be that guy.

But as I stare at him, I realise that doesn't mean I can't make myself very clear in my own way. Mags is mine and he needs to hear that from me.

"I need to get something straight with you, JJ. I know you want Mags, but—" I stop short, not able to force the rest of the sentence out with his piercing eyes fixed on me. I take a deep breath. "She and I, we're…" My mouth closes again, that sounds pathetic. We're what? Dating? Are we even? It's far more than that to me.

Shit she told me to sort my head out and I'm here to do that. Once I tell him to back off I can really let it go. I already know deep down that he is no threat to me really. He can't offer her what I can, you can tell it in every commanding move he makes. He is a man in charge, the male version of her. He would never submit for her. When I think of it like that, I wonder what I'm even doing here. If I know these things, I can be secure. I need this. I need to tell him.

"I—"

He steps closer to me. I gulp. He may not be much of a threat to my relationship with Mags, but he's a predator. He has a kind of swagger that throws me off.

"You?" He says with a roguish smile. It's a clear challenge.

"I love her." I blurt.

His face becomes more serious. "Indeed you do," he concedes.

"That's right and I'm here to tell you that you can try, but you can't have her because she belongs with me."

"I agree."

"Wait, what?"

"I agree, she belongs with you." He steps closer still.

"Well…good." I murmur, caught off guard by his cooperation. I stand up a little straighter, trying to seem in control.

"I'm not standing in your way."

"Ok, good." Now I feel stupid, maybe it was all in my head and even if it wasn't I'm making a right big deal out of it.

"I wouldn't." He says regretfully. "I know how much it hurts to want someone who can't ever be yours."

"Yeah, I know all too well," I agree.

"Do you?"

"Well yeah." I frown. "Of course I do."

He shakes his head. "See I don't think you do. You could have had her all this time. It was your choice to walk away. And now, whether you deserve it or not, she is going to give you a second chance because she loves you too. You know that don't you? She loves you."

I swallow. “I can only hope.”

“Well some of us have no hope, so count yourself lucky, because it hurts.”

I feel awful all of a sudden. “I’m sorry. I—” I don’t know what to say.

“It’s not your fault. Some things are just not meant to be no matter how much you want them.”

He stares intently at me for a long moment and the guilt weighs heavy. Then suddenly, he moves. His lips are on mine before I know what hit me, his strong hands holding my face to his.

It’s only when I hear a throat being cleared behind me that I realise, in my shock, I haven’t fought him off. He pulls away abruptly and leaves me dumbstruck.

I look up. Mags is standing there with her arms folded, looking unimpressed. JJ steps back a few paces, touching his lips.

I open my mouth to speak, though words escape me right now.

“It was just a taste Mags. I couldn’t help myself.” JJ says casually. “Sorry.”

She stalks towards us and faces him. “I hope you got a good taste because it will be your last.” She grasps my hair. “Because he,” she yanks and I hiss from the sharp pain. “Is mine.” She forces me down to my knees with one flick of her wrist.

I’m speechless, and instantly hard as fuck.

JJ grins from ear to ear. “That’s my girl.”

I can see Mags fight a smile but she manages to keep her expression stern.

What the hell? I have so many questions, but they all evaporate when she turns to me, effectively dismissing him. JJ watches us for a few seconds and then walks away, not looking back.

Mags caresses my chin, locking eyes with me when I look up at her. I have to force myself to breathe. Is this really happening? I'm not sure of anything right now.

"I thought I told you to spend the day sorting your head out."

"I was."

She raises a brow. "Really? You needed to get that kiss off your chest did you?"

"He kissed me."

She watches me for a moment. I don't know how much she heard. I hope nothing. I'm not ready for her to hear me say I love her. It's too soon, she will think I'm crazy.

"Did you say what you needed to say?"

I swallow. "Yes."

"Are you done with this nonsense?"

"I think so."

She grabs my hair again and twists.

I gasp, but my hands don't go to hers to relieve the pain, they go to my jeans to ease the pressure.

"You think so?"

"I'm sure," I wince.

She lets go. "Good, now get up and kiss me."

I scramble to my feet as fast as I can and she jumps me, grabbing my face and planting her lips on mine, while wrapping her legs around my waist. I stagger a few paces until I have her against a wall and then I really kiss her.

"Oh god," I gasp against her skin.

"Was the hair pulling too much?" she breathes, kissing me again before I can answer, her hands grasping my hair as a reminder.

"No," I groan. "It was perfect."

"Is that what you like?"

"It felt good."

"What else do you like?"

"I don't know. We'll have to find out."

"Are we really doing this?"

I pull back and look at her. "What do you mean?"

"Us. Are you ready to give us a chance?" She kisses my neck and then nips at the tender skin.

Fuck.

"Yes. I am. Will you have me?"

She moans when I push myself against her.

"Yes," she whispers. "I need you."

"Good because you're stuck with me."

"No, I mean I need you. Now."

"Now?"

"Yeah," she reaches out and slides the bolt on the stable door beside us. "In here."

"Seriously?"

"Yes, now."

I pause to look in her eyes. She means it. "We can't."

"Says who?"

"We can't!"

"Shhh. Give me your wallet."

"What? Why?"

"Tsk tsk, you won't make a very good submissive if you

insist on questioning everything I say."

I roll my eyes and she shakes her head.

"Why do you need my wallet?"

"Because if you have a condom in there, you're going to fuck me." Her hands start searching for my back pocket, but fortunately she can't quite reach.

Fucking hell. "I don't have my wallet with me." I don't know whether I'm relieved or gutted. I want her so badly.

"And there was me thinking you'd always be prepared."

"I am, there is one in there, I just ran out the house in a hurry and left my wallet behind."

She sighs. "Fine then, your mouth will have to do. Get in there."

"Mags! There are people around."

"So? Let them watch."

I groan. This is too bloody perfect for words. I step in, kicking the stable door closed behind us. There is a large blanket box to one side and fortunately, no horse. I sit her on the blanket box and try to find the fastening of her tighter than tight jodhpurs. After feeling my way around the front, she intervenes and slides a side zip down. She lifts her hips so I can tug them down her thighs. I pull them as far as the tops of her boots and abandon them, lifting her legs and ducking under. With my head between her thighs, the smell of her is intoxicating. I lick her through her lace knickers, moaning.

"Do it," she demands.

I shudder and pull the fabric aside, immediately latching on to her clit, she drops her head back and lets out a low sound.

"Oh god," she gasps.

I slide two fingers into her, making her buck and grip my

head, holding it firm while she grinds on my tongue. It's hard and fast, no time for pillow talk.

"Fuck yes," she cries.

I grunt and dig my fingertips into her soft hips, pulling her closer.

Hooves can be heard clip-clopping on the concrete floor of the stable block, reminding me there are people around. Anyone who cares to look over the half door will see me feasting on her and that's hot. Fuck, I could come just thinking about how we look right now. She tugs my hair, urging me on. I am so hard, it hurts, and there is no relief as one hand holds her tight and the other teases her slick hole.

"That's it," she breathes. "Good boy."

I moan at that name and my cock twitches. It makes me work extra hard to please her and in seconds she is coming as she rides my tongue. Her gasps and moans fill the air. Someone has to have heard us.

Just outside the door a horse makes one of those deep rumbling horse noises. Mags lifts her leg over my head, releasing me and hops down from the box, wriggling back into her jodhpurs. I need help. I need her touch. I'm so turned on right now.

I'm about to ask, but she leans her head out of the stable and laughs when she finds her horse tied to a metal loop in the wall.

Oh my god that's awkward, someone, probably even JJ actually came to the door while we were…

Shit.

Then it occurs to me that I got so caught up with Mags that I didn't fully digest what happened with him. Suddenly it hits me. JJ kissed me.

I look up to see Mags leading the horse in. I back up into the corner and stare at it.

"Good boy," she soothes.

A pang of jealousy takes hold of me. That's what she just called me and I loved it.

Great, now I'm jealous of a horse!

Focus.

"Mags?"

"Mmmm?" she replies, distracted by the beast.

"What was that with JJ?"

She turns and bites her lip, "I did try to tell you he had no interest in me."

"But—"

"It was never me he was into, Will. He likes men, more specifically, he likes you."

I open my mouth to speak, but close it again because I know I'll just make some incoherent sound.

"But he can't have you."

"No he can't. And you knew about this?"

She nods, smiling.

"What on earth? I haven't seen him for years." I shake my head. "And let's face it, I've never been very nice to him."

"Maybe he likes the treat 'em mean approach." She laughs. Then she can see I'm not laughing. "He liked you from afar, but he knew it was one sided, plus you were taken. That's all."

"That's all? I've despised the guy for what? Ten years nearly? And all because I thought he was after you."

"You should have been honest with me," she giggles.

"No, hang on, you should have told me! Especially the last

few when I've been throwing accusations around."

"He wasn't out back then. He trusted me with his secret, I was the only one he felt he could confide in, even though he was in love with my boyfriend. I couldn't betray that. And just recently, the way you were behaving, you didn't deserve the truth."

I throw my hands up. "So now what?"

"Well now, I'll be having words with him about kissing what's mine."

"Oh shit." I hide my face in my hands.

"What?"

"You did all that hair yanking in front of him didn't you?"

"Wow you really were in another place. Yes, I did. So?"

"So? What must he think of us?"

"He loved it I'm sure." She laughs.

Then I recall a detail. "Wait, what was it he said? That's my girl?" I shake my head. "Seriously Mags, what is going on here?"

"Relax will you. JJ has read my books. He loves all that stuff. He was happy to see me finally coming out of myself I guess."

I fold my arms with a huff.

"Oh what's up now?"

"I'm bloody last to know everything and anyway, I thought you hadn't seen him in years."

She frowns. "I didn't say that. I haven't seen him in ages, but we have kept in touch, he looks after my horse. He's a good friend Will and he's no threat to you whatsoever, so you should let it go."

The horse twitches beside her and starts shuffling around

the confined space. "Ssshhhh, easy." Mags strokes the animal's long neck and looks in his eyes and he settles. "Good boy," she murmurs.

I swear the horse actually looks at me over her shoulder, like, ha! That's my name. I scowl at him and Mags catches me.

"What's wrong?"

"That's what you called me and I loved it. Now I hear you saying it to him and it doesn't feel special anymore." I pout, fighting a smile.

Mags' face lights up and her demeanour changes. She stalks towards me and doesn't beat around the bush, her hand cups the still semi hard bulge in my jeans and strokes. "He *is* a good boy, he does as he's told. If you're a good boy, I may call you that again."

I let out a shaky breath and try to press against her hand for more friction, but she removes it.

She turns and busies herself adjusting some leather straps in their buckles, tugging sharply on the stirrup when she is done. I stifle a groan. Watching her working the straps so efficiently and the smell of her pleasure still all around me has me achingly hard again despite myself. She moves around to the other side of the horse and I listen to the creak of the leather and the clink of the buckles. When she yanks again to test it, the horse has to shuffle to right himself and I imagine her pulling straps on me. Bloody hell, this place is no good for me.

I press the heel of my hand against my erection and breathe. Then I look up to find Mags watching me.

She raises a brow. "You ok there?" she asks, then picks a short riding crop off a rack on the wall and walks towards me.

I swallow. "If I'd known this place was so erotic, I would

have come here more."

Mags runs the tip of the crop up the inside of my leg, pausing when it meets my balls. I take a breath, but there is no air left anywhere.

"Interesting."

"Is it?"

"Yes, I'm looking forward to finding out what it is you like."

I adjust my stance because my cock is painful against the zip of my jeans and the tip of her crop lightly digs in.

Focus Will.

"We can find out together," I reply.

"I can't wait." She pulls the crop away and I half dread, half pray that it will land sharply on my body somewhere, but it isn't to be. She tucks it under her arm and smiles almost innocently. I flinched though and she saw, if the look of satisfaction is anything to go by.

"Noted," she whispers.

I just stare.

"Now, you have work to get to, don't you? And some thinking to do."

"I thought I'd done all my thinking?"

"Yes, but I'd say this morning has given you lots more to think about, wouldn't you?" She grips my bulge again and leans in. "You have a good long think today, ok?"

I nod. "Ok. Will I see you later?"

She grins. "If you're a good boy." Then she kisses me quickly and turns away, taking the horse by the reins and leading him out of the stable.

Fuck me, I'm done for.

The drive to work is short and sketchy. Even as I signal and turn, I'm not quite sure how I'm managing it with my head so full of images. I'm still hard, I need some relief, but I'm on my way to the site. All my windows are open and the wind is whipping in, but it's doing nothing to dampen the flames. She really grabbed my hair and forced me to my knees in front of JJ. Shit. I should apologise to him for that… that and all the other stuff. Fucking hell what a mess.

My mind wanders back to watching her with those straps. Is it ok to get turned on watching her tighten a saddle on a horse? And no, I'm not interested in the bloody horse, just the sounds of the leather and buckles and how hard it made me. I didn't realise that kind of thing would have such an effect on me. I guess I have a lot to learn about what really turns me on. And the crop, did I really want her to hit me with it? I don't know how I feel about pain. I thought my fantasies were more about control. Being owned.

I look up to find myself parked in the driveway of George's home. Jesus, I shouldn't drive when I'm this distracted. I wince as I get out of the car. Shit, turning up to work with a raging hard on isn't cool. I take a few deep breaths willing it to go down. But I'm dreaming, it's never going to happen. I'm going to be stuck with this all day. Adjusting it, I decide it's barely visible and walk as casually as I can manage.

"All sorted?" Spencer asks, coming up behind me.

"Yeah," I reply, but my grin is uncontainable.

Spencer clocks the grin and narrows his eyes. "Did you get some?"

"No." My hand inadvertently adjusts again and I wince.

Spencer pulls a disgusted face and glances down at my err…predicament. “Gross.” He states simply and then walks away.

'I hope you've been good.'

All day, I've been thinking about the way he responded so readily to me. It's everything I've ever fantasised about and it's with Will. I can barely even believe it. I'm worried I got a little carried away, but he seemed to love it. I was surprised. It's like a floodgate has been opened and I'm scared that I will go too far. My phone chimes.

'Define good.'

Ooooh I like the sass.

'Ok, well, a good boy wouldn't have touched himself no matter how turned on he was.'

Shit can I really send that? I mean the poor boy was hard as a rock when he left. He probably went straight home and took care of it. Who could blame him? And if he did, I don't want him to be disappointed with himself. But then I think about the look of hope on his face when I had my crop pressed into him. I think he was genuinely hopeful I'd use it on him and here I'm worried about sending him a harmless text. I hit send, re-reading it as it goes. Screw it, why stop there?

'Because he would know that belongs to
me and he needs permission.'

I blush. See, the floodgates! What am I doing? What is he going to think? We didn't discuss any of this yet. I'm just rolling with it. I don't know how far he wants to go. Hell, I don't know how far I even want to go. We need to talk about it. A reply comes through.

'Then I was good.'

I hug my phone. Yes! Giddy with relief and power, my head swims with all the fantasies I've allowed myself to explore in my mind and on the page. But wait, he has read all of that now…he has expectations. I panic. Maybe I should just tell him once and for all that's not really me, it's just some clever words and a tumblr addiction. However it excites me to think like that. To create the minds of those dominating women. They are extreme, but in each of them lives a piece of me that's never really supposed to come to fruition in real life.

Maybe I can just be myself and see if it's enough. There are no rules. We can find our own boundaries and play our own game. What am I afraid of? Rejection? I didn't really think this was a side of myself I'd ever use for more than a story. I never imagined being with someone I could open it up to. But it's different with Will, it always has been.

I take a deep breath and push through my fear.

'Hmm, then maybe you should get a reward.'

'I like the sound of that.'

'You must have suffered today, you were so hard.'

'It's been torture. I'm still hard now.'

I bite my lip. Just thinking about him hard all day gets me wet. I want to see it.

'Show me.'

Giving him a minute to let that sink in, I move to the window, hoping to catch sight of him. I'm disappointed to find he isn't in view though.

'I'm all dirty and besides I'll be done in an hour, then I can shower and come and see you. I was thinking of taking you out to dinner.'

'I like you dirty. Show me.'

'Serious?'

'Very.'

'Okay, give me a minute.'

'Will.'

'Yes?'

'Show me now!'

'Alright, alright. I'm coming.'

I smile. I can almost hear his exasperation from here.

'No.'

'No? You just said you were serious.'

'I am serious, but you don't have to come in here. A selfie will do.'

There is a long pause.

'A selfie? You want me to take a picture of my dick?'

'Yep.'

'I think you're confusing me with Spencer.'

'No, obviously I was confusing you with a good boy who wants his reward. My mistake.'

'No, no, wait.'

I wait patiently, but I don't respond. Keeping him in this state of fear will get me what I want…I think.

I don't really want a dick picture. What I want is for him to do as he has been told. The gauntlet has been laid. Now it's up to him.

The next thing that comes through to my phone makes my knees go weak. Not because it's his dick, although it's a beautiful dick, standing out hard and ready and as I think about sliding down on it tonight, my insides clench. My knees go weak because he did it. Not only that, but I can tell from the surroundings in the photo that he did it right where he stood inside the extension he is building, where anyone could see him. He didn't duck into a bathroom, or hide away somewhere, he took a risk on a busy site, full of his mates and his cousin.

For me.

He did it to please me.

'Have you been that hard all day?'

'Not quite but close.'

I grin, I love the thought that he has stayed horny and frustrated for me.

'So you gave it a little stroke to get it like that for the picture did you?'

'Just thinking about doing what you asked, and making you pleased with me, did it. No touching necessary.'

Holy shit. I have to sit down. I can feel the heat of my sudden arousal spreading.

'You have pleased me.'

'Good. So can I take you out tonight?'

'No.'

I wait and he says nothing. He is very restrained, it's amazing.

'I'd like to cook for you, I have the house to myself for the night, will you come over?'

'Try and stop me!'

'Actually, no, don't try and stop me because I'll have to do as you say and I want to see you.'

'Need some relief?'

'That's not why I want to see you. I've lived with a near constant hard on since you came back. I just want to be with you.'

I try not to grin too hard but it's face-splitting.

'Hurry up then.'

'I'm just going to go shower and change, give me an hour.'

'Ok,'

'Oh and Will.'

'Yes?'

Come on Mags, you can do this.

'Careful in the shower, ok? That cock is hard for me, so I get to play with it, not you.'

I squeeze my eyes tight shut. I can't believe I just said that.

'It's yours and only yours my goddess.'

Oh my. I groan and drag myself to the bathroom. I need to

get ready.

An hour later, he knocks at the front door and I run to open it. I'm so excited to see him and nervous, any pretence of being anything other than a lovesick girl is gone. I open the door and the smell of him hits me, making my knees tremble. He grins and steps inside, his demeanour is totally different from earlier, confident and on top. It seems for a moment like we both slip back into the more traditionally accepted roles of boy and girl. Boy sweeps girl into his big strong arms and girl melts when he kisses her.

I actually love it.

It's confusing as hell, given the fact that I've been trying to psych myself up into a dominant frame of mind all day. Old habits die hard and it feels so good to have him hold me.

"Hey," he murmurs.

"Hey," I grin.

Bloody hell we're like a couple of teenagers. Snap out of it Mags.

"Come on, I need to stir dinner, you can open some wine."

He follows me into the kitchen and hops up onto the marble work surface beside where I'm working. Reaching over to the chopping board and pinching a slice of cucumber, he grins as he bites into it. "What are we having? It smells amazing."

"Just pasta, something I made up. It doesn't have a name." I'm caught seriously off guard by his confidence. Compared to last night and earlier today, it's just such a contrast.

"Goddess Pasta," he says decisively and grins, reaching out to pull me between his legs.

I let him hold me, amazed at how vulnerable I feel.

"What's the matter?" he says softly, pulling back.

"Am I that obvious?" Surprised he can read me so easily.

He chuckles and kisses me again. "You tensed."

I offer a small smile. "I was just thinking."

He presses the back of his hand to my forehead, feigning concern and pretending to take my temperature. I smack it away, giggling. "Very clever, wise guy." I move away from his hold and stir again.

"What were you thinking?"

I frown, not wanting to bring the mood down.

Now he frowns, concern etched on his face. "What?"

"It's nothing, just…" I look up into his crisp blue eyes and shrug. "It's confusing all this isn't it?"

"What do you mean?" he pulls me back to him, holding me in front of him so he can listen closely to what I'm going to say.

"I mean, today I had you by the hair, kneeling on the floor, in front of JJ." I run my fingers gently through his hair, blushing at how crass that sounds. "Now I feel like a nervous teenager and you're so confident." I blow out a breath.

"Why wouldn't I be confident? I have you."

"Just like that?"

"Just like that." He nods. "You don't feel that way?"

"I do, but it can't be that easy can it?"

"You're confusing me now, am I missing something I should be worried about?"

"I don't think so. It's just been feeling so impossible for so long, I suppose I'm in shock that with so little discussion, we're just together and that's it."

He jumps down from the counter. “You’re right.” He walks over to the sink and reaches over, plucking a bright pink rose from the vase of fresh flowers my dad has delivered weekly. He strides confidently back to me and gets down on one knee. My insides turn over, knowing deep down it’s not an actual proposal, but panicking involuntarily just in case. On his knee, one hand tucked neatly behind his back and the other extended offering the flower, he doesn’t look to have an ounce of submission in him. It’s quite amazing.

“Mags?”

“Yes,” I reply, trying to steady my voice.

“Will you be my girlfriend?” He beams, knowing how silly this all is, but putting on the display for me.

“Yes.” I accept the rose and laugh as he gets to his feet and kisses my hand.

“There,” he exclaims triumphantly. “It’s official.” Then he hops back up on the counter and steals another slice of cucumber.

I narrow my eyes at him and assess him.

“What?”

“It’s all of this.” I wave the rose in my hand in his general direction.

“All of what?” He looks down, then back to me.

“All of this confidence. I don’t get where it’s come from. You’re never like this.”

His eyes go wide. “Is it bad?” he asks apologetically, visibly deflating.

“No!” I insist, stepping between his legs, resting my hands on his thighs. “I like it, it’s just taken me by surprise that’s all.”

He looks relieved and takes my hand, holding it level

between us, about my chest height. “In every day life, I’m around here, confidence wise.”

I nod as if I know where he’s going with this.

“Around you, I’m down here.” He lowers my hand as far down as he can reach.

“Oh thanks.” I snatch my hand back.

“Hear me out,” he soothes, taking my hand again. “Around you I’m down here, because didn’t think you wanted me as much as I wanted you. And because I was the one who fucked it up and I didn’t know how to fix it. I thought no matter what, I would lose. Add to that the fact that you are so damn irresistible all the time, I was a mess, it’s a wonder I could leave the house.”

“O-kay. But what about the other night? Didn’t that show you I wanted you?”

“Oh the other night was amazing, put me about here,” he lifts my hand to his thigh.

“Still not up here?” I raise it to the level he says he is in ‘everyday life’, which I take as ‘around everyone but me’.

“No,” he shakes his head. “Elated, but full of doubt.” He pushes my hand down a notch. “Scared of getting heartbroken again.” My hand goes down another notch. “And sure you would never want a guy who—”

“A guy who—?”

“A guy like me,” he finishes quietly.

“One who submits?”

“Well yeah, only I’ve never actually submitted before.”

“Just fantasised.”

He sighs regretfully. “Really all I’ve ever let it do is make me feel like less of a man.”

I watch him relive that feeling and want to make it better for him, but he snaps out of it and pushes my hand the rest of the way to his thigh.

"So I was here."

"Then what?"

"Then I saw you with JJ," he says with a half-smile.

"Oh," I say as seriously as I can manage, his mistake is highly amusing. "So back down here again?" I reach as low as I can without bending.

He shakes his head. "Nope, lower."

"Really?" I ask surprised.

He nods gravely. "Through the floor."

I try not to laugh.

"So how did you get out of the floor?"

"It was a series of factors really," he states as if he is being interviewed about global warming or something. "First, I removed my head from my arse."

I laugh. "I see."

"No actually, first I punched Spencer, then I removed my head from my arse."

"You punched Spencer?" I stare in disbelief.

"Yes but he deserved it, now focus."

"Really? You tell me something like that and expect me to focus on the rest of the story?" Fine. I'll tell me later.

He continues, ignoring me. "Next I realised you might actually be someone who wouldn't view me as a lesser man."

"You read my book you mean?" I correct.

He reaches for my hand again, placing it back on his thigh. "Then I got the impression you might just give me another chance." He smiles wide and brings our hands up to his ‘everyday life’ level.

“But that doesn’t explain this level of confidence.”

“Oh that? Yeah, that was, me telling JJ to back off.” My hand goes to my head height. “Me discovering JJ was never even a threat.” My hand goes up over my head.

He looks from my hand to me. I can’t help but smile.

“And then you made me eat you out where anyone could see!” He pulls my hand up until I’m on my tiptoes. “So you see now?” He lets go of my hand and holds me close to him.

“It doesn’t make you a lesser man,” I try to reassure him.

“One taste and I think I see that now.”

“One taste was all it took?”

“Each small thing seemed to make it sink in a little more. You pulled my hair and I felt owned. You ordered me to take you in the stable and pleasure you and I felt like it was specifically me that you needed, that only I could do that for you. Then you called me good boy and I felt accepted. It wasn’t demeaning like I feared. It was an honour like I hoped.”

“So now you’re bouncing off the walls.”

“Yeah and it doesn’t seem like you are.” He sighs.

I have to admit my fears. He has, it’s only fair if I do too. “I’m scared it’s just about kinky sex.”

“It’s not. That’s just the cherry on top. I can live without cherries if I have to. I just want you.”

I feel the panic subside.

“It’s not just about that at all. It’s about this, us.” He kisses me, taking his time, letting his tongue explore mine.

I don’t know how I feel about this new Will, I barely even get my head round him wanting to submit and the next thing is, he is sweeping me off my feet.

"Just enjoy it," he whispers, seeming to know my thoughts.

I nod. I'm going to.

"Let me take those," Will jumps up, trying to help me clear the dishes away.

"Sit!" I snap, trying to stop him. It wasn't meant to sound like an order. It never even entered my head. I was trying to be a good host. I just want him to sit and relax, but the way he sat straight back down, clearly he thought it was. I covertly glance at him, while pretending not to notice. His hands fidget in his lap and his eyes don't meet mine although he obviously isn't sure where to put them. Seemingly without any acknowledgement, I leave him sitting out on the terrace and take the plates into the kitchen.

I wonder how it feels for him, sitting there waiting? Thinking I didn't even notice his submission. I would hate that. I guess that's the difference between us. I glance out through the living room and he hasn't moved. It's really quite admirable. He is perfect. I never thought I'd have anything like this with anyone. It's a fantasy, pure and simple. One I spin for others to enjoy, I've let myself drift into that world of what ifs on occasion, but it was with him in only my wildest of dreams.

And there he is, sitting out there waiting perfectly, for me. His hands now rest calmly on his thighs and his eyes are cast to the floor, kinda like he has given himself a little pep talk. Fuck that's hot.

Imagining what I could get him to do, I get such a thrill. I don't want to let him down. I don't know what he wants. I take a deep breath, telling myself not to start freaking out. One step at a time. Keeping with something we've become familiar with, I pull my white silk scarf off the coat rack by the back door and run it between my fingers as I make my way out to him.

He doesn't look up when I approach. I feel guilty for barking an order at him, but he responded this way, it must be what he wants. I close in behind him and lean down to whisper in his ear.

"Which would you rather keep tonight, your eyes or your hands?" I hold the scarf in front of him to clarify.

For a second, I think he isn't going to reply. Maybe we need to set rules about this stuff and that fills me with dread because I don't bloody know how. I'd rather feel our way. But luckily, before I have to say something cringe worthy like 'you may speak', he replies.

"You can take both." His voice is hoarse, he is more affected than I anticipated.

"If I take both it will make it too easy on you. If you keep your eyes, you won't have to use your own restraint to stop your hands from getting you what you need, but you will have to watch me torture you. It you keep your hands, you won't have to see your dick passing between my lips, but you will have to fight with yourself not to reach forward and force me to give you more. It's your choice. Which is the lesser torture? Which will you keep? You have to work for it a little."

"My hands then," he replies.

I smile, placing the silk around his eyes and wrapping it securely until I can tie off the ends.

His breathing is laboured, it's visible and it excites me. I reach down and take his hand, encouraging him to stand and he threads his fingers between mine, holding on tight, like he fears I will let go.

I gently pry my fingers free and whisper. “It’s ok.” I take hold of the hem of his t-shirt.

“Whoa what are you doing?” he asks, trying to clamp his elbows to his sides as I start to lift it up. “Out here?”

“No one can see. Dad left for New York this morning, Jazz is staying at yours and there isn’t a neighbour for acres and acres and even they face the other way. It’s totally private here, I promise.”

He stills, but doesn’t relax.

“Do you trust me?”

“Yes,” he replies and with that, he relaxes his arms and lets me pull his t-shirt over his head. I drop it on the table and go for the button of his jeans. His breathing hitches, but he doesn’t resist me. I kneel as I lower them to the decked floor and help him to step out of them and his shoes. He is hard under his boxers and I lick my lips. Reaching up, I slowly peel them down, revealing him gradually until he springs free.

He lets out a small moan.

I stare at him standing there naked, putting all his trust in me. His hard length standing proud in front of him, his hands poised, but self-controlled, by his side. I want a taste, but I’m not ready to spoil him.

“It’s been a long day.”

“Long and hard,” he manages. I see the faintest hint of a smile turn up the corner of his lips and have to admire him for being able to make a joke right now.

“So hard,” I murmur, almost brushing my cheek against his sensitive skin as I get to my feet. He holds his breath. I can feel him willing me to touch him. But he doesn't ask. I push his chair out of the way so he doesn't trip, and lead him across the terrace to the sofa area. The fire pit is already lit and the warmth coming off is not strictly necessary for such a warm evening, but it's nice I'm sure, on his naked skin. And the crackle fills the silence, making it seem less imposing. I sit him down among the soft cushions and encourage him to part his legs for me, placing his hands beside him.

He blows out a breath, he has been waiting hours for this. I'm amazed at his restraint.

Slowly, I lift my hand. His whole body flinches when I touch him.

"Fuck," he chokes, overwhelmed and trying hard to get it under control.

I let my hand form loosely around him and barely apply any pressure as it slides down his length.

"Oh god," he groans.

"You've been waiting for this all day."

He nods, pressing his lips together and looking pained. He is so engorged. I imagine it's almost painful.

I increase the pressure, working my hand up and down and he whimpers.

A few more strokes and he sucks in a sharp breath. "Mags," he warns. His hands flinching, but he keeps them by his sides, gripping the sofa cushions. "Mags," he gasps more urgently. "I'm close."

Good boy, the words are on my lips, but I refrain, I can't get caught in the trap of calling him that one thing. I don't know yet what feels right. I release him right on the brink and he visibly deflates.

He catches his breath, his perfect body, taught and defined under the strain.

When his breathing calms, I lick my lips and let them slide over his head. He tenses, too wound up to make a sound, his fingers dig into the cushions at his sides. I play my tongue around the tip, learning every detail of him. Something I never did before. After several minutes of teasing, which has him twitching, but not begging yet. I part my lips and slide them slowly down his length. I take my time so that he can feel each delicious inch of him slide deeper and deeper. I want him to feel it all.

He curses when he meets resistance and I hold him there. A lesser man would not be able to fight the urge to grab my hair and shove past the resistance, but Will waits. His hands come to his thighs, where he tucks them under his body to keep them from temptation and then, when he has got himself completely under control. I press forward, triggering my gag and quickly pull back.

Will cries out, but I don't stop there. I take him into my mouth again immediately and work him up until he can't catch his breath and chokes on his words trying to warn me to stop. I push him beyond that point until I can see it's almost too late and then I pull away and go back to toying with my tongue around his head.

I continue like this, edging him countless times, until sweat beads on his abs and his chest heaves.

"Please," he begs when I let go again.

"Please what?"

"Please don't stop," he sighs, coming down from the crest of the wave again. His head drops back and he pushes his hips forward, seeking some friction. "Let me come," he whispers.

"Maybe," I reply, taking him in hand again.

He lets out a resigned moan and throws an arm across his face, twitching and writhing more freely with every stroke. I know he can't hold out forever and I could let him go now, but I'm selfish and I want him. I don't want to waste this magnificent hard on. I think of all the ruined orgasms I've watched on the internet in the course of book research. Maybe we can play with that in the future, but tonight I want mutual satisfaction. Trying to get in the head of a sadistic bitch is fun, but I realise now, that is not the kind of dominant I will be. I could never get into the humiliation and the degradation. I'll leave that to the hardcore.

"Please," he begs. "I need—" he swallows and gasps for air. "I need—"

"You need to let go, I know." I slide my hand from him. I have to let him have his release.

"No, I need you," he reaches forward blindly and feels for me. Making contact with my cheek, he grabs me and drags me up his hard body, kissing me fiercely. I slip my thumb under his blindfold and peel it off him, discarding it. He blinks in the light of the fire and focuses on me, smiling. "I need you so badly."

I barely notice rolling under him until he lifts himself off me. When I look up, he is standing over me, his hand outstretched and his dick begging. I take his hand and let him lead me quickly through the house, the shift between us is exciting. I like these moments when he assumes control and I let him to see where it leads. He is so swollen and hard from a day of mental and physical teasing that there isn't even any sway to his erection as he walks up the stairs. It just juts out, rigid, leading the way. I'm transfixed.

He shoves open my bedroom door and drags me over to the bed, stopping to pull my short black dress over my head. "Oh shit," he stops short when he sees my purple silk underwear.

I smile flirtatiously and that seems to snap him out of his trance. He throws my dress over his shoulder and pulls me against him, groaning against my lips when his over-sensitive dick gets pressed between us. He ignores it, unclasping my bra, while he kisses me.

"Condoms?" he asks urgently.

I nod, turning to get them out of my drawer. When I turn back, he scoops me up and places me on the bed, crawling on top of me. I want to refuse him and make him lay down while I ride him, but I've tortured him enough today…maybe. I reach out for him and grip his shaft loosely, he thrusts his hips forward, trying to use my hand for more than I give. I let him, watching him try to get himself off, but knowing he won't really go all the way, not when he is this close to being able to fuck me.

He is panting and working himself harder and harder, then suddenly, he freezes. "Stop, stop, stop," he insists.

I let go immediately and reach for a condom, tearing it open and positioning it at his tip.

"No, no." He hisses, "too close."

"You'll be ok, trust me. You won't come."

He forces out short, sharp breaths, trying to keep control and I gently start to roll the condom down.

"Please," he begs, "I can't hold off."

"Yes you can." I don't need to say the words, 'you're not permitted to come', he is so eager to please, I can't imagine him doing so without permission. Suddenly, it hits me. I get to give him permission! This is one of those fantasy moments. I change my mind about voicing it. "You can't come unless I tell you to."

I finish rolling the condom down and position him at my entrance.

He takes a deep breath and presses forward slowly, his eyes close as he sinks in. He is beautiful like this, so raw and desperate, but holding it together for me. I urge him on and reach down to touch myself. The brush of my fingers gets his attention and he looks down at me and moves my fingers away, replacing them with his own. I let him take over.

Watching him as he barely moves inside of me, but yet somehow does enough to really hit the right spot, its almost enough on it's own. But his fingers. God his fingers. I quickly lose my grip and close my eyes, flaunting my freedom to let go. I gasp and try to find something to hold on to, grabbing at the pillows and the sheets. Nothing seems enough until my hands find him. He is everything I need and I sink my nails into his thighs, claiming him as he pushes me nearer.

His breath hitching pulls me out of my own head and I focus in him kneeling above me, barely able to hold back.

"You can come," I whisper.

His eyes widen a fraction and determination sets in his jaw. Instead of pounding into me like I expect, he doubles his efforts on me and within moments, I am coming. As soon as the first wave hits, he lets go, falling on to me and rocking into me with each pleasure filled wave.

His moans are my reward. His face buried in my neck, I wrap my arms around him and ride it out with him until all the tension bleeds from his body. It feels like that wasn't just today's tension he let go of, that release was a long time coming.

After we've laid there, wrapped in each other for a few moments, he lifts his head and kisses me. He doesn't have to say a word, his smile says it all.

"I should go and lock up," I whisper, annoyed that real life can creep into our bubble. I just wanted to snuggle in with him for the night, but everything was left open downstairs.

"No let me, you relax," and he quickly gets up and leaves the room so I can't argue.

A few minutes later, he sets a glass of water on my bedside table and crawls into bed with me.

"Thank you."

He snuggles into me from behind, wrapping me in his arms and nuzzling my neck.

"I liked it when you said I could come," he says a few minutes later, into the silence.

I grin. I liked that too.

I turn in his arms and brush my nose against his. "I liked it that when I said it, you did."

"I had to take you with me though. Ladies first, always."

"I loved that part."

"I just want to make you happy," he smiles.

I stare at him for a moment. "You already are."

I wake with a start, but finding Mags draped over me, my panic subsides.

Then into the despair in my head, she reached out and silenced it all.

Yesterday was life changing. It was simple, nothing fancy, but it was perfect. Someone understands me. SHE understands me. I can finally open myself up to exploring my real self with someone I trust. That was the reason I was so on top of the world last night, why I feel like I could move mountains today.

I stroke my fingers down her spine lazily and she stirs.

"Mmmm," she purrs, her voice thick with sleep. Her hand lifts up, while her eyes stay closed and she gently feels her way up my body to my face, squeezing my features lightly.

"What are you doing?" I ask through squished lips.

"Just checking."

"Checking?

She lifts her head and props her chin on my chest, smiling at me. "That this is real."

"I hope it is."

"You hope?" she smiles, raising herself slowly onto her hands and knees. "That doesn't sound like the confidence you were full of last night."

"Oh you liked that did you?"

"I really liked that." She presses her soft form down on top of me.

"I was high on life last night."

"Hmmm, we will have to figure out why so we can get you there again."

"Pleasing you seemed to have an effect on me."

"You were a very good—" she pauses kissing the end of my nose, "boy."

Pure bliss settles inside me and works its way through me to form a sleepy smile. "I don't think you know what that name does to me."

She rotates her hips, drawing attention to the fact that not all of me is sleepy. "Oh I think I'm getting an idea." She makes a point of grinding again, making me harder still. "So," she says pinning one of my hands to the bed above my head. "I will have to think of lots of new ways you can please me, to keep you high on life." She takes my other hand and holds it down into the mattress beside the first. Looking into my eyes, she slowly rubs up my length. I catch my breath as she pauses with my head at her entrance. Just a tilt of my hips and I could sink right in.

A bang and a clatter startles us both of us, Mag frowns and glances over her shoulder at the closed bedroom door.

What the—?

Drilling resonates through a nearby wall.

"Shit." Mags sits back on her heels.

"What time is it?" I sit up with my hands propped behind my back, searching around for a clock.

Mags looks at her watch, "Nine fifteen!"

"Holy shit!" I lift her off me, trying to put out of my head that I was almost inside her. I should have been at work over an hour ago. I'm going to get so much shit for this.

"Fuck," Mags gasps as I jump out of bed. "I undressed you outside."

"It's ok, I picked up my stuff when I locked up. It's over on the chair."

"Oh thank god."

I begin throwing on my clothes as quickly as possible. The drilling stops and hammering begins. It's almost as if someone is making a point.

"Fuck, fuck, fuck," I grumble trying to hop into one of my socks. Spencer is going to be even more unbearable than usual. I can't believe we overslept. I can't believe I woke up in such a relaxed state that work wasn't even a consideration.

Normally I wake up and start meticulously planning the day, obsessively making a mental to do list and worrying over things I can't control, before it's even light out. I haven't needed an alarm clock most of my adult life. It's been even worse lately, knowing I'll see her every day. So it never even occurred to me I could sleep past the start of my work day. How could I have been so relaxed? Me?

"I've got to go." I say absently, grabbing my shoes. "I'm sorry." I look up and she's sitting where I shoved her. Naked.

I swallow.

She always had the ability to take my breath away, but now she has that knowing look on her face, I can almost feel her hands around my throat. I feel like she will decide when I take my next breath and I love it.

I don't know what's going to happen next and for some inexplicable reason, I'm perfectly ok with that.

What the hell is happening to me?

"What's the matter?" she laughs. "You look like you're having an argument with yourself in your head."

"I'm just trying to work out what you've done to me. I'm all..."

"What?" she frowns.

"Relaxed."

"Oh." Her body visibly relaxes. "I thought you were going to say something bad."

"Lying in bed with you and blowing off my job isn't exactly good."

"It could be worse, at least you won't be in trouble with the boss."

"No it's so bad. What kind of example am I setting to the boys? Fuck," I curse, trying for the third time to get my foot into my shoe. "And the worst thing is, I've got to go out there and face Spencer."

"Ergh." She pulls a face. "Yeah that's going to suck."

I look up from wrestling with my shoe and find her standing right in front of me. I didn't even realise she had got up. Her scent is all consuming. She is so close I could reach my tongue out and— bloody hell, no, I can't. I sit back in the chair trying to move my mouth away from temptation. She doesn't move. I glance at the door. I need to go, but I can't get up without coming into full body contact with her. And she knows it. She is relying on it in fact, I can tell by the suppressed smile she's wearing.

"Aren't you going to be even later if you don't get going?"

she asks innocently.

I stare at her, my heart pounding.

She leans forward, grasping my wrists in her hands, pressing them together and holding them tight. "I could always call Spencer and tell him you got tied up...doing something for me," she says seductively, her smile growing as she brings my hands towards her.

I inadvertently ball them into fists to keep my fingers out of harm's way. But when I make eye contact, she shakes her head. Eager to please, too eager probably. I uncurl them and she nods her approval. Then I watch, frozen as she guides them between her lips and slides them up and down, coating them in her arousal. Some irrational part of my brain must take over, because my fingers become animated of their own accord as I watch, helpless. My thumb circling her clit and two fingers sinking in to her.

My god she's wet.

She moans immediately and I feel a swell of pride. I love that she responds so freely. It's what I want to hear, that I did that to her. I brought her that pleasure. Now I know what that sounds like, I would walk over hot coals to hear it again.

She halts my hand and removes it slowly. I look up, worried I have disappointed her, but she doesn't look displeased. She looks like she wants more.

"Go to work."

"But—" I start to object.

She presses a finger to my lips.

"I just wanted to make sure you'd be thinking of me all day," she says, bringing my fingers up to my face so that I can catch her scent on them. "And now you will," she grins.

I close my eyes and groan.

I find I'm breathing hard. I'm not sure if it was my rush to get ready, her intoxicating scent, or how overtly sexual she is? Maybe it's all of it.

I would have caught her scent from my fingers and been overcome with desire later, that's a given. But to say it like that...to actually make me smell my fingers that have just been inside her. It's just so...in control. I think stuff like that all the time, that's the stuff I keep locked in my head. If I ever let it out of my mouth, I always find myself in the wrong company and end up embarrassed. She makes it look so easy. I've always wished I could be like that. Like Spencer I guess. It isn't me.

I'm starting to see I didn't need to be that way at all. What I needed was for someone to be that way for me. To give me a safe place to be me.

"Now go."

Pulled from my thoughts, I look up and blink. She has stepped away, freeing me to go and leaving is the last thing I want to do. She is standing there naked, how can I be expected to work?

"Will?"

"Huh?" I realise I was just sitting, staring. "Oh, yeah," I shake my thoughts from my head. "I'm going." I force myself out of her chair and step towards her to kiss her before I leave. But I falter, suddenly unsure if I need permission for something like that or if I can just do it when I feel like it. Until now, I would force myself to 'be the boyfriend', not that there have been many girlfriends, trust me. It's just that girls expect certain things of the guy that have never come naturally to me.

It just feels strange not having to pretend anymore and now I'm not sure what I should do.

Just do it Will, you're being ridiculous.

Forcing myself forward like there was no issue, I wrap her in my arms and stare down at her for a second, smiling that she is mine…that I'm hers…whatever, we are together and that's the amazing thing. We will work through the rest.

"Are you going to kiss me?" she whispers.

"I'm working my way up to it." I laugh. She giggles and when her eyes meet mine I seize the moment and capture her in a slow kiss that stops her still.

"Ok, I really have to go," I murmur against her lips.

"I know." She extracts herself from my arms since I seem incapable of letting her go voluntarily.

"I'll see you later?" It's more of a plea that a statement.

"Of course," she replies.

"Ok." I make myself head to the door, turning back briefly before I open it. "Bye."

When I close the door behind me, I feel exposed and as if I have been forced out of my bubble, but the drilling starts up again, reminding me why I had to leave and I fly downstairs to the front door. This is all bad enough, but I can't face going out the kitchen door straight into the site, where they can all jeer and have a dig. I let myself out of the front door and head to my van to change into the work boots I keep there.

As casually as I can, I walk around to the side of the house dreading who I will see first, but no one is around. I can hear work going on inside the extension, so I head to the garage where we are storing our tools. Staring at the machinery and materials though, I struggle to even remember what I do, let alone what I specifically should have been doing for the last hour.

My phone vibrates from my back pocket and while my conscience says, get on with work you slacker, I take it out to delay the inevitable.

‘Thinking about me?’

I smile. That familiar hit of adrenaline washes through me just like every time she comes to mind. It’s somewhere between fear and elation and I hope it never goes away.

‘I’m always thinking about you.’

‘That makes me happy.’

“Well look what the cat dragged in.”

I jump out of my skin and spin around to face a gloating Spencer, sliding my phone into my back pocket as subtly as I can.

“What sort of time do you call this?”

“I’m sorry, I was...err.” Fuck, I shut my mouth before I start feeling as pathetic as I sound.

His eyebrows wiggle up and down in the juvenile way that he applies to everything. “Oh yeah, I bet you were.”

“I just over slept that’s all.”

“Mmmhmm. Late night was it?”

“Leave it will you. I should get to work.”

His smug face forms an amused frown. “Dressed like that?”

I look down at myself. I put on my work boots, which will save my nice shoes, but I'm wearing my favourite jeans and an expensive T-shirt, which kills me, and he knows how much it will bug me to ruin them. I'm going to have to suck it up, I don't have time to go home and change. So I style it out and shrug. "Yeah, why?"

He almost fully suppresses his smirk, not a bad effort for him, I'm impressed. "Ok then. Give me a hand with these bags."

I look down at the dusty bags. Bastard. This day is going to blow.

When I find the time to sneak a look at the messages I have felt come through while I've been gingerly trying to work my arse off while not wrecking my clothes. My stomach churns.

'I have a question…'

'Why did you hesitate before you kissed
me?'

'Are we moving too fast?'

Fuck. Why would she say that? Of course we aren't moving too fast. If you ask me, we aren't moving fast enough. I want to shout it out, tell the world I'm in love with the most incredible, perfect girl in the world. Not only that but she is the girl I have loved since I first discovered what that word really meant.

'No not at all, we can't go fast enough for my liking.'I type.

And then I stare at it and scrub my face. Maybe I shouldn't say that.

I'm suddenly overcome with doubt.

Telling her how I feel seems to end up burning me and I can't get burned this time. I told her how I felt once before and then it all fell apart. I know there were many reasons for us crumbling, but I never really shook the feeling that I freaked her out and the rest was a result. There I said it. I was jealous, I felt left out, but I had also laid myself bare and I felt like the same didn't come from her.

I delete the message. The fact that I don't want to get burned is not the reason I hesitated, I turn my attention to that question and brush the rest under the carpet.

'I wasn't sure if I should.'

'Why?'

I feel my face flush just thinking about having this discussion.

'Will, are you having second thoughts
about us? Please be honest with me if you
are.'

'No, God no. I just wasn't sure about taking
the initiative that's all.'

There is a long pause before she starts typing again.

'I'm confused.'

Damn this is embarrassing to put into words.

'Because you didn't want to lead me on?'

Oh Jesus, I need to spit it out before she falls in to a spiral of doubts.

'Because I didn't have permission.'

I know I'm red with embarrassment. Thank fuck she can't seem me. Maybe this is the best way to have this conversation.

'Oh!'

'Not that I needed permission. I just wasn't sure. We had been playing, you know?'

Ugh god. This is painful. This is precisely why I kept it all in.

'You can always kiss me Will.'

'Okay.'

Shit that sounded dismissive.

'Thank you.'

Aaaannd that sounded pathetic.

'Unless I've gagged you.'

I need to sit down. Leaning heavily against the only solid object near me, the wall, I swallow hard. My mouth is dry and my dick is working on a permanent denim imprint. I just stare at her message, not sure how to respond without looking like a teenage boy.

'I mean you seemed to like it when I fed
you my underwear, but you should say if
that's not your thing.'

I almost drop my phone scrambling to type a reply.

'No, no, no, it is. It is!'

I look at my screen in my shaky hands and huff. Yep you nailed it. Nothing 'desperate teenager' about that response at all. Idiot.

'Lol! Ok. We should really talk about this
stuff shouldn't we? Find out what the
limits are.'

My insides seem to be on a spin cycle already and her use of the word limits cranks it up a gear. Fuck. To be actually talking about this stuff like it's normal is just amazing. Suddenly feeling bold, I reply.

'I can't think of any.'

'Everyone has limits, Will.'

'I guess you'll have to test them to find out.'

I can't believe this stuff is coming out of me. I have held it in so long I get gripped with panic every time I see the words on the screen, as if I have accidentally broadcast my secret to the world.

'I need some clue though.'

It's heartwarming to see her uncertainty. But I know she can figure it out.

'I liked everything I've read so far.'

'Oh god, I keep forgetting you read my books.'

'Why is that a problem?'

'It's just embarrassing.'

'You shouldn't be embarrassed, you are an amazing writer.'

'You're biased.'

'Hey I'm in one of them, I'm allowed to be biased. Is that going to be a series too?'

There is a long pause and I start to think I pushed my luck.

'I thought it was going to be a standalone,
but maybe there's more to the story.'

God I hope so.

"Is that Mags?" Spencer shouts across the shell of a room I'm standing in.

"Fuck." I jump out of my skin. Trying to put my phone away and look busy, to no avail.

"Tell her she left her drawers on the patio furniture while she was fucking your brains out last night."

He is gone before I process what he has said.

What the…?

Oh shit! I dash out of the open doorway and round our well worn path to the rear of the extension, trying to recall Mags taking anything off out here. I know she stripped me, but I got all of that. I'm wearing it now. Did she undress? No, I took her clothes off upstairs. He's bluffing.

I round the building only to find Spencer, hands on hips, staring down at something strewn on the outdoor furniture.

Fuck, shit, bollocks.

A couple of the other guys disperse, chuckling as I approach, but Spencer doesn't move. I peer over to see what he's staring at. Oh fuck. It's the scarf she used to blindfold me. She didn't untie it. She just pulled it off and tossed it there. It's obvious how it was used, the head sized circle of fabric. The knot. Kill me now.

"It's a beautiful, beautiful thing."

"What is?" I frown, peering down at it, wondering what on earth is so lovely about any of this.

"Your spiral out of control," he says, without taking his eyes off the slip of fabric that has his attention.

"My what?" I snap. Playing right into his hands.

"You're getting uncharacteristically sloppy, William. Your head is all over the place. You leave early, come in late, do dirty work in your favourite clothes, which I know must be killing you by the way, and now this." His hand leads my eyes back to the offending article. "It's just beautiful, that's all. Thank you."

I lean down and snatch it up to spare Mags' blushes. It's far too late for me.

Staring him down, I find some fight. I know what we used it for, but he doesn't know any of that. Mags could have tied her hair with it for all he knows. So I recover myself and laugh, slightly more nervously than I would have liked, but I'll have to live with it.

"It's a scarf you moron."

He looks at it for a long moment and a slow smile tells me I have won nothing.

"Indeed it is," he nods. "Indeed it is. But…" He places one of his paws on my shoulder and squeezes at a level somewhere between misplaced affection and a Vulcan death grip and laughs. "The way you came running out here says it could definitely have been undies, so it was worth it."

"You're such a dick."

"I accept that," he turns to me and grins. "But for once it's not my dick that is providing the entertainment around here, just let me enjoy it." With that he slams me on the back, knocking the wind out of me and starts to walk off, plucking the scarf out of my hands as he goes. "Coming for lunch?" he calls over his shoulder.

I groan, but follow him. Lunch would be good, I didn't even get a cup of tea this morning and I also need to nip home and change.

Spencer pauses as he passes the kitchen door and opens it, leaning in.

"Maaaaaaags!" he bellows.

"Yeah?" I hear her call from inside the house.

"We are going to see Jazz and get lunch, you wanna come?"

My eyes widen in surprise and I watch him with suspicion. Who is this guy? Maybe I knocked some civility into him when I punched him. I'm not complaining though, I get to spend lunch with Mags.

"Coming!" she yells back and he dutifully waits holding open the door.

"Hey," she smiles as she comes into view.

"Hey," I offer her a tight smile in return. Not that there is anything wrong, I just don't want to beam like an idiot in front of Spencer. But of course she has doubt in her eyes in an instant. Why wouldn't she? I'm doing a fantastic job with the mixed signals recently aren't I? Spencer is right, I'm falling apart.

"You left this outside where you were screwing my cousin last night," Spencer says casually handing her the scarf.

I cringe, why does he have to be so...related to me?

Mags on the other hand seems to rise to the challenge. "Oh thanks, I was looking for this, I'd hate to lose it, it's part of a set. The white ball gag and cuffs look all wrong with a black blindfold," she deadpans.

My jaw drops…I can't even.

Then I risk a look at Spencer and find him in much the same state. Fuck me. She silenced Mr. Answer-for-Everything. Could she be any more incredible?

"Are we going then?" She breaks the silence, unpicking the knot and wrapping the scarf artfully around her neck like it's nothing, establishing herself even further as a force to be reckoned with.

"Hey, what do you think you're doing? Shotgun is mine," Spencer shouts, catching up with us after putting his tools away.

"Ha, yeah, nice try," I shout back, planting myself firmly in the seat.

"Take the van. I'm going home to change after lunch," Will tells him.

I can hear Spencer grumbling as he turns back towards the van, which makes me laugh.

"You're incredible," Will whispers as he slides into the driver's seat and leans over to nuzzle my neck.

"I have my moments," I reply. In truth, I just enjoy seeing self-assured men floundering.

"Well, that was a great moment." He pulls back and focuses for a second on getting the key in the ignition. The car starts and he sets off down the driveway, then he looks back at me. "Are you really going to wear that scarf to lunch?"

"Yeah, why not?"

He groans and grips the wheel. "No reason."

"Does it bother you?"

"No it doesn't bother me, I'll just keep thinking about last night that's all."

"Like you weren't already?"

He laughs. "Yeah ok, guilty."

"Well this will just give you something to focus on."

"Brilliant."

"You can look at it and think about how many times I took you to the edge and wouldn't let you fall."

"I'm practically there right now."

I can't help looking straight at his crotch and smile with satisfaction when I see he isn't exaggerating. I lift my hand and move it slowly towards him. He watches me warily while trying to keep one eye on the road. The little sound he makes when my finger traces the pronounced length of him currently constricted in the leg of his jeans, makes me ache to have him beneath me.

"Mags please," he whispers.

I pull my hand back and he takes a shaky breath, calming himself.

I cut him a break as he pulls in behind Mary's. I shake my head, I have to stop thinking of it as that, it's Jazz's place now. Spencer pulls up beside us and jumps out, not waiting for us. We both climb out of the car and I watch, amused, as Will tries to make himself more comfortable, his jeans hiding nothing.

We enter through the back door and find Spencer already trying to make Jazz his lunch.

"This is a nice surprise," she sighs, while he bites and kisses her neck.

"We came for lunch." He tells her, between kisses.

"What are you having?"

"Depends what you're offering" He growls, lifting her to wrap her legs around his waist.

She yelps and wriggles. “Not me! It’s against health and safety regs.”

He huffs and puts her down, still looking like he might eat her. “Oh well, in that case I’ll have my usual and 30 minutes of your time to eat with me.”

“Your usual? How am I supposed to know what that is?”

“Let your minions sort it out, come sit with me.” He grabs her by the hand and leads her through the kitchen and into the front of the shop.

Will slips his hand into mine and smiles sweetly when I look up at him. I can see that he envies Spencer’s confidence, when he really shouldn’t. It’s not confidence Spencer has, it’s arrogance, and there is a fine line between the two. Confidence is strength, arrogance is weakness and Will is strong, he just needs to embrace it.

We follow Spencer through the tables and sit at the one he chooses, waiting while he takes over the ordering of the food and drinks. When things settle down, I put my hand on Will’s thigh, offering him a comforting squeeze. While with the other hand I twirl the end of my scarf to tease him.

He side-eyes me and swallows.

I love toying with him.

“Why are you wearing a scarf Mags?” Jazz asks innocently, not knowing how perfect her timing is. “It’s like, a million degrees out.”

Spencer chokes on a laugh and Will covers his face with his hands. I can’t help but laugh.

“What did I miss?” Jazz eyes us all suspiciously.

“Nothing.” I’ll tell her all about it later.

Spencer however, isn’t going to let it slide.

"These two fucked on the garden furniture last night."

"Oh?" Jazz smirks.

"Yeah and they left their kinky props laying around."

"Oh God," Will groans, wrapping his arms around his head in an attempt to disappear.

I turn to Jazz who is understandably intrigued. "We had *dinner* on the terrace, that's all." I tell her, shooting a glare at Spencer. "And I left my scarf on the sofa, which Spencer seems to take as a sign that there was some hanky-panky going on in the great outdoors."

Jazz rolls her eyes and digs her elbow into Spencer's ribs. "Leave them alone will you."

"You weren't there when I found it. It was fucking hilarious. Old Captain Obvious over here busted himself out. You could tell from the panic on his face it could have been anything I found lying there, which tells me stuff went down."

Jazz looks at me expectantly and I lightly shrug, making Jazz have to look away before she laughs.

"See! They fucking did! I can't even get you to use the sex orange and he gets to fuck her outside."

Will's head snaps up and he looks at Spencer aghast.

"Aww, still no sex orange action for poor Spencer." I laugh, making Will turn his look on me, before he looks back to Spencer.

"Where on—" he lowers his voice and glances around once more to be sure. "Where on earth are you going to put an orange?" His eyes are wide at the thought. "No actually…" he holds up his hand. "I do not want to know."

"I'm not going to put it anywhere, you freak."

I tense. I don't like Spencer calling him that. Partly

because I don't like him the name calling, but mostly because I'm certain he'll believe it.

"Jazz is going to use it to get her daily dose of vitamin C while also getting a protein shot. Am I right?" he turns to Jazz enthusiastically for confirmation.

"In your dreams."

Spencer huffs. "Come on, I'll do that thing you like in front of the mirror..."

"Spencer," Will hisses, looking around. "Will you keep your bloody voice down?"

"Why Will?" he whispers loudly. "Are you embarrassed?"

"Yes!"

"Well, it was your exploits that lead us to have this conversation, not mine. Maybe you should think about that the next time you do...whatever it is you do."

Will growls in frustration, but quits before it gets worse.

Spencer smirks triumphantly and turns his attention back to Jazz. "So I was thinking, we should go away for the weekend. I'm sick of this place having its claws in you."

Jazz laughs. "Already? It's been less than two weeks, Spencer."

"Yeah, two weeks with no day off, you leave at the crack of dawn and you fall asleep at nine pm."

"Aww, are you feeling neglected?"

"Yes!"

Jazz's expression changes from amusement to understanding. "I know I'm working a lot, but it's kinda soon for me to be taking time off don't you think?"

"No, I don't think. You can't work 24/7 Jazz. You need time off. Just tell them you're going away for the weekend."

"I can't just leave."

"It's your business. If you don't establish a work/life balance now, you'll never have one. Tell her Mags."

Jazz looks at me with a smug, 'this'll be good' smile. Counting on me, her best friend and person who took the plunge and started this business for her when she was too afraid, to back her up. But I did it so she would have a happy future, not no life at all. "Sorry Jazz, but I think he's right."

She rolls her eyes. "Ugh, not you too."

"Thank you," Spencer barks loudly, slapping the tabletop. "You need to establish your working week and include time off in it. You can't work nonstop, you'll work yourself into the ground."

"But I'm still getting the hang of things and won't it look bad to the staff if I'm not here every day."

"If you're here every day, what do you even need staff for? You pay enough people to run the shop so that you can have time off just like everyone else," I point out.

"Yeah, I guess you're right," she sighs. "I'm just still getting to grips with things and making plans. I don't want any of them to think I'm not dedicated. Give me a couple more weeks and I'll make a schedule where I get some days off."

"You want me to wait a month Princess?" Spencer reaches over and scoops Jazz up, lifting her across into his lap. "I don't think I can."

"Spencer," Jazz squeals, hushing herself when she remembers her surroundings. "I have customers," she scolds.

"So? They get to see you all the time. It's about time they shared." Spencer tucks his face into Jazz's neck and regardless of who is watching, starts kissing her there.

"Okay, okay, I'll take Saturday off, will that do?" Jazz giggles.

"It's a start," he replies, his words muffled by her neck.

Jazz groans openly and then suddenly Will grumbles something incoherent and scrapes his chair away from the table, getting to his feet. "Can you get my lunch to go and take it back to work. I need to go and change," he says to no one in particular. Then he walks to the kitchen without looking back and leaves through the back door.

I turn to look at Spencer and Jazz, my mouth hanging open.

"What was that about?" Jazz asks, pushing Spencer away and straightening herself up. Although she makes no effort to get out of his lap.

"I have no idea," I reply. "Did I say something?" I scan back through the last few minutes thinking I must have said something insensitive, but come up empty.

"It's got nothing to do with you," Spencer interjects. "He turns into a little baby whenever he sees over the top PDLs."

I look at him puzzled.

"Public displays of lust." He clarifies, grinning and then sinking his teeth into Jazz's shoulder.

Jazz yelps and gets up, giving him a playful shove.

"It's because he's jealous."

I doubt that, but maybe on some level he does wonder why I'm not all over him in public too, I should stop wondering and go and find out. "Can you bring my lunch back too please Spencer?" I make to stand.

"Just leave him to sulk," Spencer insists.

"No, I need to talk to him." I pick up my bag and turn to Jazz. "I'm sorry, I'll see you later."

"Don't worry, go sort it out," she replies.

Sure he would already be gone when I get to the back door, I'm surprised to see his car still there. But he isn't in it. I stare at it for a minute wondering why he walked home when he had to walk right by his car, but as I turn to go back in the kitchen, I spot him sitting on an upturned crate, between the back of the shop and an outbuilding, with his head in his hands. I have no clue what his problem is, but he can't run away from me and leave me wondering.

I march over and stop in front of him, waiting for him to look up.

"I'm sorry," he murmurs, keeping his eyes to the floor.

"You want to explain to me what that was all about?"

"No, not really."

"Well that isn't going to work for me. You can't storm out with no explanation. You've got me thinking I did something wrong."

He looks up. "No you didn't do anything."

"Yeah well, I know that, but you throw a fit and storm out, I'm going to wonder."

"It's me, I'm sorry." He shakes his head looking back down at the ground.

I glance down at my feet and curse my relaxed summer vibe. Perhaps I should have a 'never leave home without heels' rule and then I wouldn't get caught short in flip-flops when it counts. Oh well, flip-flops it is. I lift my foot and press my toes into his chest, forcing him to sit up straight and look at me. "That's not good enough, Will. I need to know what's got you like this."

"It's just him," he sighs.

"Spencer?"

He nods. "He can do whatever the fuck he likes and no one blinks, but I get to have some actual fun for the first time ever he not only catches me out, but he has to make a big joke out of it."

"Oh come on, it wasn't that bad."

"Easy to say when you haven't had him on your case your whole life."

"That's a bit of an exaggeration."

"Is it? Spencer can be as much of a dick as he wants and everyone loves him for it. Even my family. When we all get together, Spencer is the golden boy and it just becomes this..." He searches his thoughts looking for the right words, then he shakes his head. "You know what, it doesn't matter."

"Oh no you don't, tell me."

He looks me straight in the eye.

"What?" I demand, leaving him nowhere to go.

"They kind of pick on me," he says quietly, deflating.

"What do you mean? Your parents are lovely." I frown.

"Yeah, I know they are. With family though, it just all gets...Oh I don't know, it sounds so pathetic when you say it out loud." He huffs.

"You can tell me," I urge.

"They just have rose tinted glasses for Spencer. They all see him as this amazing achiever. You know? They tell everyone he's an architect, because they think that sounds more important and they don't feel they need to understand the difference. His mum has totally ignored the fact that he is now doing labour out of choice, she just tells everyone he has his own company, even though we are equal partners and the whole damn thing was MY plan. And now they are all ecstatic that he has a girlfriend because he might settle down, like that was all he needed, a good girl. Not that he needed to grow the fuck up and stop pissing around. Just that he needed to find a nice girl and it would all magically be ok. They don't see that people have sacrificed so fucking much to see that he got to this place and it doesn't matter what I do, how well I do, it goes unnoticed. And If I try to tell them, they all turn it on me, like I'm jealous or trying to get attention, and it's all a big laugh at my expense. And I know I sound like a stupid spoiled kid. But it's been happening since we were kids, so that's how it still makes me feel."

I stare at him for a moment. I've never seen him like this.

"See? It's not attractive is it?"

"Not really." I laugh.

He looks at me in surprise, but then nods in resignation.

I want to rip into him, but I can see he's feeling low and I know it won't help. Instead I try to get to the root of the current problem. "So what has got to you today specifically?"

"It's just that we had a great time last night."

"We did." I smile.

"It was amazing." He returns the smile, but it quickly fades. "And I can't just have a great time without him catching on to it and rinsing me for it. But then it's fine for him to maul his girlfriend in public and no one says a word."

"Why don't *you* say something? Give him a taste of his own medicine."

"Because with Spencer it doesn't work like that. He is always on top and I'm always the scapegoat. Even when I think I have the advantage, he manages to turn it around on me."

"Maybe the problem is you," I venture.

"Thanks," he says dropping his head forward and resting his elbows on his knees.

I don't think, I just act. Poking my toes in his chest again, harder this time. Forcing him back up and shoving his back to the peeling wall. His eyes the last thing to come up. "Don't do that. This is about you, not any of them."

"You don't know what it's like," he starts and I cut him off.

"You don't think I've ever been in that situation? I come from a big family with plenty of money and endless opportunities. My cousins are all in the family businesses, earning their places as partners and directors and CEOs, with their degrees and diplomas, and I write smut. I avoid family get togethers because I'm the fucking sideshow. All I ever get is, 'So tell us about your books,' in that tone that is morbid curiosity, jealousy and distain in one neat little package. I mumble apology after apology for missing polo matches and fundraisers, because I don't want their life and I accept that I am a constant disappointment. It's just that when we get together, I don't give them any chance to make me feel bad about myself. This is what I choose to do, they do what they choose to do. I don't judge them, so I don't let them judge me."

"It isn't because they judge me, it's because they just don't see me."

"Well, maybe you need to come out of the shadows and show them what you've got."

"They won't notice trust me." His shoulders slump.

I shove again, forcing him back up. "You're right, it really is unattractive seeing you like this."

"I told you. Why do you think I walked out?"

"So what are you going to do to change it?"

"I don't see what I can do."

I release him and put my foot back to the floor, and he looks disappointed. He isn't the only one. "What happened to all that confidence you were bouncing with? It was only yesterday, Will. How can you have lost it so quickly?"

He shrugs. "Maybe I never really had it."

"Bullshit." I can see he's low but there's no excuse for this level of self-pity and I'm not going to let him wallow in it when it's so unnecessary. "You just need to ignore him and focus on you. Be more like him if that's what it takes."

"Mags, I can try and pretend but I'm never going to be like him. Fucking hell, he thinks he's God's gift to women. He's had them throwing themselves at him on social media for so long he actually thinks that 'being kind of a dick' is an attractive personal quality. And I can't even really blame him. He's just the monster they created. They're shameless. Have you seen them?" He posts a selfie and he gets a hundred comments, he shows me. 'Oh Spencer, you're so hot,' 'oh Spencer, you're making me wet,' 'oh Spencer, I'm gushing just thinking about you.'"

I raise my eyebrows.

"Okay, I made that last one up, but the first two were real. I mean, what is wrong with these people? He doesn't even hide that he is in a relationship now. And does it stop them? No. Some of them will even talk to Jazz to get in with him more. It seems like all you need to do is have a dick, be a dick and post enough pictures of some skin and they can't fucking contain themselves."

He shakes his head and stands up, dusting off his jeans. "Honestly, I feel like he could start strangling kittens and his little pack would all be like, 'Well you know, kittens are a real problem these days aren't they? Good for him for taking action.' It's just a joke. His arrogance is out of control and he is just celebrated for it."

"He is kind of a dick on Twitter, I'll give you that."

"No regular Spencer is kind of a dick. From what I've seen, Twitter Spencer redefines the word."

"Yeah," I chuckle. "But it's all just an act. You could do that, be a Twitter dick and let the mob massage your ego. I wouldn't mind. I think I'd find it quite entertaining."

"You think I've got all those shirtless selfies in me?" He laughs grudgingly. "I don't."

Pushing him against the wall, my lips hover over his. "You look fabulous with your shirt off," I tell him as I feel for the bottom of his shirt.

"Not here Mags," he whispers, caught off guard.

"Why not? I thought it gave you confidence to do what I tell you. That's what you need right? Confidence. And if following orders reminds you that you can give me something no one else can and shows you how valued you are, then I'm happy to oblige. Now take it off."

"Mags," he moans.

"Do it, Will."

"Fine." He yanks it over his head and tucks it into the waistband of his jeans to keep it off the dusty floor. Looking around, he steps further out of sight between the buildings just to be on the safe side.

I smile and pull my phone out of my bag.

"What are you doing?" he asks trying to put his hand up to stop me.

"Taking a picture for you to post on Twitter."

"Stop it Mags," he tells me turning slightly away. "I'm not even on Twitter."

I lower my phone without having hit the shoot button. "What?" I ask, aghast, as if it's the most shocking thing he could have possibly ever said. "You're not on Twitter?"

"Nope." He shrugs.

"Really?" I can't even…

"What's the big deal?"

"Nothing, just that I hadn't realised that's all."

"It's just Twitter, I don't see the appeal."

"Don't knock it, all that business with Spencer and Jazz happened because of Twitter. It never even occurred to me that you weren't part of it."

"I don't see the point. What would I use it for?"

A slow smile spreads across my face. "I can think of some things." I press myself against him and he gasps like I've stolen all the oxygen from round him, my thigh lightly brushing the front of his straining jeans. "You should take a leaf out of your cousin's book. Twitter can be lots of fun."

He swallows as I deliberately rub my thigh on me again. "Can we not talk about Spencer right now? I'm sick of him."

"I'm just saying, it might do you good acting like him on social media. There's a reason he loves it." I push.

"I am not Spencer," he snaps. Rage finally spilling out of him like hot lava.

"You got that right," I agree, glad to finally see some fire from him. "Fucking finally!"

"So why are you pushing me?"

"Because it's all you ever talk about, Spencer this, Spencer that. Don't you think that there's more to life that how you compare to The Spencer Ryan?"

He studies me, finally seeing my point. "There should be."

"But there isn't?"

"It hasn't felt like it until recently, no." He frowns, realising the weight of his words.

"And there is now?" I ask flirtatiously, trying to lighten the mood and remind him he has good things happening right now if he can see past his pity party.

He tries to keep his shy smile in check, but he can't hide it, "yeah," he says sliding his hands around my hips to my back and pulling me tight against him.

"Good." I let hold me, it feels nice. "Because I don't want to date @TheSpencerRyan's cousin. I want you."

He squeezes me a little tighter in acknowledgement.

"Who are you?" I ask abruptly, pushing his hands off me so that he can't snuggle his way out of this breakthrough.

"I'm just Will," he replies, shrugging. He tries to grab me back.

"For fucks sake." I slap his hands away. "You're not JUST anything. Why do you do that? Don't you dare make excuses for yourself. You are Will. Better than Spencer. More in every single way. You're *my* Will. Do you get that? *Mine.*"

The modest little dip of his head and the uneasy smile just tells me how closed off he is to that concept. How he has programmed himself to believe he is second best in everything. The hint of colour on his cheeks shows me that my words have worked their way inside. Now I just have to make him believe them.

"So, I'll ask again, who are you?"

"I'm Will," he tells me, squaring his shoulders.

"Whose Will?" I prompt.

"Your Will." He smiles.

"Mine," I whisper, pulling the scarf off my neck and wrapping it around his. I let him put his arms back around me, his eyes never leaving my lips. I make him wait for it. Feeling the tension build between us before I pull on the scarf to draw him in for a heated kiss. I feel him relax and let go of the scarf I'm using to hold him close to me. Leaning in more to the kiss, I push him against the wall and my hand instinctively reaches up and closes around his throat. His moan is drowned out by my own as the feeling of being in control, of being controlled, overcomes us both.

His hands fall away from my hips and he gives in to the feeling I know he wants.

Being owned.

And it gives me an idea.

I tighten my hold on his throat for a second, claiming him, before loosening my grasp and trailing my hand down his chest. I pull back and study him, wanting to see his eyes glazed with pleasure, my reward for giving him what he needs. I'm not disappointed.

"Wait there," I tell him, moving back a few steps to my bag and rummaging around.

"What are you doing?" His voice is raspy and full of need.

"You'll see," I reply, finally finding what I need and returning to him.

He looks down at my hand and frowns. "What are you going to do with that?" he asks, nodding at the lip pencil.

I pull the cap off the pencil and smile, pushing him back against the peeling wall. With him watching me intently, I select the place where I want my mark. His firm left pec, right over his heart. "I'm staking my claim. Isn't that what you want? To feel owned?"

He nods, not taking his eyes off the pencil in my hand.

'#Hers' I write in soft waxy crimson.

"There." I slide the top back onto the pencil and take a few steps back to get him in the frame. "Look at me," I tell him, zooming to line him up on my screen.

"What's it for?"

"Your Twitter profile picture." I reply, distracted by filters and trying to get him perfect in the frame.

"Mags I told you," he huffs. "There's no point. I wouldn't know what to do, what to say, hell, I couldn't even pick a name, so I decided it wasn't for me. I'm just not that interested."

"I said, look at me," I demand, shutting him off. Reluctantly he does as he's told and looks into my lens. His hair is perfectly ruffled and his eyes show me a hint of defiance. He isn't doing this for him. He is doing it because it's what I want. I see there is a pleasure in that for him and I can see it there on my screen. I take the picture and smile at the result.

Will doesn't even ask to see, he just shakes his head and walks towards me.

"Thank you," he says cupping my face in his hands.

"What for?"

"For knowing what I need, even if I have no clue."

"It's what I'm here for," I reply, letting him kiss me. The fact that I'm totally guessing shouldn't matter if he thinks I'm getting it right. It certainly makes me feel good to know he does. It gives me the confidence to push harder. "But don't make a habit of this," I warn him, poking my finger at his chest. "I need a man who is sure of what he's worth."

"Yes," he agrees.

I decide it's time to start pushing for more. I know he has it in him, it might even help him. "Yes what?"

A slow smile spreads over his face as he catches my drift. "Yes, Goddess."

I can't control my satisfied smirk as I pull his T-shirt out of his jeans and help him on with it, rolling it carefully over my mark on his chest. I touch it lightly through his T-shirt. "Don't wash this off. I want my claim on you all day."

"Ok," he whispers.

"Good boy. Now go get changed. I'll see you later."

He looks disappointed. He'd obviously hoped I might go back with him and scratch the itch he's had since he had to run out this morning, but I think it will do him good to have a little time to think about what I've said. He leans in and places a light kiss on my lips and I smack his arse to send him on his way.

I pick up my bag and walk back inside without looking back and my phone buzzes in my hand with a message.

'Mags?'

'Yes Will?'

'I have an important question I need you to answer in a way you think I can handle.'

'Okay...?'

'Where does he want to put the orange?'

My laugh barks out in the kitchen, startling one of the girls who is quietly working. When I compose myself enough to reply, I see he is typing again.

'Seriously, if you think I don't want to know, just say so. I've dealt with more TMI's over the years from him than I can stand to remember. I'm just baffled. It seems too kinky, even for him.'

He is funny. I could put his mind at rest, but toying with him is way more fun.

'If you're lucky, I'll show you later.'

'I'm cringing.'

'*Cackles*'

I put my phone in my bag and I hear him start his engine.

"What's so funny?" Jazz asks, walking in with two empty plates.

"Nothing." I chuckle. "Just messing with Will. Did Spencer go back to work?"

"Yeah, he took your lunch back with him. I thought you'd be back at Will's making naughty."

"No, we talked outside. He just left."

"Everything okay?"

"Yeah," I blow out a pent up breath.

Jazz frowns, looking torn between wanting to help her best friend and needing to get back to work. "Why don't you come help me make a batch of Dark and Stormy? We can talk about it."

"Jazz, don't worry, you're busy I don't need—"

"*I* need." She cuts me off. "I need to know what's going on with you. I need to give you advice. I love this place and I'm so happy you pushed me to do it. But I don't want you to learn to cope with your troubles without spilling it all to me. I want you to need me too. I want to be the pillar of strength that keeps you standing."

I bust out laughing. "Okay, okay, you can cut the amateur dramatics, Jesus. I'll come and help you, share my troubles. Just promise me tea and chocolate."

"Can do." She smiles.

I follow her through into the purpose built chocolate kitchen that Spencer worked tirelessly on to get it just right for her. Since we are on display to the customers, I refrain from hopping up onto the counter to watch her work, which might have been my usual habit. Instead I pluck an apron off the hook and tie it round myself before washing my hands.

"So come on, tell me your woes," Jazz puts on the kettle she keeps here for her refreshments, rather than going to the main counter to make tea.

"They aren't woes exactly."

"Is it not working out?"

I look up her, surprised that she would say that. "Yeah, why? Does it not look like it is?"

She tilts her head, studying me. "I don't know. I know I've been distracted, but you've looked tired, like you're carrying a huge weight around lately."

"I'm just finding my feet in very new territory that's all."

"Oh come on, you can do this with your eyes closed. You know this stuff, you've researched every inch of it."

"Yeah, but that doesn't prepare you for entering into it for the first time with someone you…"

"Someone you what?" she asks as she bends down to get some equipment from a cupboard. When I don't answer, she comes up quickly, dumping a bowl on the counter, her eyes wide with glee. "Mags Goldsmith, are you in love?"

"Sssh!" I look around to see which of the village gossips are listening in, but find to my relief, only the slightly deaf old lady who helps with the church flowers left after the lunch crowd. And she seems oblivious.

"Are you?" Jazz demands. When I don't answer she goes on, "Oh my god you are!"

I don't know how ready I am to admit that. I haven't felt this way in a long time. The last time I felt it, I was certain and I got my heart broken, so I'm not exactly jumping to offer it up again. "I don't know how I feel yet, it's too soon to say."

"Bull. Shit. You're smitten kitten. Admit it."

God I hate it when she's so right, but that doesn't mean I have to give her the satisfaction. "What happened to, 'Who says this has to be so serious?' Remember that? You said, 'Maybe this *should* be more about sex. Enjoy each other. That's what life is for.' Am I ringing any bells?"

"That was to get you to take the plunge. Now it's open season. I call L-O-V-E, luuuurrrve. The only bells you'll be ringing missy are wedding bells." She holds a tea towel over her head like a veil and bats her eyelashes.

"You shut your trap!" I laugh sulkily, grabbing it out of her hands and screwing it up in a ball.

"Make me," she taunts "Mags and William, sitting in a tree, K-I-S-S-I-N-G."

I throw my hands up and lean against the counter. "You're such a child and you're enjoying this way too much."

"Oh and you got no joy out of my misery with Spencer I suppose."

"There were some moments of joy," I admit.

"Turnabout is fair play."

"What does that even mean?"

"I don't know, it's something my dad says because he's old. You had your fun now I'm having mine, I guess."

I roll my eyes.

"You are having fun aren't you?"

"Yeah," I sigh, feeling the heaviness settle again.

"Mags?"

I look up to see that concern has replaced amusement in her eyes.

"No, I am. He's just working through a few things that's all."

"Oh?"

"I think he just feels like he lives in Spencer's shadow and doesn't realise that not everything in life is measured in comparison to Spencer Bloody Ryan."

"Ah."

"Yeah."

"He shouldn't compare himself to Spencer. He is everything Spencer isn't."

"I know. And you and I can see how much of a good thing that is in some areas and all he sees it as is failure."

"God. I'm not sure how you're supposed to cure that. We don't need two Spencers in the world."

"You're telling me." I laugh. "Anyway, I'm working on it."

She catches my eye and I involuntarily give her a conspiring smile.

"This sounds like something I need the details of."

"You don't need all the details."

"Oh come on, give me something."

I shake my head but decide to toss her a bone.

An hour or so later when I stroll up the driveway, I can see Will working. He doesn't see me, so I watch him as I get closer. Back in his work clothes, he looks far more at ease and knowing that he has my claim to him written on his skin under there makes me smile. Which reminds me. I need to set him up a Twitter account. I'm not going to force him to be on there, I'm not that overbearing. It occurred to me if he had an account I could tag him in things I post there from tumblr. Unsolicited porn on your phone at work is never not fun.

Chuckling, I open the front door and head into the kitchen. My lunch is sitting on the counter, so I grab it and head out to the terrace to sit in the sunshine.

'Download the Twitter app.'

'I will when I get home.'

'No do it NOW.'

'Jesus.'

'Would you prefer me to demand something else while you're working.'

'No! Give me a minute.'

'*Waits*'

'Okay, I have it, now what?'

'Sign in as @HerWill1. Password is my initials and my date of birth...a little challenge for you.'

'Pft! That's no challenge!'

I wait, while he enters the information and sees his page for the first time. The picture is the one I took and the bio reads:

Will Middleton
@HerWill1
'There's a thin line between confidence and arrogance. It's called humility.
Confidence smiles, arrogance smirks.' - Unknown #Hers

I followed him and followed myself back, setting notifications for my tweets. I'll leave the rest for him to figure out.

'You can change the password to something secret obviously, I just wanted to help you set it up.'

'I don't have secrets.'

I can't help but smile.

'So what do I do now?'

'I'll show you later.'

'That's the second thing you've said you'll show me later.'

'Looks like I'll be busy then.'

THURSDAY 3RD SEPTEMBER

"Morning," Mags says to Spencer and Jazz as they file into the kitchen.

As we all exchange greetings, my eyes fall on the cutting board by the sink. It has the top and tail of an orange and the pithy centre, still laying on it from when Mags came down late last night so that she could show me the wonder that is the sex orange.

I go to grab it and chuck it away before they see, but Mags puts her hand on my arm to stop me and when I look at her, she shakes her head slightly and has a sadistic grin. Reluctantly, I leave it, and go to sit at the table.

Jazz takes a seat beside me and Spencer goes over to the kettle.

"Sleep well?" Jazz asks me.

"Very well, you?"

"I'm making toast, want some?" Mags offers, opening the loaf of bread.

"Sure," Spencer responds, with his usual manners.

Jazz shakes her head, seeing the same thing I did. "Toast would be lovely, thank you," she replies, pointedly compensating.

"What the—?" Spencer turns around, the ends of the

orange in his hands and a look of accusation. I can't quite tell if it's directed at Mags and I for doing it, or Jazz for not having done it. But Mags was right, leaving it there was so worth it.

I look at her to let her know how much I adore her and she winks before she turns her attention to him. "Oops!" she exclaims. "I didn't mean to leave these out." She takes them from him and picks up the board, brushing past him in false haste to clear the evidence into the bin. Then ignoring his speechless stare, she busies herself washing the board and knife.

Jazz snorts beside me, trying to stifle her laugh.

"So fucking out of order." Spencer sulks. "Why does he get to do it? I discovered it."

"You don't have dibs on all the fun Spencer." Mags smirks, going back to loading the toaster with bread.

"I should. I am the most fun, I should have the most fun."

"Not one to blow your own trumpet though are you?" Mags teases, ruffling his hair.

I adore her.

"Jazz is in charge of blowing my trumpet. I just tell it how it is."

Jazz screws up her nose. "Gross."

"Oh shush, you love blowing my trumpet."

"Can we please all stop talking about blowing Spencer's dick please?" I drag my fingers through my hair in despair.

Spencer comes to the table with two cups of tea, "Once again mate, we're talking about my dick because you left your sex props laying around where anyone could find them. If you can't stand the heat, tidy up the fucking kitchen."

"It was me that left the evidence, he was…indisposed."

Mags brings a plate full of toast over and takes a seat.

"Ergh! TMI," Spencer shakes the thought out of his head and opening the butter.

"Hypocrite," I mutter.

"What was that?" Spencer challenges.

"Nothing."

Mags nudges me and simply smiles, snapping me out of the dark. I smile back.

She's amazing in every way, but the way she handles Spencer is perfect. She leans across and opens the butter, gouging her knife into the centre and lumping it onto her toast, completely oblivious to the divot she has left behind that is making me cringe. I reach over and scrape my knife across the surface of the butter evenly. Trying hard to ignore the hole. It will be gone in a day or so, it doesn't matter. I take a deep breath to quash the feeling.

Mags dives straight back into the butter as soon as I have finished and digs out another chunk, spreading it on her toast. I press my lips together, but can't tear my eyes away. It soon becomes apparent that she took too much and I watch in horror as she scrapes what's left on the knife, crumbs and all, onto the side of the pot.

Holy shit.

Mid-scrape, she looks up, suddenly aware of the silence. Everyone is watching her. Me, trying not to have a panic attack. Spencer, fully aware of my impending freak out and I'm sure morbidly amused by my silence. And Jazz just intrigued by the level of tension suddenly in the room.

"What?" she asks, looking at us in turn.

"Nothing." I force a smile.

"Blood-dy hell." Spencer swallows

"What?" Mags demands.

"I've seen people killed for less."

"Less than what?" Mags is confused.

I would love to be as carefree as her.

"That." Spencer points to her knife in the butter.

I watch it dawn on her. She remembers now. I have issues that run well beyond food in the bed. "This?" she does an extra swipe on the edge of the pot.

"Yep, that," Spencer replies gleefully.

Mags waits until I look her in the eye, then she uses her knife to ruck up the surface of the butter, quirking her brow in a challenge.

I tense, but resist closing my eyes to shut it out. It's just butter. It doesn't matter.

"Oh shit," Spencer hisses under his breath. I can hear the admiration for Mags in his voice.

I keep her eye contact. It's a silent command. I'm bound by it just as if she had tied me down. She's pushing my buttons again and it's turning me on.

Fuck. All eyes are on me now and I have a hard on.

Mags digs her knife into the centre of the butter and leaves it there, standing up. "Anyone else for butter?" she asks innocently, while not breaking eye contact and offering me another of her sadistic smiles. She is as turned on as me by this. I find it shocking as the penny drops, but she really is.

It's such a rush.

She pushes the butter towards Jazz and continuing to stare, picks up her toast and takes a bite. Then like it never happened, she looks away. "So did you get a day off booked in this weekend?" she asks Jazz, while I sit and die a little.

"I'm taking the whole weekend off actually."

"Are you really?" Spencer perks up.

Jazz nods, biting the corner of her toast. "Yeah. The girls are fine. I just have to finish training them on the chocolates today. So eat up, I want to be in early."

Spencer crams his toast in his mouth and stands up, eager to do as she asks if it gets him a whole weekend. "Come on then, you can take that with you."

"Alright, alright, I'm coming."

"Oh here, Spencer." Mags tosses him an orange out of the bowl as he makes to leave. He catches it without thinking. "In case you're hungry later."

"Bitch."

Jazz laughs long and hard. "I love you," she calls out to Mags from the hallway.

"Well I hate you all." Spencer huffs. "We're using this later," he says going after Jazz.

The front door slams and Mags gets up, standing over me.

She lifts her leg, straddling my legs and lowers herself slowly into my lap.

"Mmmmm." She purrs, licking her lips. Flashbacks of last night when she had those lips wrapped around me while she worked me with that orange, tear through my mind.

"You may be a butter gouger, but you really are incredible. Have I told you that?"

"No actually, I don't think you have." She grinds on me again.

"Well you are." I slide my hands into her hair and bring her lips to mine, taking my time to show my appreciation.

She lingers when I finish, her lips brushing along mine. "Tell me again," the whispers.

I kiss her again, this time more urgently. My hard length pressing against her harder with every measured thrust. I curse the clothes stopping me from driving inside.

She pulls away panting, rocking against me once more, just to watch my reaction. I drop my head back and moan. I swear, I could come just from this. I push up, begging for a relief I know I won't get and that just makes it better.

"Come on, we should go too," she says, starting to get off me.

I grab her arse and hold her down. "No we shouldn't."

"Yes, we should. You have work and I'm going for a ride."

"Oh?" I try to stop my pout, but I know I'm unsuccessful.

"What's the matter?"

"It's nothing." I sound like a child again. I'm fully aware of that.

"Will, I thought we sorted this whole JJ misunderstanding out. He isn't interested in me."

"No I know. Believe me, I know." I laugh nervously when I think about the way he devoured me. Now the way he looks at me makes far more sense. How I never realised will remain one of life's great mysteries.

"So what is it then?"

I pout again, this time not bothering to play it down. "It's that animal of yours."

She laughs her throaty, bewitching laugh and I stifle a groan. It's a sure sign, I've come to realise, that I've just made things worse for myself. Or better, depending on how you look at it.

"Jealous of my steed again?" she asks flirtatiously.

"Yes!" I press my lips together in an attempt to stop yet more punishable nonsense spilling out, but it's fruitless. "He gets all the fun. He gets to be between your thighs, when I can't be. He gets to have your body wrapped around him, feel you rocking against him, your hot—" I close my eyes. Easy Will, you're talking about a horse, don't take it too far.

"My hot?" She leans in so that I can feel her warm breath on my neck.

"It doesn't matter," I mumble, refusing to open my eyes.

"Hmm."

"And you call him good boy." I say barely above a whisper.

"He is a good boy." She laughs. "Always."

I wrinkle my nose. Bastard.

"Although, sometimes he needs corrections, like all good boys. And when he does, he feels the bite of my crop."

I shudder. I know without opening my eyes that she is wearing a delighted smile. She knows how to work me up.

"Nothing too serious, just enough to remind him who is boss."

I nod, knowing I can't trust my voice right now.

"Perhaps you need some correction."

I swallow hard.

Her breath moves closer to my ear and she steals a nip at my sensitive skin with her teeth.

I jump, startled by the sensation.

"Oh, you'd like that wouldn't you?"

I nod again, incapable of any other movement.

She pinches my nipple and I gasp, forcing my eyes open

since hiding from it is getting me in deeper.

"I can't hear you," She twists the skin between her fingers.

"Yes," I hiss.

"Yes what?"

"Yes, I would like that."

She chuckles, almost out of character, which I find quite comforting.

"That's not quite what I was looking for, but I'm sure you'll remember your manners with a little correction." She cups my chin with her free hand, still maintaining pressure on my nipple with the other. She studies my face at close range for a moment, then releases me. "Now," she says all business again as she gets up, leaving me shaking. "I'm going to take my good boy for a ride, and if you play your cards right, you'll be next."

She blows me a kiss and then she is gone.

The doorbell rings and I smile. He's so formal. Spencer just waltzes in the kitchen door. My heels cut a brisk path to the door and I pause before I open it and pick up the little treat I brought him home. Taking a deep breath to get in the right mindset, I open the door.

He smiles, colour staining his cheeks. "Hey."

Excellent.

I've been posting porn all day on my Twitter feed, so he has been flooded. I'm pleased to see it's had the desired effect.

"Hey." I return his smile, but mine has a hint of what is to come. "Come in." I reveal the crop in my hand, extending it to point the way. He freezes, eyeing it up.

Perfect.

He steps inside and waits for me to close the door.

I circle him, looking him up and down. I want to make him feel scrutinised, vulnerable. I want him to need me to build him back up.

Stopping in front of him, he watches the tip of my crop as it touches his calf. He tenses as it explores the contours of his inside leg until it meets the apex of his thighs and he sucks in a breath when I use it to caress the bulge there. I love how quickly he gets hard for me, it makes a girl feel good. I bite my tongue though. If he wants to know how much he pleases me, and I know he does, he will have to earn it. Instead I choose to address it in a way that will leave him wondering.

"Hard already?" There's no feeling in my tone.

He doesn't answer immediately, I'm certain he doesn't know how. He doesn't know if being hard is what I wanted, or if I disapprove.

When I lift the crop, his eyelids flutter. But I only want to press the soft leather under his chin, to force his eyes up. I could get lost in their sea of uncertainty…but not until I've made some waves.

"Answer me, boy."

There's a part of me that can't believe that sentence made it out of my mouth, but I'm pretty proud of myself. Now I appreciate what it takes for him to call me Goddess. We are discovering a whole new comfort zone together and it puts the rest of the world on the outside of our connection.

I want him to say it again, over and over.

He swallows, his Adam's apple nudging the leather pressed to his throat. "I can't help it if I get hard every time I see you," he finally replies. "I can only hope it pleases you, my Goddess." His body quivers with repressed desire as he speaks.

I'm so proud of him that a smile breaks out. Shit, no. Hold it in.

He spots it though and does a much better job of controlling his than I did. While the masks have slipped briefly, he raises his brows seeking approval, and in a moment of weakness I nod, letting him know he's doing great.

Then I snap the mask back on. "Now follow me," I

demand, and turn on my heel to head for the stairs. I can feel his nervous energy following me as I cross the hallway to my room and I motion him in, closing the door. Although Jazz has promised not to come home tonight and leaving it open might add a risk element for him to worry about. I just want it to be us. Intimate.

"Strip," I command, walking to my dressing table and not looking at him. From the corner of my eye, I can see him in the mirror. He hesitates, staring at my back, probably wondering if this is play or if I'm cold for a reason. Come on baby, you can do it, have faith and strip for me.

Baby… that's interesting. Boy and Baby in one evening. I wonder if I can make it work.

He pulls his shirt off and reaches for his shoes, snapping me out of my head and I turn my attention to the items I have gathered to use tonight. These things will have to do for now, but if we are serious about this, I need to do some shopping. We will be making a list.

When I look up, he is naked, standing stock still where I left him, waiting. I turn around slowly, having to stifle a groan at the magnificent cut of his lean body and the unadulterated need in his eyes.

I approach him slowly, bending the crop between my hands. His chest rises and falls rapidly as I close in.

We need to lay some ground rules, but I can't help wanting to see him tremble. I stroke the tip of the crop down the centre of his chest and appreciate every jump and twitch of his body as it strokes between his abs and lower, lower, until it ghosts along the hard cock, standing out proud from his hips.

He stares down at it, his whole body reacting when I round

the head, a near revolt, but he holds it together. I step to the side of him for a better view and continue my journey along the underside, until I have the crop under his balls, caressing them the way I had through his jeans when he arrived.

God do I want to smack them. I don't know where that desire comes from, but it's strong.

"Give me a safe word."

He jumps like he forgot he had company. I love that he was zoned out because of me. "I don't need one," he hesitates.

Okay, perhaps I put him in the zone too soon. We need to sort this out. Breaking out of the hardness I had established, I drop the crop and move in close to him bringing his face to mine, holding him there. He visibly relaxes, the doubt etched in his worry lines softens and he lets some of the tension out of his body. "You have to have a safe word. There might be things you don't want me to do." I pull back from him slightly so that I can read him.

The corners of his lips turn up in a hint of a smile, as if he's imagining all the things he'd never ask me to stop doing to him. "I can't think of anything I wouldn't want you to do."

I roll my eyes. "That's what they all say, until you get the knives out."

He lets out a nervous laugh. "It's kinda hot that I don't know whether to take that seriously or not."

"Which totally proves my point."

"You can do what you like to me. I want you to."

"But Will, you never know until that moment. It can even be something you thought you were perfectly comfortable with and suddenly you want it to stop."

"Then can't I just say stop? I know you'll listen."

I sigh. We will figure this out eventually, but not tonight apparently. I decide to move things along. "Sometimes ignoring you saying stop might be part of the fun. I might want to hear you beg me to stop, knowing I have full permission to ignore it and carry on. A safe word allows us both to let go. But tonight, I don't plan to play those games, so stop will be fine."

I turn away from him, gathering my crop from the floor and put my cool demeanour back in place before I turn around.

He searches my face, but I give him nothing and sure enough, that tension returns. I eye him, stepping from side to side, inspecting his body, putting him back in that vulnerable state. Taking my crop, I don't waste my time making my way to my target this time, I return it straight to where I left off. Weighing his balls with it as if he is nothing but an object.

I give them a light tap, relishing the jolt he can't control.

Stroking them again, I lean in. "Stop is your safe word tonight. Do you understand?"

"Yes," he whispers.

I pull back a few inches and give them a much harder tap. "Yes what?" I demand.

"Yes Goddess!" he barks, trying not to choke.

I could have gone harder, but I'm learning and I want to see the range of reactions I can pull from him. "That's better, boy. You'll have to remember your manners if you want rewards."

"Yes, Goddess."

"Sit here," I tap the chair I set in the centre of the room before he arrived.

He obeys and sits.

"Hands behind your back."

Obliging, he stretches his arms out behind the chair and clasps his hands together, settling into a comfortable position.

I return to the dressing table and collect the scarves I will have to make do with.

"I wish I had my box here." I mutter to myself, separating his hands and tying the right wrist to the right side of the chair back as best as I can with my good old silk scarf, luck I have a few.

"Your box?" he replies, thinking I was talking to him.

"I have a box of toys at home," I inform him.

"Like dildos and stuff?"

"Among other things. I'd have something better to tie you with if I had it here."

He falls silent as I move around to tie his ankles to the chair legs. It dawns on me that I might have made it sound like I've had other men tied to chairs. I have already told him I haven't though, I don't need to explain again.

Standing up I am taken aback by how he looks when he's at my mercy. His dick is so hard it's standing straight up. I want to climb on it now. But it's too soon.

Collecting my crop, I run through my plan in my head. I made sure today that I warmed him up for this experience. I posted images I wanted him to think about. Taking the crop, I tickle up his arm and onto his shoulder, then down onto his chest. His eyes follow. So I use it to lift his chin. "Eyes on me."

When I take the crop away from his chin, his head stays up, so I go back to his pecks.

Not giving him eye contact, having told him to keep his

eyes on me, gives me more power than I realised and I can reward him with the odd glance. I like it. A lot.

Running the tongue of leather under the line of his pecs, I lift it away and pause. This is the moment of truth. Do I hit him with it?

I want to.

I need to.

Before I can analyse it any more, I land it on his chest, above his nipple. It isn't too hard, but it makes a delightful snapping sound and he jumps. His breath coming short and sharp as he calms himself. I use the leather that just stung his skin to soothe it too. Then before he can come down, I hit the opposite side with a similar blow.

As he breathes through it, I graze his nipple and he stills.

"Did you like the picture of the sub with the clamped nipples?"

He sucks in a breath and nods. Without hesitation, I land my crop right on his nipple. He grunts through gritted teeth and breathes hard.

"I'll ask again, did you like the picture of the sub with the clamped nipples?" I move the crop to the opposite nipple to make my threat clear.

"Yes, Goddess," he answers urgently.

"Have you ever had your nipples clamped boy?"

"No, Goddess."

I use the corner of the leather to stroke the tiny bud and watch him shudder. "Are these nipples sensitive?"

"Yes, Goddess," he sighs.

"You think they can take a little pain?"

"I think so, Goddess."

"You think so?" I challenge, landing the crop harder on the other nipple. The resounding smack is followed by his yelp and it sends a shiver of excitement down my spine.

"Yes Goddess, they can take some pain," he cries.

"Excellent." I tuck the crop under my arm and walk to the dressing table, picking up the small pad of paper and pen waiting for me. I turn back to him watching me, panting. "Let's make a shopping list shall we? Nipple clamps," I say aloud as I write it on the list. Then I place the pad and the pen on his trembling thigh. The pen immediately rolls off. "Oops," I grin, stooping to pick it up. "Here, hold my pen boy." I offer it up to his lips and he obediently takes it between his teeth.

Fuck he's perfect. I'd need a change of underwear, if I was wearing any under this tight skirt.

"So…" I return to his nipples with my crop, sending fresh shivers through him. "Some nipple play is on the list. Does that excite you?"

"Yes, Goddess," he replies through his teeth clenched around my pen.

I smile and reward him with a tap, tap, smack across one nipple, then a tap, tap, smack across the other.

He openly groans.

Moving my crop lower, I continue my tap, tap, smack on each of his abs, soothing each one with a stroke of the leather before I move on to the next. Left then right, lower and lower. My smacks gaining in intensity with each pair.

The hiss of his gasping breaths through his teeth is music to my ears.

"Did you like the picture of the man being flogged?"

"Yes, Goddess."

"Would you like to feel the bite of a flogger on your skin?"

"Yes, Goddess."

I raise the crop and deliver a blow across his abs. "I think you are forgetting to say please."

"Please!" He cries out. "Yes PLEASE, Goddess."

"Lovely." I smile and pick up the pad, taking the pen from between his teeth. Voicing the words as I write them down. "Item two. Flogger…and other nice things to make skin pink." I jab the full stop with a flourish and don't give him any attention, simply returning the pen to his mouth and the pad to his leg.

"We already know you like the scarves don't we boy?" I ask, circling him and tapping my way up his lower arm, delivering a smack to his shoulder.

"Yes, Goddess," he hisses.

Repeating the same on the other arm, I smile at the way he tenses before the smack.

Leaning close to his ear, I continue. "You love to have your sight taken away don't you boy? You love not knowing what's coming."

"Yes, Goddess."

"And you like to be tied up don't you?"

"Yes, Goddess."

"You just love to have the control taken away from you don't you?"

"Yes, Goddess."

I grasp his hair, yanking his head back. "You love it boy," I growl in his ear. "Tell me."

"I love it."

I release him completely and take the pen from his teeth,

inspecting it. Then I say the words I write down for his benefit. "Blindfold…cuffs…maybe a nice ball gag? I saw the way you got off on having my knickers stuffed in your mouth." I peer over the pad and smile.

"Yes, please," he moans.

"And you're leaving teeth marks in my pen." I laugh. "Anything else?"

"Rope," he replies cautiously. "I'd like to try rope."

I look up at him, hope in his eyes.

"You're a bad boy aren't you?"

He scoffs and looks at me, shaking his head regretfully. "I wish I was, Goddess."

I analyse him, of course he turned that around on himself, this is his whole problem. But I won't baby him. He has to see for himself. I throw the pad and pen down and take my crop, raining it down on his chest, stomach, and finally his thighs. The blows harder than before, the sounds from him pulling more and more strength out of me. I can do this. I can show him. Working my way up his thigh, his cock bouncing with each strike, I pause when there is no more leg left to smack.

He knows that there's nowhere left for me to go and watches the crop intently, gasping for breath.

I run it gently along the underside of his cock.

"Bad boys are a dime a dozen." I take another long sweep up his length and watch it bob trying to chase the sensation. "It takes a real man to be a good boy." Lifting the crop, I hold it above his cock and wait. I wait for him to look up at me. I wait for him to believe. I'll wait as long as it takes.

Finally, the moment comes.

His eyes meet mine and I smile. "Are you a good boy,

Will?"

"Yes, Goddess," he answers knowing what it will bring and I land my crop on the head.

He roars, but it feels more like triumph than pain.

I take a deep breath. I got off track, but it took us to a good place.

I drop the crop and move in close, his eyes focusing back on me as the pain clears from his mind. As he blinks up at me, I peel my top off and cast it aside. Turning my back on him, I reach behind and find the zip of my pencil skirt and slowly lower it. His breath hitches when I lower it all the way down to the floor, revealing that I was wearing nothing underneath. I let his cock brush my bare arse as I come back up and adore the whimper it draws from him.

Turning back to him, naked but for my bra, I place my finger under his chin. "Now that we've established you're a good boy," I tell him, lifting one leg to straddle him and then the other. "I think I said I would ride you next."

"Yes Goddess, you did."

Lowering myself, my lips skim over his. "I'm on the pill," I tell him. "I want to take my ride bareback, is there any reason not to?"

He shakes his head. "None," he replies. Then he reaches his lips up to mine and using the first contact I've allowed him, absolutely melts me with his burning kiss.

I can't wait any more. "Good," I reply and sink down on to him, seating myself fully in one stroke.

He cries out.

I throw my head back. "Oh god."

Straining to take advantage of my exposed neck in his

reach. He nips at my throat and thrusts his hips up, realising it's mostly in vain.

Gripping the back of the chair over his shoulders I roll my hips to my own pace and groan. "You can't take the control boy. It's mine." I fuck him possessively. "I own you."

"Fuck," he growls, surrendering. His head rolling back.

I grab his throat, applying only enough pressure that he can feel the thrill of being controlled. "Perhaps, when you can show me you deserve to wear it," I gasp. "One day you can have a collar to remind you whose good boy you are." He lifts his head fixing me with his glazed eyes and I catch the look of surprise through his haze.

"It will remind you that you belong to me." I thrust, pushing my point home. "I own you, I control your pleasure, I say if you come or…" I let him see the sadistic amusement in my slow smile, before I grind the word, "don't"

His head falls back again with a resigned groan.

I slap his face, pulling his head back up. "Don't you give up on me. Beg for it."

"Please, Goddess," he whimpers.

"Please what? Do you need to come?"

"Yes, Goddess, please, I need to come."

"You don't get to come until I come. Do you hear me?" I command, my voice overcome with lust as I take my pleasure.

"What was that noise?" Will hisses, sounding completely out of the zone.

"Focus boy. If you want your release you'll—"

"Mags, I'm serious, what was that noise?"

It takes me a moment to realise he has come completely out of the scene, or whatever it is you would call this thing we are doing. I stop moving in his lap and listen. “I don’t hear anything.”

“I heard the front door. Do you think Jazz came home?”

“No, she promised she wouldn’t.”

“There! Shhh.”

I strain to hear. “What?” I whisper.

“A man’s voice.”

“I think you’re hearing things.” I start to rock against him again, dismissing his paranoia, when I hear it too.

“See?” he hisses. “Is your dad home early”

“No definitely not, he’s in New York…or is it Dubai now? What day is it?” I frown.

“Untie me.”

“No, wait here.”

I climb off him and head for the door, grabbing my silk robe off the hook and slipping it on.

“Mags.” He whispers loudly.

Ignoring him, I open my bedroom door.

“Dad!” Seeing him crossing the landing talking on his phone, startles me. He stops and tells whoever he’s talking to that he has to go. “What are you doing home?” I pull my door shut and step towards him to stop him discovering Will. How much he heard I don’t know.

“Dubai got cancelled, Hello sweetpea.” He draws me in for a hug and kisses the top of my head.

I feel dirty knowing what I was just doing. “Hi.”

“Have a cuppa with me before I hit the hay?”

Shit.

“Actually Dad, I was just…” I point back towards the bedroom.

"Oh," he holds up his hands. "Say no more. If you were working, don't let me disturb you. I'm beat, I'll just shower and crash out."

"Ok,' I smile, nervously.

"Let's have breakfast though. That was Anne, she managed to book in a meeting in Frankfurt, so I'm heading out again tomorrow."

"Sure," I reply, feeling sorry for my dad's long-suffering assistant having to rearrange travel night and day. I smile, waiting for him to walk away before I open my door again.

"Goodnight." He waves over his shoulder as he disappears down the long corridor to his master suite.

"Goodnight," I call back.

When I'm sure he has gone, I slip back inside my room and turn the lock just to be safe.

"Fucking hell. Untie me," Will demands. "Did he hear us?"

"I don't think so." I go over to him. "I'm sorry. He wasn't meant to be home."

"It's not your fault, just untie me." He pulls at his bindings. "I shouldn't have thought I could do this without getting humiliated."

"You didn't get humiliated, he didn't see."

"Being stuck tied to the furniture with your dad outside the door is a pretty humiliating experience, Mags."

"Well it was just a one off. In the future I'll lock the door."

"In the future, maybe we should just not do this nonsense."

"What?"

"Well, I'm not really cut out for all this am I?"

"Baby, you're perfect at this. You just have to trust me." I quickly straddle him again. Taking him in hand between us.

"Mags please, we should just leave it for tonight. Untie me."

"Did I say you could speak?"

"No, but—"

I clamp my hand over his mouth. "Ssshh."

He nods, his dick hardening in my hand as he follows my command and shuts up.

"That's better." I stroke. "Now, we are going to finish this and you are going to keep it silent, unless you need to use your safe word. Are we clear?"

Will nods.

I lift up and position his head at my entrance.

"Do you want to use your safe word?"

He shakes his head, then blows out a long breath as I slide down onto him.

Within no time, I have us right back to where we were, only this time there are no cries of pleasure, only our staccato breaths.

I bring his face to mine and press our foreheads together. It helps connect with him. Looking him in the eyes, I move, harder faster. I can feel him tensing and I'm getting closer. I don't know if I can do it in silence, not with his cock hitting the spot like this.

I hold his face, gazing into his eyes. I want to scream, but instead, I kiss him deeply, silencing my inner cry.

When I can't hold on any longer, I manage to whisper, "Now." And resume our kiss as I come hard around him. His tongue strokes mine while he lets go, coming deep inside me.

FRIDAY 4TH SEPTEMBER

A picture message comes in and I stare at it for a moment not quite knowing what I'm supposed to be looking at. 'Thank you for your order' it says. I frown. Then I scroll down and read the order it's thanking me for.

Holy shit! She ordered all the stuff on the list.

My cock twitches at the memory of the list.

'Oh my god. You are amazing.'

'Well we can't use scarves forever can we?'

'I don't know, they've been pretty great so far.'

'Oh, so shall I cancel this order?'

'No way!'

'I thought not.'

'When will it come?'

'LOL. Monday, so we'll have to make do until then.'

Now I'll feel like a kid waiting for Christmas…only three more sleeps. Except she did say she had some kind of box at her apartment. Maybe…

'Unless…this box…does it have anything I would like in it?'

'Box?'

'Oh my box of tricks at home. Yeah I think you would like a few things in there.'

That's something we're going to have to talk about. She's still calling it home. I want to know if or when they will start calling it home here. I mean, Jazz won't really want to be anywhere else now right? Unless Spencer fucks it up. Great, why do I feel like my happiness rides on Spencer not being Spencer, again?

'Maybe we should go and get it tomorrow.'

'That's actually a really good idea. We could have some time alone. No interruptions this time.'

'I like the sound of that.'

'Clear your schedule, boy, you're going to be tied up all day.'

God I love her.

'I have good news, and bad news.'

'Go on…'

'I told Jazz that we were going back home to get some stuff tomorrow and she thought it was a great idea. She wants to come.'

'What? No!'

'I can't stop them, it's a free country.'

'Them?'

'Yeah, that's the good news. Spencer is coming, so they will take their own car and more or less leave us alone.'

'I think we need to work on your definition of good news. Spencer is never good news. Especially when I'm on a promise of some incredibly hot sounding alone time and now he wants to tag along.'

'No, it is good. He's coming to help her, she'll be faster, so we can get rid of them. We can tell them we have lunch plans or something and then they will go and leave us to our alone time.'

'It will be fine trust me.'

She still has so much to learn, but I want her to know I trust her, so instead of arguing with the inevitable, I just say ok.

SATURDAY 5TH SEPTEMBER

"I swear, I'm going to kill him."

"Shhhh, no you won't," Mags soothes. "Just look on the bright side."

"Bright side? What fucking bright side?" I demand, setting down the suitcase I just brought up from the car.

Mags approaches me seductively. "Well, there's the fact that you've been horny all day."

"How is that a bright side?"

"Because now it's going to be all the better when I get your clothes off."

"That's the problem though," I hiss, aware that Spencer and Jazz are just across the hall. "They are *still* hanging around! They've followed us all day. You plan lunch to get rid of them and they invite themselves along."

"Your face though," Mags covers her mouth to mask her smile.

"It wasn't funny."

"I'm sorry." Mags straightens her face. "I'll make it up to you."

I shake my head. "It's fine. Maybe the universe is trying to tell me something."

"Like what? That you're a big moany baby?" Spencer

quips barging in.

"Fuck off, Spencer."

"Oh sure, right after I put down all this shit I've carried up from the car for you. You're welcome by the way." He puts down the pile of boxes he is carrying.

I snarl at him, but he ignores me and turns to Mags, tipping his imaginary hat.

"Will that be all Ma'am?"

Mags giggles. "That will be all," she plays along. "You are dismissed."

"Thank you, Ma'am. My lady friend and I will be in the jacuzzi for the next couple of hours. Do not disturb." He backs out of the room bowing like an arse. Mags laughs.

"Just make sure you drain it after." She pulls a face at the thought of using their water after they've…eww, whatever.

We hear Jazz yelp as Spencer chases her out of her room and down the stairs. And once again, it's envy I feel. He wants to fuck Jazz in the jacuzzi, so he just puts it out there. By the way, I'm going to have my dick out in the jacuzzi and I'm going to be playing hide the sausage with Jazz for a while. I'd stay away if I were you.

Boom.

Just like that.

Me, I bite my tongue all day and let them tag along, rather than admit I was even thinking about getting it on. There is something very wrong with this picture.

"That moment when your cocky cousin carries my box of toys upstairs for me and has no clue what he is carrying." Mags laughs.

"Huh?"

"Never mind." She takes a few things off the lid of the blue box and then looks up at me, smiling. She starts to stalk towards me. "So, I'm going to ask again. What is your safe word going to be?" she asks stopping in front of me.

I roll my eyes and earn myself a light slap to the cheek, which sends tiny sparks of pleasure all through me.

"Stay," she purrs, pressing a single finger into my chest and I do as I'm told, waiting by the door.

Mags lifts the lid of the toy box, turning it so that the raised lid obscures my view of its contents. She makes a big show of selecting something and closes it, approaching me with her hand behind her back. She stops before me and raises a brow expectantly.

"I don't need one," I repeat for the tenth time.

She produces a bundle of rope from behind her back and my dick twitches.

"No safe word, no play," she says firmly. "It would be a shame to think we went and got my box of tricks for nothing."

I draw in a shaky breath. "What else have you got in there?"

"I wouldn't want to torture you with the knowledge of my toys, if you weren't going to get to see them."

"Fine, we'll have a safe word." I huff.

"Good boy," she smiles. "What's it going to be?"

I screw up my nose. "Fuck I don't know, I couldn't even pick a Twitter handle. You pick it."

"No, it needs to be something you pick. It won't be me saying it."

"I won't be saying it either."

Mags laughs. "Fine, pick a word and we can play a game."

“A game?” I perk up.

“Safe word.”

“Ugh, I don’t know.”

“Just pick a word you would never, under any circumstances say during sex.”

“Spencer,” I blurt. I want to take it back as soon as I’ve said it, but she is already laughing. “No let me think of something else.”

“Oh no, Spencer is perfect.”

Fuck. “I’ll never say it anyway.” I tell her defiantly.

“Wanna bet?”

“I won’t. It’s a fact. You can do whatever you want to me.”

“Oh there are other ways I can get you screaming his name. It’s not all about what you do and don’t want me to do to you.”

I frown, I have no clue what she means, but I’m resolute. That word will never pass my lips while we’re…

“Take your clothes off,” she demands.

I oblige, aware that she hasn’t shut the door, but Spencer and Jazz are long gone, I guess we have some time.

Mags circles me, eyeing me up and down. I feel conscious when she passes behind me, but her possessive look when she comes back into view, makes me feel hers. To feel owned from just her look alone is more than even I fantasised about.

She unravels the rope and my chest tightens. I’ve been tied up before, it’s no biggie. But that was with scarves. This is rope. This is really happening. I watch her do her thing with the rope and try to ignore her familiarity with it.

Once she has organised the rope how she needs it, she steps towards me and I freeze. Who did she learn this with? It shouldn’t matter. It doesn’t matter. It means she’s the surprising, stunning, perfection she is today and I shouldn't question how. Rational thinking has gone south, with most of my blood flow.

"When did you learn to do this?" I try for nonchalant, but sound more like a pathetic child.

And when? When? Like it matters. That was an interesting way to go Will. I guess it beats, tell me who you have done this with, I want names and locations and marks out of ten. My breathing is heavy by the time I get a hold of myself.

"I took a course," she says. "I needed to for book research. I made Jazz come with me as my subject, she bitched the whole time about me being too brutal and whined about pinching. So you'll have to let me know if I'm hurting you."

"You won't." I manage not to show my relief, the edge is taken off by the idea of her being brutal. Just the thought…

"Let's see shall we, Jazz seemed to think I took joy from her discomfort."

"Did you?"

She looks up at me through her dark lashes and one corner of her mouth curls into a sly smile. "A little."

I skim my hand over my straining length, making a bad job of silencing my groan.

"I think you'll enjoy it more than she did."

"Well I doubt she was ready to come just from the sight of you with rope in your hands, so I think we are off to a good start."

She gathers my wrists and holds them together, wrapping the rope around. I'm no expert, but I've watched a YouTube how-to or two. She does a nice job of cuffing me. She handles the rope with confidence and I'm trembling by the time she takes the two ends of the rope, side by side and ties a knot in them. I stare down at my bound wrists with a few inches of rope hanging from them and a heavy knot at the end and wonder what she is going to do. When I look up she is waiting, for what, I'm not sure. Maybe for me to take it all in?

"Ready?"

I nod slowly.

She takes the knot and lifts it above my head, placing her hand on the centre of my chest to guide me back two steps to the door. Draping the rope over the top of the door, she wedges it shut, trapping the thick knot on the other side. I test the restraints and feel the pleasure of the security deep inside.

Mags smiles and walks back to her box, picking out a couple of things and returning to me. Slowly, she gets to her knees, my dick leaps in anticipation, but she chuckles and lowers herself to my feet. Pushing them together, she binds my ankles. I try to adjust myself to keep balance, but I realise it isn't necessary, I'm steadied by the rope in the door. I can't move, I'm safe and I'm already floating.

And then her tongue flicks over my head.

My eyes snap open. I hadn't realised they were closed.

She takes me deep into the back of her throat in one swift, shocking moment as soon as my eyes meet hers and I choke back my cry. My head hits the door and my eyes roll closed, but she doesn't indulge me long and pulls back.

"Watch," she says.

I look back down at her and her fingers close around me, slipping easily down my shaft.

"Are you going to edge me again?" My voice is gravelly, it's a wonder I could get a word out as her tongue curls around the head and her fingers continue to glide up and down. It's shocking I had the nerve to even ask.

She shakes her head and smiles. "Not today," she says taking another lick. "We're going to test out your safe word."

"I told you, there's nothing you can do I'll want you to stop." She is killing me already and I sound half drunk as I speak.

"Really nothing?" she teases.

"Well, other than gross stuff, but I don't think I need to be concerned with that, do I?"

She shakes her head. I'm not stupid. I know her fairly well. There's very little I don't think I could predict her preference on and that's all stuff I'd be willing to explore anyway.

"I mean unless you're planning on dumping me, I'm not ok with that."

She chuckles and her hot breath on my skin makes my entire body twitch. "So you're up for some pain?" She rolls my balls with a tug, making me jerk involuntarily. It wasn't a pain so much as a slight sick feeling in my stomach, but I can take that, and more.

"Yep," I reply regaining my voice, but forgetting myself.

Her hand slaps down on my dick and I choke on the pain.

She waits.

As soon as I have my breath I blurt, "Yes Goddess."

"Hmmm," she mumbles disapprovingly. "Well as good as that is to know. The safe word is not a bad thing. You can use it any time and it doesn't mean we have to stop if you don't want to." She takes my dick in her hand again. "It just means that thing is too much. You're treating it as failure."

"Ok, I get it." I groan when her hand falls away and I'm

left with nothing. "Don't stop,"

"I've already seen you respond very well to short term denial." The lightest of touches on the very tip and I'm straining for more. "What's your long game like, boy?"

"What do you mean?"

She raises her hand and I correct myself. "Goddess!"

"What if I said that you can't come today?"

"If it's what you want, Goddess. I want to please you." I try not to let my disappointment show.

"What if I forbid you to come today and if you do, you don't get to come for a week?"

I swallow. I could do a week. It's obviously not what I want, but I could. If I slipped up that is, which I don't plan to. If she says don't come, I won't.

"Hmm no, that's too easy. You could survive a week."

"I've been years without you, survival is my specialty, Goddess."

A warm smile breaks through her game face and I return it. I love her surprise when I'm open about how I feel. It seems like she is never expecting it.

Quickly she rearranges her features back into her dominant expression. "Of course you could survive a week. You need more motivation than that. Let's make it a month. If you come without permission today, you don't get to come for a month."

"Like I said, I've gone longer."

She rakes her nails down my chest and I hiss. "Yes but you didn't have me making it hard for you then." She leans in and the skin on my neck prickles in anticipation. "So hard," she purrs as her fingers meet my begging cock.

I whimper. She's right, I didn't, and a month of this would

be hell. A delicious hell on earth with Mags as the devil herself. I could think of worse ways to spend eternity, but I'd rather not chance it. "It won't be a problem, Goddess." I manage, trying to sound confident. "I'm not going to come until you say I can."

She strokes her hand down the side of my face. "Good boy," she whispers.

My eyes roll as I groan. She is going to make this impossible.

Lowering herself to her knees again she takes me slowly in hand, licking the head as she works the shaft. I swallow back my groan, it's too early to show that I might not have the willpower I dream of. In my head I'm certain. I can do this. But with her mouth and hand performing a slow torture, I'm not sure my body will get the memo.

I try to stop thinking and just sink into the rope. It doesn't help. The feeling of freedom that comes with being properly restrained is one I want to explore more, but I have a feeling if I think about how great it feels too much it will be my downfall.

God I wish my brain would just shut down.

Her free hand moves back to my balls and I brace myself for pain, but she is gentle in her caress.

"I wonder how much of this you could take?"

I draw in a long breath, not trusting my voice to answer as she twists her hand over my cock and strokes harder.

"Something tells me you could fight this for a long time," she says pushing her hand right to the base so that my aching head is left exposed to the warm breath coming from her parted lips, just an inch away. "I think I would have to up the ante to get you begging me to stop." I watch it slip between her soft lips. She continues to stroke her hand up and down and I feel my resolve take a big hit when she starts to suck.

I moan, not stopping to think it might encourage her. I realise my mistake too late. Her smile is clear, even wrapped around my cock. I calm my breathing, centring myself. I need to get on top of this or I'll lose. She must feel the way my body changes as my grip on my control tightens, because she pulls her lips away and looks up, impressed. That moment of unspoken praise is everything. I'm flying. This is everything I imagined submitting could be and I know we have only scratched the surface.

"I think I'll have to get creative to push you to your limit, won't I?"

I half shrug, not easy with my arms over my head, but words are useless, they will only give her ideas.

Her eyes flash with glee. She takes my shrug as defiance and I regret it immediately. Her hand squeezing my cock until I gasp. "I need to take you somewhere you've never been before, if I want to break you."

I stare, afraid to fuel the fire.

"Won't I?" she demands.

"Yes, Goddess," I whisper. It's acquiescence, it's surrender, it's a plea.

Her silence draws me out of the place I lost myself to. A place where my hope has started to blossom far beyond the idea of this life I'd always dreamed of, to things I can now see are worth letting my imagination explore. Her face, when I focus, has that same look. She is imagining what we could discover together.

Her fingers, still caressing my sac, curl under. My ankles are bound together, but I still involuntarily clench when one slides into the tight space between my thighs.

"Shhh," she soothes, stroking the sensitive skin there. God that's incredible. When I relax into the sensation of her playing there and stroking my cock simultaneously, she speaks.

Her brows raise. "Ever been licked from here…" her finger reaches as far as I think it can, almost reaching, but not quite. She drags it back through my legs and up onto my balls. "…To here?"

My head shake is barely perceptible.

"Ever thought about it?"

"I—" my voice all but fails me and I clear my throat.

She puts two fingers in her mouth, slicking them. Then she slides them between my thighs again, curling them slightly, giving me a taste of how a tongue would feel. I whimper. I thought she reached as far as she could go but I was wrong, she strokes my cock harder and reaches her fingers back further, circling my hole. Her tongue circles the head of my dick at the same moment and I swear my heart nearly stops.

"Ever been touched here?"

I shake my head and swallow.

"Ever want to be?"

I nod vigorously. Maybe too enthusiastically, but no one has ever asked me before and her fingers are already there and they feel like heaven, so I can't fake denial.

"Ever think about having something in here?" She presses her finger against the tight ring, but my position won't allow her to enter. I'm half relieved.

"Yes," I sigh.

"Oh really?" She asks, her tone more surprise than flirtation.

I nod, conscious of how much of myself I'm exposing, but caught up in the pressure of her fingers.

"God you're perfect." She grins and I hold my breath waiting for her next move. She circles once more, stroking my cock too. "We will have to explore that." She slides her finger away, tracing her path back out. "Not today though. We'll start with my tongue first, work up to it."

My eyes close and a groan creeps out.

The feel of her pressed against me snatches me from my thoughts, I open my eyes and she is gazing into them, smiling.

"You're full of surprises."

I offer a shy smile, feeling fully exposed.

Mags turns her back to me and skims her arse over my hard cock, laying her head back on me and torturing me with a light touch. I strain against my bonds, trying to rub against her, getting any friction I can, my cock grinds between her cheeks through the fabric of her maddening little skirt. I finally get something to rub against when she moans and pushes back, but before it can come to anything, she moves away.

"Easy tiger, remember you don't get to come today. Unless you want a month of torture."

A low growl comes from me, so unlike me that she turns around to look. I've never felt this need before. Need for what, I don't know? I need to get off, but I can't. I need her to keep me in this state even though I might die. I just need it not to end. Ever.

Mags sees the need in me and goes after it like it's her prey.

She reaches for a bottle of lube and I watch as she drizzles it onto my straining length. “You liked that did you?”

My dick jumps and her hand smoothes the cool lube over the whole length of me. “Yes,” I hiss, trying to hold it together.

She turns her back to me again, flipping up her skirt, revealing to me for the first time that she has had nothing on under it this whole time. I want to tell her off for it. What if a gust of wind had lifted it? It’s a tiny floaty thing. Spencer was around. I don’t even want to think of him catching a glimpse. He would be insufferable. But damn, she is so beautiful.

She runs her soft arse over me, letting me grind my lubed cock between her cheeks. For a moment she lets me have my fill, thrusting and sliding over her, but then she presses back, taking control of the motion, pushing my back to the door.

“Ever taken a girl’s arse before?”

I shake my head. I have no words.

Mags rocks back against me. “Ever wanted to?”

My moan answers for me. If she carries on with talk like that, I’m finished. She can’t tease me like this. I need something. “Please…”

“You want to try?”

Oh no, that’s not what I meant. I would never presume…I and it’s a big deal…not everybody…I just meant…

Of course, I can’t get a word of this out as she reaches behind her and lines my cock up with…oh my God, she’s serious. I pull against the rope. I can’t move, not even my feet, I can’t do a thing. I’ll never last if she does that.

“Shouldn’t we talk about this?” I stutter.

“Talk about what? You’ve thought about what it feels like to sink into a girl’s tight arsehole before haven’t you? Wanted to try? And now you can, with me.”

She emphasises the 'with me', like it's supposed to help. It's the very fact that it's with her right now that doesn't help me at all. This is Mags. The girl I have longed for, lusted after and above all else, cherished for as long as I can remember. And this…this seems so…disrespectful. So dirty. I'd want to make sure she's ok with it. Hold her, talk to her.

"Are you saying you don't want to?" she asks innocently, rubbing my head up and down her seam so I can't think.

"No, I—" I try to pull away but it's futile. I'm backed right up to the door and I couldn't move if I tried.

"Good," she says triumphantly, lining me up so there is nowhere else to go.

"No, no, no!" I don't know where it came from, it just burst out. I'm so close to losing it on first contact like a horny teenager. She knows I can't survive this surely?

"You have the safe word for a reason, Will. Do you need me to stop?"

"I need—" I choke on the words. I don't know what, I just know I need.

"Do you want to know what it feels like?"

I nod. There's no denying it.

"Think you can handle it?"

God, no, I don't think I can. I don't respond. I've never wanted something more and yet, less, in my life. I get the sense that I should get used to this feeling.

She leans back slightly and tests the resistance, but not enough for me to push in. I'm frozen. Every cell in my body wants me to push forward, but I'm not allowed to come and this is only going to end badly for me.

"You see, the safe word isn't only for times when you

object to what I'm doing, it's sometimes about how much of it you can take."

I tense. She is going to force my hand.

"I can take as much as you give me," I slur, doubting my own words.

"Is that so? You can take this can you?" she gasps, pressing back so that my dick slips in past the tight entrance. "And still follow a simple instruction?"

I almost black out from the pleasure.

She is murderously tight. Worse than I imagined. It's as if all of me is inside her, I feel it in every raw nerve ending, right down to my toes. I'm never going to survive. I should have been careful with my wishes, but I never expected this. I didn't wish things that happen to normal people.

Yet here I am with my dick in her arse, tied to her door, no control. I'm going to lose it.

She pulls slightly away and the battle within me not to surge forward, chasing her, is intense, but thankfully short lived. She presses back again, making me realise I might have been better off with her pulling away. The war that wages while she rolls her hips, ebbing and flowing, while my dick glides inside her— No. I can't think it. I'm going to blow the next month if I can't hold it together.

"Mags, slow down." I gasp.

She doesn't. I need to get away. I yank at the rope, but it's futile.

"How does that feel?" she moans.

Hearing her pleasure triples mine.

"Mags I can't…please…"

"You can't what?" she purrs, rolling her hips in a way that

almost finishes me. “You can’t believe how good it feels?”

I can only whimper in reply.

“It feels so goooood.”

For a second, I almost let go. But then I think about how long a month will feel. That’s it, I can’t. I have to stop her. “Stop, Mags, please.”

“You want me to stop?” She almost sounds disappointed, but I can hear the tease in her voice and I know she is toying with me and loving it.

“Yes…please.” I can feel myself coming undone.

“I’ll stop any time you like.” She slams home. “All you have to do, is say the word.”

Fuck.

I can’t.

No.

She’s relentless.

Everything inside me tightens and I can’t hold it back any longer.

“Spencer,” I whisper.

Mags pauses.

“Spencer,” I repeat, trying to use the idea of saying his name to put the brakes on my impending release.

She starts to withdraw immediately but there’s no way to pull out of her without stimulating me more. I’m going to come if she doesn’t get off quickly.

“Spencer,” is all I can get out to show the urgency. “Spencer, Spencer…PLEASE! SPENCER!”

Mags pulls away that last inch and turns to face me. I’m left trembling, on the brink of orgasm and sag with relief.

“Will?”

My eyes snap up to Mags in horror.

“Will? Are you ok in there?” Spencer shouts, concerned, from the other side of the door. He tries the handle and I feel his attempt to push the door open.

“No, no, no!” I shout, trying to stop him. But he pushes the door harder.

“The fucking door is stuck,” he calls out. “Hold on.”

“Spencer, no!” I yank at the ropes for my life.

My objections are not heard and I hear a loud bang as I’m thrown from the door and land with a thud face down on the floor.

“What the fuck is going on in here?” He demands.

I want the ground to swallow me up. This can’t be happening.

I watch in horror as Will falls to the floor, not even able to defend himself because of how I've tied him. Lucky for me, my skirt fell back into place, but Will is naked and lying face down on my carpet.

Spencer scans the scene, still pumped from busting in to help us in what he assumed was some kind of emergency. He takes a good look at Will and then he turns away. Like completely away. Faces the wall and everything. I press my lips together. Now is not the time to giggle.

Jazz appears behind Spencer and covers her mouth with both hands. I can tell from her eyes it's to spare Will her laughter.

"I can explain," says Will, sounding pained.

Spencer shakes his head at the wall. "No mate, you can't. And please don't ever try."

Jazz and I both erupt. We should know better than to make eye contact in a situation like this.

"I thought you were in the jacuzzi?" I chuckle.

"We came in to get some wine," he replies indignantly. Clearly, this had thrown a bucket of cold water on any more fun he was hoping to have.

"Oh."

"Well, if you don't need me, and I'm hoping to *fuck* you don't, I'll be going." Spencer turns to Jazz, "Come on, let's go back to mine. It's less weird there."

Jazz tries really hard to hold it together and flashes me the 'good luck' eyes as she closes the door behind them.

"When you've finished laughing, do you think you could untie me?" Will asks, his face still pressed to the floor.

I kneel beside him, composing myself as best I can and encourage him to turn over.

"Are you alright?"

"Oh yeah, I'm brilliant," he says with a degree of humour. I manage to stop a laugh from bursting out of my chest, but I can't hide my struggle. He closes his eyes and nods, resigned. "That's it, have a good old laugh. You know, people like me shouldn't explore their fantasies. I've resisted it my whole life and then when I actually think, yeah, this could be cool, and let go…I end up flat on my face with my arse on display along with all my dirty laundry."

I cover my lips with my fist.

"I mean I didn't just dream that, did I?" He opens his eyes and looks at me. "Spencer, just came in here and saw me like this." He holds up his bound hands.

I nod. I probably don't need to tell him it was Jazz too. "It was just unlucky that's all. We weren't to know they'd come back in."

"And your dad the other night? Just bad luck too, or is the universe sending me a message loud and clear?"

"Here, let me untie you." I pick at the large knot I'd tied in the end of the rope. Unfortunately, it has been pulled so tight in Will's struggle that I can't gain any slack in it. "Shit." I mutter under my breath. I try a different tactic of feeding the rope through so I can at least loosen the cuff and slip his hands out. But the knot is too big to pass through the loop I'd made.

Such a rookie mistake.

"Please tell me you can undo it." He's hopeful, but I can see the resignation.

"I'm trying." I keep picking at the knot. "I'm such an idiot. I'm so sorry. I wasn't thinking it would get pulled this much. The guy told us all this stuff about quick release and I haven't listened to any of it."

"I was struggling for my life." Will finally laughs. "I guess my life is over now, so it makes no difference if I have to stay like this. I can't ever look him in the eye again, so you may as well keep me tied up here."

I giggle and lean forward to place a soft kiss on his lips.

"But don't expect me to be your sex slave." He glances down at his dick, which is currently as deflated as his ego. "No chance I'm ever getting that up again."

I grin. "If you can get it going again, I'll let you fuck me."

He smiles, then sighs. "Thanks, but I don't think my pride can take anymore submission today."

Oh my god.

I. Feel. Terrible.

Then I get an idea. "Stay here." I jump up and head to the door.

"Where are you going?" He calls after me, but I ignore it and run down the stairs. I'll be back that much faster if I don't stop to reply.

Jazz and Spencer seem to have made a quick exit, so I head straight to the kitchen. I know we used to have these massive scissors around here. They were fabric sheers. Really sharp and heavy. I'm sure Dad must have kept them. I find them in the second drawer I rummage in and test them out. They should do the trick. I start back towards the stairs, then stop. Just in case I can't cut through it with these, I grab one of the Japanese chefs knives from the block.

When I walk back in to my room, Will is sitting up, pulling the rope off his ankles with his restricted hands. It seems that wasn't as hard to untie. He looks up and his eyes go wide when they fall on the weapons I have brought back.

"Whoa, whoa, lets not get crazy. I can't defend myself."

I kneel beside him and set the knife on the floor. I hold up the sheers, "I brought them to try and cut the rope off, it will be quicker than trying to unpick it."

"And what's the knife for."

"In case I'm not strong enough with the scissors."

"If you can't do it with the scissors how will you do it with the knife?"

I nod to the knife as I slide the blade of the scissors under the ropes on his wrists. "These are just for fabric. That thing is some special Japanese steel. It can cut through bone."

He looks at me with fear in his eyes. "Then please be strong enough with the scissors!"

I smile and concentrate, snipping through the rope easier than I expected.

"Oh thank fuck," he says, rubbing his wrists.

"I'm so sorry, that whole thing was my stupid fault. I didn't think."

"No, it's not your fault. I should know better. This is just a fantasy, it should stay that way."

"The hell it should." I frown. He's serious and it shocks me.

"No, come on Mags, I should just get over it."

"And what about me? Have I got to get over it too?"

He shrugs.

"I know what you need."

"What's that?"

"You need to take charge."

He laughs, but there is no mirth. "I'm not particularly good at that."

"No, maybe not." I get to my feet and hold out my hand. "But you are particularly good at taking an order, right?"

"I guess." He looks up at me and takes my hand.

I wait for him to stand and look me in the eye before I issue it. "Fuck me."

He looks at me, unconvinced.

"I mean it. Fuck me."

"I don't know Mags, I—"

I cut him off before he can make excuses. "Did it feel good with your cock in my arse?"

He blushes, it's so adorable.

"It felt good, right?"

"Amazing."

"Don't you want to finish what we started?"

"Yes but—"

I hold up my hand. "I'm changing the rules. You will get to come today…on the condition that you take charge, pin me down and fuck me." I let that sink in for a few seconds. He looks like he is considering it. I just need to give him the final nudge. "And if you don't, you don't get to come for a month."

Something snaps in him. He reaches for my top and yanks it over my head. My head rolls back when he bites at my neck and slips a hand under my skirt.

He pulls back to look at me when his fingers slip inside me and he has a glint in his eye. “You are really bad. Where did your knickers go?”

“Who said I put any on this morning?”

He gives a disapproving frown. “With this skirt, you always put some on, okay?”

I raise my eyebrows.

“In fact, if you are going to be around Spencer, no matter what you’re wearing, you need underwear at all times.”

I chuckle. “I didn’t know we were going to be around Spencer that long and besides, he only has eyes for Jazz. He isn’t perving on me.”

“Spencer is totally in love with Jazz, no matter what he says. But he is also a massive dickhead and will dine out on it for months if there is a gust of wind and you flash him a bit of arse…or worse.”

I wrap my arms around him, grabbing his naked behind and pulling him against me. He drops his forehead to my shoulder and groans. “I don’t think you are in a position to lay down the law about flashing arse at Spencer, do you?”

A growl rumbles in his chest and he swiftly picks me up, taking a few steps to the bed, dumping me down and bending me over the mattress.

“Like this?”

“Yes.” It’s bloody hot. His hand stays between my shoulder blades, holding me there and I feel my skirt lift and my bare arse exposed. He growls again, running his hand around the curve of my bottom.

"Why didn't you wear underwear?"

Giving a little wiggle, I contemplate avoiding the question, but I think he will like the answer too much. "I was thinking maybe I might jump you somewhere risky. I wanted to be ready."

His hand strokes and grabs at my flesh, I can feel his hunger.

"Damn it, I was going to spank you and tell you off, but how can I argue with that defence?"

"You can't." I grin into the mattress. "But feel free to spank me anyway."

"Where?"

"Wherever you like."

"Nooo. Where were you going to jump me?"

"Oh! I don't know, just if there was an opportunity. The toilets, the bushes, hell, maybe I would have just sat on your lap at lunch and let you slide in."

He makes a sound in his throat, I know the face that goes with that sound. It says 'bloody hell, you will be the death of me' and I love making him do it. "Why didn't you?"

"Jazz and Spencer ruined it. Maybe I should have just done it anyway."

"Yeah, I think things are bad enough between me and Spencer, he certainly doesn't need to see me come."

"You're assuming I was going to let you come." I laugh.

His hand lands with a sharp smack and I soak up the pleasure. I actually enjoy submitting, but I top from the bottom so badly. I can't help it. With Will though, I don't think it will ever be a problem.

"Fucking hell, you're killing me here." He soothes the spot he just smacked, stroking further down. "Next time." His fingers find my pussy and tease softly over the skin. "Find a way." His demand sounds more like a plea.

I like it.

"Will."

"Yes?"

"Fuck me."

He slides a finger inside me.

"Not there."

I hear his breath catch. He slowly slides his finger out and sinks to his knees, pausing. I wait.

"Are you sure about this?" he asks nervously.

A giggle escapes, and I feel like maybe I sound nervous to. He needs me to be strong for him right now so I have to keep that in check. "I'm totally sure. It's you who doesn't sound certain."

"No…I—" he clears his throat. I love it when he has to get himself together to speak, it makes me feel powerful. "I am, I want to, it's just…" He curses under his breath.

"You really don't have to." I start to get up. "I shouldn't have—"

"No." He pushes me back down firmly. "I want to."

He sounds determined and in control, just like how I wanted him to feel. This is what he needs right now and I congratulate myself for recognising it.

"I'm just making sure you're ok with it because it's a big deal to some people. I wouldn't have dreamed of suggesting it."

"But you want to do it?"

"Oh yeah."

"You're just too considerate, aren't you?"

"I suppose."

"Interesting. So we need to work on getting your secret desires out of you and fulfilling them, don't we?"

"One thing at a time, let's just concentrate on this first."

I rock my hips, pushing my arse back. "I'm waiting."

"Quiet you, I'm thinking."

"About what?"

There is a long pause and even though I'm waiting with my arse in the air, instead of pushing him, I wait for him to come to it by himself.

"What it feels like to have it licked."

I smile. "I look forward to showing you. It's amazing."

Waiting for him to reply, I'm shocked when his tongue meets my tight ring. "Oh God," I gasp and fist the sheets as the pleasure washes over me. He doesn't hold back, years of imagining probably, so I am treated to his full exploration. My god he is gifted with his tongue. I thought it already, but this is some next level amazingness. My legs start to shake and I know much more of this and I'll come.

My moans are swallowed by the bedding and I'm on the edge, when the tip of his tongue presses against my entrance and pushes in a little way. "Such a good boy," I gasp.

His finger tips dig into my flesh and his moan is music to my ears.

Caught between the sub he wants to be and the 'man' he so wrongly thinks he should be, might just be where he is best. He would do anything to please me. But he fights with this image of manhood, and it isn't a damn competition. I'm overwhelmed by the need to be the one to show him that he is perfect.

I'm ready to beg, I need him to take me. Just when I think I can't stand to wait any longer, he gets to his feet. His finger circles for just a moment and I push back with need. Then finally I feel him there. He hesitates and I have to force myself to resist taking control. And then he presses forward.

Slowly at first, he edges in. Going slow is more intense than slamming home, I need him all the way inside me. Being stretched, but not filled is torture, it's more than I can take and gasp sharply.

Will freezes. "Did I hurt you?"

"No, more, I need more."

"Are you sure? I don't want to hurt you."

"Fuck me," I demand. Only it sounds more like begging as I hear the words out loud.

Like a good boy, he obeys.

"Oh God." I moan as he finally sinks inside me fully. Unable to stop the sounds of pleasure spilling from me as he starts to thrust, I rock against him trying to get what I need.

"Fucking hell, you're so tight," he whispers, grasping my hips to slow me down.

I push back even more, I need it harder.

Will pushes me down until I'm pinned to the bed by his firm hand. "I thought you said I was in charge?" He says leaning over me. I can hear in his voice what an effort it is to speak through the sensation.

"I did, but I need—" I suck in breath as he withdraws painfully slowly.

"Tell me what you need."

"I need more, slow is too intense." Holding my breath as he pauses, I wait for him to give me what I asked for. But he doesn't. Instead he pushes forward slowly. Painfully slow. I cry out.

"Too much?"

"No," I whimper. "Yes…"

"You want me to stop?"

I shake my head.

"Then take it."

I groan. I love him like this. So capable of taking control, yet delighting in the fact that he can do so under order.

He fucks me at his own pace, it's too slow to take at first but I helplessly let him have me. The sounds coming from him make it worth it.

"You're so amazing," he moans. "I can't believe you're mine."

"You're mine," I correct.

"Right now, you belong to me."

"Yes."

"Come for me Mags."

And as I come undone, I am his.

"I can't do it." He backs up before he reaches the corner and refuses to turn into the pub.

I squeeze his arm. "Yes you can. You have to face him some time. You've already spent the day hiding out in my bed. You can't hide forever."

"Yes I can. And admit it, it was the perfect way to spend a Sunday. Just you and me, pretending the rest of the world doesn't exist…Let's go back there." He swivels us around and tries to start walking in the opposite direction.

I pull him back. "Oh no you don't. You're going to put your chin up and we are going in there. Now come on."

"You can't make me."

"I could if I wanted. Do you want me to?"

"Um, no."

"Come on you big baby." I tug him forward a few steps, taking pity on him. It was a pretty embarrassing ordeal, so I'm not going to make it worse. He can't hide forever. Maybe if I offer an incentive. "If you suck it up and get in there, I'll make it worth your while."

"Oh yeah?" He softens immediately and sidles up to me, is gentle eyes focused solely on me and it almost makes me blush. His undivided attention never fails to make me feel special. It's an interesting power exchange we have going on.

"Yeah," I reply softly, inhaling his sent as he enters my space.

"What are you offering?" The corner of his mouth turns up suggestively. He knows he's pushing his luck.

I give him a lascivious grin. "We could try that little fantasy of yours we uncovered yesterday."

He looks puzzled for a few seconds and then his eyebrows shoot up. "You'd do that?"

I shrug my shoulder, "It's a fantasy for me too."

He hooks his thumbs into the belt loops of my jeans and pulls my hips so that we bump together, then he presses his lips against mine in a brief kiss, before flashing me a wicked look and smiling wide. "You've twisted my arm."

He clamps his arm around mine and marches me through the gate and down the path, into the pub.

"Jesus, what's the rush?" I frown, trying to keep up.

"You made me an offer I couldn't refuse."

"You're so funny." I laugh.

Spencer and Jazz aren't in the bar, so we walk on through to the garden at the back and find them sitting at a table in the shade.

"Here we go," Will mutters, squaring his shoulders and setting off more tense than I have ever seen him and that's saying something.

"Oh there you are," Jazz calls out as we walk over to them.

"Sorry we're late." I don't offer any explanation because there isn't one, other than Will didn't want to face Spencer.

Spencer mumbles a greeting and stares into his pint.

Will takes a deep breath and sits down opposite him, then to my surprise, addresses him directly. "Spencer I think I should apologise for what happened last night. I—"

Spencer looks up at him. "No mate, what you should do is pretend yesterday never happened. Burn it from your mind, god knows, I'm trying to."

"Yeah, okay." Will looks down at his fingers intertwined with mine on his lap.

"And buy me a fucking drink will you. I think you owe me that much, I tried to save your arse!" Spencer's laugh gets Will's attention.

He looks up and some of his tension falls away as he sees Spencer's mirth.

Spencer shakes his head, touching on it a little more even though he forbid Will to. "Fucking hell mate, whatever you've done for me in the past, I think you just put me even."

"Yeah alright—" Will attempts to agree.

"Ah!" Spencer interjects. "I said don't talk about it."

"But you—"

"Ahlalalala!" He covers his ears so that he can't hear.

Will sighs. Infuriated, but probably relieved that Spencer addressed the elephant in the room without forcing him to relive it.

I'm not going to pretend he'll get over last night easily and Spencer will make damn sure he suffers I'm sure of it. But I do feel a little less terrible now we've got that bit over with.

"Who wants a drink?" I ask, feeling a bit lighter.

"Me," Spencer replies sharply.

"Me," Will agrees. "I'll get them," he says, waving off my offer to come with him, grateful, I'm sure for the escape.

MONDAY 7TH SEPTEMBER

"Delivery!" Shouts Spencer, over the din of our crew working hard.

Mags is out riding this morning.

"I'll get it!" I yell. Realising what it might be in the box. I drop everything and scramble past Spencer making sure I get my hands on it first.

He looks at me suspiciously and I try to act nonchalant as I walk quickly over to the garage where we keep our tools to store it safely. I wish I could lock it in my car but that will just draw too much attention to it. Hopefully Mags will be home soon and she can take it and spare me any extra humiliation this week.

I try to concentrate back on my work but the thought of those things in that box is just filling my head with too many images to concentrate. I don't know how I'm going to last the day.

'A package came for you, I signed for it.'

'Oooh! Our toys.'

'I put it in the store with the tools for safe keeping.'

'Good.'

As I type I watch Spencer cross the driveway to the garage and disappear inside. This is not an unusual occurrence, but the way he glances over his shoulder at me before he goes him has me worried. I panic.

'It wouldn't say anything incriminating on it would it? Spencer is in there with it right now!'

'LOL.'

'Mags I'm serious. I didn't look closely I just tucked it away.'

'Calm yourself. It's fine.'

'Are you sure?'

'Yes I'm sure, the box will be totally unmarked.

'Thank fuck for that.'

'Open it.'

'I can't!'

'Yes you can.'

'No.'

'No?'

'That's right. It's staying sealed. If I open it, I will get caught, there's no doubt about it, look at our track record. These guys will crucify me. I can't do it.'

'Will?'

'Yes, Goddess, I know there will be punishment for my disobedience, but I'm not doing it.'

'I'm messing with you.'

'Oh.'

'But there will be punishment for your disobedience.'

'I figured.'

'You love it.'

No, I love you, I think to myself. But of course, I pussy out of saying it. Right now I need to distract Spencer.

"We need to line something up for when we finish here." I ponder aloud, as I enter the garage relieved to find that Spencer is nowhere near the package. "We've probably only got a couple more weeks, we really need to get organised. We can't afford to be doing nothing when this job ends."

Spencer looks up and nods. "I have been thinking about it actually. What if we bought your mum's house?"

I frown. I only opened the conversation as a distraction, and he throws buying a new house at me. "You want to move?"

Spencer rolls his eyes. "Not for us genius. As an investment."

I think about this for a minute. "It's been on the market for a month and not even had a viewing. Do you not think that's a bit risky?"

"No, I don't actually. I was thinking about it a lot while I was hiding out there. It's a pretty big four bedroom cottage, in a highly desirable location. No offence, I just don't think your mum's dated and dusty décor is really what the rich out-of-towners are looking for, do you? And plus that agent uses Evan to do their photos." Spencer does a really exaggerated eye roll and sticks his fingers down his throat. "That dickhead couldn't make a Kardashian look sexy, how is he going to make a house look good?"

I can't help but laugh. Spencer is never going to like poor Evan. "What? So you're saying do it up, sell it on, make a profit?"

Spencer shrugs. "Yeah, it's what everyone else is doing. There's money in it, especially around here."

"Can we even afford it?"

"I think we can. We've got equity in the house, some savings, and my old uni mate is a mortgage broker. I reckon we could swing it."

“But it’ll take ages. We need work in a couple of weeks. Shouldn't we just follow up with some of the interest we had at George’s party?”

“It won't take that long to get mortgage. We can just ask them to take it off the market and do a private sale once we have the money in place. I bet it would still be quicker than waiting for a buyer. And your mum and dad would let us start work straight away, you know that. Think about it, that's all I'm saying. I think it's a really good idea. They’ve priced it as a fixer upper, we could turn a nice little profit. And no agents fees for any of us, it’s a win/win.”

I nod, my mind already racing.

Will seems relieved when I arrive home and is quick to handover the parcel.

"Wanna come and look at it with me now?" I offer.

He looks pained. "I really want to, but I have to finish this today, the plasterer needs to get in where I'm working tomorrow. I think I'm going to be staying late tonight."

"Did you remember I have that podcast thing tonight?"

"I remembered. I'll finish up by six at the latest, so you won't hear any banging or crashing."

"Thank you," I lean forward and place a kiss on his cheek. He is all dusty so he can't grab me for more. "I'll see you later." I back away from him, smiling at his disappointed pout.

"Okay."

Walking towards the house, I see Spencer inside the new building, watching. Why is it whenever I turn round we have an audience? No wonder Will finds it so hard to come out of his shell. Then I have an idea. I take out my phone as I'm entering the house and dump the big box on the kitchen side so that I can concentrate on my call.

A few minutes later, I'm headed outside to find Spencer with a big smile on my face.

"Checking up on us?" he teases.

“I don't want you slacking” I reply looking around pointedly as if I suspect they have been.

“I think you’ll find it's all above board, milady.”

I narrow my eyes. He knows I hate his lady of the manor jokes. “Actually, I just wanted a quick word,” I tell him.

“Fire away.”

I hold out several folded notes.

He takes them cautiously and looks at them confused. “I don't know what you’ve heard about me, but I don't dance…anymore,” he smirks.

“I’ve booked you a table for tomorrow night at Scarlett’s Grill. I want you to take Jazz and treat her to a nice night out.” Spencer frowns, he takes my hand and shoves the money back in it, looking puzzled.

“First of all, I don’t need your money and secondly good luck getting a table there. The partners at my old firm used to entertain big client there and it gets booked up months in advance.”

“I know it does, you will be sitting at my dad's usual table.”

Spencer scoffs. “Money doesn't talk that loudly.”

“His does.” I laugh. “He is the majority investor. Scarlett was my mother’s name.”

Spencer’s jaw hangs open while he processes that information. When he finally believes me, he changes his tune. “I’ve heard the steaks at that place are amazing.”

“You get to find out tomorrow don't you?”

“Thank you,” he says hesitantly, wondering what the catch is.

“Are you sure you don't want this?” I hold out the money. “I wasn’t trying to offend you, but those steaks don't come cheap, and I’m kind of springing it on you.”

“No honestly I'm fine, but thank you for getting us in. What's the catch?”

“The catch is, I need you to stay out of our way. Don’t come back here. Take Jazz out, show here a good time and then take her home to your house.”

“No way,” he says to my surprise.

“Fine then, come back here if you want a repeat of Saturday night. It’s your call.” I shrug, knowing this threat will be enough.

“You can have your alone time,” he says. “But if we’re doing you a favour, then we get the Jacuzzi.”

“You and that bloody Jacuzzi.” I shake my head.

Spencer doesn't look fazed. “I’ve had some good times in that Jacuzzi, take it or leave it.”

“Yeah, whatever. You bring her back here, we'll be at yours. Come home at entirely your own risk. You have been warned.”

He wrinkles his nose at the thought.

“Do we have a deal?” I hold out my hand.

“We have a deal.” He shakes it.

TUESDAY 8TH SEPTEMBER

She chases me up the stairs as soon as we get home making me lose my grip on the big box I'm carrying. She drops her bag on the landing beside where it fell and I make it to the bathroom before she catches me. Out of breath I turn on her laughing and drag her dress over her head.

"What are you doing?" She giggles.

"I've just finished work, I'm disgusting," I tell her. "I need to shower and you're going to shower with me."

She laughs kicking off her shoes and wriggling out of her underwear while I switch the shower on. When I turn back she's naked and I drink her in. God I want to touch her. "Are you sure they won't come home?"

"Positive. We have the whole night."

"You are fucking amazing." I quickly take my clothes off and bundle her into the shower.

Fifteen minutes later, we finally make it kissing and touching into the bedroom with dripping hair and towels hastily wrapped around us. I drop her bag I picked up from the landing floor and place the box on the desk, returning to lock the door behind us, because, yeah… I'm scarred for life.

"Paranoid, boy?"

"Always."

"Would you like me to help you relax?"

"Mmm, what do you have in mind?" I pull her close, zeroing in on her luscious lips, and lining up to take a kiss.

"Help me unpack this box and I will show you." She swivels away from me before I can close the distance to her lips and she has the box and is sitting on the bed before I can mutter my objection.

I sit with her on the bed and watch as she slowly pulls the rip tab on the box. She does it deliberately, prolonging my agony.

She pulls out handfuls of screwed up paper from the top and drops it on the floor without a care.

I ignore it, a little proud of myself, and stare down at the contents. For some reason I expected it all to be tacky but I should've known that Mags would shop in some nicer places. The only toy experience I've ever had was a vibrator an old girlfriend had, that came in a plastic blister pack with a photo of a busty porn star on it. This stuff is packaged so nicely.

"Well?" she says softly, making me aware that I'm gawping.

"It's not what I was expecting," I tell her honestly. "It looks like a box full of Apple products."

See grins and strokes the side of my face. "Only the best for my good boy."

My chest tightens. If she sees me melt, she ignores it.

"Let's have a look then," she says going back to her bossy tone.

I pick up the biggest box and slide the sleeve off it. Lifting the lid, I gasp at the set of cuffs. Four of them, two for my wrists, two for my ankles. The gold buckles and rings shine in stark contrast to the brown leather. Also in the box are a variety of straps and double-ended trigger clips. I lift one out and touch it, feeling instantly aroused by the smell of the leather and the clink of the metal. Suddenly, I remember I'm being watched and look up guiltily.

"Sorry," I tell her, realising, I was hogging. "Do you want to see?"

She smiles. "The look on your face was enough. Do you like them?"

"They are really nice." I show her. "Thank you." It feels awkward to thank her for such a thing. It makes me sound kept. She bought them for us, not for me, but she's chosen really nicely and I just wanted her to know I appreciate it.

"I thought they would be. I'm excited to see you wearing them."

Oh God, me too. I return the cuff to the box, noticing four small padlocks and a set of tiny keys as I do. Now, you don't get all locked in for a five minute quickie, and the thought of hours of play in these things makes me absentmindedly press my hand into my crotch to relieve the pressure. I replace the lid, putting the box aside before I think too hard. One item at time, I unpack a flogger, a pair of nipple clamps and a ballgag—as promised—with a shiny red ball just the way I imagined. Holding it in my hand I open my mouth inadvertently, envisaging it there forcing my jaw into an open position.

"Put it back in the box Mr. I want to be the first to gag you," she warns playfully.

I look up at her. She smiles

"You're going to look so perfect," she purrs, and I can see

it's getting to her as much as it is me.

She gets up and takes the box from me, placing everything on the floor by the bed. She pulls her towel off, using it to dry her hair. I feast on the sight of her. Her tattoo still steals my breath.

She drops her towel over the back of my desk chair and turns to face me, beckoning me to stand. She uses a finger to unhook the towel around my waist and lets it drop to the floor.

"The safeword is still Spencer," she informs me, not able to hide her amusement.

I roll my eyes, but nod anyway. It's not like I'll ever forget it.

"On the bed," she instructs.

Obediently, I climb on the bed and lay in the centre waiting.

Mags collects the wrist cuffs and some straps from the box and climbs on the bed with me. I watch her buckle them around my wrists, already floating even before she straps them to the posts of my bed.

"I think I want to get a four poster bed," she says completely out of the blue, while figuring out the best way to secure me.

"I can make you one," I tell, her being pulled back from my floating by images of kinky beds I've seen.

"You can?"

"I made this one."

She sits back for a second and looks at the headboard, then at me. "You made this?"

"Yeah."

"Wow. It's beautiful." She bends down and kisses me.

"You're so talented."

I smile. "I could make it with special secret places to tie me to if you want."

"Oh my god, I want!" she claps, excitedly.

"I'll make you a bed, Goddess," I promise.

She caresses my face. "You are a good boy," she purrs, going back to securing my other wrist.

Once my arms are securely spread across the width of the bed, she gets the ankle cuffs and repeats, leaving me tied down spread eagle style. The only part of me not down is my eager cock, which is standing to attention crudely.

Next, she gets the new blindfold out and places it on the bedside table. She removes the nipple clamps from their box and sets them with the blindfold and looks at the ballgag with a smile, before placing it there too. Then going to her overnight bag she pulls out something large, which I don't quite see, and puts it on the bed between my feet

"What was that?" I ask.

"You'll see," she smiles and I shiver with anticipation.

"Are you going to fuck me?" I ask.

She throws her head back and laughs. "You aren't ready for me yet, boy."

And then she carries on with her preparation. And I'm left wondering, which was obviously her desire.

Finally she tosses a bottle of lube on to the covers besides me and crawls on to the bed with me.

This is the most vulnerable position I have ever been in, I have never been so open to her. To anyone. And my heart is racing.

She reaches for the eye mask and slips it over my head and

immediately my pulse starts thundering in my ears. Not being able to see gets me going anyway, but with all these new things we've discussed, that are now on the table. Proper cuffs holding me down, creaking in that certain way. A leather eye mask with fur lining that feels great and blocks out everything, not like the scarves we've used. The other new things sitting just beside me like a threat. Or is it a promise? And let's not forget the lube and some mystery object in the mix, I'm really on edge. So when she touches me on the thigh, I jolt so hard that I make a pained sound.

"Fuck, are you ok?" she asks concerned.

"Yeah, fine," I gasp, trying to catch my breath.

"Do you want me to let you out?"

"No!" I jump again, not helping my case.

She lifts off the blindfold and hovers above me, assessing my face. "Really? Because it seems like you're having an anxiety attack. Breathe in through your nose and out through your mouth." She demonstrates and I listen to the rhythmic sound trying to replicate it.

"I wouldn't call it anxiety," I tell her, blowing out each breath as I feel like I'm getting it under control. "It's far more pleasurable than that. It's almost orgasmic. It's like being on the brink of an anxiety orgasm." I laugh at how ridiculous that sounds.

"An anxiegasm," she exclaims laughing and the sound eases me down enough to catch a full breath.

"Yes!"

"Do you want me to stop?" she asks getting serious for a second.

"You haven't started yet," I protest.

"I know but look at you."

"I'll be fine, please."

"Okay, but you stop me if you need to."

"I will."

She goes to put the blindfold back over my eyes.

"Mags," I stop her.

"Yes," she looks concerned again.

I take a deep breath. "I love you."

She stares at me, without giving a clue as to what she is thinking.

Anxiety, without the orgasmic haze hits me hard. Why did I say that now? Panicking, I try and smooth things over. "I'm sorry I probably shouldn't say it for the first time when I'm like this," I tug at my wrists cuffs. "It isn't the right time, but I need you to know. I've been feeling it since you came back, more and more every day. I just look at you and I don't know how to say it. I know I feel it, I feel it bone deep. You have me tongue tied when you have me in the palm of your hand. It might be too soon and you don't have to feel the same way, but I have always loved you and I just wanted you to know."

She straddles my chest without a word and places a finger under my chin, leaving me no place to look but into her eyes. Some of her dark hair falls in front of her face and I wish I could reach up to tuck it behind her ear. She doesn't seem to notice it as she just stares. Seconds tick by and the dread builds. Then she takes a breath to speak.

"You are the only person I have ever loved. It killed me when you went away and I promised myself I wouldn't let myself feel that deeply again. Then the moment I saw you in that pub, I knew that my whole carefully constructed plan to guard my feelings would be shattered. Because I still love you." She pauses, staring at me.

I swallow hard.

"And I'm afraid I always will."

"That's nothing to be afraid of," I tell her. Wishing I had my hands to hold her, but I realise that maybe having me bared to her like this, body as well as soul is what she needs in order to handle this moment. She has her quirks, I have mine. Being in control is something she needs. Maybe I did that to her, made her need to control what happens to her heart by controlling the person who holds it. I don't know, but I'm happy to let her roll with it if that's what she needs.

"No, it just means you're stuck with me," she smiles, leaning down, her face an inch from mine.

"I can handle that."

"I hope you can, because I'm going to test you."

I nod slowly, not sure if she means physically or emotionally, but I am ready for both.

She moves down my body, biting my nipple with no preamble.

"Fuck!" I grunt, realising that today the test is going to be physical. She soothes the bite with a lick and then moves on, down to where I can feel her warm breath on my cock. I think she's going to lick it, when she sits up.

Shit.

"Are you ready?"

"I'm ready." I promise breathlessly, already starting to get that feeling again.

She watches me, gauging. "I won't use this," she says tossing the blindfold she still has in her hand, onto the bedside table.

"No please," I blurt. "I want it. I want it all."

"If you're sure." She leans over me to retrieve it, but instead comes back with the ball gag.

My heart rate increases and my breathing becomes even shakier.

"With this in your mouth, you won't be able to use the safe word." I can feel her start to doubt herself.

"I know," I whisper. It's dark, but that's why I like the idea so much. "I can still let you know if I need you to stop, I'll shake my head a lot. It will be ok. I trust you."

She nods. Looking at the gag like she is still deciding. Then I see the 'fuck it' moment and she lifts it to my mouth.

I lick my lips and open wide. Fuck, this is it.

I try to adjust to it while lifting my head as much as I am able to let her buckle it at the back. It's awkward, but comfort isn't supposed to be the aim.

"There," she says and I lay my head back down.

I'm more aware of my breathing now and how rapid it is as I get used to the intrusion.

Next come the clamps and she holds them up waiting for a nod before she sets to work. She pinches my nipple up and I wait for the agony, but it never comes. There is a pinch and I can feel the pressure, but it isn't what I expected at all from such a vicious looking contraption. I watch her do the other one and then she looks at her handy work.

"We won't leave these on for too long the first time," she tells me. "It's taking them off that is the fun part."

I've watched enough porn to know that, and I sort of can't wait.

She plays with the tiny bud of my nipple that is protruding through the clamp, with her fingernail, and I feel it straight in my cock. Fuck! It's like the clamps have rewired my nerves. I moan past the gag and the sound just adds to the scene. This is really me, I remind myself as I watch her reach across to the table. No more wishing, or wanting, or hiding what turns me on. It's now.

She slips the blindfold over my eyes and the circle is complete.

I feel her leave the bed. Trying to relax and surrender to whatever is coming, I test the bonds and the ball between my teeth and it feels incredible to know how powerless I am. I start to float again. I'm not as tense as before, but I still jump when a strange sensation brushes across my belly. It takes a second sweep for me to realise it is the soft leather fronds of the flogger I had forgotten was in the box. It disappears again, only to return, lightly tickling across my sensitive nipples. I pant trying to measure my responses, because I know this is just the beginning.

Tracking her around the room in the moments when there is no sensation is not easy. When her voice comes from the foot of the bed, it startles me.

"You look incredible," she says, stroking the flogger down my right leg. "So perfect." She strokes it down the left leg.

Then with no warning, it lands on my thigh.

My muffled cry is the most primal sound I have ever heard. It wasn't painful, just a sting and a shock, but the release it gave me to cry freely like that was incredible.

She let's me come down, before dishing a second one to my other thigh. The built up tension lets rip from me with the sharp sting. This time she continues laying blow upon blow up and down my body until it's hard to breathe. Then she stops abruptly leaving me gasping and trembling.

"Breathe, baby." she coaches, closer to my face than I realise and I flinch.

My whole body is thrumming with tension and I can feel the sheen of sweat that has broken out.

Fuck, I feel so alive.

The bed dips and Mags positions herself on top of me. She strokes my face. "Shhh. Deep breaths. In-2-3, out-2-3."

I try to.

"Better?" she asks when I calm.

I nod. Then I feel the clamp on my nipple move as she touches it, sending a zap of pleasure straight through me and I moan.

"Deep breath," she warns and I suck in a breath and hold it.

The searing pain as she releases the clamp is something I am not prepared for at all. I roar, pulling at the cuffs keeping me restrained.

"Good boy," she purrs. Her soft warm tongue tries to soothe the pain, but it is so raw even that causes me to cry involuntarily. It makes no sense, how can something feel fine all the time if it's biting into you and then agony once it's gone? I feel the other clamp lift and I freeze, holding my breath. But then nothing happens so I let it out. That's when she does it. Faster this time, more brutal, but over in a flash. My scream echoes through the empty house.

She takes her time with her tongue though, soothing it until it feels good. Fuck yes, I moan. I love how much more sensitive they are now.

I feel her lift up, kneeling over me. “You’re doing great. Are you ready for more?”

I nod slowly, not knowing what more she has up her sleeve, or if I am ready. I’m shocked when I feel her line me up and start to sink down onto me. I thought it would be more pain, not this.

She moans.

I can feel how wet she is. It is a surprise to me every time, this thing I fought for such a long time, can actually bring pleasure to someone else, not just me.

She stops with my dick just inside her.

“Does that feel good?”

I nod, attempting to push into her more. She lifts up as I do making it impossible to gain any ground.

“Just the tip,” she whispers. “That’s all I need.” Her hips start moving and she sighs.

Like this she uses me to take her pleasure. It's torture, I need more. I need to sink in all the way. I try in vain to thrust up, but she doesn't allow it.

“Just the tip,” she repeats breathlessly.

I whimper.

Suddenly, there is a click and a low buzzing sound fills the air. I have no time to work out where it’s coming from before intense vibrations flood my senses.

I moan uncontrollably and so does Mags. That must be what she got from her bag. A vibrator. She has it pressed to her clit as she rides just the tip of my cock, so part of it is brushing my shaft and I can feel the vibrations inside her too. Fuck, it’s amazing. I can’t stop myself chasing more of her, trying to get deeper.

"Is that enough to make you come?" she teases.

Whimpering, I shake my head and thrust again, but she is good at rolling with it and stopping me getting anywhere.

The vibration increases. "How about now? Could you come from this?"

I'm finding it hard to breathe, I need more.

"If you can boy, you may come," she teases. She knows I won't be able to. It isn't fair. "Poor baby," she continues, adding to the torment. "It's enough to make me come." She lets out a long moan. "This is all I need, just you hitting the spot like that and a girl's best friend vibrating away on my clit. Fuck it feels good."

She turns the vibration high and I bite into the ball gag growling. It's so good, maybe I could come. If I just had enough—.

"I'm so close baby. I'm going to come." She cries shattering my hopes, and I feel her come as she moans with pleasure.

The vibrations leave me and the buzz stops. I moan in frustration. Maybe if I had long enough it would have made me come.

Mags moves down my body, not concerned with depriving me. She retreats until she is kneeling between my legs and her hand strokes my cock once and then it's gone. I lift my hips wanting more.

"It's too bad you didn't come baby," she says with mock sincerity. "Perhaps I could try something else."

I still haven't caught my breath and I feel like I'm going mad with desire. All I can do is moan.

The snap of the lube cap refocuses my attention. Her cold fingers run my seam and I can't help but try and pull my legs up to open myself for her. Of course I'm tied down, but my legs are spread enough for her to slip easily between my cheeks. I hold my breath.

Her other hand starts stroking my dick as she circles my hole and I let out a sigh, trying to relax myself.

I feel her press and her finger pushes in.

I bite down on the ball between my teeth, grunting, but when she withdraws I cry out.

"Relax," she says softly. Then she lets go of my cock and reaches up, using the leather strap to pull the gag out of my mouth and letting it fall around my neck.

I gasp for breath and she goes back to stroking my dick and starts working her finger inside me.

"Oh my god." I moan.

"Does that feel good?"

"It feels—" without warning she twists her finger around and brushes a part inside me that makes my head swim. "Fuck!"

"I take it fuck is good."

She strokes that spot again, more deliberately this time and I choke on the words.

Her hand glides up and down my shaft in sync and my mouth goes dry.

"This is your prostate, boy. How does it feel to have it stroked?"

"So amazing," I whisper.

"I can't hear you."

"Amazing!" I cry as she presses on it. "I'm…I'm…" Shit

I’m so close.

“You’re what, boy?”

“I’m going to come.” I yell, trying to warn her.

“You think so, don’t you?”

“I am, I am!”

Her hand that was wrapped around my cock opens out and I’m left rutting against her open palm.

“Fuck!” I cry in frustration.

She grips the base of my cock and rubs harder with her finger inside me. “Think you can come without me stroking it, boy?”

“Please,” I beg. “Please Goddess.”

“What do you want, boy?”

“I want to come Goddess, please.”

“Alright then,” she says reluctantly. “I hope you’re ready.”

Her hand grips me again and I am overwhelmed. I’ve never feared an orgasm before but as I feel it build I know it might break me. Gasping for breath, I surrender to it and hear the creak of the leather as I yank at the tethers currently holding me down.

“Fuck!” I roar.

"It's so peaceful isn't it?" I lift his hand, linking his fingers between mine.

"Yeah, it's lovely," he says stroking our fingers together. "I wish it could be like this all the time."

"We both have the wrong best friends for a quiet life." I laugh. "You know that."

"We do, don't we?"

"Shall we just ditch them and move to a desert island??

He laughs. "I wish."

Chuckling with him, I sigh. "We do need some space though, don't we?" As soon as the words leave my mouth, he seems to tense. Silence falls over us and I listen to his heart beating overtime in his chest. Maybe I shouldn't have said it like that. It sounded like I meant we need our own place. Of course I didn't mean that, there's no pressure, we've only been together what, a couple of weeks? I think admitting our feeling were so strong was probably enough to last us a while. "Are you okay?" I ask, lifting my head.

His hand grips mine and he flips me quickly onto my back, pinning my hand to the pillow and hovering over me with a lustful look in his eyes. "I feel amazing," he says with a slow smile. "You are amazing, what just happened was amazing. Life…" He grins uncontrollably. "Is amazing!" He dips his head and licks his lips looking ready to devour me and I wait, willing to be devoured. "I love you," he whispers. "It feels so good to say that." Then he moves in, taking my breath away.

"Space is exactly what we need," He says coming up for air and rolling off me. He flops back onto the pillows, and I settle beside him.

"I just meant that it would be nice not to constantly have to arrange our private time around our friends."

"No I agree, we can only get alone time if they're taking alone time. And I like alone time."

I watch him, smiling to himself with a faraway look. Perhaps he is thinking about some of the things we've tried so far, or maybe some of the things we might try soon. And with that, the worry I have started to feel lately snakes in to the back of my mind.

"What's wrong?" he asks.

"How do you know something is wrong?"

"You breathed differently, like you wanted to say something, and then changed your mind."

"You don't think…" I wrinkle my nose, doubting whether I should even say anything.

"What?" he prompts.

"You don't think we're rushing things do you?"

He sits up quickly, a look of concern appearing on his face.

"I don't mean with us," I quickly reassure him. "I mean play stuff."

"Why would I think we're rushing into play stuff?

"Because it's only been a short time and we're trying all these things, I don't want to get carried away and rush into something you aren't ready for."

"Mags, listen to me. I am so ready. I was ready for you, and I am ready for your games," he says salaciously.

"I'm serious, Will. I know we're having a lot of fun, but I don't want to do something you might regret."

"Okay seriously." He straightens his face to show that he is not messing around now. "I promise you I will tell you to stop if I feel that it's something I might regret." Then he makes doubly sure that we have eye contact to prove that he is telling the truth. "We have that godforsaken safeword, I used it remember? We all know how that turned out. But at least you can trust that I will use it if I need to."

I smile. "Alright then, tell me what you want to try next."

"Now?" he looks alarmed.

"No, not now, silly."

"Jesus, I thought you were trying to kill me."

I laugh and lay back down.

"I'll try anything, surprise me." He lies back down, turning onto his side to face me.

"What's the one burning thing you have on your mind now though?"

"You know what it is, I told you."

"Tell me again now that you're not begging to come."

"I want you to fuck me," he says confidently. I don't see an ounce of doubt. "I thought you might do it tonight."

"Why would you think that?"

"Because you got that toy out, I didn't know what it was."

"Oh!" I laugh. "That explains why you were wound so tight."

"I just didn't know what was coming, what was that thing?"

"That was my Smartwand. It's my favourite." I reach over the side of the bed and pick it up off the top of the pile of discarded restraints, lifting it to show him.

"Bloody hell!" he exclaims. "It's huge."

I hand it to him and he weighs it, wrapping his fingers around the gold handle while he examines the black silicone body. He presses a button on the handle and it clicks into life. "Whoa." His other arm reaches around me so that he can touch the bulbous head. He speeds it up all the way and tests how it feels with his fingers. "We could have some fun with this."

"I thought we just did."

"We did," he smiles, switching it off and dropping it beside him so that he can focus on me. "And I loved it."

"Anxiegasmic?" I laugh.

"It was! Fuck."

"Well, sorry to disappoint you, I don't just have a strap-on lying around."

"I realise that now I'm thinking clearly. I'm glad you don't. I'm happy you haven't done it with anyone else."

"Exactly." I stroke his chest and we fall silent, just enjoying being so relaxed with each other. "Looks like I need to do some more toy shopping."

"Does that mean we need to make another list?" he asks suggestively.

"Oh baby," I stroke my fingers into his hair softly and look into his eyes. Then I grip firmly. "You haven't earned the bite of my crop again yet. You enjoy it too much for me to give it freely. You understand, don't you?" My tone is so teasing, I nearly giggle.

His eyes close. "Yes, Goddess," he hisses.

"Good. Now is there anything else I need to buy?"

"I don't know really." He thinks for a moment.

"Why don't we get the laptop and browse together?" I suggest.

He is up out of bed so fast, something tells me he is into this idea.

FRIDAY 18TH SEPTEMBER

Will emerges from the pub with an ice bucket and a handful of glasses and to my surprise, JJ in tow.

"Fucking hell Mags," Spencer says semi-discreetly. "Looks like your competition is back."

I shoot him a look, to find that he is smirking. "You weren't supposed to know about that." I turn my glare on Jazz, who holds her hands up and shrugs without a hint of regret. Nope, she's right, it was too good not to tell someone. Hell, I told her. So now everyone knows that JJ kissed Will. Poor Will.

"Look who I found," says Will cheerfully, completely oblivious to the looks being exchanged on his approach.

"What are you doing here?" I ask, getting up to greet JJ.

"Hey Shrimp. I was just—" He kisses one cheek. "On the date from hell." He kisses the other cheek. "And this handsome man came to my rescue." JJ winks at Will, who rolls his eyes. "He was dull as shit, I can't thank you enough."

"I didn't really do anything," Will insists.

"You came in at just the right time."

Will takes out the bottle of champagne and begins to open it.

"Are you sure you don't mind me joining you? Will insisted, but you're celebrating."

"You can celebrate with us," Will tells him, handing him the first glass, then passing the others out to us.

"Thank you. So what are we celebrating?"

"To the end of our first job." Will holds his glass up and we all repeat the toast and lift our glasses with him.

"And a bloody good job we did too," adds Spencer.

"You sure did," I tell him. "So much so that as soon as the interior people are finished in a couple of weeks, the house is being featured in a national magazine."

"Oh wow," says Jazz.

"Venomous Veronica?" JJ asks knowingly.

"Yeah," I turn my nose up.

JJ's nose wrinkles too. "Worst luck."

"I know, but needs must. She's been onto Dad for a year for some kind of spread and he keeps turning her down telling her work is too busy, but you know she's going to get bored and start using her imagination if he doesn't agree. So he threw her the house renovations as a bone."

JJ nods. "Smart."

"Who is Venomous Veronica?" Will asks confused.

"Veronica Stapleton. She's a society journalist and by that, I mean blood sucking hack."

"Sounds lovely," Spencer laughs, taking a drink and then screwing up his face and looking at his champagne glass with contempt, before putting it in front of Jazz and picking up his beer.

"Hey what happened to the date?" I ask JJ, changing the subject.

"I told him Will was my little sister's boyfriend and I'm not out to my family, so I hustled him out the door."

"Poor bloke."

JJ shrugs. "He should learn the art of conversation. I knew online dating was a mistake."

"Oh don't get me started with online dating," Jazz pipes up.

"Right?" Laughs JJ.

"What do you know about online dating, Princess?" Spencer frowns.

"Plenty."

Spencer narrows his eyes, but doesn't question it further, turning his attention to JJ. "So was this a Grindr thing?"

"I didn't take you for a Grindr man Spencer," JJ teases.

"No, Spencer is more of a Twitter whore," Jazz laughs, ruffling his hair.

Spencer bats her hand away and fixes his hair. "I know what's going on in the world thank you very much. And you," he points at Jazz. "Are not exactly a Twitter angel now are you?"

That shuts Jazz up.

"This all sounds very interesting." JJ leans forward, putting his elbow on the table and props his chin up on his hand.

"Spencer and Jazz met on Twitter. It's old news," I inform him.

"Ah social media love." JJ sighs.

"Hardly," Will scoffs. "They almost killed each other."

JJ looks intrigued.

"Just a bit of light criminal damage." Spencer smiles salaciously, pulling Jazz onto his lap, eyeing her hungrily. "There was never any mortal danger."

"So you thought," Jazz replies trying to get out of his grasp.

"Wow, and I thought my love life was interesting." JJ muses, throwing a knowing look Will's way.

"Hey, can you get off me," Jazz kind of snaps at Spencer, shuffling back to her seat.

"Sorry Princess, I just get all worked up thinking about you tunafishing my pool table."

"Is that a straight thing I'm not aware of?" JJ whispers loudly to me.

I just laugh. Jazz looks annoyed for some reason, but she's trying to play it down.

Spencer doesn't do 'playing it down.' "You're hot in a rage."

"And you're going the right way about seeing it again," she throws back.

"Promises, promises, Princess."

Jazz huffs and stands. "Whatever, I'm going to go get a drink."

"Will just brought a bottle of champagne." He slides her glass closer to her.

"I'm just going to get some water, I don't actually feel too well."

Ah, that explains the snappy mood, she gets all kinds of crabby when she's under the weather.

"I'll come with you," I call after as she walks away. I'd better just find out if she's ok.

FRIDAY 18TH SEPTEMBER

Spencer watches Mags and Jazz walking into the pub and I can see his filthy cogs turning. He doesn't show any concern for his girlfriend who just said she doesn't feel well. He's practically drooling.

"Seriously Spencer, sort it out."

He drinks from his pint and wipes his mouth with the back of his hand. "What did I do?"

"Your tongue was hanging out of your damn head."

"I was just admiring the view."

"Well, admire it more subtly, it's disrespectful."

"Sorry, Your Holiness, I didn't realise there was a law against appreciating my *own* girlfriend."

"Uh huh."

"And her hot friend," he mutters under his breath.

I roll my eyes. "She said she's not feeling good, aren't you bothered? And by the way they happen to be two very intelligent women, one of whom climbs into your bed every night, for her sins, and the other, I'd prefer you keep out of your lecherous thoughts, thank you very much."

"Oh really? And what lecherous thoughts are those exactly?"

I roll my eyes, trust him to try and come over all innocent.

"Don't even. I know just the sort of disgusting ideas you have rattling around in that head of yours."

"Such as?"

I shake my head. "You know what you were thinking, you don't need me to sink to your level to prove it. Just cut it out is all I'm saying. They both deserve better."

He folds his arms across his chest. "No come on, this should be good. Let's hear it."

"I'd actually quite like to hear it too," JJ laughs.

What the hell is going on here? I'm not having JJ on team Spencer.

"Oh I don't know," I wave my arm, dismissing them. "My mind doesn't live in the gutter like yours, I can't just come up with this stuff off the cuff."

"You've made a big deal of it now. I want to hear what you've got."

Rolling my eyes, I think for a minute. "Ugh fine. It would be something disgustingly crude like…" I puff out my chest and do my best arsehole impression. "By the time I finish with her, she'll have a face like a painter's radio."

"Wow!"

I look up to see Jazz looking pretty aghast and beside her, Mags has her eyebrows raised in amused shock.

I hold up my hands. "Oh no, no. I was just doing an impression of Spencer."

Both girls turn their distain on him.

"Don't fucking look at me! I have never said that." He looks at me with nothing short of admiration. "I bloody wish I had though, that was brilliant, but it was all you mate." He slaps the table. "There's hope for you yet."

The girls look back to me and I've got nothing. Their amused faces soften the blow slightly, but fuck my life. I set out to do the chivalrous thing and end up looking worse than Spencer.

"I don't get it." JJ frowns, looking confused.

"Oh lord." Spencer looks withered, like he has to carry the burden of manhood singlehandedly. "Allow me to explain." He throws an arm around JJ's shoulders. "He means…"

It's at this point that it dawns on Spencer that he has a real life gay man in his arms and he is about to talk in detail about ejaculation. I see his split second battle and expect him to drop JJ like a hot potato, but to my surprise he does an almost indiscernible shrug and carries on.

"He means, when he has finished with them, their faces would be all splattered with jizz, resembling the paint splatters on a painter's radio. You get it?"

"Oh!" exclaims JJ. "Ewww."

"Yeah gross," Jazz agrees sitting back down with her bottle of water.

"For the record, I don't mean I would, I mean…you know what? Forget it. Let's just pretend this whole conversation never happened."

"Do you not have that?" Spencer asks JJ.

"Do I not have what?"

"No, I mean, do men not do that to each other?"

"Oh for the love of god!" I sink my face into my hands and groan.

"What?" Spencer doesn't get the issue.

"Do you not have that?" JJ repeats, testing out the concept, amused. "You ask like it's some brand of mayonnaise I can't get in my country."

Spencer bursts out laughing and I look up at him, begging him with my eyes not to say anything else remotely Spenceresque. "Mayonnaise!" he barks regardless. "Good analogy, I like your style." Then he holds up his hand to high five JJ and to my horror JJ, amused, accepts the invitation.

"So let me get this straight—wait, no, that's wrong." JJ laughs. "You want to know if gay men come on each other's faces?"

"Well…I wouldn't say I want to know. But yeah, I'm interested. Do you do that? I have no clue."

I begin banging my head on the table.

"Jesus Christ, Spencer," Jazz shakes her head. "I'm sorry about him," she tells JJ.

"No, It's fine," he tells her. "It's quite entertaining. We do 'have that'," he informs Spencer. "I mean, no one is holding a gun to your head, but it happens. It's just our 'radios' have dicks too."

"Are we still doing this?" I groan from my hands. Looking up, I fix JJ with my look of disappointment. "I thought I could rely on you to at least not be on his side."

"He's quite funny once you get past all the…" he waves his hand in a circle towards Spencer. "All the Spencer."

"Thanks, I think." Spencer looks perplexed.

"You see, Spencer?" I feel vindicated. "He doesn't even know you and he sees what a knobhead you are."

Spencer holds up his middle finger and defiantly turns to JJ. "So when you're in the sack…" he asks.

I choke on my beer, killing my chances of stopping him going on.

"Who tops?" he finishes.

"Oh wow," JJ rolls his eyes.

"Spencer!" Jazz snaps.

"What? That's what you call it right?"

"It is," JJ replies amused. I can see he's giving Spencer just enough rope to hang himself.

"See," Spencer nods to Jazz, proud of himself for getting the term right.

I'd be proud of him too if I didn't know his endless capacity for putting his foot in his mouth.

"So who's 'the man' then?"

And there it is.

JJ, to his credit, remains amused. "Why do people think it's ok to ask gay people that? You wouldn't ask a straight person what they do in bed."

"Erm, because it's perfectly obvious who tops in a straight couple."

"Is it?" Mags and JJ answer at the same time.

My stomach flips as all eyes but Spencer's turn on me. And I try not to think about the strap on we ordered that we still haven't used, in case they can all tell what I'm thinking.

Spencer continues to look at Mags, a challenge clear in his eyes. "Look, whatever freaky shit you two get up to, his cock goes in your pussy. So he tops. Period."

"Oh my God," Jazz hangs her head.

"Oh Spencer," Mags leans across to grab his face and give it a squish. "You have so much to learn." Then she smacks him hard.

"Ouch."

Man, that should not do things to me.

"You deserved that," Jazz grumbles.

"What for?"

"For being an idiot."

Mags leans in to me.

"Take me home," I whisper, suddenly feeling the need to get out of here.

She wiggles her eyebrows. "You going to redecorate my face?" she whispers back.

I start to screw my face up, then realise she might be serious. "I, er…if you want me to."

Mags laughs. "If you're a good boy I might let you." She murmurs. "Or I was thinking we could prove Spencer wrong about the topping thing."

I try to keep my response subtle and not grab her and drag her home, but Jazz's rant at Spencer that we had tuned out cuts into our moment.

"What's crawled up your arse?" he asks her with no concern for the repercussions.

"Nothing," she replies, backing down. "I just don't feel too great and you're really getting on my nerves."

"Well what's wrong?" Spencer asks with a sigh, finally acknowledging it.

"I don't know. I just feel really queasy all of a sudden and I could do without you being a twat."

"Pft," He scoffs at the very idea. "You'd better not be pregnant."

It was typical Spencer flippancy, but the scowl that forms on Jazz's face tells me it's something he will live to regret. I almost feel sorry for him.

"And just what the hell is that supposed to mean?" she

snaps.

Spencer doesn't even have time to think of a reply before she lets rip on him.

"You know what, save it. If that's your attitude, I don't want to hear it."

"But—"

Jazz stands abruptly, effectively cutting him off and turns to leave.

"You're not are you?" Spencer blurts, sounding uncharacteristically desperate.

Jazz turns around and glares, emotion about to spill over. "Would it matter? Doesn't seem like you'd be interested anyway."

With that, she storms off.

Ten seconds of stunned silence follows.

"I'd better go after her," Mags says, getting her bag.

"I'll come with you." I don't hesitate, getting up with her.

"Sit," she commands.

I sit down instantly, staring at her in disbelief. Did she just Domme me in front of everyone? My cheeks flush and my dick gets hard.

Fuck.

She probably didn't mean it that way, but so what?

I nod, speechless, and stay in my seat. When I look at JJ, he looks surprised.

"Impressive," he nods in approval. "I always knew she had it in her."

"What the fuck was that?" Spencer asks oblivious, as I watch Mags disappear into the pub.

"You were just an idiot." I shake my head, trying to push

aside my need. “Big shocker.”

JJ takes a sip of his drink, looking as if he feels like an intruder. I feel awkward for him. This is not a good introduction into our group dynamic.

“Sorry, it’s not usually like this,” I offer.

“It’s fine. You did me a favour getting me out of that date, this is decidedly more appealing, trust me.”

“Is she…” Spencer drifts off and stares in the direction she went. “She couldn’t be p—” He swallows, forcing out the word. “Pregnant. Could she?”

“Sure seems like you touched a nerve.” JJ grimaces.

“Just let Mags calm her down. And for fucks sake get your shit together before you next open your mouth.”

You can see the moment when he closes in on himself and can’t process any more. “I’m going home,” he mutters and gets up slowly, dragging himself home with the weight of the world on his shoulders.

JJ whistles, shaking his head. “And I thought my date was bad.”

Surveying the damage, as I walk down the hall into the kitchen, I decide to check on Mags before I clean up. I pull out my phone and open a text.

‘How are things there?’

‘Well let’s see…Jazz threw up. Then she
cried. Then she started packing while
crying and now she’s throwing up again.’

'Packing?'

'Yep, she's convinced herself she needs to go back to London to think.'

'Shit.'

'Yeah.'

'She's adamant. I don't think I can stop her, she's really upset. I think I'll go with her, just for the night. I'm worried about her and I don't want her to be on her own.'

'Of course, you should definitely go with her.'

'How's Spencer?'

'We need a new living room door.'

'Oh shit.'

'And judging by the dent and the glass everywhere and the beer still dripping down the wall in the kitchen, I'd say he got himself a drink and then decided he wasn't in the mood.'

'Fuck, Will please don't get in his way. I don't want you to be the next thing he punches.'

'It's okay Mags, I can look after myself.'

'Where is he now?'

'Shut in his room, he was already there when I got home. You don't think she is do you?'

'Pregnant? No. She is on the pill. She's just in shock at his reaction.'

'Not 100% though is it?'

'No, I guess not. She is highly emotional and puking. Maybe when we get home I'll run out and get a test to be sure.'

'It's probably a good idea. It will put this whole mess to bed to know she's not.'

'Will it though? Even if she isn't, he can't take that reaction back.'

'I know. He's a dick.'

'Yeah he is. Look, I've got to go. I'll let

you know we got home ok.'

'Okay, drive safe.'

Mags

SATURDAY 19TH SEPTEMBER

"I'm really sick. I can't come in while I'm like this." Jazz tells whoever has answered the phone in her weak voice. "Yeah I know…will you guys be ok?…A couple of days at least, I can't be around food prep right now…I'll let you know…Okay, call me if you need anything…Thanks, bye." Jazz hangs up the phone and flops back on her pillows.

"Everything okay?"

"Yeah, they'll be fine for a few days."

"Good, now we just need to sort you out."

Jazz groans and pulls the cover over herself.

She isn't in any fit state to talk right now, so I back out of the room. I only let her call in sick herself because she demanded the phone and got all teary when I tried to argue. Apparently, she's the boss and should be setting an example so the apology needs to come from her. I've never seen her this emotional. She can play down her feelings for Spencer, but this speaks volumes.

As soon as I shut the door, I hear her feet thump to the floor and run to the bathroom, but I leave her to it. I can't do anything but watch and who wants that? Besides, I'm here for her, but I'm determined not to get sick.

I flick the switch on the kettle and set one mug on the

counter. She is hardly keeping water down, so she won't be having tea. Taking out my phone while I wait for the water to boil, I contemplate what I'm going to tell Will. Jazz isn't pregnant, she has a fever and a stomach bug. She'd have to be seriously unlucky to be knocked up on top of this crap. She doesn't want me to tell Will though because she thinks he'll tell Spencer. She wants him kept in the dark to punish him.

I'm not sure that's fair though.

Mostly because I know Will is going to ask me and I'm not going to lie to him.

So here I am, not talking to him so I can avoid the conversation.

This is bullshit.

We're adults. I can put my concerned boyfriend's mind at rest and ask that he doesn't tell anyone.

Fuck, I could order him not to tell anyone and it would be ironclad. But I'm not going to do that. I don't need to. We have trust. Right?

I shiver when it occurs to me that I just called him my boyfriend. I know it's a fact, I just haven't really had chance to test the title out. It seems a bit juvenile, like it's not significant enough for what he is. But I think it's too early to be thinking about alternatives. For now, boyfriend it is, and the sappy teen in me likes it a lot. I don't know why it hasn't dawned on me I can call him that. I guess I've just been wrapped up in all the other things I've been calling him. I like those too don't get me wrong, but those are for us. Boyfriend, that's for everyone else. And yeah, he's mine, so I'm going to text him right now. If Jazz wants to punish Spencer, she can, but I want to say good morning to my *boyfriend*.

'Morning.'

'Morning, how is she?'

'She's okay. She's resting.'

'Did you get her to do a test?'

'No, I didn't need to. She really is just sick, she's had a fever. I just haven't seen her cry that much in a long time. Don't say anything to Spencer though, they need to talk it over themselves. What's he saying?'

'Nothing. He hasn't left his room since he got home from the pub.'

'Oh shit, he is still there right? He hasn't run off again?'

'I thought that too, but the car is here and I've heard him moving around.'

'Thank fuck.'

'Yeah.'

'Are you ok?'

'Yeah, I'm fine, just tired.'

'Didn't you sleep?'

'No, I slept like shit.'

'Why?'

There is a long pause before he starts typing.

'Yesterday was playing on my mind.'

'Don't worry, Jazz isn't pregnant. She was throwing up all night and shivering, this is a stomach bug.'

'No not that part. They can sort themselves out.'

'What then?'

A couple of minutes pass and he doesn't even start typing. All kinds of things start running through my head trying to think what it could be. Did I upset him?

'Will?'

'It's selfish of me. You need to be there for Jazz.'

'Are you upset with me for being here?'

'No, not at all!'

'Well what then?'

'It's just that you called it home. You said, I'm going to go home with Jazz.'

'Oh.'

He goes quiet again and I don't know what to say. It's hard to reassure him when I haven't spoken to Jazz about this stuff yet. So much has happened, I was just waiting for things to settle down before we discussed finding a place to live. I don't know what she wants to do yet. When I look down, he is finally typing.

'I'm being stupid, it's good that you had somewhere to go if Jazz felt like she needed to get away. It just makes me feel like you being here is temporary.'

'I don't see it as temporary.'

'Well if it's permanent, you won't need to keep that place anymore will you?'

I grin. It's a slow realisation that he is showing me what he really wants. He wants to know that I am there to stay, of course. But he could have just asked straight up. I think he's giving it to me with a pout like that so that I'll know how to treat it. He could have gone about it a different way, but he's sulking and sulking is something he needs to be corrected on.

He's pushing me to get what he wants.

When he feels insecure, he wants me to be an authority, not a comfort.

God this is a responsibility.

My silence has obviously added to his insecurity because he's typing again.

'I'm sorry, I don't mean to push you. I
know you'll do what you think is right.
I'm just overthinking.'

'I like to know what you're thinking.'

'I'm thinking about you. You're never off
my mind.'

I grip the edge of the counter for support. Wow. Right when I need to summon the Goddess, I squee on the inside. It's not very dominant of me I know, but it does things to my inner romantic that he thinks like this. Luckily he can't see me because I have a role to play and I really think he needs it right now.

Fuck, it's hard to just take that loveliness and not return it.

Come on Mags, he's thinking about you, you're never off his mind, that deserves a reward, and not the lovey dovey kind. Do it.

'Good. Now, I'll be HOME soon, but I'm going to stay here with Jazz today. You'll be ok without me won't you?'

'No. I'll miss you.'

'*Fists your hair* You wouldn't be pouting would you boy?'

'Oh god.'

'I think you'll find it's Goddess actually.'

The clock tells me it's 4 pm and I sigh heavily. I hadn't realised how accustomed I had become to working in my spot on the terrace, but these four walls are closing in. Knowing that I have already bled out all the words I'm likely to get for now, I close my laptop and get up to make more tea. I was at least disciplined enough to leave my phone on the counter, so my word count isn't bad today.

After making a tea, I check my phone. There's a message from Will.

'I've been thinking about this mess all day and I'm so disappointed in Spencer. The way he reacted was terrible and I don't blame Jazz for hating him. I just wanted you to know, if that happened to us, you would never have to wonder if I would be

there for you. I love you. I would never let
you go through something like this alone.’

I almost drop my tea. I put it down on the counter with a bump, spilling a good amount. Shit. Throwing my phone down, I clear up the mess, even though it really isn’t important, it just seems like the most important thing right now. It seems easier than processing what he just said. One minute he needs me to help through how he’s feeling and the next he knocks me completely off my feet with that. Holy shit.

I need to sit down.

I slide to the floor and drop my head back, hitting the cupboard door with a loud thud. “Ouch.”

“You okay?” Jazz croaks, shuffling into the kitchen looking dazed and confused with her duvet wrapped around her.

“Yeah, I’m good.”

She looks down puzzled, trying to figure out why I’m on the floor, but it’s too much for her to think about, so she sinks down opposite me, curling up in her duvet.

“Why are we on the floor?” she asks, closing her eyes.

“I just needed to sit down for a minute.”

“Sure you’re okay?” she asks, her voice heavy with sleep.

I look down at my phone again and blow out a breath. “Yeah, I’m fine, how are you feeling?”

Jazz lifts her head and peels open one eyelid, eyeing me suspiciously. “You don’t sound very fine, did something happen?”

I allow a small smile to form. “Nothing bad.”

“Oh?”

I reach forward and check her temperature with the back of my hand. "You look a little better. Would you like something to eat?"

She shakes her head. "I'll take a tea though."

"Go and lay on the sofa. I just need to send a quick text, I'll bring you one in."

"K," she replies, half heartedly trying to get up.

I have to help her to her feet before I can send her into the living room, then I turn my attention straight back to my phone.

'I love you too. So much. I'm sorry I didn't reply, I put my phone down to write.'

'That's ok, I guessed you had. I just wanted to tell you, that's all.'

'It was a lovely message to come back to. Thank you.'

'Will you be coming back tonight?'

'No, she's been sick all day, she won't be up to it, so we will stay here, sorry. She just woke up. I need to see if she is ok.'

'Alright. Tell her I hope she feels better.'

'Text me when you finish work?'

'Okay.'

I'm sure he's disappointed that we aren't coming home, but I can only deal with one thing at a time.

I tip the rest of my tea in the sink and make two fresh ones, carrying them into the living room. Jazz is half sitting, half curled in a ball at one end of the sofa, so I put her tea down on the end table by her head, taking a seat at the other end of the sofa.

"Thank you," she says softly, without opening her eyes.

"How do you feel?"

She lifts her head and slowly forces herself to sit up enough to lift her tea. "Like crap." She sips it and swallows, pausing to see if that changes how she feels. When it seems to have no effect, she looks at me. "I haven't thrown up for a few hours though, so that's something."

"Have you thought about talking to—"

"Don't say his name." Jazz stops me in my tracks. "He's done."

"Just like that?"

Jazz calmly drinks some more tea. "He showed me who he really is. I can't unsee it."

"But you aren't pregnant, Jazz."

"And what if I was huh? Accidents happen Mags and he just showed me I would be totally on my own if I was."

"Maybe not. It was a flippant remark. You don't know what he would do if it was true."

"Does he know it isn't true?"

"No."

"Well, I don't see him anywhere," she says waving around

the room. "Do you?"

"No." I have no choice but to concede on that point. If he thinks she is pregnant, he isn't by her side.

"Has he asked about me?"

"Not that I know of," I admit.

"Well that's that then, isn't it?"

"I doubt it very much." It's never going to be that simple with them.

Silence falls over us. What if she's right? What will that mean for Will and I if Jazz and Spencer go back to not being able to be in the same postcode?

"Don't worry," she says as if reading my mind. "I'm not bailing. I have everything I want there. My shop, you, Will. I'm not going to quit on that because Spencer's mask slipped and I saw the real him. He'll have to just avoid me, because I'm not going anywhere." She drinks her tea quietly. "This is good."

I nod and wrap my hands around the warm mug. I feel like I need the comfort.

"Care to explain why were you on the kitchen floor when I woke up?"

Chewing the inside of my lip I try to decide if I can tell her I was just blown away by my boyfriend telling me he would never do to me, what her boyfriend is doing to her.

"Spill," she says spotting my hesitance.

"It doesn't matter, I just got a nice message from Will and it…"

"Melted you to a literal puddle on the kitchen floor?"

I giggle. "Yeah, that."

"Aww, let's hear it then."

"No."

"Oh my god, why not?"

"I…"

"Mags, we share everything, secrets are not acceptable," she demands.

"But, you…"

"No buts. Don't do that tiptoeing shit you do to protect my feelings. You know that pisses me off way more than what you are trying to protect me from."

"But your boyfriend is being a wanker, you don't need to see mine being all sweet."

"I need to see it especially because he's being a wanker. I need something to cheer me up. Now hand it over."

"Ugh, my God you are so demanding when you're sick. Here." I hand her my phone, open on the messages from Will. "Don't say I didn't warn you."

She takes my phone and reads through the thread of messages. Her eyes bulge out,

"See, I warned you."

"No, it's not that. Since when are we on I love you's?"

I think about it. "A couple of weeks."

"Couple of fucking weeks? And you didn't think to tell me?"

"I was going to. I've just been getting used to the idea."

"Mags, it's so obvious you're head over heels for each other. We're used to it, why the hell aren't you?"

"Because…it's a bit soon isn't it?"

"Not for you two, no."

"Really?

Jazz drinks her tea, thinking.

"Can I share an observation?" she asks cautiously.

"Sure," I shrug. Like I could stop her.

"It turns out there was a lot I didn't know about you, when I thought I knew every bit of you."

Okay, that's possibly true.

"Everything made so much more sense when I found out about Will."

"So?"

"So, stop dicking around and roll with it. Jesus!"

"I am."

"No, you're hiding it from me, which means you're hiding from it."

"It's a few words."

"A few words," she scoffs. "They are *the* words. Poor Will," she mutters shaking her head.

"Why poor Will?" I huff.

"You know why. You are the most loving, giving person I know Mags, but you haven't let anyone into your heart in all the years I've known you. I know Will was the one that made you guard it so fiercely, but are you really going to keep it guarded form him now?"

"I'm not keeping it guarded. I'm really opening it up."

"And that terrifies you?"

"Completely. But I'm letting it happen."

"Good."

"Now, what about you?"

"What about me." She frowns.

"Do you have some words you need to say to a certain dickhead I'm not allowed to name?"

"I have nothing to say to him."

"Is it okay to just let him think you might be pregnant though?"

"It's ok with me. He deserves to sweat."

"I don't know," I confess. "Sure, let him sweat over your anger and whether he has lost you. I'm not sure if it's fair to use unplanned fatherhood against him."

"If he bothers to ask, I will put him straight. If he's as selfish as he looks right now and doesn't try to find out, I'm not going looking for him."

"Jazz?"

"Yes?" she snaps.

"Why are you so angry?"

"Because," she huffs. "You heard what he said."

"I did. Can I have a turn with the observations now?"

"Whatever."

"Maybe you need to say *the* words as well."

"What? No! I have no plans to make any declarations. Especially not now."

"I get that. Here's the thing though. If there's no love lost, his stupid comment last night could have been handled very differently. Your reaction tells me you love him."

Jazz scoffs.

"You were gutted because even though you aren't in that place yet, he just shattered your dream."

"I am not dreaming about getting knocked up by that bastard."

"Liar. You may not have actively thought it, but somewhere in that brain of yours there was hope for the future, even if you didn't know it." I nod, marking my words as fact. "You say you feel sick and he hits you with a warning you didn't even know you needed. And it scared you. Now you feel as though you can't trust him to support you if you need him to."

She looks bored. "And your point is?"

"You love him. And maybe you should tell him that so that he knows what you want from him."

"I don't want a thing from him. We've been together a month Mags. One."

"So? Will just said it to me and we've been together half that."

"Oh please, you and Will have years behind you, you're on the fast track."

I raise my eyebrows. "You and Spencer have been dancing around each other for what? Three months, longer maybe. So what that you only stopped playing games a few weeks ago, it's not like you just met, these feelings have been building for a while."

Jazz picks some imaginary fluff off the duvet and flicks it away.

"He's great with the boyfriend/girlfriend stuff. You're his, he's yours, he gets to have sex with you any time he wants and he isn't even looking at other girls. But that's an unformed state, it can't go on like that endlessly. He needs to know how you feel, at least then he would know what the expectations are moving forward. I don't think he would have been so careless with his words if he knew."

"I don't think it should make a difference. I shouldn't have to explain to him that I expect him to support me when I need it. If he cares even a little bit, he should do that anyway."

I hold my hands up. "You're right. He should."

"Thank you."

"But people say and do things in the heat of the moment that they shouldn't. You of all people should know that. Please don't write him off until you see what his next move is."

Jazz lets out a heavy sigh.

SATURDAY 19TH SEPTEMBER

"We have a situation," I say urgently into my phone.

"What is it?" Mags sounds concerned.

"Spencer just announced he's going to go and talk to Jazz and left. That's the first thing he's said all day. I thought he was stewing, but he's perfectly calm, kind of contrite in fact. He didn't ask if she was home, he just assumed. I don't know what to do. I don't know how he will react when he realises she isn't at the house, but he is going to ask me a whole bunch of uncomfortable questions."

"Oh shit."

"What am I going to tell him when he comes back?"

"Tell him we aren't there and that he should call Jazz."

"You think she will answer?"

"I have no idea, but it isn't our problem."

"Yeah, well it's going to be my problem in a minute because he'll know I've talked to you."

"Just tell him to call Jazz and let them figure it out. She told me she would be honest if he bothered to try and find out how she was."

I hear Spencer's car pulling back in to the driveway. "Okay, I gotta go," I tell her hastily, pressing end on the call.

"Where are they?" he demands.

Here we go, this is going to be rough. I straighten up, trying not to look like I know too much. “Jazz was pretty upset mate. She took off last night, Mags went with her to make sure she was okay. You should call her.”

“What? Why didn't you tell me?”

“You haven't said shit since the pub. I was just letting you cool down.”

“I was letting *her* cool down.”

“Do you think that was a good idea?” I ask, genuinely interested. I just can’t fathom not being there for someone if I thought there was even the smallest chance they were pregnant with my child, but that’s just me.

He looks at me at a loss for a moment, then scratches his head. “Where are they? The apartment? Her parents?” he asks, calmly ignoring my question. “It will save me a lot of time if you tell me.”

“Just call her mate.” There’s nothing else I can really say. I turn away and head upstairs, because this is not my problem. I do feel really bad for him. He pulls out a chair and sits at the kitchen table. I was expecting more of a fight, maybe he is going to call her.

Jesus those two are a mess.

‘I’m back.’

‘How did it go?’

‘I told him to call her and I think he might.’

‘That's it?’

'Yeah, I mean he might be calling her now, is she with you? '

'No she's in her room. We have to let them sort out.'

'I hope they do it soon. I want you to come home.'

I open up my contacts, and choose Mags, looking at the photo of her I picked for her contact image, then I take a deep breath and hit video call.

"Hello?" Her voice plays into the air before her face appears on screen.

I wait until I can finally see her before I say, "Hi."

She smiles shyly, it's something she only does when I take charge of the situation, which is not very often. I fucking love it, because it's a break from wondering if I'm acting the right way. She wasn't expecting me to call, especially not video, so I get to see her off guard which is a nice turnaround.

"I just wanted to see your face."

"I miss you," she says. "I know it's only one day, but I miss you."

I smile with relief. "Oh good, it's not just me then."

She shakes her head. "I can't wait to come home." She emphasises home like she did in her text earlier and my stomach churns.

Apologise you nit-wit.

"I'm sorry, you didn't deserve that stuff about home this

morning."

She brings the phone closer so that just her face is in the frame and she looks straight into the camera and my eyes, cutting me off. "Please don't apologise, Will. Not for that. You were right, this isn't really my home anymore." Then her face softens with a smile again. "I just want to see you."

"I want to see you too, can't you just come back?"

"I thought about it," she looks guiltily over her shoulder at her bedroom door, which I can see is closed. "I really should be here for Jazz though, and besides, I'm trying to be a grown up. I should be able to last a couple of days without seeing you."

"No you shouldn't." I smirk. "Adulting is overrated."

She shakes her head, laughing disapprovingly. "Are you sulking again boy?"

Hearing her say it so naturally and not in the voice she puts on for play, makes me groan involuntarily.

She lowers her voice. "Such an easy thing to get to you."

I laugh nervously and try to relieve the strain in my jeans subtly.

"You should take those off if they're uncomfortable," she says casually.

I stare at my phone wondering if she's serious, knowing deep down of course she is. I resist my natural questioning response and decide for once to live dangerously. Without saying another word, I get up and lock my door, turning to face her. Her silence tells me she is as surprised as I am that I'm going to do it, but that just makes it more exciting.

Slowly, I strip my top off and then unbutton my jeans dropping them to the floor.

"Are you hard?" she asks.

"Yeah," I reply, stroking myself through my boxers.

"Show me."

I love how her simple commands affect me, even over the phone. And I love it even more that following them feels so freeing. I slide my fingers into the waistband of my boxers and slide them over my erection and down my legs.

"Mmmmm," she hums. "Touch it."

I wrap my hand around my shaft as I walk towards her, crawling onto the bed and kneeling in front of her.

"Shuffle back a tiny bit, I want to see all of you."

I do she says and sit back on my heels settling into position.

"That's better, now stroke it for me."

I want to ask her to take her clothes off too. I want to hear how wet she is when she slides her fingers in and out of herself. But having her full attention on me like this and performing for her, is almost better than doing it together might be. I decide to say nothing and just enjoy this feeling. My mind wonders as my eyes close.

When she speaks it startles me.

"Imagine my hands on your body while you touch yourself."

My breath catches and I nod.

"Where do you see them?" she asks.

I say the first thing in my head. "My throat."

She makes a sound of approval. "I love that," she whispers. "Where is my other hand while I squeeze your throat?"

Her voice gives away her need, but I can't look her. I can't open my eyes. Instead I let my hand move unrestrained and my mind go free, as if I was alone. There, I find an answer.

"My balls," I manage in a gravelly murmur.

"Hmmm and what would it to be doing to them?" she asks seductively.

I don't know how to answer, I feel gripped like her hand is really wrapped around my throat and the intense pleasure of my hand jerking my cock is too distracting. She answers for me before I have to think too hard.

"Am I stroking them? Hmm? Caressing them gently to heighten your pleasure."

"That's good." I sigh, feeling it like she is really here.

"Or would you like them tugged a little. Just enough to make you wince?"

I flinch slightly and hear her sadistic little chuckle.

"You'd like that too wouldn't you?"

I nod vigourously. "I don't know what's wrong with me," I whisper. "The wrongest stuff gets me going."

"There's nothing wrong with you," she reassures me. "You like to be dominated that's all. You like me on top."

I nod again working my hand faster.

"And it doesn't matter who puts what where, no matter what *he* says, trust me I own you."

"Oh god," I moan too loudly.

"You're mine." She growls possessively.

"I'm yours," I whisper.

"Hmm, where should I stroke after I've finished with your balls?" She ponders deliberately, it's obvious she knows her next move already. "Would you like to feel me to stroke further back?"

"Oh god yes." I shudder.

"Two fingers this time?"

"I want them… inside me," I stammer, grasping for air, while I bring myself closer. I find no shame in saying it either. Only need.

"Yeah? Tell me about that," she demands.

"I want…I want…" I can hardly get the words out, I feel ready to come and I'm fighting it hard.

"Tell me," she demands firmly, helping to bring me back to her from where I was lost somewhere close to the edge.

"I want you to finger me," I manage. Somehow the thought becomes easier to deal with as soon as it's out.

"Oh fuck," she sighs. "That sounds really dirty."

I squeeze my eyes tighter because if I look at her I will lose it.

Now that I've found my voice though, I find I have more to say. And random thoughts in my head are now lining up to be heard for the first time. I slow my hand to allow me to focus and once I feel I have it under control, I open my eyes to see her reaction when I tell her what I want.

I swallow. "I want you to fuck me."

"With my fingers?" she asks wondering if she understands me correctly.

I shake my head. "You know what with." Referring to the brand new strap-on she bought which has so far stayed in the box.

She makes a throaty sound and leans in close to the camera. "Are you sure you can handle it? Most men couldn't."

I allow my hand to move faster again.

"Yes," I gasp. "I can handle you fucking me. I want you to."

"We'll see," she teases.

"Oh fuck," I groan. I'm so close, I lean back resting my free hand on the bed behind me, and thrust my cock into my hand as it twists over my head and back down to the base, again and again. Mags watches me like this for a minute until I'm about ready to blow. I don't ask. I know she will tell me when.

"Feel my hands on you," she tells me softly. "Your throat," she pauses. "Feel that?"

And I do, closing my eyes I do feel her hand on my throat. I nod once in confirmation.

"Good boy," she whispers. "Now come."

Shuddering I let go. Stroking myself through my release. It's a struggle not to collapse back onto the bed, but I want to stay where she can see me.

"I could watch you come all day," she says. "Maybe one day we will have to see how many times I can make that happen."

I can only moan between panting breaths, that's all I'm capable of right now. I try to sit back up, but find I need to fall forward onto my hand for support because my trembling legs won't hold me, all the while still stroking my dick slowly.

"That was good," she says encouragingly.

Yeah, it was. Very good. "I don't know what's happening to me," I pant. "The stuff that used to make my toes curl from embarrassment, like the thought of having phone sex for example, video phone sex no less, now seems perfectly okay. And with Spencer downstairs as well. Jesus." I shake my head. "We need some time alone."

"Yeah, that would be so nice," she agrees.

I try to focus on her now that I can breathe. "I'll work on

it, I promise."

SUNDAY 20TH SEPTEMBER

Sitting at the garden table, pouring over Spencer's draft for the house plans, I'm startled by her voice.

"Knock knock," she says with a hint of humour standing behind me.

"Who's there?" I laugh.

"I missed you."

"I missed you too." I smile jumping up.

She steps forward throwing her arms around my neck and laughs. "No silly it's supposed to be 'I missed you who'."

"Who cares, just kiss me."

Her lips meet mine and I relax into the safety of her arms.

Spencer gets up quickly and I hear him collect his keys from the hook inside the kitchen door on his way out through the side gate, the way Mags let herself in.

I slowly lift her up, so that her legs wrap around my waist.

"I've missed you so much," I whisper against her lips.

"Show me how much," she whispers back.

I kick the chair out of my path and take her inside the house, setting her down on the kitchen table.

"He didn't come home last night. So either they made up, or she murdered him," Will says stroking my back.

"She hasn't murdered him," I assure him. "Trust me, if she had she would have called me to help her dispose of the body."

"Good point." His chest rumbles beneath my head with his laugh. "I hope she hasn't. If ever there was a person capable of inspiring homicidal thoughts, he's the man, and I don't want you doing any time."

"Don't worry we wouldn't get caught. You feed it to the pigs, they eat everything. No evidence."

"Okay…" he says warily. "That's…reassuring."

"Not just a pretty face," I laugh. "Don't you need to get up?'

"I should, I just don't want to."

"I should go home and see how Jazz is."

"No, leave them to sort it out," he growls wrapping his arms and legs around me in protest. "Spencer is still there. You'll be intruding."

As the words leave his mouth, we hear Spencer letting himself in downstairs

I burst out laughing at the irony.

"Fine, go," he sulks, throwing his arms open.

I turn to him, poking the tip of his nose. “There’s a good boy.”

“How are you feeling?” I ask Jazz, finding her sitting in the kitchen when I return home.

“I’m feeling so much better,” Jazz says. And I can hear it in her voice.

“Good I'm glad. Now you better hope that you haven't given it to me,” I narrow my eyes at her.

“That's what Spencer said. Bastards. You’re all so full of sympathy.”

“Awwww, I'm sorry, little one.” I ruffle her hair. “So, did you make up or break up?”

She sighs and smiles.

I chuckle shaking my head. “You two are the absolute worst I swear. What did he have to say for himself?”

“Let’s just say, it was enough,” she says being cagey.

“You wouldn’t be hiding from it would you?” I accuse her, using her words from yesterday against her.

“No,” she groans. “I’m not hiding from anything, it’s just that I’m still processing what he said and it feels wrong not holding it close for a while. Do you know what I mean?”

“Funnily enough, I know exactly what you mean.” I give her a flat look and she winces.

“Touché, I’m an arsehole.”

“Bingo.” I click my fingers and laugh.

“You’re an arsehole too.” She laughs.

“Yep, now did he really say enough? I don’t want you cagey because deep down you know he didn’t say what he should have said.”

"He said enough." She smiles fondly. "He said more than he needed to."

My eyebrows raise. "Any declarations?"

She shakes her head. "Not *the* words no, but in his way he let me know that I'm the most important thing in the world to him."

"Okay." I nod. "If you are satisfied, then I am too. But this won't be happening again," I warn her.

"He is disgusted with himself Mags. He said that it was some knee-jerk reaction that he would have come out with five years ago around his mates, when pregnancy scared the shit out of all of them and his school friend had screwed himself out of his late teens by knocking a girl up with twins. That's not how he feels now, he just didn't think. It won't happen again."

"That's good." I walk over to where she's sitting and pull her face to my chest, hugging her. I'm glad it's all sorted out. Fucking relieved if truth be told. She wraps her arms around my waist and I can feel her relief. "Why did he take so long?"

"He said he realised he'd fucked up right away and there was a moment he was so angry with himself that he broke some stuff, which he isn't proud of," she says breaking the hug. "He realised that I might really need his support and be out there, potentially pregnant, angry and alone and he was so disappointed in himself, he couldn't face me.

"So then why didn't he call you when Will told him to?"

"He said he was taking some time to think about whether he could really be the person I would need if in fact I did need him."

"And?"

"And he's ready"

"For what?"

Jazz blows out a breath. "From the way he was talking last night, ready for anything."

"Uh oh, sounds like someone wants to put a bun in that oven."

"I think now that the idea is out there, he thinks it's on the table. But trust me, this oven needs pre-heating first."

I roll my eyes. "Men!"

"I know right?"

"You don't hate the idea though, look at your face!" I laugh and she shoves me.

"Arsehole."

"Takes one to know one."

FRIDAY 25TH SEPTEMBER

"Okay, see you then. Thanks. Bye." Mags hangs up the phone and sighs deeply.

"Everything alright?"

She jumps a little and touches her hand to her chest. "Oh you scared me."

"Sorry, I came in and you were on the phone. I didn't want to interrupt you."

She smiles holding her arms open to me. Except, when I step into her embrace, I don't feel any warmth. Her body is as tense as her voice on the phone sounded and I start to get a bad feeling. Truth be told, I've had it all week. It's small things.

Like Monday, when I had to go down to mum and dad's with paperwork for the house that I need them to sign. I wanted to see her when I got home, but she told me in advance I'd be tired and she could see me Tuesday. I felt at the time I could decide for myself if I was too tired or not, but I let it go because maybe she had work to do that she was too polite to mention.

Tuesday, she had a headache and didn't want me to look after her, she just wanted to sleep.

Wednesday, I was busy. She didn't seem to mind.

Thursday, I managed to get some time with her, but she seemed quiet.

And now here we are Friday and I don't know if I'm just looking for it, but I definitely feel something is off.

"You seem tense." I soften in her arms, hoping she will do the same, but to no avail.

"I'm fine," she says semi-cheerfully, pulling away and busying herself filling the kettle.

"Mags."

She turns, looking preoccupied.

I frown. "What's wrong?"

She gives me a tight smile. "That was the magazine people, just arranging times."

"Is that why you're so tense?"

She sighs. "I guess."

I slip my arms around her waist. "Can I help?"

"It's fine," she says quickly. "I just need to get it over and done with."

"When is it?"

"A week today."

"I could be here if you like? Make sure they don't stress you out too much."

"No!" she blurts, almost urgently. "I mean, you're busy, you don't need to hold my hand. I can handle Veronica."

"Okay," I pull her against my chest and I decide to drop the subject for now, trying not to feel too concerned about what could just be an off week.

Will
FRIDAY 2ND OCTOBER

I feel like I've barely seen Mags since we finished the job at the house. First we had the Spencer and Jazz drama. Then between driving up and down from mum and dad's with paperwork that needs to be signed and working on plans for the new house with Spencer, I've barely had a free evening. We have had a few heated debates about the spec I'm pushing for. Spencer thinks I'm aiming too high and I'm not budging. I want this house to be the best it can be.

Mags has been writing more which is great, because I think I've been taking her away from that a little too much lately. But it still sucks.

I decided I'm taking advantage of an unscheduled day off today, to go and surprise her. She's got the magazine people there and I know she said she doesn't need me, but I want to give her some moral support.

I let myself in to the kitchen as always and walk through into the hallway. A young girl and man are running through a checklist and making notes. "We've done the pool and the new wing. They are just finishing up with the rooms down here, we just need the kitchen as soon as the food arrives and the upstairs bedrooms," the girl says to the man. She looks up from her clipboard and eyes me with suspicion.

"Is Mags around?" I ask, purely to justify my presence.

"She's in the study."

"Okay, thank you." I walk on through and reach George's office as JJ is coming out laughing, followed by George and Mags and a very sharply dressed woman. Behind them, I can see a photographer and as assistant packing up equipment. "…thanks to this fine young man," George tells the woman, patting JJ on the back.

It's a harsh flashback to a time when my world changed in an instant. Things are different now, I remind myself. Mags loves you.

The group notices me standing there like a spare prick at a wedding.

"And who is *this* fine young man?" the woman, who is easily twice my age, asks flirtatiously, offering her hand.

"Hi, I'm Will," I shake it. "I'm—"

"Will is the builder who has done such a wonderful job on the extension," Mags interjects.

Spiky woman mutters congratulations but obviously loses interest immediately as soon as she finds out I am nobody and turns to George. "Well thank you for fitting me into your busy schedule George, it's a pleasure as always. I won't keep you from your flight, we will carry on shooting the rest of the house."

"Pleasure, Veronica, thank you." He air kisses her cheeks and she returns to her assistants in the study.

I am left speechless and my heart has sunk to my feet.

The builder? *Will is the builder…*

I see. JJ is a 'fine young man,' and I'm 'the builder.'

"What are you doing here?" Mags hisses, taking my elbow

and leading me back into the entrance hall and more specifically, the front door. I catch JJ and George exchanging an awkward knowing look as I am dragged away, which only adds to my humiliation.

"I came to give you some support, but…" *But you clearly don't want me here…But you're ashamed of me…But I knew I'd never be good enough for you when it counted…But of course, I won't say a word of this to you.* "But you're busy, so I'll go."

The worst part is, she doesn't try to stop me. Instead, she just says, "Okay. I'll see you tonight," as I make for the front door.

"Will, stop," JJ calls out as I jog down the steps. Painful memories of having had my heart shattered in that entrance hall once before and having to make exactly the same hasty escape, fill my head. Deep down, I knew this day would come, and yet I still wasn't ready.

"It's fine, JJ, Don't worry, I've got the message." I dismiss him without stopping or turning around. I have to get away from here.

"Will you wait up?" I hear his footsteps close on me and his arm wrapping around my shoulder. It's all I can do not to shake him off and hit him with all the frustration I feel.

"Please, just leave it, I'm fine."

He steers me away from my car and towards the garages. I glance down the driveway, where I can see my escape from this hell in the distance, but I don't have the energy to stop him and soon find myself being forced to sit on the bench behind the garage buildings where the gardener sometimes eats his lunch. At least we're out of sight of the house, so I feel like I can breathe a little.

"It's not what you think," he says pacing in front of me.

"She told that reporter woman I was the builder and couldn't get rid of me fast enough."

"She did it to protect you." JJ takes a seat beside me, his body turned towards mine.

I choke on a bitter laugh. "I'll be honest, I've never felt less protected." I stare out cross the acres. "It's funny, you never know when it's going to be over, do you? I really thought everything was fine. How stupid was I?"

"Don't jump to conclusions."

"I'm not JJ, she's been getting distant the last couple of weeks. I let myself think it was work and this interview stuff building up. I guess it was more than that."

"You have to understand, this isn't something she wants to do. She hates this aspect of her life."

"I don't understand. Why did they do this magazine thing then, if George knows Mags hates it so much."

"It's just something she has to do."

"Is it? Really?"

"It's necessary once in a while."

"But why?"

"Because, if you give them nothing, they will look for things. And if there is nothing of any note to find, they will make something up."

"Keep them sweet you mean?"

"Exactly."

"It's not exactly the tabloids JJ. It's a relatively classy magazine."

"That doesn't mean they won't dig around for gossip."

"Well why couldn't she just be honest and tell them she has me?"

"Because that Veronica is an absolute viper. She would be all over you to find a story."

"I have nothing to hide."

"No, but are you really ready for the invasion into your personal life? *If* you're squeaky clean, the very least you can expect is 'Millionaire Heiress Trades Down' type headlines." He waves his hand in the air to indicate the size of the headline. "Picture it, you're in the post office and you glance over at the magazines and see, 'Margot Goldsmith, sole heiress to the Goldsmith fortune, dates builder."

It cuts like a knife to hear him say it aloud.

"They're only words Will, don't think they matter for a moment. You love each other, that's what counts. Your face right now though, as pretty as it is, tells me you couldn't handle seeing it left and right. Think about it, you'll have to call your mum and warn her not to listen to what they're saying. You'll have to brief your entire family about sly journos calling them up to get some dirt from the weakest link. It's no fun, trust me. Why do you think I'm still single?"

I sit in silence, all my old, seemingly irrational fears realised in one horrifying conversation.

"So it's hopeless? Is that what you're telling me?"

"Not at all. She is protecting you, that's all."

"How do we move forward though? She will always have to hide me, it can't work can it?"

"She only needs to protect you this time. Once they print this little glimpse into the Goldsmith life, they will leave them alone for a year or two. By then you'll be in a different place.

You'll be so far down the line that you won't care and old venomous Veronica won't be able to throw shade on a long established relationship. Who knows, the next time you have to deal with her, you might be choosing to share some happy news." JJ winks.

"I admire your optimism JJ, but there is a long way to go before any of that could happen. I mean, I don't know how George really feels about Mags and I being together. I've barely seen him since we became official and he hasn't expressed any kind of opinion. I mean, he is fine with me and happy with the work we did, but as for dating his daughter…to be honest, I don't even know what Mags has told him and I'm too afraid to ask. Maybe he thinks we're just friends. Maybe I'm just kidding myself."

JJ laughs loudly. "Something you need to know about Mags is how close she is with her dad. If it's happening in her life, he knows about it."

"Doesn't mean he's happy about it. It's not me he calls son," I return pointedly.

JJ inclines his head. "A man can have many sons, Will."

I try not to sound bitter when I laugh at his suggestion. "Please. You're the son he never had, I'm just the one he could get lumped with."

JJ raises his brows. "George Goldsmith does not get lumped with anything, or any one."

"Until his daughter has a chance meeting with an ex he was probably glad to see the back of, you mean."

Shaking his head, he puts his hand on my shoulder. "You really think that was a chance meeting?"

My brow furrows and I watch him closely.

He says nothing.

"Are you saying it wasn't?"

"Let me ask you something. Did George, or did he not, seek you out to do this work?"

"He did."

"Did he, or did he not ask Mags to supervise the work and live in the house while he travelled a lot this summer?"

"He did."

"Well then." He nods. "I think it would be a gross underestimation of his intelligence to not assume that your chance meeting was in fact put into motion by a father who could see his daughter was missing something in her life and recognised exactly what that something was."

"Me?" I ask, placing my hand to my chest. I can't believe what he is saying.

"Yes you." He smiles.

"No way."

"It's true."

"So *you* think." I scoff.

"So George *told* me."

"Oh my god."

"No, not God, George, although they do share some qualities." He laughs.

I stare into the distance.

"All I'm saying is, if it's approval you're looking for, Will, you've had it all along."

I have no words.

JJ looks at his watch. "I'd better get back in there. As soon as they're finished, I have to take them to the stables to shoot there. Just think about what I've said." He pats my knee. Then he stands and without another word, he walks back to the house.

I handled everything wrong. My heart aches and I want to cry, but I know it won't help him or us. I have to tell him how sorry I am. I have to find him first. I grab my keys and head out the door, stopping dead when I see his car parked in front of the garages.

He came back?

I walk over to the car, expecting to find him sat in the driver's seat, but the car is empty. Maybe he took a walk home to think. Who could blame him? He had a lot to think about. JJ told me that he talked to him, but he couldn't promise me things would be ok. I've been worried sick and it took forever to get rid of Veronica and her team. They are finishing off at the stables now.

I was going to his house to look for him, but since his car is here I doubt he would be there. The last thing I want to do right now is have any kind of conversation by text or phone, but I have to find him. I call him. My heart sinks when it rings and then goes to voicemail.

Now what?

I decide to go back in the house. Maybe I need to involve Jazz and Spencer. I'm just not ready to admit to them what I did to him.

I open my contacts again once I am inside, hovering over Jazz. Perhaps I should just try texting him first. Even if he doesn't want to talk, he deserves to know how sorry I am.

'Will, I'm so sorry. I'll explain if you'll let me. Just please know how much I love you and that I did it for us.'

I put my phone on the coffee table and throw myself onto the stupid cushions arranged 'just so' by dad's interior designer for the shoot. Fuck the shoot, I sit up and hurl a cushion across the room. The next cushion is only saved by the buzz of my phone.

'I know you did. JJ explained it to me.'

'I should have told you myself.'

'It's done now.'

My chest tightens. No it can't be done. I have to see him, prove to him that I was trying to protect him.

'Where are you?'

'Down at the pool.'

I leap up, but then stop myself. Face to face we never seem to say what's on our minds. If I go down there, we might lose this chance to be honest.

'What are you doing there?'

'I needed to let off some steam, but I didn't want to go too far. I hope you don't mind.'

'Of course I don't mind.'

'Leaving felt too final.'

My eyes fill with tears and my hands shake.

'You've been distant.'

'I've been scared.'

'Scared of what?'

'Scared of losing you if this side of my life came too close to us.'

'I've felt you pushing me away, I've been trying to ignore this feeling of impending doom, but it wouldn't go away.'

'I haven't meant to. I'm so sorry.'

I know exactly what he is referring to. We got a new toy and it's still in the box. He keeps hinting at using it, but I kept putting him off. It just felt like more than we were ready for when I was so worried about getting past today.

'Will you come back in?'

'Can you give me a few? I just need to run, let it all out. I will come in, I promise.'

'Okay.'

I want to see him, but if he needs to let his frustration out first, I understand. I decide to go and get changed before he comes. I hate how I look for pretences today. I don't need him to see me like this and live the bad memories again. I want him to see the real me. *His* Mags.

In my bedroom, stripping off the clothes I'd used to become that 'society girl' today, feels fantastic. I select some underwear and slip it on. Some black lacy-edged boy shorts and the matching bra. I'm not trying to dress to seduce him. I'm really not expecting anything from him tonight. Just being here is more than I can ask for, I'll earn the rest back slowly.

When I look up and across the dusk lit garden, I see him on the treadmill through the window of the pool house. He is running full pelt.

I've never seen him running before. He has his t-shirt off and it's sexy as fuck the way his lithe body moves. I want to see it closer up. I know if I go down there, I won't be able to resist him. I'm aching for him just watching him from up here.

I want to watch him let go of his stress, help him unwind

and soothe his pain away and I want to be the one who gives him what he needs, not that treadmill. Suddenly, I abandon my plans to earn it all back slowly. If he turns me down, I'll be sad, but I'll understand. Though I don't think he will. Because I think he needs to do this as much as me. It's what we both need.

I don't bother to find clothes after all. Instead, I slip on my black silk robe.

I slip in through the door to the pool house quietly. I can hear the treadmill going and the pounding of his feet. I approach slowly. The way his body looked from up in my bedroom is nothing compared to the sight of it close up. He is spectacular. All the definition of the muscles on his back shining with sweat. Perfect.

I set my things down in the changing area. I don't know if he will want to play and I don't want him to think he has an obligation.

Leaning against one of the pillars I fold my arms, just watching, waiting. He is too beautiful to interrupt.

Eventually, he slows the speed down to a jog, and then to a walk. Finally, he stops, and breathlessly grabs a towel to wipe his face and his sweat soaked hair. When he looks into the mirrored wall in front of him, he notices me for the first time. His chest still rising and falling rapidly from the exertion, he stills and stares at my reflection.

I push off the pillar and walk towards him, taking the towel out of his hand and losing it on the weights bench behind him.

"Did you get what you needed?"

Will shakes his head. "I could run forever and it wouldn't

help. What I need is you."

I smile. And reach up to his face.

He pulls back, "I'm all sweaty."

"I don't care." I pull him in close, but let him close the distance. I'm desperate to know things will be ok, but I hurt him. It has to come from him.

His lips meet mine softly, hesitantly. Then his hand slips under my robe and he breaks the kiss when he feels skin.

He pulls at the tie and lets it fall open, eyeing me greedily.

I half shrug. "I was getting changed when I saw you running out of my window and had to come down."

"You have a thing for sweaty men?" His flirtatious tone gives me hope.

"I do if I'm making them sweat."

"Is that an offer?"

I'm unsure. The guilt is still weighing heavily on my mind and I feel uneasy after today, just going back to playing like nothing happened. "It's your call," I tell him hesitantly.

He levels me with a look. "That's kinda not how this works."

I take a deep breath. "Will, I hurt you today, I don't think I can be who you need me to be until I make it right."

"You didn't try to hurt me, there's a difference," he tells me trying to reassure me with his eyes.

"No it was the worst possible thing I could do to you, given our history."

"Mags, JJ explained it all to me. I get why you did it; you were protecting me."

"We need to talk about it though, you need to understand why I was distant, and I was. I was pushing you away, I admit that. Veronica couldn't know about you; she would have torn us apart for a story. I'll be damned if she is getting that power. The guilt of telling her I was single to protect you was unbearable, so I guess I have held you at a distance. Knowing I was going to do it, I couldn't take things even further with us. You wanted something I couldn't give. There's no way I could let you surrender something so huge and then pretend you don't exist. I just couldn't do it."

He strokes my face. "I understand. You felt you had no choice."

"I did have a choice though. I could have talked to you."

"Perhaps," he nods. "Or perhaps I wasn't in the right place to understand."

"And you are now?"

He smiles. "I am."

"Are you sure?"

"I'm sure," he kisses me softly. "Now was that an offer?" he says trying to keep the mood from bombing.

"It's a promise." I grin.

He pulls me back in for a deep kiss and I let the robe slide off my shoulders.

"Are you ready to play boy?" I ask when he lets me go. I want to look him in his eyes and seek more reassurance that he does truly understand, I can't stand the thought of hurting him further. But this is what he needs, it's what I need too. This is a part of our healing.

"Yes Goddess," he whispers hungrily, confirming that I'm right.

My confidence floods back through me.

"Get on your knees," I order.

He looks at me like it's the nicest thing I could ever say to him and lowers himself to the floor. I stroke his hair. It seems like a lifetime ago that he dropped to his knees after he found out about my writing. We've been through so much since then.

I turn away and hit the switch that closes the blinds. Going to where I left my collection of things and selecting what I need to tie him.

His face lights up when he sees what is in my hands.

"I came prepared." I smirk.

He lifts up his wrists willingly in response. I can see that I'm not pushing him, this is something he truly wants. Whether he will think that in a minute is another matter.

Once I have buckled them into the cuffs I tell him to stand and strip the rest of his clothes off, laying the towel out on the weights bench. "Lay here." He obediently gets settled on the narrow bench and watches me. I cuff his ankles and then take out the rope, threading it through the loop on his wrist cuff and then binding it to the frame of weights behind his head. I do the same on the other side. Next I thread rope through the loop on his ankle, and his still laboured breathing picks up when I lift his leg slightly allowing me to tie the rope just above where I tied his wrist. Once he is tied, his legs are raised and spread open for me and his hands are out of temptations way.

"So perfect," I mutter, trailing my fingers down his leg. I have paid no attention so far to his dick, but it doesn't matter, he's as hard as ever.

He fidgets, getting used to his position.

"Look." I nod to the side, towards the mirror, showing him how he looks.

He groans when he turns and sees himself.

While he's inspecting my handiwork, I turn and collect the last two things. I'm keeping this really simple, no extra props, just the restraints and this, I pick up the strap on and step into it, pulling the harness tight around my hips.

"Let me see." Will's raspy voice comes from behind me.

I turn and he gasps. I stroke it without thinking, it feels so natural. Like it's part of me. The weight feels right and I have this strong urge to hold it, stroke it.

"So beautiful," he whispers.

I picking up the lube I walk towards him, watching him take in the sight of me.

"Are you sure?" I ask, before he loses rational thinking.

"Please," he breathes.

That's it. No more doubts. I open the lube and drizzle it along the shaft…*my* shaft.

"Stroke it again," he pleads.

I smile and stroke the lube up and down spreading it around.

"Fuck," he curses under his breath.

He makes it feel real, the way he responds to me touching it. The voyeuristic pleasure he gets. I always thought I would feel like I was just wearing a dildo, but it's more than that.

I straddle the bench and settle between his outstretched legs. Ignoring his cock, I put the lube on my fingers to good use, slicking his exposed hole.

He whimpers, then sucks in a sharp breath as I push a finger inside. He screws his eyes shut trying to adjust to the discomfort and then I stroke his cock.

The moan it pulls from him is such an erotic sound.

For a moment, I lose him to that place and I let him enjoy

it, not holding back. Then when he is nice and relaxed, I add a second finger.

"Fuck!" he cries, tensing around me.

"Too much?" I ask, trying to stroke him through the adjustment.

He shakes his head, not opening his eyes.

"Relax."

He breathes deeply and blows out, managing to relax a little.

"Good boy," I soothe.

I watch, mesmerised. "Look at that," I whisper to myself, watching his arse open for me and grip me tight. I was planning on making him take three, but as I slide two in and out of him, I realise three will be almost as much as my cock and I want my cock to stretch him. I want him never to forget how it felt to be fucked for the first time. I really want him to feel it.

"Fuck," his back straightens as I stoke over that sweet spot.

"Look at me."

He opens his eyes.

"Are you ready for my cock?"

"Yes," he replies.

I press on his prostate and he lifts up off the bench, his cry echoing off the walls of the pool house. Then slowly, I withdraw my fingers.

I line the head up and he holds his breath.

"You have to breathe," I tell him.

I push forward, letting just the head slide inside him. I watch him tense and curse.

"Breathe, Will." I push in another inch.

“Oh my fuck,” he grunts.

Knowing all too well the feeling, I try to let him get used to it, before I give him more, but I also know that everything feels a lot better when there’s some other source of pleasure and I watch him pull at the ropes, instinctively wanting to touch his cock to ease the pressure.

He moans in frustration, I use the chance to slowly slide home.

He chokes on his cry and his eyes screw shut again. I can’t stop now I’ve started. I pull out until only the head is still inside, and then watch it sink back into him. He lays there stretched open, hands behind his head and can’t control anything. He belongs to me.

“Open your eyes.”

He obeys, but his eyes tell me his mind is elsewhere. His wrists pull at their bindings and his body tenses and flexes as I slide into him again.

“Will, come back to me.”

“I’m here,” he whispers on a pained gasp.

“No,” I thrust deep to get his attention. “You’re not.”

He lets his frustration show in his cry.

“Your eyes drift closed when your mind starts to wander.” I continue to thrust gently. “Focus on me. Nothing else.”

“I am. I’m all yours,” he mutters.

“I know you’re mine. I’m trying to make you believe it.”

He moans at my words, but then closes his eyes and gets lost back in his fantasy place the second he stops hearing my voice.

He twists his wrists again unconsciously. “You’re doing it again. Getting lost in what ifs. That’s what fantasies are. What ifs. Imagining what you would do with your hands if I let them free. How you could roam my body or add to your own pleasure. What would you do Will? Would you stroke your cock?" I take his cock in my hand and stroke it in time to my languid thrusts. "Were you imagining how this would feel? Wishing for it?"

"Fuck," he manages, almost choking on the word. He loses himself in the double pleasure of me fucking him and stroking him simultaneously.

"You don't have to imagine Will. I've got you. That's my cock inside you, you feel it? Stretching you, claiming what's mine. You're so tight. So fucking amazing for taking it."

He desperately tries to keep his eyes open and on me.

I continue to stroke and thrust. "You have to trust me. My job is to know what you need. Stop wishing, and feel. I don't want you to miss any of it lost in your own head. Feel it all. You're mine. Focus only on me. On how I have control of your body." I lean forward and wrap my free hand around his throat, pressing my thumb and fingers into flesh either side of his windpipe, harder than I have done before. I feel him swallow, but he doesn't panic. I smile, proud of him and I know he sees it.

As he climbs higher and higher, he closes his eyes and I lose him again, but I know this time he is entirely focused on what I'm giving him. I feel him become harder in my hand and I know he is close. I adjust the tilt of my hips so the strap on brushes his spot on each thrust and he can't do a thing but draw in the next shallow gasp. His eyes flicker open, glazed and far away. He moans and it's an unmistakable plea.

I smile.

"Feel me, that's all there is, nothing else matters."

He tenses beneath me.

"You're mine, Will. I own you. Now let go."

As I slam home, he cries out and comes hard, shooting on his chest, neck and even on his face.

I slowly pull out and lean over him, still stroking him, keeping him in that lost place. He is lost in me. I did this. I gave him what he needs. He really is mine. I reach out my tongue and lick over his cheek, cleaning up the pleasure I fucked out of him. I lick along his jaw and dip down to his neck. Coming up, I bite his ear lobe and whisper, "Mine."

He sighs.

I pull back and study him. He looks at me in wonder. I smile, but he's still too speechless to return it. I lower my face to his and take another lick, until I meet his lips and sink into a deep and tender kiss.

SATURDAY 3RD OCTOBER

"Morning." Mags smiles, her face only inches from mine. I become aware that I'm wrapped in her as my body starts to wake up and unfurl and it's the perfect way to ease into a day.

"Morning," I reply, sleepily, remembering last night as I stretch.

"How are you feeling?" she asks.

"Fantastic."

There is a loud bang and I lift my head off the pillow. "What was that?"

Mags looks at her watch, unconcerned. "That, is the stealth-like arrival of the ever graceful Jasmine Parker, home from your house, where she spent far too many of the night's hours riding your cousin and is now late for work, in need of a shower and probably a Redbull."

"Ah, is this a regular occurrence then?"

"You could say that."

"Aren't you glad we aren't like them," I joke. After yesterday's drama, it's good to see the funny side.

She laughs and snuggles in to me. "We'll never be like them."

"Thank fuck."

We fall silent and I think about yesterday and what could

have happened.

"Are we alright?" she asks.

"Of course we are." I pull her even closer and hold her tight. "You don't have to ask."

"Well, after yesterday—"

"Yesterday should be struck from the record."

"I respectfully disagree," she says light heartedly.

"Oh you do, do you?" I tickle her and she squeals.

"Yes!" she shrieks, wriggling away from me and holding my hands away from her body. "I do actually." She manages to get out from under me and pin me to the bed by pressing my hands into the pillows. She mounts me and presses her chest against mine, hooking her feet under my legs so I am stuck, unless I really want a fun fight.

"Why?" I challenge. "You said something I was too weak to hear and I, predictably reacted like a scared child." I raise my eyebrows daring to come up with a better argument.

"Or," she counters. "You could say that we needed it. You could argue that you needed to see that not everything on that side of my life is what you assume. That I choose you above everything. That I will get myself into very sucky situations to protect you. And that I'm incredible with a strap on and you can take it like a champ."

"Say that again," I ask, going serious.

"You take it like a champ…?"

"No not that part, the part about choosing me over everything."

"I do."

"Say it again then."

She looks down at me, her morning hair falling all in her

face, and she smiles softly. "I choose you over everything." She dips her head and places a tiny kiss on the end of my nose. "And you take it like a champ."

"Thanks." I have to laugh at her refusal to get serious today.

She beams from ear to ear. "Let's try not to have any more days like yesterday, even though it ended fun," she suggests,

"Okay," I agree.

She releases one of my hands and pinches my nipple, hard.

"Ouch."

"I think you mean yes, Goddess."

I rub my nipple with my free hand. "Yes, Goddess," I grumble.

"That's better, boy."

"And let's not make the same mistakes our friends have made recently."

I give her a looks that says 'oh please,' but she returns it with one that says, 'just agree will you,' and tweaks my nipple sharply again. "Bloody hell, yes Goddess. Agreed."

"Good boy," she grins. Then she studies my face and her face turns serious after all. "I'm so lucky I got a second chance with you, I don't know what my life would be like if you hadn't come back into it. You've already changed things to a point where I hardly recognise myself. I don't ever want to lose that." Then she looks at me with a troubled expression, like she is weighing up something huge. I'm about to ask her what is wrong, but then she smiles and the weight is lifted.

"Marry me," she says suddenly. It's more of an order than a question.

All the breath leaves me and I close my eyes.

My heart is thundering. I don't know where it came from, but I really mean it.

When he opens his eyes and looks at me again, it is with pained sadness.

"Spencer," he whispers.

Things start to spin when he lifts me off him and sits up. He stands without saying a word and pulls on his clothes.

Did he just safe word?

Oh my god, he just safe worded my marriage proposal.

I'm speechless as I watch him. He turns to me and opens his mouth to speak. And then he just shakes his head and leaves.

No!

I sit in stunned silence and try to figure out what just happened, then I hear the front door slam and my world comes crashing down around me.

He's gone.

The tears start to fall.

"Mags, can you do my z—" Jazz pauses in the doorway. "What's wrong?"

I cry harder in the place of words, because I can't even

think about what this means.

Jazz climbs on the bed with me and wraps me in her arms without hesitation. She holds me there for a long time. When my body shaking sobs subside, she carefully moves the hair from my face. “What happened?” she asks softly.

“I think it’s over,” I sniff.

“What? Why?”

Fresh tears start to fall. “I’m so stupid,” I sob.

“No, you’re not. Will loves you, I’m sure whatever happened was just a misunderstanding.”

“I asked him to marry me.”

“What??” she yells in disbelief.

“I didn’t plan to, it just felt right so I went for it.”

“What did he say,” she asks wearily. I can tell from her tone that she is wondering what the hell I was thinking too.

I sigh and sit up. She sits up as well and slowly starts to pick off the strands of hair that are plastered to my face for something to do while I gather my thoughts.

“We have a safe word,” I tell her.

“Safe word,” she frowns.

“Yeah to stop…stuff, if he feels it’s going to far, or hurts, or whatever.”

“I know what a safe word is silly, I have read your smut. What does that have to do with this?” she uses her sleeve to wipe some tears away, but I’m a snotty mess and she soon realises she is out of her depth, so she gets up quickly to grab the box of tissues from my dresser.

I pick a few tissues from the offered box, but just hold them in my lap. “He used it.”

“He used it when you asked him to marry you?” She picks

her own tissue out and wipes a few tears.

I nod and spring fresh ones for her to mop up.

"Oh my god, why?"

I shrug. "Because it was too soon. Because it's not what he wants." I start to sob again. "Because I'm an idiot."

"You're not an idiot." She soothes. "I don't know what just happened, but I see how much he loves you. Don't go thinking this is over."

"What else can it be, other than over?"

"You need to talk to him and find out."

"But he left me. He's gone again. I don't know what to do." my tears are free falling and my voice is higher and louder with each painful sentence.

"Give him some time to cool down and then talk to him. Maybe it is too soon, but that doesn't mean it has to be over."

"It's over Jazz, I just made a proper fool of myself, there's no coming back from that." I sniff and finally use the tissues in my hand to stem the flow. "This is why I don't do feelings Jazz. Exactly this. I'm fucking done with it."

"I know." She dabs my cheek. "It's easy to live like that when you only do superficial and meaningless. But Will is different."

"Was," I correct. "Was different."

There is a knock on my open door and we both snap our eyes to see a very shell-shocked looking Will standing there.

He addresses Jazz softly. "Can we have a minute?"

Jazz nods and gets up from the bed, leaving me feeling very exposed and raw. I pull the covers up into my lap for comfort and protection. Jazz walks towards Will and puts her hand on his shoulder as she passes him, he nods.

He steps into the room and closes the door, approaching the bed cautiously, but with determination. He sits on the edge, his body turned to mine.

Panic rises in me. I feel so stupid for what I did. "Will before you say anything, I'm sorry."

"Mags I—"

"No, you're right I shouldn't have done it, it's way too soon."

"Just—"

"I feel like an idiot, I—"

"WILL YOU LET ME SPEAK!" he shouts.

I shut my mouth.

"Thank you," he says more calmly taking a deep breath. Then he places a small box on the covers between us.

My instinct is to back away from it. This is all wrong, it shouldn't be like this.

"Will you don't have to—"

He lifts his finger to stop me, but I can't let him do this just because he feels forced.

"You don't want to, I get it. Don't do this just b—"

He presses his finger to my lips. "Do I need to gag you?'

I shake my head.

He sighs. "You really do like to control everything don't you?"

I nod, still silenced by his finger.

"If I take this off, will you let me speak?"

I nod again and he lifts his finger off.

I raise my hand a little, "Can I just say one thing?"

"Am I going to be able to stop you?"

"Don't do this," I gesture to the box. "Not like this. If it's what you want one day, do it then, not because I've forced your hand. I want it to mean something."

"And it would have if you'd let me do it like I planned."

"Huh?" I frown. Planned?

"I had it all planned, but you went and—"

"I—" He growls at my interruption and grabs my leg, pulling me so fast, I don't know what's happening until I'm laying with him over me, pinned to the pillows by my wrists, exactly how I had him a little while ago.

"Shut up for once will you. I love you. Don't you get it? I need you. I know you and I trust you. I know you want me. I know you think I still don't believe that, but I do. We are forever. I was hoping to show you that myself. I wanted you to know how sincere I was. But you went and got there first."

I stare at him, shocked. And the tears well up again. "You said the safe word," I whisper.

"Because this isn't part of our game, Mags. I need you to believe that I know I have you. I need you to know that nothing else will make me doubt you. No reporter, or dashing billionaire or even average Joe will steal you away from me because you belong with me. We belong together, I am yours and you are equally mine. And I can't make you believe that I see that, if I do it from inside the game."

I swallow hard. I've never seen him like this.

He backs off me and pulls me up to sitting, then he searches on the bed for the box. As soon as I see it again, my heart starts racing.

"Now, I've had this for a couple of weeks. I was going to wait for a couple of things to fall into place before I gave it to you, but since you're so bossy, you're going to get it now."

"Will, I—"

He shuts me up with just his look.

"Do you want it or not?" he asks sternly.

I nod, unable to fight the beginnings of a smile.

"I have the ring, I have the house, I—"

"The house?" I gasp.

Will rolls his eyes. "Yes, if you let me finish. I've been pushing for big things with the new house, because when it's finished I want it to be ours. I haven't told Spencer yet. I wanted us to buy him out to free our equity back up for a new project. If you agreed that is."

"I—"

"Let. Me. Finish." He blows out a long breath.

"Sorry."

"So I wanted to sort that out, but it can wait. And there was just one other thing I really wanted to do first."

"What's that?"

"I wanted to ask your dad's permission."

I cover my mouth with my hands and I feel tears prick my eyes again. I shake my head. What have I done? He had this whole amazing plan and I wrecked it all. "I'm so sorry." I reach for his hand. "Do it. Wait until you can do what you planned and I won't say another word." I zip my lips closed, lock them and toss the imaginary key over my shoulder.

"It's too late now."

"Please Will, dad would love that. Ask him."

"I did."

"What?" I frown. "But I thought you just said…"

"I called him when I ran home to get the ring. Woke him up at three am in Chicago. Great start to the, 'can I ask for your daughter's hand in marriage' conversation." He chuckles.

"What did he say?" I gasp.

Will picks up my other hand and looks me in the eyes. "He said nothing would make him more delighted."

Tears spill down my cheeks and I can't do anything because I don't want to let him go. All I can do is smile and cry.

He lets go of my hands and picks up the box. "Mags. My Goddess." He swallows. "Would you do me the honour of becoming my wife?"

"Yes!" I blurt it out before he even opens the box and grab his face to kiss him.

He sinks into the kiss and pulls me to him, so I'm straddling his lap. Then he pulls his lips away. Reluctantly, I let him go.

He brings the box to the small space between use and slowly opens it. I gasp. It could be a ring of foil from a chocolate bar for all I care. But it is beautiful, vintage judging by the age of the box, and delicate. Just what I would have chosen for myself. "Oh my god, I love it."

"It was Nana's. Grandad bought it from a flea market somewhere in Europe during the war, she has convinced herself that it belonged to a Russian princess, but there is no truth to that whatsoever. I want to take you to see her, just nod if she tells you."

I laugh, the tears still rolling down my cheeks. "Okay."

He lifts it out of the box. "He gave it to her right on the docks when he returned home from D-day and it fit perfectly. They were married sixty-one years before he died. She says if it fits, it's a sign that we will have as long and as happy a marriage as she did." He picks up my hand and prepares to slide it on my finger. Then he looks up at me. "I say, if it doesn't fit, she's an eighty-four year old woman with very few marbles left and we'll get it resized."

"Okay," I giggle. Then I hold my breath as he slips it on, because I *really* want it to fit.

"Holy shit, it fits." He laughs. "It's definitely a sign."

I kiss him and throw my arms around his neck. "Definitely."

"That means at least sixty years of wedded bliss, can you handle it?"

"I can, can you?"

"Yeah I think so."

I pull away and study the ring on my finger. "It really is beautiful. How come you get it?"

"Because she had two daughters who each only had one child. So it goes to me, or Spencer and well…"

"Yeah." I laugh. "I see.

I stare at it again. "I wish I had something to give you."

"It's ok, you don't have to."

"Are you kidding me? I want everyone to know you're mine." Then it hits me. "Oh! I have something." I jump up and cross the room. "Although you might not want to wear it to work." I laugh.

"I'll wear it anywhere you tell me to."

"I wouldn't be so sure about that," I tell him going to my wardrobe and delving into he box he hasn't yet seen.

"Why not? What the hell is it?"

"On your knees boy," I order, turning around with a collar in my hands.

His eyes go wide and then a slow smile spreads across his face. He gets up off the bed and crosses the room towards me, stopping half way. And then he sinks slowly to his knees. “Yes Goddess.”

SATURDAY 3RD OCTOBER
EPILOGUE

"Can I do anything?" Mags asks, slipping her arms around my waist and making it hard to chop.

"No, I've got it all under control. Spencer will be here in an hour, Jazz will be home from work soon."

"Did he suspect?"

"No I just told him we had a ton of food here that needs to be eaten so I'm going to BBQ."

Mags peeks around me to the prepared food I've been amassing as I work. "It is a lot of food for four people, you went a bit crazy."

I twist around, knife still in hand. "Look, did you promise to leave this to me, or not?"

She surrenders with her hands in the air and steps back smirking. "I'm just saying it's a lot of food. That's all. Not taking over."

"Good. Now leave me to marinate these prawns and go an get ready."

"You're marinating prawns? Will it's Spencer and Jazz. Burger, ketchup, bun, and done."

I narrow my eyes at her. "I got engaged today," I tell her. "I had a whole plan and it all got turned on its head by my bossy fiancée."

She bites her lip.

"Therefore, if I want to celebrate with too much food and marinated prawns, I will. And my bossy fiancée will remember that she's reached her quota of bossy today."

"Are you putting your foot down?"

"Yes, I am. Is there a problem?"

"Nope," she grins.

"Good. Now go to your room." I smile back. I haven't really stopped smiling all day.

Mags fights a laugh and manages to look coy. "Oh my. Do I have to call you Daddy?'

God, I love her. I shake my head, laughing. "Please don't. We may never recover."

She lets out her dirty as hell laugh and then turns on her heel and leaves me wanting to run after her. I close my eyes. No. I've been wrapped up in her half the day, if I want tonight to be perfect, I need to get on with it.

"Wow, this looks amazing," Jazz says slapping Spencer's hand away from her arse as they both come out onto the terrace. I heard them both arrive about half an hour ago, but apparently Jazz needs chaperoning in the shower.

"Of course it does, Princess. We built it." Spencer tells her, making his way across to the outdoor kitchen area that he planned with George to turn it into more of an entertaining space out here.

It does look amazing. Especially since the interior people did all their finishing for the shoot. In the evening light, with the fire pit crackling and perfect lighting glowing from every precisely planned recess. It works perfectly. I'm proud of him.

Of us.

I hand Spencer a beer and offer Jazz some champagne. “Goodness, champagne? What’s the occasion?” She says with unconvincing innocence. Mags told her first thing. We couldn’t let her worry all day about how she left us this morning. I wanted to explain, and apologise. But she promised she would let me tell Spencer.

Mags steps in beside me and I put my arm around her. Despite Jazz already knowing, I have to take a deep breath. I’m worried he’ll think this is crazy. “We, um, kind of have some news.”

Jazz grins from ear to ear and Spencer lowers his beer bottle even though he was just about to take a swig.

“We’re getting married.” I tell him.

“Are you serious?”

“Of course they’re serious you idiot.” Jazz rolls her eyes, opening her arms to celebrate properly with her best friend. They hug and squee and bounce and then look at the ring. Spencer and I watch then for a second before we turn to each other.

I brace myself for the speech. The one where he tells me I’m being a twat, we’ve only been together a few weeks and marriage is for losers.

“Fucking hell! Congratulations mate.” He shocks me by holding out his hand to shake and then stuns me by pulling me in for a backslapping hug.

“Thanks,” I manage. What the hell?

He doesn’t let go right away. He holds me. Then he pulls away and shakes his head.

Here it comes.

"I can't believe you didn't tell me you were thinking about asking her."

"I knew what you'd say."

Spencer nods regretfully. "I imagine you thought you did. But I'm happy for you mate." He finally lifts his beer to his lips. "Bit jealous actually."

My eyes snap to his. "Jealous?" I ask, lowering my voice. "You're not thinking…" I glance at the girls then back to him.

He shakes his head. "I think that would be pushing it right now, don't you?"

"But you're thinking it."

He shrugs one shoulder. "I've done a lot of thinking recently. It turns out I'm not as dead to the idea as I thought I was." He watches Jazz talking excitedly to Mags as he spills his heart. Then he shakes off the melancholy. "I'll just let you set the example and see what happens."

"Shit." I'm speechless. He has been quieter since the big fall out with Jazz, but I had no clue that was the reason.

He hugs Mags when they remember we are still here and she holds out her hand for him to see the ring. "Is that Nana's?"

I feel a huge pang of guilt since no one ever thought he would have any use for it after swearing off commitment for life. "Yeah." I wince. I should have talked to him. I probably would have eventually, I just wasn't expecting to do it today.

"It's perfect." He smiles graciously. The throws his arm around my shoulder. "I'm proud of you cuz. You've set the benchmark pretty high. Hopefully I'll be able take a leaf out of your book one day."

"Not yet, obviously," Jazz cautions, sliding under his other arm.

Spencer lets go of me and wraps her up in both arms. "Not yet, Princess," he agrees, kissing the top of her head. "One day."

I'm a little bit in shock to see him like this and a lot in shock to hear him say he's proud of me and hopes to follow *my* lead. Mags catches my eye and smiles. 'See,' she mouths.

"So when are you thinking of doing it?" Jazz asks.

Mags and I look at each other. She nods her encouragement.

"Great question!" George's voice comes from behind us.

We turn to see him coming out of the house with JJ behind him.

"Dad? What are you doing home?"

I didn't tell her he was flying home. I thought it would be a nice surprise. Just like I didn't tell her I invited JJ.

"My only child gets engaged, you think I'm going to stay in Chicago for a business lunch? Hell no. I got on the first flight home this morning."

She rushes to him and he picks her up and crushes her with a hug.

"Congratulations Will," JJ says coming to stand beside me and watch George and Mags having their father/daughter moment.

"Thank you." I shake his hand. "I'm glad you could make it."

"Thank you for inviting me. I wouldn't miss it for the world."

George approaches, Mags still by his side, looking so happy. He holds out his hand for me to shake and I stare at it, wondering how I'm so lucky that he trusts me to make Mags as happy as he thinks she deserves to be. I take it with confidence though, because I know I'm up to the job. I'm only person in the world up to the job. Because I'm the only person in the world who loves Mags as much as George.

He pulls me to his chest and hugs me briefly. Letting me go but still shaking my hand. His free hand grasps my shoulder and he smiles. "Welcome to the family, son."

I smile. "Thanks, George."

"Oh please, call me dad."

Before I lose it completely, I'm saved by JJ. "We need champagne!" he shouts.

"I was just about to open some," I tell him, pointing to the bottles I have on ice.

"Allow me," he says in that way he does, when he's in his element, fitting right in and impressing everyone.

After the garden party, and the way I felt that day, I instantly want to reply, 'no, allow me.' But when I think about why I feel such a need to prove my worth, it all seems so pointless. So I allow him. It makes him happy, what's wrong with that?

Mags slips her hand into mine and gives it a light squeeze. I squeeze back without looking at her. I know she is smiling with pride. I know I don't have to explain all that to her because she gets me. And for the first time ever, I feel like I really fit in.

I think maybe I always did. I just needed to see it.

"So when is the big day going to be?" George asks.

Mags looks at me and nods.

"Soon we hope," I tell him.

He looks pleasantly surprised.

"We were thinking about Valentines Day," I admit.

George smiles fondly. He and Mags' mum married on Valentines Day. "Sounds perfect," he says, a little emotion showing in his strong exterior.

"That's only four months away!" Jazz gasps. I suspect not because she thinks it's too soon to be rushing into it, but more because that's not long to plan what she has in mind.

"I know. It's okay, we can plan it in four months," Mags assures her.

"But Valentines Day? Everything will have been booked two years ago."

"Not where we want to have it."

Jazz relaxes as it dawns on her. "Here?"

"If it's ok with Dad," Mags turns to him.

"Oh darling, of course it is."

"I don't want hundreds of people. We just want it small and beautiful."

"It will be," he promises.

"Where will you live?" Spencer asks suddenly. Reality sinking in that this means the end of our sharing arrangement.

"I wanted to talk to you about that. I'm hoping Mags and I can buy the new house when it's done. I've worked out how it can work. I'll show you my figures and we can talk about it."

"Okay," he nods. I can tell he wants to talk about it now, but it doesn't need to be tonight.

"Wait, where am I going to live?" Jazz pipes up.

Mags laughs. "I'm sure you'll find somewhere," she says giving a Spencer a dig in the ribs.

Spencer's face lights up. "You can stay with me for a while," he tells Jazz, sounding like he is doing her a humungous favour, while really you can tell he is over the moon.

"Well, I suppose I could, just for a while." Her smile is difficult to hide. "I'd pay my own way, of course."

"We'll split things 60/40 Princess. 60% for you, 40% for me. Okay?" he jokes.

"Hey! Why do I have to pay more?"

He sweeps his arms around her. "Because, my Shoegirl, your shoes are going to need their own room."

"I could get rid of them if that's what you'd prefer," she teases.

"Whoa, whoa, let's not be too hasty."

"Well I'll have to do something to get the rent down."

Spencer flashes her his most salacious look. "I'm sure we could come up with a payment plan, Princess."

"Ugh," she slaps him in the stomach to general laughter.

JJ starts to hand around champagne and I catch George's eye.

I feel I have so much I need to say.

"I know it's all fast," I say to him quietly, hoping I can reassure him.

"Fast?" he laughs. "You know I proposed to Scarlet after two weeks and married her after four?"

"I didn't know that."

"Her father was furious. But we got past it. In the end, you have to set your own pace and if you stick to your guns and make it work, people will respect you for it. "

"We will make it work I promise you. I know I might not be not what you had in mind for your daughter. But I swear to you, I will never hurt her."

"I know you won't son. I think you have the wrong impression of what I want for Mags. I want her to be happy. That is all. I had to watch the love of my life fade away and not one penny I had in the bank or one diploma on my wall could do a damn thing to change it. Just love her and always be there for her, that's all I ask."

"I will."

"Good, because you two are meant to be together. It was always my hope that you could rekindle what you lost. I confess that's why I jumped at the chance to get you working here for the summer. It seemed like the perfect way to bring you together after you had avoided each other for so long. A father knows."

"Thank you." There aren't really any other words.

"Nonsense. You did all the hard work, I merely put the pieces into place. And look at what I got in the deal," he waves his arm across the addition to the house.

He does that shoulder squeeze thing again and I look up and catch JJ's eye. He gives me that 'I told you so' look and raises his glass to me. I raise mine back.

Mags slips her arm around me. "You ok?" she whispers.

"Never better," I whisper back.

"I'd like to raise a toast," George says. "To my beautiful daughter and her future husband."

Our friends raise their glasses.

"And to a beautiful house and having Veronica Stapleton out of our lives for a while," he adds.

"Oh god." Mags tenses.

"What's wrong?"

"You're going to have to see that horrible article where I

tell them I'm single. I'm so sorry."

"That's ok. I don't care."

"It's not ok. I don't want them to have that control over my life any more."

"Darling, you know they will just dig for detail. Give yourselves some time to enjoy this."

"But they are going to find out and dig anyway. Wouldn't it be better coming from me?"

"Us," I correct her.

"Maybe, but it's going to be something they are very interested in, are you prepared for that?" George warns.

"No," I admit. "But I'm ready to face it." I wrap Mags in my arms and she looks up at me. "Tell her the truth. It will be okay."

"Are you sure?"

"Positive."

George nods and to my surprise, pulls his phone out of his pocket. We all watch while he dials and waits. "Veronica? George Goldsmith. I have an announcement for you to add to the article…yes. But we do it on our terms…Can you come back Monday?…Excellent." He hangs up the phone. "It's done. Let's celebrate."

"Thank fuck," says Spencer. "I'm starving."

ACKNOWLEDGEMENTS

I am so very thankful…mostly for finishing this book!

I can't say that working with these characters has always been a pleasure. It felt like they fought me every step of the way. But great things take time and I think these characters are great. Even if they are elusive, stubborn arseholes at times.

I truly love each of them for all their flaws, and I so enjoyed letting my inner psycho out to play. Part of me would like to live in their world forever. But for now, I'm done with these fools!

As for my thanks. You know who you are, and you know what you did. Whether you pushed, or pulled, I couldn't have got here without that help. Thank you always, from the bottom of my heart.

Printed in Poland
by Amazon Fulfillment
Poland Sp. z o.o., Wrocław